A TRIAL OF BLOOD & STEEL

Tracato

JOEL SHEPHERD

an imprint of Prometheus Books
Amherst, NY

Inquiries should be addressed to
Pyr
59 John Glenn Drive
Amherst, New York 14228–2119
VOICE: 716–691–0133
FAX: 716–691–0137
WWW.PYRSF.COM

14 13 12 11 10   5 4 3 2 1

Library of Congress Cataloging-in-Publication Data

Shepherd, Joel, 1974–
    Tracato / by Joel Shepherd.
        p. cm. — (A trial of blood and steel ; bk. 3)
    Originally published: Sydney : Orbit, 2009.
    ISBN 978–1–61614–244–5 (pbk. : alk. paper)
    I. Title.

PR9619.4.S54T73 2010
823'.92—dc22

2010024686

Printed in the United States on acid-free paper

Also by Joel Shepherd

Crossover
A Cassandra Kresnov Novel

Breakaway
A Cassandra Kresnov Novel

Killswitch
A Cassandra Kresnov Novel

Sasha
A Trial of Blood & Steel

Petrodor
A Trial of Blood & Steel

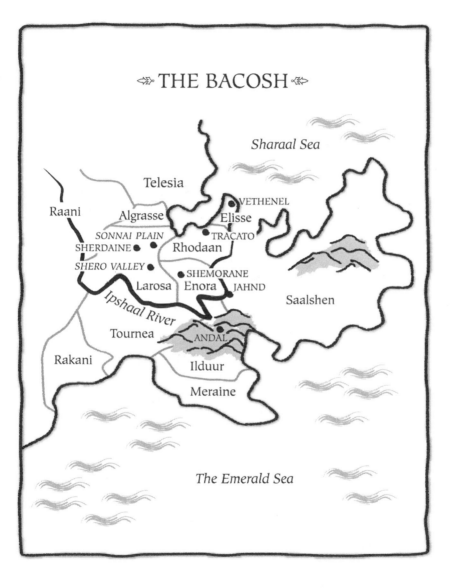

THE BACOSH

Sharaal Sea

Telesia

Raani

Algrasse

VETHENEL

Elisse

SONNAI PLAIN

TRACATO

SHERDAINE ●

● Rhodaan

SHERO VALLEY ●

● SHEMORANE

Larosa   Enora   JAHND

Saalshen

Ipshaal River

Tournea

ANDAL

Rakani

Ilduur

Meraine

The Emerald Sea

One

"I DON'T LIKE THE LOOK OF THIS," said Sasha, leaning on the *Maiden*'s railing. Behind them, she could see three ships, triangular foresails billowing, masts rolling in the swell. "How far away, do you think?"

"Five leagues," said Errollyn. "They're no faster than us, I doubt they'll catch us."

Sasha turned to look across the deck, the wind whipping at her short hair, tossing the tri-braid across her cheek. Huge canvas sheets thudded and strained against their ropes as sailors ran on the deck, or crouched, and kept a wary eye to their knots and loops lest something abruptly break. Waves rolled across their path. The *Maiden* surged as the swell lifted behind, white foam spraying as her bow rushed through the water. Then slowed, riding high atop the wave, mast tilting back to the left as she slid down the rear side, losing half her speed.

Port side, Sasha reminded herself. Port was left, starboard right. It was her seventh day at sea, and she'd not been as sick as she'd feared, despite the weather. Half a year in Petrodor and much experience fishing, rowing and sailing on small boats had granted her enough sea legs that she wasn't green and hanging over the side, like some others she could name.

"I'm not real keen on learning naval warfare right now," she said, scanning the horizon for other sails. She saw none besides the three, but the haze and rolling seas could conspire to hide things even from eyes as sharp as Errollyn's. The three pursuers were almost certainly Algrassien, though it was too far to see the colours. They were past Algrasse now, and it was the Larosa coast that occasionally showed its dim shadow through the distant mist to starboard.

Soon, the captain hoped, they would meet a Rhodaani or a Saalshen patrol, and the pursuers would flee. They were little more than pirates, in the face of serrin naval power. Blockade they had threatened, should Elisse be attacked, and now, blockade they attempted . . . three vessels at a time, preying on freighters alone or in small groups, never daring to face warships bow to bow. There was too much traffic in the Elissian Sea for all freighters to be guarded all the time, and a few had been lost. Sasha only hoped that this particular Rhodaani freighter was as fleet on the downwind run as her captain claimed.

She wondered if they shouldn't be hugging closer to the Elissian coast. Elisse was no more friendly to her cause than Larosa or Algrasse, but it had been under attack for weeks. If the latest tales were true, the Rhodaani Steel had bypassed the port city of Algen and were laying siege to Vethenel further north. Given what Sasha had heard of the Rhodaani Steel, she had little doubt that, if true, Vethenel would have fallen by now.

But the Elissian coastline was rugged in parts, its waters treacherous, and its navy had not been entirely smashed, or so the *Maiden*'s captain feared. More likely its surviving remnants were in hiding, he claimed, in hidden bays known only to local sailors. He chose for his ships a more westerly course, down the centre of the Elissian Sea. The great Rhodaani port city of Tracato lay barely a day and a half ahead, so long as the wind held to this direction.

Off to starboard, *Windsprite* heaved and foamed, keeping pace measure for measure. To port, *Radiance* appeared to be struggling a little. Sasha saw men about her foresail ropes, adjusting tensions, with much gesticulating and pointing. Three against three.

"You're the master tactician," Errollyn told her. His bow was unstrung in his hand as he leaned on the rail. "What would you do?"

"Hope they don't have artillery," said Sasha.

"Doesn't seem likely. There's no room to fire past those foresails."

"They won't be carrying cargo either," Sasha countered. "We're heavier."

"But better built."

"Enough to make a difference when we're so much lower in the water? They're bound to be a bit faster, at least, and they probably will have artillery somewhere amidships, though they'd have to draw alongside to use it."

"We might have to start throwing things overboard," Errollyn suggested. He stood up from the rail, took a firing stance, and practised drawing an imaginary bowstring. Testing his balance, as the ship slowly heaved back and across to port.

"Fine," said Sasha. "I'll start with Alythia."

Errollyn just looked at her, half amused, half wary. The wind blew ragged, dark-grey hair about his face, framing brilliant, deep-green eyes. "Maybe you're getting enough practice at naval warfare already," he suggested.

Sasha snorted. She turned and made her way past the captain's wheel, down a short flight of steps to midships. Her balance was fine now, even with the ship rolling so heavily . . . but then, balance was always her strong point. She'd been sick the second day after leaving Petrodor, but pretty good since then. Cool wind, sea spray and a view of the horizon all helped—she was much better above decks than below. Also, it was a relief to be finally free of Petrodor. Half a year in the primary port city of Torovan was her absolute limit, and while the ocean was nothing like the Lenay mountains and forests that she craved, its far, open horizons calmed her nerves and unknotted a winter's worth of accumulated tension from her muscles.

Kessligh sat with Dhael upon the raised decking about the main mast, talking. Sasha sat beside Kessligh, and gazed up at the pair of heaving, triangular foresails. Their conversation was about sails, boats and winds. Sasha found more interest in Kessligh's left leg as he sat with his it stretched out before him, the knee nearly straight. He seemed to find it more comfortable that way. The crossbow bolt had gone straight through the meat of his thigh five months before. The wound had healed well and the stiffening had not affected his movement as much as Kessligh had feared. But it was bad enough, and the limp was now permanent. A long, smooth staff rested at Kessligh's side, his constant companion.

Dhael was Rhodaani, of an age with Kessligh, but considerably taller. He had long, greying hair, but a handsome, lean face, as little weathered by middle age as was Kessligh's. He wore a black cloak against the spring chill, and seemed unbothered by the ship's motion—unsurprising, for a merchant. Dhael Maran, however, was far more than just a Rhodaani merchant—he was a Tracato councilman, an elected leader of Rhodaan. Strange concept *that* was. Such concepts the serrin had introduced to the three Bacosh provinces of Rhodaan, Enora and Ilduur, after the fall of Leyvaan the Fool two hundred years ago. Normally the serrin had not the force of arms to invade their neighbours, but following the demise of Leyvaan's armies, those three provinces in particular had been left with little to defend themselves. The armies of Saalshen had invaded, and met with many friendly peasants only too happy to be free of their feudal overlords.

Rhodaan, Enora and Ilduur now made a wall of serrin/human civilisation, protecting Saalshen from the savagery of those arrayed against her. Sasha had often wondered why the serrin had stopped where they had. Elisse, too, would have been largely undefended, following Leyvaan's fall, but the serrin had opted not to invade. Meraine also, and perhaps even parts of eastern Larosa. But many in Saalshen seemed discomforted even at their present, limited conquest, and neither Saalshen nor their Bacosh allies (known most everywhere as the Saalshen Bacosh) had invaded any foreign territory in two centuries since. Until now.

"Algen should come up soon to port," Sasha remarked. "There should be some ships in the vicinity."

"Perhaps a blockade," Kessligh agreed.

"I don't think anyone will be stupid enough to try to assist Algen by sea," said Dhael. They spoke Torovan, and Dhael's accent was lovely—all soft Larosan vowels and lilting consonants. Rhodaan retained its own native tongue, but Larosan was the tongue of nobility and civility in most Bacosh cities. Of all the Bacosh kings, Larosa had supplied approximately half, over the endless, bloody centuries. Most Bacosh nobility traced their lineage back to Larosa at some point. So much conquest had its rewards.

Now, a new Larosan ruler had proclaimed himself regent of the Bacosh. He would no doubt have claimed himself king, had Verenthane nobility not declared that title forbidden . . . until the one who would claim it had retaken the Saalshen Bacosh from the serrin, and reestablished human dominion there. Regent Arrosh was massing an army in Larosa, by far the largest yet assembled for such an assault. Kessligh and Sasha had hoped to stymie such a development from Petrodor, but Petrodor's conflicts had only seen the emergence of a new king of Torovan, as there had never been a king of Torovan in seven hundred years. Torovan was marching. The united Bacosh was marching. The Army of Lenayin was marching. And the Rhodaani, unwilling to be threatened on two fronts simultaneously, had struck first— into Elisse.

"Might some of the Elissian nobility try to escape across the sea?" Sasha wondered. "They've allies in Algrasse."

"Perhaps, from further along the coast," Dhael conceded. "But they'll not risk Saalshen's navy nearer the ports. I hear many of the Elissian nobility fled in advance of the Steel, even as they were exhorting their armies to stand fast and fight. They heard talk from across the border, Rhodaanis muttering that they should not repeat in Elisse the same mistake the serrin made in Rhodaan."

"Leaving the nobility alive?" Sasha guessed his meaning.

Dhael nodded. "They say Saalshen was too kindhearted two hundred years ago. If they'd put all Rhodaani nobility to the sword then, as was done in Enora, Rhodaan would be much more stable now."

"It wasn't kindheartedness," Kessligh replied. "They just didn't see the point. The serrin consider no conflict resolved until the opponent has been convinced of his own wrongness. To kill a person to win an argument is not only abhorrent to them, most serrin believe it only loses you the argument, or postpones it to a later date."

"That didn't seem to bother them in Enora," Sasha remarked.

"Serrin killed very few in Enora," said Kessligh, "and mostly only those who would not put down their arms. The killing there was done by the peasants and townsfolk. Lord Gilis of Enora was a brutal man, and the Enoran peasantry had long been the most friendly to Saalshen. They were closest to the Ipshaal, and many knew friends or family who had slipped across the river, and could testify to the kindness of the serrinim.

"When Saalshen's warriors came to Enora instead of the returning armies of Leyvaan, the peasants were thrilled. They rose up in a force too powerful for Saalshen to control, and Saalshen did not wish to offend their new friends and rob them of their new-found liberty. But the mobs killed every noble they could find, man, woman and child."

"And a good thing too," Dhael sighed. "They erased every claimant to the Enoran throne. Now, Enora is at peace. Rhodaan, however, is always crazy."

Sasha had heard as much. Enora was the site of the Enoran Grand Temple, holiest of the Verenthane holy sites, and the greatest single cause of the current troubles. But Enora itself was peaceful and secure, with villagers and townsfolk volunteering to form the impassable barrier of the Enoran Steel—one-third of the greatest fighting army ever known to humanity.

Rhodaan, however, was even more powerful. It had ports, ships and trade. Thus, Rhodaan had gold, and lots of it. The Rhodaani also had competing factions, powerful old families clinging to old loyalties from before the coming of the serrin, and a tendency to solve such disputes through force that continued to exasperate their more peaceful serrin friends.

"This was a smart move, though," said Sasha. "If they'd waited until the regent had mustered all forces on Rhodaan's doorstep, they'd never have had the strength to defend the Elissian flank. Best to deal with Elisse first, and get it out of the way."

"No," said Dhael, shaking his head. "It's a terrible decision."

"Terrible?"

"When the serrin came to Rhodaan," said Dhael, "my ancestors hoped that it was a new dawn. The serrin do not like war, and never engage in it by choice. Many of us have striven to make Rhodaan a place that will never resort to war. Least of all a war of aggression like this one."

"Aggression?" Sasha stared at him. "Regent Arrosh gathers the largest army ever seen in the Bacosh to assault you and your allies and Lord Arshenen of Elisse declares his support for them, and yet you claim this *defensive* action is a war of aggression?"

Dhael shrugged. "We attacked them. We crossed their border and invaded their lands, attacked their armies. . . ."

"Semantics," Sasha snorted.

"You are Lenay, and Lenays like war," Dhael sighed. "Alas, even the grace of Saalshen has not swayed enough of my people from their love of bloodshed."

"Nor their will to defend themselves," Sasha retorted. "What you describe is suicide. How can you claim to love your people if you will not fight to defend them?"

"I love my people and I serve their interests," Dhael said shortly. "I was elected to the Council by my peers. It is not for you to question whether or not I love my people."

He got up, steadying himself as he found his balance, and departed. Kessligh shook his head. "I can't believe I brought *you* on a mission of diplomacy."

"He's supposed to be schooled in the learned tradition of serrin debate," said Sasha. "That means he's not supposed to walk off in a huff when I make a strong point."

"I'm quite sure you could walk into a Council of the most gentle and wise serrin thinkers," Kessligh said drily, "and have them all baying for your blood within the hour."

Sasha grinned. "You say the sweetest things." She rested her head briefly against his shoulder. Kessligh snorted. She was enjoying being more affectionate to Kessligh these days. In so many ways, he'd been her truest father, much more so than her blood father, King Torvaal of Lenayin. Their relationship had been turbulent, as the master swordsman had attempted to whip the wild brat tomboy into a passable swordsman and Nasi-Keth uma. He'd been the one man whose approval she'd truly craved, while at the same time resenting the power that gave him.

Lately, though, the resentment had faded. Much of the wisdom she'd questioned at the time had turned out to be wise after all, and while she continued to disagree with his outlook on many things, she had gained a new-found respect for the reasoning behind his views. He no longer intimidated her like he once had, which was partly because she had grown, and partly because they had reached a deeper understanding. She was a woman now, and a blooded warrior, a person to be feared by her enemies. And she knew now for certain that Kessligh loved her, however gruffly he might express it. He might have difficulty showing his feelings, but that did not mean *she* should.

"Dhael is an idealist," said Kessligh. "He knows serrin teachings well. He believes that if followed, humanity can become a peaceful race, like the serrin."

"I doubt it. Serrin are just different, they don't think as we do. If humanity is to find peace, we must find our own path to do so."

Kessligh shrugged. "Even so, it is important to understand his position. There are many like him, in the Saalshen Bacosh. The Bacosh has had so much war, and people look for solutions."

"Utopias," Sasha corrected.

"Some might say Saalshen itself is a utopia," Kessligh replied.

"But the serrin don't understand the concept," Sasha argued. "The serrin were always astonished that any human should think them so perfect. But serrin don't even understand a concept like 'perfection' either . . . or rather they understand the idea, but they just can't accept it. It's always humans who come up with these stupid, simplistic notions, whether it's Verenthane fanatics who think serrin are evil, or pacifist fanatics like Dhael who think that somehow by imitating serrin ways they can make humans more serrin. I mean, he's crazy . . . it's *imitation*. Any fool can decide to be pacifist, but if he doesn't understand *why*, like the serrin know why, what's he actually achieved?"

Kessligh smiled. "They're only human," he said. "One could argue that it's better to be a peaceful idealist like Dhael than a ruthless pragmatist like Regent Arrosh."

"No, it's *not*!" Sasha exclaimed. "Because if the peaceful idealists won't defend themselves, then the ruthless pragmatists will kill them all! And if the peaceful idealists are all dead, what can they possibly offer the next generation? The first imperative is survival; the dead offer nothing to anyone."

"A moral example?"

"Of what not to do," Sasha snorted. "And besides, Dhael hasn't abandoned pragmatism entirely. Did you hear what he said about Enora? It being a good thing they'd killed all the nobility? Some pacifist."

"You noticed. Good. That's a rationalisation, Sasha. Those are the most dangerous of all."

"Break a few eggs to make an omelette?"

"Exactly. Or in this case, 'We must kill a lot of people now in order to ensure we don't have to kill even more people later.'"

"I don't know," Sasha said glumly. "Enora is more stable now than Rhodaan, and it needs to be, considering its enemies. Maybe killing all the nobility was the right thing to do. It's made their politics so much less destructive."

"Quite possibly. Even flawed logic can arrive at the correct conclusion by accident. But that doesn't make the logic any less dangerous. Because if that becomes the way Enora deals with all future problems, it could easily become a nightmare."

Sasha used to find such philosophical ponderings exasperating. Kessligh seemed to make every discussion needlessly complicated. Since then, however, she'd seen the horrors of simple thinking. The northern Verenthanes of

Lenayin, who had decided that the last remaining pagans in their midst, the Udalyn, should be exterminated. Lord Krayliss of the Lenay province of Taneryn, who had been prepared to see all Lenayin burn in civil war in order to see the return of the ancient ways to dominance. The power-hungry Patachis of Petrodor, who knew only wealth and swords, and respected no other currency.

This was the world that Kessligh had sought to escape. These were the simple thoughts and ideals he had striven to find answers to.

He glanced over his shoulder. "Are we being caught?"

"Errollyn doesn't think so."

"And Errollyn knows much about boats?"

Sasha shrugged. "Rhillian did. Rhillian's uma was a boat builder, amongst other things. Rhillian told Errollyn quite a lot." She gazed up at the flapping, heaving foresails, her mood suddenly dark.

Kessligh put a hand on her shoulder. "Rhillian chose her own path," he told her.

"I know," Sasha muttered. "She's a bloody fool."

Meals on the *Maiden* were not as bad as Sasha had initially feared. The beef in the stew was salted and tough, but there were good vegetables too, and fruit, and even some half-fresh bread and cheese. The run from Petrodor to Tracato rarely took more than twelve days, but with this roaring tailwind the captain was confident they could do it in nine. Food kept well enough over such periods, and Nasi-Keth warriors like Sasha and Kessligh, and *talmaad* warriors like Errollyn, were somewhat particular about what they ate.

They weren't the only ones. Also aboard the *Maiden* was a lieutenant of the Rhodaani Steel, and two *dharmi*—footsoldiers of the Steel. Sasha had sparred against all three, and had been impressed. They used shorter swords than the Lenay warriors she was accustomed to, and she'd been expecting them to show less competence when fighting alone. Instead she'd found them a comfortable match to most Lenay warriors she'd known, untroubled by the shifting deck beneath their feet, and probably more practised at contesting her own style, too.

Sasha had taken the opportunity to speak with all three men at length, and had learned a great deal. The Steel were serrin metalworking, weapons and armour, combined with serrin philosophies of motion and tactics, and the human knack for logistics, pragmatism and ruthlessness. One of the *dharmi* was half serrin by parentage, a common enough thing anywhere in the Saalshen Bacosh.

The lieutenant's name was Geran, and he had travelled to Petrodor to speak with the Nasi-Keth, and assess lessons from the great battles that had wracked the city. The Steel, Sasha learned, were like that—always learning, always trying new things. Councilman Dhael had travelled on similar business, and to meet with the new king of Torovan's representatives (those who would deign to see a councilman from a nation Torovan was busily preparing to make war against). Being a merchant as well, he was also conducting trade. Nothing stopped the trade, it seemed. Not even war.

In addition to Dhael's three travelling retainers, there were five other passengers aboard, all Rhodaani. And, of course, there was Sasha's sister Alythia.

Alythia was now busily charming Councilman Dhael at one end of the passengers' table. She laughed and smiled between mouthfuls, dabbing daintily at the corner of her lips with a napkin, in such a way as to draw attention to their fullness. She wore a red gown of flowing folds that fanned from the waist, with white, lacy trim. It enfolded her in a tight corset about the torso—a current fashion of the Bacosh. Alythia's assets, Sasha noted drily, were just about spilling out, and the men at the table were staring. Dhael was married with four children, yet Alythia's eyes, and breasts, seemed positively fixated on the man. Sasha knew only too well what that meant.

Sasha finished her meal, and took a pear and her water flask up steep, narrow stairs to the deck. She held onto a rail where she thought she couldn't possibly get in the way, and ate the pear, listening to the rushing, roaring heave of the sea. The air smelled an intoxication of salt and freshness, as though alive. Cold, perhaps, but her sheepskin jacket was thick, and she had layers beneath . . . and she was Lenay, after all, and well used to cold.

After a while on deck, she tossed the pear stem overboard and returned below. The galley table was clear, and she followed the narrow corridor up to the forequarters and the only half-decent guest lodging available on ship, up near the bow. The door was closed, and she recalled her manners at least long enough to knock before entering.

She found Alythia struggling with her corset. Her sister looked annoyed that she'd entered before being invited, but also a little relieved. "Oh, Sasha. Could you help me with this? I can't reach the laces properly."

"I can see," said Sasha, amused. She shut the door, and stepped behind her sister. Alythia was taller, and her bundled hair tonight added to the effect. To say nothing of her boots, which Sasha saw only now were red leather, high with big heels. "Dear Lords, where did you get those boots?"

"These? Oh, there's so much for sale along the docks if you look, Sasha. You never looked. You lived in Petrodor for six months and you missed everything."

"Everything meaning clothes, jewellery and perfumes," said Sasha drily. "You lived there for six months and you never once went out fishing."

"I leave fishing to men and tomboys," said Alythia, unconcerned.

"I leave dresses and jewellery to flirts and whores," Sasha replied, loosening the laces with difficulty. Once, Alythia would have flown into a rage at such talk. Now, she might even have smiled . . . only Sasha could not see her face from behind.

"Your opinion of fashion does not truly interest me, Sasha," Alythia said mildly. "I'll not take tips from someone who wears more dead animals than a Lisan sailor."

"Skins are the Lenay tradition," said Sasha, straining to get the middle laces loose. "Of course, I wouldn't expect you to know what that means. How in the world did you get these laces so tight? Considering you can hardly reach them?"

Alythia smirked. "I had Lieutenant Geran come and help me into it. He was most accommodating. His hands are so strong!"

"So the plan was to have Lieutenant Geran dress you, and Councilman Dhael undress you?" The laces finally came loose, and the corset shifted, loosening visibly. Alythia let out a small gasp.

"Councilman Dhael is a very interesting man," Alythia said, struggling out of the dress. "If I am to be located in Tracato for the next Gods-know-how-long, the least I can do is learn how the city functions."

"Councilman Dhael is a very influential man," Sasha corrected. "What are you plotting, 'Lyth?"

"Plotting," Alythia snorted. "You have a devious little mind."

"Isn't it slightly beneath the dignity of a Lenay princess to be a councilman's mistress?"

"Don't *you* talk to me about dignity," Alythia snapped. "If you knew the meaning of the word, you'd not walk around in pants with a sword on your back. Talk about being a blight on the dignity of Lenay princesses, you've got some nerve."

She shrugged the corset down her body and finally stepped out of the dress, which revealed curves that might have turned a less self-conscious woman than Sasha green with envy. Alythia, as most men seemed to observe, had a body made for sin. Sasha didn't mind. She had a body made for war, and Errollyn liked it just fine.

"So what did he tell you?" Sasha asked, bouncing onto Alythia's small cot. "About Tracato?"

Alythia took out a plain, brown and white dress from her chest, and pulled it carefully over her head. "It seems a strange place," she said, muffled under her dress. Watching her, Sasha noticed that Alythia wore a knife in a sheath strapped to her shapely thigh . . . and Sasha wouldn't have wagered good coin on the odds of *that* six months ago. "No kings nor queens, just the Council and the High Table. I'm not sure how it all works yet, but I understand more than I did."

"Kessligh says the idea is to give the ordinary people a voice," said Sasha. "Instead of just petitioning their lords, they have actual representatives in the halls of power."

"Oh, Sasha," Alythia said crossly, "for such a ruthless general, Kessligh can be so woolly-headed sometimes. It would never work, and there's no way of truly telling who the people want as their representatives anyhow. People are so fickle." She began letting down her hair, one pin at a time.

"Is that what Councilman Dhael thinks?"

"Don't be daft, Sasha. Never ask a man what he thinks. Let him tell you of his own accord, that way he'll never know which of the things he's told you are valuable to you."

"I didn't ask whether you asked him his opinion," Sasha retorted. "I asked whether you *know* his opinion."

"He thinks Tracato doesn't work very well," said Alythia.

"How doesn't Tracato work very well?"

"Oh, all this talk about 'representatives of the people,'" Alythia said dismissively. "Councilman Dhael speaks prettily enough of his ideals, but truly, he's just a merchant. Few enough of the Council are truly common folk, whatever their pieties; most are just schemers out for power. It's so much simpler, Sasha, when the people know who's in charge. But in Rhodaan, *everyone* thinks to be in charge, and stand on the shoulders of the other person to get there."

"Aye," said Sasha, sarcastically, "because the nobility are so much more well behaved."

"You make fun," Alythia said mildly, as dark curls unbundled down her back, "but in truth, they are. It is the natural order of mother nature, Sasha. Even wolf packs have leaders."

"Aye, they rise all the way from the bottom of the pack. It takes more than being a pack leader's daughter to become a pack leader oneself, *Princess* Alythia."

"Aye, and if wolves owned lands, you'd have a fair analogy," Alythia retorted. "But we can't have everyone scrambling for power all the time, can we? Fighting over titles for lands? It would be a bloody massacre. It seems poorly enough in Rhodaan. Humans need structure, Sasha. Royalty and nobility serve their Godly purpose. This Rhodaani experiment seems ill advised indeed. The meddling of idealistic serrin and Nasi-Keth dreamers."

Sasha thought about it as she lay in her hammock later that night. She was sleeping in the general quarters, as there was precious little dedicated space for high-class passengers on the *Maiden*. Councilman Dhael had the only other quarters, though he had graciously offered them to Sasha . . . her being a princess too, in her previous life at least. Sasha had, of course, declined. It was her own little snobbery, perhaps, that she did not need such luxuries. She liked being tougher and less refined than women like Alythia, or men like Dhael. It made her smug.

She, Kessligh, the three Rhodaani soldiers, Dhael's three retainers and five other passengers all slept in the main quarters with the sailors. Privacy of sorts came from old sheets and blankets draped over ropes between hammocks. Being the only woman, she'd been allowed the forward-most space, up against the wall that separated main hold from forequarters.

Sasha lay with a blanket folded three times over her to ward the chill. Boards groaned and creaked, and above decks men shouted direction. Frequently there were footsteps or conversation over by the crew hammocks, as tired sailors changed shifts, or returned below decks for things they needed.

More footsteps, and then Errollyn pushed past the hanging blanket. He looked a little tired and grim.

"I was up the rigging," he answered her unasked question. "The captain wanted a better look at the lights on our pursuers. He thinks to know them better by their nightshift."

Sasha nodded. Serrin could see by night nearly as well as humans by day, and Errollyn's sight was sharp even by serrin standards. "Do they draw closer?"

"No." Errollyn removed boots, socks, bandoleer and jacket, stowing them in their saddlebags against the wall. "The captain fears a trap."

Sasha nodded, biting her lip.

Errollyn climbed into the hammock beside hers . . . an unusual arrangement, which had caused some consternation amongst some crew and passengers, and some mirth with others. Sasha was usually bothered by little where lewd or stupid remarks on her gender were concerned, but this was different. Some called her "whore," she knew, and it worked on her temper as such things never had before. Well . . . before Errollyn she'd been a virgin, so it had hardly been applicable.

She was one of only two women aboard, and she was sleeping with (or alongside, at least) a man who was not her husband . . . and was serrin, even worse. She'd thought a Rhodaani crew, with their superior affection for all things serrin, might not be bothered by this arrangement, but she was learning that humans were more similar from land to land than she'd have liked. Errollyn, they were fine with. Some might have even respected him more, for appreciation of his "conquest." It was her they called the slut.

Errollyn pulled his blankets up, and reached across to put a hand in Sasha's hair through the hammock netting, as she scowled at the ceiling. The motion of the ship made their bodies swing in time, barely touching.

"Why the face?" he asked her.

"It's nothing."

"Alythia?"

Sasha shook her head. Errollyn reached his hand beneath her blankets to grasp her own. Then he put it on her thigh. Sasha removed it. "That's not like you," Errollyn teased.

"Just rest it for a moment, will you?" Sasha said. Errollyn sighed, withdrew his hand, and laid his head back to sleep.

"I'm sorry." Sasha wriggled sideways in the hammock. "I didn't mean to snap."

"You always snap. I'm used to it."

Sasha could have argued, but didn't. Denying her own temper was foolish. If she wanted the man she loved to stay in love with her, at some point she was going to have to stop picking unnecessary arguments.

"This ship annoys you. Very few serrin women would envy you, being what you are, here amongst humans."

Sasha smiled. Of course he understood. He always understood. She reached, and took his hand. Her frustrations had hardly kept them abstinent, of course. The hammocks were not suitable for a couple without the privacy or patience to experiment, but the cargo hold was usually empty. Which had been hardly romantic, with no space between crates and bags to lie down, but they'd managed nonetheless. As svaalverd warriors both, they shared an interest in physicality, and discovering what their bodies could do together—in positions that did not involve lying down—had been an entertainment all of its own.

There came a round of unpleasant coughing from behind the next partition. Sasha swore lightly, and slid from her hammock. The other reason the hammocks were unsuited was that Kessligh bunked directly alongside. She suspected he wouldn't have cared, but even so . . .

She slipped past the blanket, and found him half seated in his hammock, sipping from a water flask. "You all right?"

He grimaced, nodding as he drank. There was a small pan on the floor beside the bed, just in case. "Damn ships," he muttered. "We'll be in Tracato soon, that'll cure me. What did Errollyn see?"

"They're not gaining. The captain fears a trap. Perhaps we'd best not sleep?"

"If there's an ambush, we'll have enough warning to wake, dress and arm. Better to fight rested."

Sasha nodded. "How's your leg?"

"It's fine, dammit woman," Kessligh growled. "My mother died long ago, you don't have to check on me every time you hear a noise."

"Oh, but look at you," said Sasha in consternation. "Your hair's a mess, you haven't shaved in two days . . . here, just let me . . ." She moved to comb his hair down with her fingers. Kessligh swatted at her, dangerously fast, and she danced away with a mischievous grin.

"You," Kessligh said warningly, "will find you're not too big for a spanking."

"You'd have to catch me first, old man," Sasha laughed. "Sleep well."

She retreated back into her hammock. The ship lurched and rolled, but the only twisting in her stomach was from happiness. Woman. Kessligh called her "woman," not "girl." It was hard not to grin with delight.

Errollyn noticed. "What's so funny?"

"Nothing." Sasha turned onto her side, facing him. "Say, you want to go downstairs and fuck?"

Errollyn grinned. Spirits he looked nice when he did that. Those incredible green eyes flashed, full of humour. Sometimes she couldn't believe her luck.

"You're impossible," he said. "Tracking your moods is like sailing through four seasons before breakfast."

Sasha laughed. Impulsively, she leaned over and kissed him long and deep on the lips. Then she lay back again, and contented herself with holding his hand.

"Sasha?" Errollyn asked. "I've a question. Don't kill me."

"Ah," said Sasha. "A stupid serrin question. Go ahead, I'm bracing myself."

"Do you think . . . I mean, Kessligh is like a father to you. But it's all very well to say that, it's another thing when a man hasn't had a partner in a long time, and after all, you're *not* his daughter . . ."

Sasha frowned. "You know, for a serrin wordsmith, that's an appallingly opaque question. Spit it out."

"Do you think he's ever fancied you?"

Sasha stared at him in horror. "No!" And remembered to keep her voice down. "How can you ask me something like that?"

Errollyn shrugged helplessly. "Stupid serrin question, remember?"

"We were . . . dammit, Errollyn, we've been together since I was eight! He still thinks I'm a little girl, or . . . or . . ." Only now, he called her "woman." She broke off in frustration.

Errollyn put a hand on her arm. "Don't be angry. I was just curious."

Somehow, Sasha found that she wasn't angry. If anyone else had suggested such an appalling thing, she'd have most likely hurt them. But serrin were so innocent, in some things. Not innocent like children, far from it. But they weren't offended by the notions that most humans found so terrible.

He reached, and put a hand on her hip. "Do you still want to go downstairs and fuck?"

"Gods, never again." In the dim wash of lamplight, Sasha thought she saw Errollyn's face fall. As if she'd actually managed to offend him. She grasped his hand and held it tightly. "I'm joking! Errollyn, I'm kidding." He looked a little relieved. "Just . . . maybe tomorrow. You're fine in the dark, but I'll whack my foot and break something."

"Tomorrow we may die," Errollyn said reasonably. "I'll make certain you don't break anything."

Sasha gave him a hard look. She hated it when he did that—said exactly the right thing to talk her into something she'd already decided she shouldn't do. "All right," she sighed. "It's not late yet. We'll get a lantern and go down the front way."

Sasha was up at dawn, and found their pursuers gone. What was more, the wind had fallen to a cool breeze and the seas were calming. She exercised on the deck, watching the sky change from dark to pale blue, then yellow, red and gold. To starboard, *Windsprite* gently rocked, her sails full as she cut through azure seas.

To port, *Radiance* lagged a little, and seemed to have damaged a foresail. At the captain's wheel, the night helmsman cast dark looks in *Radiance's* direction. When the captain rose to relieve him, some unimpressed gestures were aimed in the other ship's direction.

Errollyn joined her soon enough, and was delighted to find their pursuit had vanished. He pulled off his shirt, and Sasha chided him in Saalsi for his vanity. She'd have been prepared to fall for a man less pretty than this one, so long as he'd been the right man. This, however, was serendipity. And what she'd done with him in the cargo hold last night had been considerably more than that. She couldn't believe no one else on the ship had heard her. She'd tried to muffle it, but there'd been a few shrieks that surely could have been heard above a raging thunderstorm.

She and Errollyn sparred as the sailors watched them. Most Rhodaani men might have seen serrin women spar, but few would have seen human women at her standard. The svaalverd, at the level practised by Sasha and Errollyn, was blindingly fast. Neither of them missed a stroke, a shifting, circling dance of sliding feet and flashing wooden blades, the sharp cracking of wood-on-wood breaking the morning calm.

Errollyn suggested variations, and Sasha complied with flashing attacks, complete sequences but for the killing blow. She found herself actually enjoying the shifting deck beneath their feet. All svaalverd fighters were obsessed with balance, and anything that challenged it was an intrigue to be explored at length.

"Keep bossing her about, lad," said one bald, pot-bellied sailor in passing. "You can still teach her a thing or two, I'll wager."

Errollyn grinned, windmilling an arm, sweat dripping down his flexing chest and hard stomach. Sasha realised the sailor had mistaken Errollyn's suggestions for commands. "She's teaching me how not to die," Errollyn corrected the man. "If she came at me with something I was not prepared for, I'd last two strokes."

A few listeners laughed, as if thinking him joking. Or chivalrous, complimenting the girl. Watchers could not see what both Sasha and Errollyn could feel, in every flashing combination, in every clash of wood-on-wood. She was better. Not faster, and certainly not stronger. She simply translated thoughts and forms into actions faster and with greater cunning than he did. In fact, the ease with which she was coming to handle Errollyn in sparring sometimes bothered her. Errollyn was formidably good, by any standard. Perhaps, she sometimes thought, she was simply coming to know him too well. Perhaps she was not truly as superior as her results suggested. Perhaps she was only getting better at beating *him*. On mornings like this one, however, she doubted it. She could feel herself improving, and it was addictive. She wanted more. She wanted to know where the boundaries lay. And she wanted to know for certain that, the next time she met her enemies in battle, as many of them as drew steel against her would die for it, no matter what their numbers and standard.

Tracato announced its proximity approching with an increasing number of ships converging on the sea. At first one sail appeared on the afternoon horizon, then a couple more. All resolved into traders of one sort or another. Then came another pair, larger, twin-masted with huge, billowing sails. They came close, cutting the water with greater speed than Sasha had ever seen. Sailors lined their sides, and up in the rigging, most with bows. Amidships was a pair of ballista—huge things that no doubt fired flammable oils over a range many times further than a longbow.

Serrin warships. They flew no flag, for serrin had never yet agreed on the necessity of a single banner to represent their diversity. Neither was the hull painted, nor figures mounted on the bow, nor gold trim about the captain's quarters. Simple, they were, and beautiful in their sleek lines. Only the sails bore decoration, a dark embroidery on canvas white, a swirling pattern that might have made the outlines of a square or a rectangle.

"Saalsi script," said Errollyn, leaning at her side to watch them pass. Sasha took a closer look, and suddenly she could see it. Saalsi letters, overlaid and stylised.

"What do they say?"

Errollyn smiled, and shook his head. "Oh, a thousand things." Sometimes, even Errollyn failed the translation.

Toward evening, they came upon another warship, towing a second, half-size vessel in its wake. The captive's sails were blackened, some furled, others missing. Half the usual, tangled rigging seemed gone, and the masts were burned in places. As the *Maiden* heaved alongside the slower tandem, Sasha saw folk huddled on the deck in tight groups. Some appeared injured, others sooty. Yet others with swords stood over them, guarding, and even from this range Sasha could see that those were serrin. She could tell from the way they stood, and grasped the blades in their hands. And some appeared to be women.

This time, it was Kessligh at her side as she watched. "Elissian refugees," he said grimly. "Nobility, by the look of them."

Sasha nodded. Only nobility would have the money to pay such a passage. Trying to cross the Elissian Sea, only to be intercepted and captured. "Heading for Algrasse or Larosa," she agreed. "They must have been scared. Perhaps they recall what happened in Enora."

"I'm sure they do."

The *Maiden* reached Tracato shortly before midnight. The place did not look like much from out to sea, not after the gleaming slopes of Petrodor. Two dancing lights burned brighter than the others, reflecting double off the dark water. Some smaller lights above burned, and the flickering glow of many boats bobbed on the water like firebugs upon a Lenayin lake. To either side fanned the tall, dark cliffs of the Rhodaani coast.

Only when the port city drew closer did the scale of those two fires become apparent. Each was a great bonfire, burning atop a huge, square-sided tower of stone. Sasha stood amidships as the *Maiden* passed beneath the port tower, and stared up at its walls in amazement. Never in her life had she seen a structure so large. The twin fires lit the harbour mouth to near-daytime glare, and cast unearthly shadows across the rigging. Protruding from each tower's lower wall, Sasha could see the links of an impossibly huge steel chain. Within each tower would be winches, she knew, having heard tell of this particular defence. If under attack, the chain would be pulled tight, to keep invading ships out. To gain entrance to Tracato harbour, the towers would need to be captured first. From the sea, that didn't seem likely.

Within the harbour mouth sheer cliff walls loomed above a wide circle of sheltered water. Here, as sailors scrambled to fill out the sails in the dying breeze, Sasha could see the city lights—the lanterns on the docks, the mid-slope lights from the occasional house window, and the dancing line of torches above the great wall of Ushal Fortress. Tracato was barely a quarter the size of Petrodor but, many said, considerably more beautiful. Houses climbed the hill from Dockside toward the fortress that loomed over all— save the spires of the Heleshon Temple, lower and to the right—from this harbour view. But the dark robbed her of the sight of flying banners and colourful commotion on the docks.

Tracato was known to be windy, yet so sheltered was the harbour that barely a breeze pushed at the *Maiden*'s sails as she drifted slowly to an available mooring at the end of a long pier. There were many tall ships, lashed close together along the piers, frequently two abreast on either side. It made for a unique sight, so many masts and forests of tangling rope dimly lit from below by the nightwatch lights on deck. There seemed to be quite a few guards, Sasha noted, seeing the armed figures standing on the decks, or down on the piers.

The sailors worked fast, lashing sails and securing ropes. Sasha went below decks to fetch her small bag, and by the time she reemerged, a wide planking had been raised to the *Maiden*'s side. The captain was already on the pier, talking to a man in a wide black hat and a long red coat flanked by a pair of equally important-looking guards, who Sasha took for the Tracato Blackboots. They wore blue coats over mail, and their boots were indeed tall and black. A separate militia, to keep order in the city. She'd never seen their like before either.

Kessligh disembarked first, walking staff-in-hand, his saddlebag of luggage over his shoulder. Then went the three Rhodaani soldiers, and Councilman Dhael with his retainers. Sasha looked about to find Alythia standing close, wearing a flowing green gown with a laced back.

"Where's all your luggage?" Sasha asked. Alythia's hair fell in rich, black folds down her back and shoulders, her lips painted red, her nails long and sharp. Who she thought she would be making such a grand entrance for at this hour, Sasha had no idea.

"Councilman Dhael has arranged for his servants to collect it for me," she said mildly. Alythia, of course, had not come travelling with just a saddlebag. How she'd managed to accumulate so many possessions, after everything she'd brought from Lenayin had been lost in the fall of House Halmady was also a mystery.

Sasha disembarked after Errollyn, with Alythia behind. Soldiers and gathering dockworkers on the pier stopped whatever they were doing and stared. And not at *her*, Sasha noted.

The man in the red coat finished his business with the captain, who turned and made his way back up the plank to his ship. Sasha expected Councilman Dhael to announce himself first, but he stepped aside for the three Rhodaani soldiers. They thanked Dhael, conversed briefly with the red-coat, showed him a tattoo each had on their upper arm, and passed. The Steel were respected in Tracato, if even a councilman should step aside for them.

Dhael then introduced himself. The red-coat barely glanced at his face, made a mark on the parchment he carried flat on a writing board, and waved him and his retainers on. Dhael spoke with the senior-most of his retainers, striding down the pier without a glance behind. Sasha could just smell Alythia's annoyance.

"*Ur nahrom?*" the red-coat asked Kessligh. "Your name?" Sasha reckoned that was. She'd learned a little Larosan over the last six months in Petrodor.

"Kessligh Cronenverdt," he said, and continued in Torovan: "This is my uma, Sashandra Lenayin, her sister Alythia Lenayin and our companion Errollyn Y'saldi." Sasha winced inwardly. Errollyn never used the second name. It meant things that most humans did not understand. Here, it was formality.

"I shall ask them their names in turn," said the red-coat dismissively, also in Torovan. He peered at Kessligh, apparently unimpressed. There was little politeness about him. "Prove that you are Kessligh."

"Prove that I am not."

The man's nostrils flared. "Here in the great city of Tracato, all are answerable to the Council of Rhodaan and the High Table. Their appointed officers wear red coats, like mine. You shall answer my questions, or you shall not be allowed entry. Prove that you are Kessligh Cronenverdt."

"He could chop your fucking head off," Sasha snorted in Lenay. "That'd prove it."

"He could indeed," responded the red-coat in flawless Lenay. Sasha blinked. She'd not expected any in this part of Rhodia to understand her. "But it would not gain him entry to this city."

"Dear Lords, Sasha," Alythia exclaimed in exasperation, also in Lenay. "You're such a mindless unsophisticate, I can't believe you're my sister."

"Me neither," said Sasha, in Saalsi. Alythia frowned, uncomprehending.

"You speak Saalsi too?" the red-coat asked Sasha, also in Saalsi.

"Better than you, I'm certain," Sasha replied in the same.

"I quite doubt that, young lady—all the red-coats of Tracato are schooled in the language of our serrin friends since childhood." Sasha stood sullenly. His Saalsi *did* seem rather good. "You certainly do have the reputed appearance of Sashandra Lenayin . . . but these things are known to many, and could be imitated."

"Our languages too?" Sasha asked incredulously. "My tattoo? I'll show you that too if you like!"

"Sasha . . ." Kessligh began, with weary impatience.

"This is ridiculous!" Sasha exclaimed. "Who the hells else would we be? What kind of honourless people go about asking others to prove who they are?"

Errollyn put an arm about Sasha's shoulders to restrain her, and leaned forward. "Excuse me?" he asked, back in Torovan. "I'm rather tired and I'd like to lie down. If this is going to take a while, could I just go on and leave them?"

The red-coat looked amused. "Of course, serrin sir. Whenever you please."

"Oh that's great!" said Sasha. "Serrin get to enter whenever they please, and the rest of us must . . ." Errollyn muzzled her with a strong hand.

"I couldn't take her with me?" he asked the red-coat. "She's quite sweet with me, she only barks and growls at strangers." Sasha struggled to remove his hand, but it wasn't easy—Errollyn's right-handed grip came more from bows than swords, and had ferocious power.

"Master Errollyn," said the red-coat, "I do believe I recall you from Council sessions. How many years has it been?"

"Nearly three," said Errollyn.

Sasha finally freed herself, though it took both of her hands to do so.

"And you can vouch for these others?"

"For Kessligh, Sashandra and Alythia, yes. I'm quite sure I haven't been deceived as to their identities, by this one least of all. She's far too annoying to be anyone else." Alythia laughed like that was the funniest thing she'd heard in weeks.

The red-coat smiled grimly. "Very well. I shall require your marks on this paper, and you must report to a council officer before sundown tomorrow.

Failure to do so shall be taken as admission that your stated identities are false, and the Blackboots shall be alerted."

"Thank you, Errollyn," Alythia said graciously as they walked down the pier. "If we'd left it to Sasha, I'm sure we'd have all spent the night in a Tracato dungeon, at best."

Sasha let them talk, stalking angrily ahead. The decking felt as though it were still heaving beneath her, and it was a curious sensation indeed to take long strides and be certain that the boards were, in fact, not moving. The pier was wide: two horse-and-carts could easily have passed, making it possible to unload two large vessels simultaneously.

Fronting the docks were mostly warehouses, grim and silent, and guarded by militia men who Sasha guessed might be hired swords. There was little of the life and bustle of the Petrodor Dockside, and the water smelt foul as it lapped against the retaining wall. A sheltered harbour, Sasha realised, with no ocean currents to disperse the city's wastes.

Tracato Dockside was far more orderly than Petrodor's. The stone facades of taverns and dwellings presented a friendly face to the sea, alive with the light of lanterns.

Ahead, Councilman Dhael had walked to the forecourt of a tavern, where men waited with horses tethered to carriages to take folk up the incline. Sasha was in half a mood to walk, to stretch her legs and to see Tracato up close. But Alythia would assuredly dislike the notion, to say nothing of Kessligh's leg, so Sasha headed toward the carriages.

There were four of them, their drivers standing around a forecourt fountain, sharing drinks and laughing. And now, stepping about the carriages, were men in wide hats, matching dark tunic and pants, and tall black boots. Those men were looking at her. And now, they were coming toward her, swords swinging at their hips.

Sasha kept walking, counting ten Blackboots in all. They were spreading out now, across her path. Heart thumping in anticipation of trouble, Sasha found herself paying more attention to the dockfront windows behind the men than the men themselves. A Petrodor reflex that was, searching for archers—always her greatest concern. Swordsmen she could handle. Perhaps not ten, but maybe.

"Sashandra Lenayin!" announced the leader.

"Aye," said Sasha, with as much unconcern as she could muster. "Who blocks my way?"

"We are the Blackboots of Tracato!" he said in Torovan.

"I can see that." She stopped. A city militia, by the coin of the Council of Rhodaan, the Blackboots kept the peace, it was said. And given that the

Council was largely under the control of the feudalists these days, it was also said the Blackboots were bought and paid for by the noble families of Tracato.

"We have orders that you are to be detained."

She was not particularly surprised. There had been enough Tracatans in Petrodor of late, many of whom she'd talked to. It was common knowledge that she and Kessligh were headed this way. No surprise that someone here found the fact disquieting. But she did not like how it developed on this quiet, nighttime dock, with only a few witnesses who could be arrested, paid off or murdered.

She drew her sword. "By whose authority?"

Swords came out in reply. "The Council of Rhodaan," said the lieutenant, stony faced. Sasha looked beyond him to Councilman Dhael, now boarding his carriage. Dhael looked her way. He saw, but did nothing. He was an elected member of the Council of Rhodaan. Had he known?

Dhael's carriage rattled off.

"Now lads," came Kessligh's voice from Sasha's back, "your seniors have done you a grave disservice in sending only ten of you." He came closer, yet Sasha could not hear his staff tapping on the paving. That meant he'd drawn his blade, as no doubt had Errollyn. "I am Kessligh Cronenverdt, and this is Errollyn. If you know our identities, then you'll know that ten to three are odds greatly in our favour."

"You have no authority to defy the order of the Council of Rhodaan," said the lieutenant. "Besides which, you may wish to reconsider the odds."

More Blackboots were emerging from the tavern. Some were putting their hats on, others adjusting their sword belts. They'd been drinking, clearly, and caught off guard.

"Twenty to three?" Errollyn said in Lenay at Sasha's side, testing the weight of his blade.

"You can have the seven on the left," said Sasha.

"Oh, generous."

"Oh look, you pack of imbeciles," said Alythia, striding to stand between the groups. "Seriously, why must everyone always draw swords at the slightest provocation?" She drew herself up to her full height before the lieutenant, chin up and chest out. The lieutenant's eyes dropped, predictably. Sasha nearly laughed.

"Fear not, my friends," she said in Lenay, "my sister's breasts may save us yet."

Alythia threw Sasha a nasty look. "Lieutenant," she said, "I am Princess Alythia Lenayin."

"Princess," said the lieutenant.

"Yes, Princess! Wedded to Gregan Halmady, and widowed in the War of the King. I have come to Tracato to meet with the Lady Renine, and her son, the young Lord Alfriedo. They shall be expecting me."

The lieutenant looked wary. Not a bad ploy at all, Sasha reconsidered. The Renines were the highest rank of nobility in Tracato, direct descendants of the last Rhodaani king. Some Rhodaani feudalists, pursuing the distant dream of a restoration of royal power, called Alfriedo "The Young King." And now, come treating upon their doorstep, was a princess.

"One of these days," said Errollyn in Lenay, "you shall stop underestimating your sister." Alythia might have heard him, for she seemed to stand a little taller.

The lieutenant conferred with his men. There was hand waving, and some agitation. Alythia threw Sasha a superior look.

"Don't get smug yet," Sasha told her in Lenay, "there's still twenty of them."

"And vastly less dangerous, without a blade being swung," Alythia said. "When will you learn?"

Yells from across the dock interrupted the lieutenant's arguments. Everyone looked as down a nearby road came running young men with no apparent uniform, save the swords across their backs. But not serrin. Nasi-Keth then. The lieutenant rolled his eyes in exasperation.

The Nasi-Keth came on with no small amount of hollering and whooping, like boys on their way to a mud fight. As they came closer, Sasha saw that many of them were just that—boys, or teenagers at least, sprinting now with the enthusiasm of those who feared they'd nearly missed an excitement.

"Kessligh Cronenverdt!" exclaimed the first to arrive. This was a man, not a boy, bald with a red goatee. His blue eyes shone with lively welcome. "I am Reynold Hein of the Tol'rhen, welcome to Tracato!"

He grasped Kessligh's hand and shook, ignoring the drawn blade. Other young men skidded in, out of breath and happy.

"I'm sorry we didn't get here sooner," Reynold continued. "Our Ulenshaal predicted the winds and thought it a good chance your boat would arrive this evening, so we waited at the tavern up the road. Its owner is a good friend to Nasi-Keth; there's not the same unsavoury characters that frequent some other taverns . . ." He threw a glance at the Blackboots. "But our Dockwatcher strolled off to talk to a pretty girl who works along the way. . . ."

Catcalls and jeers came from the Nasi-Keth at an unfortunate young man who blushed red and looked at his feet.

". . . and we nearly missed your arrival!"

"Step away from them!" barked the lieutenant, brandishing his sword. "They are to be detained by order of the Council of Rhodaan!"

The Nasi-Keth laughed, not even bothering to draw their own weapons. Several danced daringly close to the Blackboots, bare handed, making faces. The Blackboots seemed concerned all the same, weapons ready.

"Oh, don't mind them," said Reynold, "they can barely use those toys they're holding. I daresay you three could take them all without a sweat, but it's really better if we don't have to kill any Blackboots tonight. . . ."

An infuriated Blackboot lunged at one young man who came too close. The Nasi-Keth backed up, laughing and hooting. The Blackboot's hat fell off in his lunge. In a flash a Nasi-Keth grabbed it and ran off with his prize, waving it in the air. Several others pursued, wanting to try it on.

"But I haven't introduced myself to everyone," said Reynold, moving on to Sasha. "You must be Sashandra Lenayin! An honour . . . and Princess Alythia!"

A flurry of introductions followed, eager young men equally pleased to meet them all. Alythia seemed a little frustrated. She'd been grooming Councilman Dhael throughout the long boat journey, and now he had ridden off. The Blackboots had seemed about to take her to Family Renine, yet the Blackboots now faded back toward the fountain and carriages, plotting their next move. Alythia sought the powerful like a river sought the ocean. Sasha, however, was more pleased with present company.

The Blackboots returned to their tavern while the Nasi-Keth commandeered a carriage. It became clear, however, that there was not a great distance to walk, and that the Nasi-Keth lads would all be walking. Sasha, Errollyn and Kessligh joined them, Kessligh insisting that his leg was fine over short distances. Alythia rode in the carriage, with three young men valiantly volunteering to accompany her. All three looked quite anxious in her presence, so Sasha did not have much concern for Alythia's honour.

"Where do all you lads come from?" Kessligh asked as they walked together up the slope.

"From all over," Reynold Hein said proudly. "We are the sons of poor folk and wealthy folk, farmers and land owners, traders, craftsmen, from all of Rhodaan to the north, east, west and south. All come to learn the ways of the Nasi-Keth in the Tol'rhen; it has been thus for two hundred years."

"And for far longer than that," Kessligh agreed.

"Oh, of course," Reynold exclaimed, as though delighted to be reminded that he was not talking to someone who knew little of Nasi-Keth history. "The Nasi-Keth have been in Rhodaan for more centuries than we know how to count. We were a persecuted movement for centuries beneath the feudals, and now we flourish. Our greatest regret is that we have not been able to spread our wings beyond the Saalshen Bacosh, into further lands. That is why we have been so excited the last few months, hearing that the renowned Kessligh Cronenverdt had come to Petrodor, and was likely to continue on to Tracato!"

"The Blackboots back there," said Sasha, "why did they want us detained?"

"Some feudalist no doubt finds your presence threatening," Reynold said dismissively. Despite his baldness, he was a young man . . . no more than thirty, Sasha guessed. Lean and fit, he moved with the lightness of a fighter. "They squabble a lot. And of course, you're both Lenay . . . or Sashandra, at least, and Kessligh is most commonly thought of as Lenay. . . ."

"I think of myself as Lenay," Kessligh agreed.

"And your army currently marches on us from the west," Reynold continued. Neither Kessligh nor Sasha replied.

"Anyhow," Reynold continued, "you are Nasi-Keth, and you cannot help the actions of the Lenay king. You are welcome guests of the Tol'rhen in Tracato. Just be warned—not every Rhodaani shall feel the same."

"I understand," said Kessligh. He seemed to walk easily enough with his staff, and the incline was not steep. "What are you all studying?"

"Us here this evening? I am a junior Ulenshaal myself, I teach history and philosophy. These are some of my students, but not all."

Some of the other lads volunteered their areas of learning. There seemed no particular pattern of interests, though philsophy seemed very common. One boy, who could not have been more than fourteen, enthusiastically explained how he was studying the applications of mathematics to stonemasonry. He hoped to become a great builder, and make grand buildings in Tracato and across the Saalshen Bacosh.

"And in Elisse too one day," someone suggested, and there were cheers. That turned the conversation to the war in Elisse. General Zulmaher was making great progress, it seemed, though there remained a worry that he would not complete his conquest before the great Larosan and Lenay armies mustered in the west. Some concern was voiced that General Zulmaher was a feudalist, and did not truly wish to liberate Elisse from feudal tyranny. Others argued that it did not matter, so long as Elisse was eliminated as a threat to Rhodaan's northern border while the Steel faced the oncoming, and far greater, western threat.

Another young man thought it wonderful that Elisse would soon become the fourth province of the Saalshen Bacosh, the first such expansion since the serrin arrived two centuries before. Sasha recalled what Councilman Dhael had said about imperial ambition, and how some felt it didn't belong in Rhodaan. None of these young students seemed to agree. Perhaps times were changing.

The road entered a grand square, with statues twice the size of a man towering before the walls. Lanterns illuminated the figures from below, stone faces aflicker, eyes wise and distant. About the facade walls were arches, and smaller statues adorned high rooftops. Sasha stared about, amazed.

"Who are these people?"

"Surely you recognise the lady here?" Reynold said, pointing to a statue of a woman in a flowing robe. She held a book before her, as though in prayer over its pages. From the faint angle of the sculpted cheekbones, Sasha thought the woman must be serrin.

"Maldereld?" Sasha said dubiously. "But she was a warrior."

Reynold nodded. "More renowned to Tracatans as a scholar, and a builder of institutions. The artists most commonly portray her with books or scrolls."

Suddenly the air clattered with hooves. Horses burst into the courtyard, men astride wearing jackets and swordbelts that glittered gold and silver in the lantern light. The Nasi-Keth lads stopped, and fell back cautiously, yet no blades were drawn. For an instant, Sasha thought the horsemen might attempt an encirclement, but they reined to a halt not far from the group, and presented no immediate threat save that they blocked the way.

The lead rider swung down from his saddle. He was a portly man of perhaps middle age, with long hair and a trim beard.

"Lord Elot!" called Reynold, with little apparent concern. "A nice night for a ride?"

"Indeed, Master Reynold," said Lord Elot. "I had heard that you may be in the presence of royalty. This caused us much alarm, for surely little would you know of how to treat a royal lady."

"And now you have blocked her path, and delayed her arrival at a meal and a hot bath, which she was surely desiring. Where are your manners, Lord Elot?"

"You have guests and you have not introduced me," Elot replied, unfazed. "Where are yours, Master Reynold?"

"Kessligh Cronenverdt," said Reynold, indicating Kessligh. "His uma, Sashandra Lenayin. Master Errollyn. And in the carriage, as befits her station, Princess Alythia Lenayin."

"Yuan Kessligh," said Lord Elot, walking to him. "I am Lord Desani Elot, cousin to the Lady Renine."

"A pleasure," said Kessligh, shaking his hand. "My uma, Sashandra."

Elot took Sasha's hand also, but seemed uncertain what to do with it. Sasha was used to that. She escorted the lord back to the carriage, which she guessed was the proper form, and opened the door. Alythia emerged, with no small drama. Elot took a knee.

"My dear Lord," said Alythia. "A true pleasure to meet one of the great line of Renine. I have read so much about you." Sasha knew that it was true.

Alythia had done considerable reading over the last few months in Petrodor on the history of Rhodaan. She knew who was in power when the serrin came, who had resisted and perished, who relinquished their feudal powers willingly to help the serrin make a new Rhodaan and who never returned at all from the forests of Saalshen.

She had also read some small amount on Enora, and had recounted with much shock her findings to Sasha. The example of Enora had frightened many Rhodaani noble families into cooperation with the serrin, and the serrin, perhaps ashamed of the slaughter, had treated those families less harshly as hindsight now suggested that they might have been. The serrin had expected nobility, awkward and antiquated concept that it was, to die a natural death. Instead, it had clung on long enough to rise again with the flourishing wealth of the new Rhodaani nation. Today, noble families were powerful once more, and although their old entitlements were stricken from Rhodaani law, that did not mean as much to some as the enforcers of the new laws believed it should.

Lord Elot kissed Alythia's hand. "Princess Alythia. An honour."

"Were those your men who tried to abduct us at the docks?" Alythia enquired mildly.

"A misunderstanding, Your Highness," he said. "Several of our noblemen heard only that some powerful Lenays were coming to Rhodaan . . . the men and women of Lenayin are not greatly in favour in Rhodaan at this time, please understand."

Alythia inclined her head, gracefully.

"I hope that they did not cause you too great an inconvenience?" Elot pressed.

"Not too great," said Alythia.

"Your Highness, I am here to offer you an invitation of hospitality, from Family Renine to you. We would be honoured for you to join us, where we can lodge you in the manner to which you are rightly accustomed."

Alythia's gaze flicked to Sasha. Smug.

"I should be very pleased to accept such a gracious offer," she said. "Would you be so good as to grant me an escort?"

"Your Highness, I am most relieved. I had feared our rash noble friends had caused you an offence. I shall escort your carriage personally."

He rose, and strode to his horsemen.

"'Lyth, you're crazy!" Sasha exclaimed in Lenay. "You've no idea who the hells he is!"

"He is nobility, Sasha," Alythia said calmly, as though that made everything fine.

"And you're the daughter of the man who leads the best warriors in

Rhodia into a war against Rhodaan! You don't think you'd make a wonderful hostage?"

Alythia did not get angry. Instead, she placed a hand on Sasha's shoulder. "Sasha, it's very sweet that you're concerned for me, but please. You know me. This is what I'm good at. You have your sword, and Kessligh has his high reputation and military mind, and I have the influence of status and royalty. Besides which, if not to make contacts of this sort, why on Earth do you think I came along?"

"Because in Petrodor you were poor," Sasha said drily.

"Exactly," said Alythia, smiling sweetly. "This is my element, Sasha. I don't tell you how to fight. Do me the same courtesy, yes?"

Two

SOFY LENAYIN GALLOPED ACROSS THE ROLLING HILLS of southern Telesia, and felt that life could not possibly be more wonderful. Everywhere the grass was rising on tall stems that lashed about her horse's legs, and flowers were blooming, yellow and purple and red across the glorious green sea.

Ahead, the land rose once more, and Sofy urged Dary faster up the rise. Perhaps she would finally discover a view down into Algrasse, and the Bacosh. But when she arrived, she saw only more hills, and lush, waving grass and flowers, far off to the horizon. The sight made her happy. She did not want this journey to end.

Further along the shallow ridge there loomed another old fortress, stark, broken walls and piles of fallen stones now overgrown with weeds. She pointed Dary that way and let him run as only a Lenay dussieh could—tirelessly, and with little sign of fatigue. She liked to ride out in front of her guard like this, and pretend she was alone on the plain, just her and her horse, and the wind in her hair. Princess Sofy Lenayin had been truly alone and in charge of her own destiny so very few times in her life.

Upon reaching the first of the fallen black stones, she reined Dary to a halt and dismounted. Immediately she heard the approach of her guard, four warriors on splendid warhorses, red capes flying, sunlight flashing on silver mail.

"Highness," said Lieutenant Tyrel of the Royal Guard, "allow us to search the ruins first before you enter."

"Oh, nonsense, Lieutenant!" Sofy protested. "It's no fun exploring when you've already checked everything for me! Besides, these things have been deserted for centuries!"

"All the same, Highness," he said, handing her his mount's halter. "There could be bandits, or scavengers."

Tyrel and another man drew their blades and climbed over the stones through a gap in the wall, leaving Sofy minding the horses while the other two guards rode the perimeter. That much, at least, they trusted her with.

She was not much of a rider yet, compared to men such as these, but she could mind horses well enough.

Soon the guardsmen came back to say all was clear. Sofy climbed gingerly over the rocks, still not entirely accustomed to her leather boots and the riding pants she wore beneath her dress. She wished she could discard the dress, but there were too many men around who would find such a thing confronting. Whatever her recent adventures, she remained a princess of Lenayin, and a princess of Lenayin could not in good conscience wear pants alone.

Within the wall, she found herself in a wide courtyard of lush grass. Rising about, forming a square, were the remains of defensive walls.

"A place for perhaps fifty men and their horses," said Lieutenant Tyrel. He pointed toward a large gap in the wall. "That would have been the main gate. They would have fetched water from the stream in the next valley." Sofy hadn't noticed a stream, but perhaps that was the difference between herself, who rode purely for pleasure, and Tyrel, who did not.

"It would be very crowded for so many horses in here," Sofy said.

"Only if they were attacked," said Tyrel. "Most other times the horses would graze free. These walls are only for defence in face of a superior enemy."

"Not from an army, surely," said Sofy. She wandered alongside the near wall, sidestepping fallen stones. On the most well-preserved portions of wall she could see battlements, where archers would have defended the walls from attack. "Fifty men behind these walls would barely last past breakfast against a determined infantry."

She nearly smiled at her observation . . . as if *she* would know such things. Well, she was learning. She'd ridden with her sister Sasha in the Udalyn rebellion, and now she found herself six weeks and counting in the company of the greatest army Lenayin had ever sent to war. Sofy was good at asking questions and listening. In the presence of so many great warriors, all pining for their wives and daughters left behind, it was not hard to find knowledgeable men who found pleasure in sitting with her over a meal discussing such things as battlefield formations, infantry tactics and the offensive deployment of cavalry.

A gleam in the grass caught her eye. She stooped, and picked up a small piece of metal covered in dirt. Brushing at it, she found it was a coin. "Oh, how wonderful! It has markings. . . . I can't read them, it's too dirty. Perhaps I'll have found a clue. I must have this cleaned." She tucked it into the little pouch at her belt.

Sofy wanted to climb to the battlement, but Tyrel forbade it.

"It's my neck on the block if you so much as twist your finger, begging your pardon, Highness. You've a wedding to attend, and I'll see that you reach it in perfect health."

A wedding. Just like that, her day darkened. Suddenly, the old walls lost their fascination, and she yearned once more for the freedom of the plains.

They rode down to water their horses at the little stream Captain Tyrel had spotted. Thick bushes grew there, and a few small, twisted trees, clinging close to the water's edge. Sofy remembered the coin and washed it in the crystal water, but the dirt was centuries ingrained, and the metal itself seemed black with age. Perhaps someone back at the column would know a way of making it clean.

Finding the Lenay column once more was not difficult—it stretched for a half day's march and more. So many men could be heard well before they were seen—a tinkle of metal, a creaking of leathers, a whisper of boots through the long grass. And coughs, whinnies, conversation and snatches of song. And, because they were Lenay, laughter. Lenay men made jokes to pass the time. Sofy had overheard some on her daily rides, and most had been coarse enough to make her blush bright pink. But that had been weeks ago; now she only smiled. She could hardly begrudge them their humour after six weeks' march, and more yet to come.

Then they cleared a rise and she could see it. The column snaked across the hillside, as untidy and irregular as the Lenay people themselves. Certainly there was little discipline in their formations, as men walked where they would and stopped where they would, and went wandering off to the column's side as they felt the urge to relieve themselves, or observe some passing curiosity. Only the banners held the broader column into its preferred order— the bannermen had been informed of the dishonour to their unit and region should they fall behind or lose their place, and so far, none had done so.

Sofy galloped to them, unable to see the column's head. Men saw her coming, four Royal Guardsmen at her sides and another ten fanning further behind and to the flanks. Cheers went up, and swords were raised to salute her. Sofy grinned and waved back, coming close and then turning across them, heading toward the front.

These here were men of Rayen, southeastern Lenayin—she could tell well before she saw a banner from the long, thick locks of their Goeren-yai men. They favoured hard leather armour, studded and decorated with roundrel-pattern adornments. Many had shields slung at their backs—a rare thing for Lenay militia, though recently made more common by their provision courtesy of the king, as a gift to all the men who marched.

The column trailed along a gentle hillside, into a low valley then up the other side. Clearing the crest, Sofy found the Neysh cavalry, gathered to the front of the Neysh portion of column—crown-funded regulars in heavier armour, and noble lords in finer clothes and family colours. They also saluted her, most of them Verenthane, save for small groups of wild-haired Goeren-yai horsemen on smaller Lenay dussiehs.

As she passed the Neysh bannermen, Sofy knew she was getting close. Now came the Ranash, and she did not raise nearly the number of cheers from them as she had from the southerners. Ranash was northern, and entirely Verenthane. They recalled the Udalyn Rebellion, and they recalled the youngest princess of Lenayin's part in it. Few appeared to blame her openly to any great degree, reserving that displeasure for her sister, Sasha. Most believed Sofy to have been in Sasha's thrall . . . which was perhaps true, Sofy admitted to herself now, but not in the way *they* thought.

The Ranash infantry were more orderly too, and far better equipped, with heavier, black uniform armour, shields, helms and even spears. There were no earrings here, no tattoos, no decorations of any kind save a greater number of banners, many denoting family symbols that middle and southern Lenayin disdained, and many eight-pointed Verenthane stars on poles or flags.

The Ranash cavalry, when Sofy reached them, gave her no salute at all. Noblemen watched her coldly beneath heavy steel helms, and heavily armoured regulars chose not to even notice her passage. There were not so many of the Ranash as the Neysh, as all the north bordered onto hostile Cherrovan, and their forces were in much demand at home. With this in mind, the north had conducted early winter forays into Cherrovan before the heavier snows set in, and had inflicted great losses. Sofy had heard tales of entire Cherrovan villages destroyed, and warbands trapped in valleys and slaughtered without mercy. Most officers she'd spoken to seemed to think the thrust would weaken the Cherrovan sufficiently to keep Lenayin secure in the column's absence. Sofy wondered how they could be so sure that it wouldn't have just inflamed Cherrovan into a more serious attack in the months ahead.

She cleared the crest of another hill, and saw on the downslope the Ranash bannermen, leading the Ranash nobility. Ahead of them stretched a long column of carts and a few carriages, perhaps forty in all. Sofy galloped past, and could now see the vanguard, a great cluster of red and gold Royal Guardsmen mixed with nobility from each province, each with their own captains and entourage. Further still, several formations of regulars on horseback fanned across the hillsides, perhaps five hundred in all, spread left and right in a great crescent wall across the grass. Ahead of them, a mounted scout made a small figure against a distant hillcrest, and there would be perhaps a hundred more riding yet further before and out to the flanks, some staying close, others now several days' journey away.

She'd barely begun to pass the central vanguard when a small horse broke from the side of a carriage and cantered to her side. Astride the dussieh was a slim girl in a light red dress over riding pants and boots. Her jet black hair was tied with multicoloured ribbons, and she rode with rare confidence for a Lenay woman.

"Princess!" she exclaimed, irritated as she drew alongside. "Why did you leave me for so long?"

Sofy smiled wickedly. "Did Lord Rydar corner you in the carriage again?"

"It's not funny!" Yasmyn retorted. "I think he does not speak Lenay so well. I tell him 'no,' but he does not understand."

"Oh. he understands well enough," said Sofy, highly amused. "He just doesn't listen."

"He is an ugly man," Yasmyn insisted, scowling. "Maybe he will listen if I cut off his cock."

Sofy suppressed a laugh. Yasmyn's threats were nothing to laugh at. She was from far western Isfayen, the second daughter of Faras Izlar, Great Lord of Isfayen. Like most of the Isfayen, Yasmyn had light brown skin, black hair and a pronounced slant to the eyes. Alone of all the women of Lenayin, Isfayen women usually went armed, and while they were rarely warriors in wars, they were as little known for gentleness as their men. Yasmyn's blade was a wicked-looking curved thing that the Isfayen called a *darak*, and she wore it shoved through the belt above her right hip. Sofy had seen her practising with it, and knew the *darak* to be frighteningly sharp. Perhaps she should talk to the overeager and rather silly Lord Rydar, before he suffered some unfortunate injury.

Yasmyn had been part Damon's idea, and part Koenyg's. All Lenay princesses in a wedding procession required handmaidens, to attend to their needs and to protect their virtue . . . particularly as this wedding procession doubled as a great army, filled with young warriors eager to demonstrate their virility. The Larosans in particular, Koenyg and Archbishop Dalryn had reasoned, would expect numerous handmaidens on such a journey, for propriety's sake. Sofy had eight, piled into various carts and carriages.

Damon, however, held a dim view of the useful attributes of most of Baen-Tar's assorted maidens, noble daughters and ladies-in-waiting. He'd wanted for his little sister a companion who might not only protect her, but actually teach her something. As it happened, Great Lord Faras had seen the war as a grand opportunity to forge closer links between his province and the Lenay royalty. Damon had suggested his daughter might become Sofy's primary handmaiden on this journey, and Faras had been pleased to appoint Yasmyn to the role. Koenyg was still unhappy about it. The women of Isfayen would hardly be seen, by lowland eyes, as models of propriety and Verenthane virtue.

Sofy didn't care. She was just happy to have some female company that wasn't scared of contradicting her.

"Prince Koenyg is mad at you too," Yasmyn added, trotting at Sofy's side as they made gradual progress up the vanguard's flank.

"Prince Koenyg is always mad at me," Sofy replied. "What did I do this time?"

"He said you were gone too long. You know he does not like it when you ride so far."

"I wasn't gone very long!" Sofy scoffed. "I was just a few hills away. I found another old fortress and went exploring. Look, I found a coin." She pulled out the coin from her belt and gave it to Yasmyn. "I'd like to get it cleaned—maybe I can discover whose it was."

"If you want." Yasmyn gave a shrug and tucked the coin into her own belt purse. "I say it was Valdryd the Reaver. He lived around the same time as these fortresses, and he laid waste to all these southern lands. The fortresses must have been raised by the inhabitants to try to stop him."

"Oh, I don't doubt they were raised to stop invading Lenays," Sofy said sadly. "But raised by who?"

"It does not matter," said Yasmyn. "Valdryd was strong. These men of the forts, they are all dead now. All fell before Valdryd." She seemed pleased with this. Sofy expected nothing else of the Isfayen. She sighed, and thought how nice it would be if her nation were responsible for making some other contribution to its neighbours other than shortening the lifespan of their fighting men.

A great, roan stallion wheeled from amidst the Royal Guardsmen ahead, its rider spurring to Sofy's side. Yasmyn wisely made way as Prince Koenyg, heir of Lenayin, brought his warhorse to his sister's side. Sofy controlled Dary's head with difficulty, as the horse towered over the little dussieh, snorting and dancing.

"That's your last ride," said Koenyg, glaring down at her. "I warned you not to stray so far."

"I can't hear you, brother," Sofy said mildly. "You're too high above me, please lean down closer else the wind carries your words away."

"Don't play games with me," Koenyg said. "I'll have enough trouble explaining this to your husband and his family when we arrive in Sherdaine. Fancy a lowlands Verenthane bride gallivanting around on horseback. You risk the future of all Lenayin with your stubbornness, and I'll not have it."

Sofy looked up at him for the first time. Prince Koenyg Lenayin was not the tallest of King Torvaal's sons, yet he made a striking figure all the same. He wore mail beneath a broad-shouldered leather jacket, and metal-studded shoulder guards patterned with the snarling image of a mountain cat. His gloves were overlaid with steel knuckle guards in decorative patterns, his boots bore steel caps and vicious spurs, and his sword pommel was a real Lenay beauty—a plain leather binding beneath a pommel head in the form of an eight-pointed Verenthane star. His face was broad and round, hard and handsome, and his dark hair, free of a helm, was short and perfectly neat. Beneath the mail and leathers, Koenyg's body was broad and square, with shoulders made for swinging swords in the Lenay style. The Stone Wall of Lenayin, some called him. His expression now suited that name entirely.

"You and Father think to marry Lenayin to the Larosa," Sofy said coldly. "I intend to make sure that the Larosans will be marrying a real Lenay, not some cheap lowlands imitation. I'll not dress like them, nor talk like them, nor behave like them should it not suit me. I intend to keep Lenay maids in court, and teach the Lenay tongue to all courtiers. Should they object, I shall protest, and all shall hear of it. Imagine the Larosan shame, that they cannot satisfy the wife of the Regent's heir, and the shame of Lenayin, to abandon her princess to such an unhappy fate. The alliance should suffer, I am certain."

Koenyg's gloved hands flexed upon the rein. Sofy knew that he was grinding his teeth. It was a while before he could speak. "You," he said in a voice that barely carried above the thudding of hooves, "are dancing on very thin ice, little sister."

"I am so tired of being pushed around," Sofy replied, with dark, even temper. "So tired, Koenyg. The peoples of Lenayin are independent, and do not cherish being stamped upon. Sasha reminded you once, and I remind you again. Stop now, before you destroy everything you claim to serve."

"You do not speak to me of service to Lenayin!" Koenyg snarled. "You are a woman! You do not wield a sword, you do not risk death in war, you live pampered and protected by menfolk on all sides. Your only sacrifice is marriage, in this case to perhaps the wealthiest and most esteemed family in all Rhodia! I think you got a bargain in this deal of life, little sister, yet you whine about it."

"This isn't about me, you big fool!" Sofy exclaimed with creeping desperation. "This is about Lenayin. You seek alliance with the Larosa, but on what terms? The people of Lenayin will never accept anything less than equality, yet the lowlanders to a man and woman consider us savages! You tell me to behave, not to ride my horse, to be a good and proper little Verenthane princess . . . is this to be Lenayin's fate too? Should we not speak our tongues, and sing our songs, and dance our dances? Should we hide in shame, and beg acceptance from those perfumed Larosan snobs? You've bossed and pushed and prodded all of Lenayin into this war, and willingly enough, thanks to the Lenay love of warfare . . . but good gods, Koenyg, you can't neglect Lenay pride. You are a commander of Lenay soldiers, how can you expect us to enter an unequal marriage bereft of pride?"

Koenyg almost smiled, grimly. "That's elaborate, Sofy, even for you." His temper had nearly faded, a hard, implacable certainty in its place. "So skilfully you turn your little personal dramas into a concern for all of Lenayin."

Sofy sighed, and hung her head. Arguing with Koenyg truly was like bashing one's head against a stone wall. She should have known better.

"Less than a year ago, you had no great love of horses, and no skill in riding. Yet suddenly, your selfish pursuit is the foundation upon which the entire fate of Lenayin is balanced."

"I've changed."

"Aye. To suit yourself, you have. I ask you to change back, to suit Lenayin. You are one person, and Lenayin is many people. My tutors taught me maths, and I can prove it to you should you wish." He touched heels to his stallion's sides, and cantered off toward the vanguard's head.

Yasmyn took her place again at Sofy's side. "I like arguing with him so much better when he's angry," Sofy said glumly. "He doesn't think when he's angry. But when he recovers his senses like that, he becomes annoyingly insightful."

"He scares me," said Yasmyn.

"Oh go on!" Sofy scolded lightly. "You, a noble daughter of Isfayen, frightened of a man?"

"A *great* man," Yasmyn corrected. Her dark eyes, shining with worship, had not left Koenyg's departing back. "All great men are frightening."

Sofy sighed again. Given some time, she might have made a convincing argument that the majority of her Lenay brethren were not, in fact, savages. But the Isfayen were on their own.

Sofy was practising her Larosan in the royal carriage after lunch when the door opened, and Damon hauled himself inside. Ulynda, Sofy's grey-haired tutor, bowed low. "Shall I leave, Highness?"

"Yes," said Damon.

"No," said Sofy at the same time. The middle-aged woman bowed to Damon, opened the carriage's opposite door and climbed down with assistance from a Royal Guardsman. Sofy frowned at Damon as he loosened his swordbelt. "Damon, truly, she has a bad knee, there was no need to tell her to leave."

Damon ignored her, pulling off his heavy gloves. Sofy's third-eldest brother had always looked slightly dark and morose, and now more than ever. He had a lean face, suited more by longer hair than the Verenthane norm. His garb was no less martial than Koenyg's, but somehow it seemed to sit ill upon his tall frame. He looked sombre, Sofy thought. Brooding, even.

She put aside her book of Larosan poems and folded her hands in her lap, waiting. Damon did this sometimes, simply imposed himself upon her company, and left it to her to probe and discover what was bothering him. He leaned his head back now, rocking as the carriage trundled over rough ground, and stared blankly out of the open window.

"How's the Larosan coming?" he asked.

"It's a nice language," Sofy replied. "They write the most lovely poetry." Sofy loved their plays, songs and poems, and had taught herself Larosan from an early age. "I would learn faster if you would not dismiss my tutor in mid-lesson so you could come and chat."

Damon let the jibe pass. This listlessness worried her. Unlike Koenyg, and the late-yet-legendary Krystoff, Prince Damon was not the most lively and positive of princes. But this was becoming extreme, even for him.

"The last scout says we will not be in these foothills beyond tomorrow," he said. "We should be in Algrasse the day after that, and then there'll be farmlands."

"And fresh food!" said Sofy. She was getting a little tired of the dried fare brought from Lenayin in the supply wagons.

Damon shrugged. "Perhaps. If Lord Heshan is true to his word, and supplies our army along the way. The lords of the Bacosh are not renowned for keeping their word on anything."

"He'd better," said Sofy. "We haven't brought enough. We'd have to forage, otherwise."

Damon rolled his eyes and grimaced. A Lenay army in the lowlands. Foraging. It seemed dangerously close to "looting." And "invasion." The lowlands had lived in terror of a Lenay invasion for centuries, an occurrence only prevented by the overlordship of the Cherrovan Empire, and the preference of the various Lenay regions for fighting each other. Leading an army of thirty-thousand Lenay warriors into the "civilised" lowlands made a great many people nervous, including some noble Lenays who did not trust the civility of their ruffian country cousins. It was a delicate matter all round. That the Larosans were allowing passage across their lands, and had encouraged Algrasse and Telesia to allow the same, was indication enough of how much the Lenays were needed in the war to come.

"So," said Sofy. "How does your journey fare? Amongst all the grand importances of the vanguard?"

"Still squabbling about who will take the centre in the first battle," said Damon. "The northerners, of course, insist it shall be them, but Koenyg insists on the importance of deploying heavy cavalry to a useful flank, and Father agrees. Furthermore, the Hadryn insist they will not hold the Taneryn flank, and vice versa; the Isfayen will have nothing to do with the Yethulyn; a grand family of Fyden have discovered they share the same house banner as a family from Banneryd, and have nearly come to blows over its ownership; and the new Great Lord of Taneryn, Ackryd, refuses to ride with the vanguard, and has headed back to his part of the column."

"Well, that's Lenayin for you. I don't know why you let it bother you, Damon. Division is the nature of our kingdom, and always shall be."

"That doesn't bother me," Damon replied tiredly. "It's just . . . I don't know how this is going to work, Sofy. Everyone fights differently, everyone's in the war for personal advantage and glory. I don't believe there's any certainty that the great lords will even obey commands from Father or Koenyg in the heat of battle, if they think they have a better idea. Or if they see the order as advantaging a Lenay rival."

Sofy did not reply. She was thinking about her sister Sasha. Sasha was Nasi-Keth, and thus loved the serrin. Sasha also loved Lenayin. Yet Lenayin was now marching to make war on the serrin . . . or at least, on their Saalshen Bacosh allies. Gods knew what Sasha felt, wherever she was now. Sofy was a Verenthane, as were all Lenayin royalty, and most of the nobility. The war was being fought in the name of the Verenthane faith. Yet for all the grand pronouncements of Archbishop Dalryn, and of the devout nobility, and from the northerners in particular, she could not feel any enthusiasm for this war.

The serrin had never chosen to make war on anyone. War had been made upon them, and the occupation of the Saalshen Bacosh had been self-defence, nothing more. They were gentle and kind, save where human aggression had forced them to fight for survival. What the serrin had helped the Saalshen Bacosh to build, in two centuries of occupation, seemed wonderful. And now, her father King Torvaal of Lenayin was leading an army of her countrymen to marry a Lenay princess to the Larosan heir, and forge a holy Verenthane alliance that would bind Lenayin's future to that of the Verenthane lowlands forever.

That alliance would necessarily mean the reconquest of the Saalshen Bacosh, and the destruction of all the civilisation the serrin had brought to those peoples . . . but that mattered little compared to the holy Verenthane future of Lenayin. The future *was* Verenthane, they were told. The Gods had ordained it.

"I'm far less worried about the squabbling of stupid nobles than what the Goeren-yai think," Sofy said. "Half of this army is not Verenthane, yet we ask them to fight and die for a cause that has not always treated them well. Many of the eastern Goeren-yai have long ties to the serrin, and do not march willingly to fight them."

"They'll fight," Damon replied. "It's a question of honour. You can question their willingness all you like, but never question a Goeren-yai's honour."

"I know they'll fight," said Sofy. "I'm just . . ." She could not complete the sentence. Dare she say it? Even here, to her most trusted brother and confidant? She swallowed hard.

"You're not certain you want us to win," Damon said sombrely. "Are you?" Sofy stared at his dark gaze, and bit her lip. She nodded, faintly. Damon took a deep breath. "These are our people, Sofy. We owe them everything—our lives if need be."

"Oh, I know that! I know that as well as anyone! But . . . some of these people are evil, Damon. These Larosans. What they've done to serrin and half-castes across the border in Enora and Rhodaan—"

"I know," said Damon. "I know. But it is the future of Lenayin at stake. We have no choice."

For a while, there was no sound but for the creaking of wheels, the thudding of hooves, and the jangling of harnesses.

"And how is your riding coming?" Damon said after the pause.

"Well, I tried using the rein as you showed me." Sofy smiled. "Dary was quite impressed. He thinks I'm a little dense, but he tolerates me."

"Koenyg complains you should not be riding a dussieh. I could get you a warhorse if you'd rather?"

"Never!" said Sofy. "I'll not trade my little Dary for anything. Besides, Koenyg was just telling me he doesn't want me riding at all. He's determined to find fault with everything he does not understand."

"Ignore him."

"I do try."

"I must go," said Damon, gathering his gloves. "Tomorrow, after breakfast, we'll go riding together. That'll shut Koenyg up." His eyes lingered on her for a moment, as though he wanted to say more. He reached and took her hand. Sofy clasped his and smiled at him. Then Damon departed, slamming the carriage door with a force that was almost anger.

Sofy sighed, picked up her book, and resumed reading. But the beauty of the foreign words escaped her now, and she stared forward instead, out of the windows.

She was not married yet, but Damon missed her already. For a long time they'd been friends. Most of his life, Damon had felt constrained, ignored, put-upon. Eldest brother Krystoff had been brash and flamboyant, a figure impossible to emulate in life, and doubly so in death. Koenyg was the hardest of hard Lenay fighting men, and brooked no dispute from anyone, least of all his younger brothers. That left Damon, awkward, gangly, misunderstood and mistrusting, suspecting all of merely liking him for his royalty, or about to stab him in the back at a moment's notice. All, that was, except Sofy.

For many years, she had been his solace, and now that solace was being married off for a cause that Damon had little enthusiasm for in the first place. It had been Koenyg's decision as much as Father's, and Damon blamed them both equally. Now, Sofy sat and gazed at the banners, and felt a desperate melancholy advancing at the thought of how much Damon loved her, and she him, and how lonely they would be apart for the rest of their lives. Even as she willed herself to be strong, her eyes filled with tears.

Jaryd's feet ached worst of all. His thighs and knees weren't much better, and his shoulders were painful beneath a weight of mail, shield and rucksack. Yet he walked, and contented himself to know that tomorrow, he'd have his horse back again. Most other men in this column weren't so lucky.

Yells from far ahead signalled the coming halt, as the sun dipped low upon the western horizon. Then the shout rose from nearby, and men spread out, found a clear patch of ground for a campfire and swung down their loads with aching groans.

Jaryd sat with one half of the Baerlyn contingent, and took the opportunity to pull off his boots. "Not near me, please," said Byorn, a hand raised to ward the smell. Jaryd removed a sock, and prodded at a new, bulging blister on his big toe.

"Wow," said Andreyis. "That's a beauty."

"Master Jaryd has soft feet," Teriyan remarked, his own boots removed and now sitting splayed-legged on the grass, as an experienced warrior might. "Like all lordlings, too much time ahorse has unmanned him."

Of one hundred and thirty-seven men of fighting age in the Valhanan village of Baerlyn, thirty-one had joined the Army of Lenayin on this march. Enough were left that Baerlyn would not suffer too badly in the months or (spirits forbid) years that they were away. The Baerlyn Council had made the final say on the number, and had refused many who asked. Some men were essential, farmers in particular, but also bakers, smiths and others.

The King had not demanded more than twenty men in every hundred capable of fighting, through all of Lenayin. Much discussion about campfires now speculated as to the size of the Lenayin population in total . . . thirty thousand marching soldiers made one-fifth of a hundred and fifty thousand fighting men. Which would be only half of the total number of Lenay men, when counting children and elders, making three hundred thousand men in Lenayin. Double that to account for the women, and there were six hundred thousand people in all Lenayin. It was a number so large, many refused to believe it. Scattered for countless centuries across their uncounted rugged valleys, so many people had divided into equally countless tribes, with differing tongues, beliefs and ceremonies. Now, thinking of just how many people Lenayin actually had, Jaryd wondered if any other human land possessed the sheer scale of fractious diversity the gods had granted his homeland.

No wonder we're always in such a mess, he pondered, gazing about at the long, settling column. There was no thought of fortified camps here on the Telesian plains. Telesia had few people, and had only escaped conquest by Bacosh neighbours because it possessed so little that anyone wanted. Mostly it made a bulwark between the Bacosh and southern Lenayin, and there was no threat to a Lenay army here.

Jaryd set his boots aside and rose barefoot. "Come," he said to Andreyis. "We'll spar while there's still light."

Andreyis looked tired too, but he removed his boots and rose all the same, withdrawing his practice stanch from within his bundled gear. They took stance on a clear patch of grass, shields laid aside, and practised in the traditional Lenay style—two hands, no shields and little mercy.

Some other men did the same, and most of those pairs were also made up of a youngster and a more experienced warrior. Jaryd now had twenty-two years, but he had once been heir to the province of Tyree, and perhaps the most celebrated sword- and horseman in that region. Since then, he had been deposed, his family dissolved by ancient clan law, his youngest brother murdered and his siblings married off. He had taken refuge in a Goeren-yai village, sought revenge, and found something perhaps greater than that which he had lost. He remained uncertain of exactly what it was that he had found. So many things, he was still discovering every day.

Sparring over, he and Andreyis returned to the campside, and took their places in the circle.

"You should train with those damn shields, lads," Teriyan told them. "We'll have to use them soon enough."

"Foundation first," said Jaryd. "Shields later. The lad has to walk before he can run."

"I can walk fine," Andreyis muttered, rubbing a bruised arm where Jaryd's stanch had caught him. "I've been doing nothing but walking for weeks."

"When I was a noble," Jaryd said, lounging back on the grass, "my father once received a travelling entourage from Larosa. Some bunch of idiot lowlands nobility seeking trade, horses and powerful friends in Lenayin. Anyhow, this lord's heir was seventeen; I was fifteen at the time. He was boasting to me about what a great swordsman he'd become, of how he'd trained with a master-at-arms from his father's army since he had barely ten years, and how he thought himself more than a match for anyone in Lenayin."

Men grinned or snorted. In Lenayin, boys held the stanch and learned footwork from the moment they could walk. "I challenged him to spar," Jaryd continued, "and beat him black and blue from one side of the circle to the other. Then I handed off to my brother Wyndal, who's another two years younger again, and not much of a fighter, but he did scarcely worse."

"What's your point?" Andreyis asked. The lad was a little touchy where his swordwork was concerned. Well, Jaryd supposed, it couldn't have been easy having the stuffing smacked out of him all through childhood by Sashandra Lenayin. Now, fate had afflicted another great and cocky warrior upon him. Probably he was getting sick of it.

"My point is that everyone can improve. That little lowlands snot thought he was great, but he learned that greatness in the Bacosh and great-ness in Lenayin are two different things. Perhaps somewhere out there is another kingdom of warriors who make Lenays look foolish with a blade. Always assume you're not as good as you will be tomorrow, if you work at it."

"Listen to the pup," Teriyan remarked, "spouting wisdom like he knows what it means. You come and talk to me when you've seen even half the bat-tles I've fought in, youngster."

"Aye," said Jaryd, smiling, "you've fought in so many battles that last time we sparred, I could hear your bones rattling."

"Sparring is not warfare, boy." Teriyan looked less than his usual good-humoured self at that reminder. "When the formations line up, and you see nothing but Rhodaani Steel from one end of the horizon to the other, then you'll learn the value of experience."

Jaryd just smiled, and stretched out on the grass. Andreyis joined him, stretching an arm above his shoulder.

"Am I better than that Larosan boy?" Andreyis asked sombrely.

"That little fool? No contest, you'd kill him one-handed."

"I know I'll never be great," said Andreyis. "I've had some of the best training of any man my age in Lenayin, with Kessligh and Sasha, and now you. I should be better than I am."

"Not true," Jaryd insisted. "Kessligh and Sasha fight with svaalverd, you'll not learn a thing from them. I think it might have hurt you, truth-fully." Andreyis looked doubtful, but did not argue. "Look, you're a tall lad, you've not filled out properly yet. Your technique is fine, you just need to get quicker, and that'll take care of itself as you get older."

"I've heard it before," Andreyis said quietly. He said nothing more, and lay on his back gazing at the sky.

Jaryd watched him. In truth, the boy had a point. His technique was quite good, and he did quite well in set, predictable taka-dans. But when forced to improvise it often broke down, and he simply wasn't very quick. Jaryd had never considered what it might be like to be born without the skills he took for granted. Andreyis's admission bothered him. In Lenayin, for a young man to admit to anyone, even his closest friends, that he did not think himself much of a swordsman, was akin to admitting himself a coward.

Andreyis was an unusual boy. He was clever, but seemed to have no particular skills at which he excelled. He was good with horses, thanks to a childhood working on Kessligh and Sasha's ranch, but even there, his natural skill with the animals was not the same as that of his younger workmate Lynette, Teriyan's daughter. Popularity in Baerlyn eluded him, despite (or perhaps because of) his friendship with Baerlyn's two most famous residents. He had fought in Sasha's rebellion, and gained manhood, but not the respect that came of a man making his own way, and standing on his own two feet.

When the Baen-Tar herald had called on Baerlyn in the winter, Andreyis had been amongst the first to put forth his name. His father ran a wagon and harness trade with an elder son, and the younger son was dispensable.

This young man expects to die, Jaryd thought, watching Andreyis now. He seemed to find it preferable to continuing to live the life he had. For the first time in his life, Jaryd found himself questioning the obvious truths that all young men of Lenayin had shared since they were old enough to understand such words as "honour," and "manhood." Andreyis would perhaps never be a great warrior, but he was a good young man all the same. Was goodness worth nothing to a man, if greatness could not accompany it?

Jaryd's fingers went to his left ear, and the rings that decorated from the lobe about the outer rim. Still they felt odd, even after the inflammation had died. The rings said that he was Goeren-yai, and no longer a Verenthane noble . . . but what did his heart say? Once he had been the heir to great wealth and power. When those were taken, he had been heir to honourable revenge. But that heirship too he had failed to claim. Was he now merely a villager, content to live out his days on a Baerlyn farm, to wed some local girl and raise half-blueblood children? And if he was to be content, why was his heart still so full of questions?

When the herald had arrived in Baerlyn, Jaryd had been second only to Andreyis in putting his name forth. His old injuries recovered, he could best even Teriyan in sparring now. He had claimed Kessligh Cronenverdt's title of the best swordsman in Baerlyn. And Andreyis, Sasha and Lynette's dear friend, would need someone at his side to look after him in the battles ahead. Jaryd had few ties holding him to Baerlyn, and fewer still to Lenayin itself. Yet all of these combined, however sincere, were not the complete and total reason for his decision to march to war in the Bacosh.

A horse and cart trundled down the column, its tray holding some of the last remaining firewood. A man in the back tossed down an armful to men from each campsite in passing. Two Baerlyn men rose as the cart approached, as men from neighbouring camps also rose, but now the man on the back of the cart stopped throwing down the wood, and the driver accelerated, whipping at the horse's reins. Men shouted at them to stop, and were met with laughter and rude words in a northern tongue.

"Wonderful," Byorn exclaimed. "Which shitwit gave northerners the firewood cart?"

"Kumaryn," Teriyan said darkly. Great Lord Kumaryn, that was. The great lord of the province of Valhanan. All the nobility were united in their hatred for the ex-heir of Tyree, who had refused to die, submit or be captured, and had converted to the ancient ways to escape the laws of Verenthanes. In Lenayin, most commonfolk agreed, the two faiths would get along fine if it weren't for the arrogant, god-spouting superiority of the nobles.

The cart thundered past, leaving angry Valhanans pondering the prospect of another cold dinner. The hard men of Lenayin were in some ways a pampered lot, Jaryd reflected with a sigh. Food in Lenayin was good and plentiful, and bad seasons rare. Already the column ranks were filled with complaints from men accustomed to going their own way, providing for themselves, and unfamiliar with orders and discipline. Figure *that* into any long, lowlands campaign. He wondered if the king and Prince Koenyg truly had.

Then he heard more hooves thundering and raised his head. Here along the column came a small figure on a galloping dussieh, skirts flying. *Skirts.* He got up, staring. Behind her came another girl in a loose red dress over slim, brown legs, black hair streaming like a banner. About them (and largely behind, to the apparent chagrin of a corporal whose expression Jaryd could observe) raced a contingent of eight Royal Guards.

A great cheer rose from the ranks, following the Princess Sofy and her entourage down the line. Jaryd stared in disbelief, as his Baerlyn comrades stood and roared with the rest. What happened next was obscured from view, but after a time of impatient waiting, trying to see over the heads of the risen column, the firewood cart reappeared, this time with a Royal Guard escort. Princess Sofy and her Isfayen companion (handmaiden seemed an inappropriate term, for a daughter of bloodwarriors) rode ahead, grinning and waving to the men along the way. The men on the cart unloaded firewood to those who wanted it, with dark expressions. Some of Jaryd's friends seemed to think it the funniest thing they'd seen in months, and had difficulty cheering through tears of laughter. Northern Verenthanes humiliated by a horse-riding girl. Again. Spirits be good.

As she came close, Jaryd fancied that the princess's wave faltered a little, her eyes seeking someone in the crowd. She knew this was the Valhanan contingent, surely. And probably she knew that Baerlyn, being eastern Valhanan, marched in the middle of the last third of the Valhanan column. Jaryd's heart began thumping, to see her come near. Then, somehow, her eyes met his despite the distance and commotion. And locked.

A pretty girl. "Beautiful," perhaps, was a word best suited to the likes of her elder sister Alythia, of full breasts and ruby lips. The Princess Sofy had now nineteen summers, and was slim and delicate to behold . . . although not quite as much as in Jaryd's memory. She wore a plain yet well-made dress over riding pants and boots, her long dark hair fell loose down her back, and her features were fine. Like a little girl, perhaps, all save for her eyes, which were large, dark and lovely. They fixed upon him now, wide and intent, her waving hand frozen in midair. Jaryd's heart seemed to stop, and his knees weakened.

And then she was past, smiling and waving to other men in the column. Had she just been staring at him? Had it been his imagination? Or had she merely imagined she'd seen him, in the spot in the column where she'd been told he would be?

Teriyan slapped him on the arm, grinning broadly as he watched her go. "She's got Sasha's blood in her, for sure. She's a good girl, that one."

"Aye," Jaryd agreed, faintly. Recalling a wild escape on horseback, her slim body pressed to his as they rode close on the saddle. Recalling warm lips against his own, and slim, clutching hands and hungry eyes. A night's camp all alone on a deserted trail somewhere on the border of Tyree and Valhanan, a blanket on a bed of pine needles. Bare white skin, and red nipples, and smooth, lovely hips. Intoxication, and desperate arousal, her cries and gasps in his ear.

"Aye," he murmured, watching her leave to the cheers of adoring men. "She's a good girl, for sure."

Andreyis was one reason to march to war. So was honour. But neither was the only reason he'd come.

Three

IN HER CORNER OF THE TRAINING COURTYARD, Sasha had attracted a crowd. Tol'rhen students clustered about her as she faced a country lad named Daish, who was fancied one of the better swordsman trainees of the institution. Wooden blades flashed and cracked, and Sasha caught him on the arm guard. Exclamations came from those surrounding. Daish shook his arm, grinning, and circled about, his feet dancing. He was only a little taller than Sasha, and had a boyish, freckled face.

He attacked again, in clever combination, which Sasha deflected, and refrained from the high overhead that would have split his head, dancing back.

"She just took your head off!" Reynold Hein called out, greatly impressed.

"She did not!" Daish retorted.

"Did too!" called several others. Sasha was pleased they'd noticed. The Tol'rhen bred good swordsmen—from the sidelines they could see even the openings she rejected.

"Watch your brace step," she advised Daish. "You put too much weight on your second step; you shouldn't anchor your balance on one leg."

Daish tried again. A few times he came close, but never quite did he lay a blade on her. Each time, save one where she again refused to swing at his head, Sasha gave him a thump on his pads or guards.

The session bell clanged and, across the courtyard, sparring ceased. Sasha shook hands with Daish—he was somewhat more sweaty and tired than she. From the onlookers, there was enthusiastic applause for both their efforts. Sasha began taking off her padded banda as students gathered around and fired questions at her.

She was finding their enthusiasm infectious. All through the Tol'rhen, there was a love of learning, whether the martial arts, or languages, or the many disciplines that Sasha could barely get her head around. She was disappointed that, as in Petrodor, there were so few women interested in the svaalverd, but pleased that the lads all treated her as one of their own. Of the hundred or so students in the courtyard this early morning, Sasha could only count three young women.

Walking back to the main building, Reynold Hein joined her and put his arm about her shoulders. Sasha did not mind—it was nothing that the young men would not do with each other, in the spirit of comradeship. Reynold was simply indicating that he considered her one of the lads.

"Sasha, we have a Civid Sein meeting in the forecourt," he said. "It would be grand if you could attend, maybe say a few words."

"I was going to go and see Errollyn at the Mahl'rhen," Sasha said apologetically. Not that she felt particularly apologetic, but it was a good excuse all the same.

Reynold just smiled. "Oh well, I don't suppose even the Civid Sein can compete with *Errollyn*."

Viewed from the courtyard, the Tol'rhen looked magnificent. It was the largest building Sasha had ever seen, as high as a grand temple, and far longer and wider. It had beautiful arching doors and windows, and columns that fanned out from the sides like an animal's ribs. Its great dome towered above surrounding rooftops. Sasha had been told that it had taken nearly twenty years to build, even after the rest of the Tol'rhen had been completed, engaging the best human and serrin minds of the time.

Ulenshaal Sevarien cornered her at breakfast.

"Ah, Sashandra!" he boomed, as he heaved his wide, black-robed bulk onto the bench. "I hope you're beating some manners into these little rascals!"

"Some of those bruises are mine," Sasha admitted, indicating the young men. "I don't know that bruises make for better manners though, it never worked on me."

"A worthy experiment all the same!" Sevarien exclaimed.

"Ulenshaal Sevarien would administer beatings himself," said Daish from Sasha's side, "but the last time he broke a sweat was in the year 850." The other boys laughed.

"Quiet boy!" Sevarien barked, but his eyes sparkled. Sevarien was as large as his voice, and had no discernible chin. He had been a butcher in his younger years, self-educated on books lent to him by a wealthy customer. That knowledge had impressed a visiting Tol'rhen recruiter enough to gain him a place as a student, from where he had risen to become one of the institution's most accomplished scholars.

"Dear girl," said Sevarien now, past a mouthful of porridge. "You have been here nearly a week. What do you think?"

"Of the Tol'rhen? It's amazing."

"Well, obviously," said Sevarien, impatiently. "Do you think it could be replicated in your homeland?"

Sasha blinked at him. That was quite a thought. "Who would pay for it?"

Sevarien waved his hand. "Details, girl! No one shall pay for it if they are first not sold on the idea! Could it be done?"

Sasha chewed a mouthful, thinking it over. "I think only as a part of a noble education in Baen-Tar."

"Why?"

"Because the provincial lords all think the Nasi-Keth teach blasphemy. The poor folk aren't interested in any education that won't make them extra coin; you'd do better teaching them to improve irrigation or cropping than philosophy or languages. . . ."

"Bah." Sevarien waved his hand again. "We had the same issue here. The poor stopped their nonsense when they realised what higher status they could attain with a Tol'rhen education."

Sasha smiled. "There is no higher status in Lenayin," she said. "If you're poor, you work with your hands and attain status with hard work and skill with a blade. The only men of letters and law are nobles, and nobility is a matter of birthright, not education."

"A travesty!" proclaimed Sevarien. "One of the greatest travesties that continues today across Rhodia. If there is one institution that we should all bend our backs to see destroyed, it is nobility. Fancy declaring that any of these lads, however bright and hard working, cannot rise to the same level as some soft-handed lackwit, simply because he had the good fortune to be born into a blue-blooded family."

"I agree."

"You know," said Sevarien, jabbing a spoon at her, "you should attend a Civid Sein gathering." Sasha repressed a sigh. "Being of noble birth yourself . . . or no, not noble. Royal! And yet you dress without fancy, and sport calluses on your hands, and ask no favour for the fortune of your birth. You *rejected* such favour, indeed!"

"She has to go and see Errollyn today," Daish explained.

"Tomorrow then!" Sevarien declared. "More of the movement enter the city every day; it would be quite something to have someone who has rejected royal heritage address them! Quite something indeed!"

"You don't really want to have much to do with the Civid Sein, do you?" Daish observed as they walked a paved hallway after breakfast.

"I didn't reject royal heritage for the reasons they suppose," Sasha told him.

It was all a big debate, here in Tracato. Two centuries ago, the serrin had innocently supposed that human society might work better on merit. In

Enora their vision had worked well, because Enora had slaughtered all its nobility. In Rhodaan, nobility survived, and now regrouped. The Civid Sein were the anti-nobility, formed largely of poor people and farmers, though not entirely. It had a strong leadership core here in the Tol'rhen, and with fears that the Tracatan nobility would rather negotiate with Rhodaan's feudal enemies than fight, more and more were moving to the city each day. To keep the lords nervous, it seemed.

When she reached the great classroom, it was full to overflowing. All chairs taken, Sasha joined the crowd standing along the walls, and found a place near the front of the chamber, where Kessligh sat with three Ulenshaals, and recounted the history of the Great War. The Rhodaanis knew it only as "The Cherrovan–Lenay War of 827," which to Sasha's ear seemed insultingly minor for so grand a conflict.

Kessligh had been telling this history the last two days, having finished his previous lectures on the nature of Lenay society and feudal power. Those had been opinions, but these were events, experienced by Kessligh himself as a young man. The Ulenshaals, and most of the Tol'rhen students, were intrigued to have the man who had made much of that history in their midst, having paid far too little attention, they admitted, to the study of Lenay and other highland histories.

It fascinated Sasha to listen to Kessligh speak. She had heard these stories many times, but in her youthful impatience, she'd always neglected to ask about the details, wanting instead to hear the grand conclusion. Now the Ulenshaals interrupted continuously, probing on this or that point of strategy, or the actions of minor players. Kessligh spoke incisively, without the troubled frown that Sasha recalled from her own discussions with him. Perhaps he found this audience more receptive. Sasha heard details of that time that astonished her—things Kessligh had done, relationships with other warriors that she'd not suspected, incidents of humour she'd never heard. As she listened, she marvelled at her own stupidity, that she'd had such a treasure beneath her own roof for so long, yet had taken it so completely for granted.

The thoroughness of the Tol'rhen's love of knowledge astonished and delighted her. Knowledge in Lenayin meant stories, told over an ale after a good meal, or crafts passed through families for generations. Here, knowledge was precious, to be treasured, stored and shared around. And to be given across classes, to poor and rich alike, and across races. Such a place could change the world, Sasha realised. And Ulenshaal Sevarien had asked her if such an institution could be replicated in Lenayin. Not a bad idea at all, she reckoned, and began thinking on it more seriously.

What amazed Sasha most about Tracato was that she felt relatively safe walking the streets. They were teeming, like Petrodor had been, with carts and handwagons, mules hauling loads, and cityfolk walking. There were tradesmen of all description, and many whose trade Sasha could not begin to guess at. There were rich folk in palanquins and carriages, patrolling Blackboots, red-coat city administrators, fellow Nasi-Keth and, of course, plenty of serrin.

Most astonishing were the buildings, rising for several storeys to either side of the road. The avenues of Tracato were like little canyons through which rushed rivers of people and commerce. Frequently these avenues opened into courtyards. There were buildings in garish colours, with ornamental designs, turrets and crenelations, grand archways and louvred balconies. The courtyards were also popular with performers and orators, who stood on platforms and denounced the workings of council, or the Justiciary, or indeed the Tol'rhen. Others warned of impending doom and rising oceans, or announced the latest news of the war in Elisse. Elsewhere, beggars lining walls crouched with outstretched hands.

"You have beggars too," Sasha observed sadly.

"Oh, lots," replied Daish, who had come with her. "Too many." He'd wanted to see the Mahl'rhen again . . . as had six of his friends. Sasha hadn't intended on leading such a large group to see Errollyn, but the Tol'rhen was like that; its students hung together and loved new experiences.

"It's just sad to see the wealthiest city in Rhodia has beggars," she said.

"Ulenshaal Sevarien blames the nobility," said Daish, pulling a coin from his pocket. "He says they hoard all the wealth and make others work for them. He says they create beggary, and there'd be less if we got rid of them."

"So there're no beggars in Enora then?" Sasha said warily.

Daish shrugged. "So Sevarien's theories aren't perfect." He flipped a coin to a beggar, who grasped it with dirty hands.

Soon they turned down a back road away from the avenues, and another world opened up. Household backyards opened onto further courtyards, some homely, others messy, and occasionally squalid. These too bustled with activity: tradesmen hammering, firing, smoking, sawing or tanning. Smells and fumes from the yards assailed the nostrils, and sometimes the eyes, and walking was strictly single file past the bustle of men and women carrying their loads.

"You know," Sasha said to Daish above the roar and wheeze of a backyard bellows, "when I first heard about the wealth of Tracato, I had an image of everyone lazing around sunning themselves, as wealthy people might. Now that I get here, I find that Tracato is wealthy because everyone's so busy!"

"I think it's a little sad," Daish replied, edging past four men hauling a huge pig carcass. "Everyone is obsessed with money, they rush and rush and think of little else."

"If Rhodaan weren't wealthy, it couldn't have survived two centuries of being attacked by its neighbours," Sasha reasoned. "Taxes from all this pay for the Steel."

"True. But I'd love to travel to Lenayin. As you describe it, life seems simpler there." Sasha thought about that, and gazed around at every new thing.

They all paused at another courtyard, to peer at the furnace beyond some guarded gates. Within, shirtless men in leather smocks fed wood and coal into a narrow mouth of flames, and the heat was so intense, Sasha could nearly feel her eyebrows singe from twenty paces away. About the other side of the furnace, men would be pouring steel, but she'd never seen it before. Very few had, for these were the great furnaces of serrin steel, or "the folding," as the serrin called it. Serrin had perfected the art in Saalshen hundreds of years before, and now guarded their secret carefully.

The Mahl'rhen, when they came to it, was a surprise. A lane ran to a courtyard, where arts were displayed at a huge market, and the laneways were alive to the chip and clang of sculptors and metal workers.

The lads finally dragged her onward, where an arch at the courtyard's far side announced in typically understated serrin style the entrance to the Mahl'rhen. Four serrin stood guard there, and gave the Nasi-Keth lads and Sasha curious looks, but made no move to stop them entering.

They entered a courtyard garden that Sasha thought looked something like a Torovan noble garden. But the square angles of human inspiration were infused with a serrin randomness, little tangles of natural greenery, and the sinewy twist of an artificial stream tumbling over small, smoothed stones.

About the garden walked mostly serrin, some in the flowing robes that they preferred in their own quarters, others in the more practical garb of city folk. Some nodded and smiled at the Nasi-Keth in passing, and the lads quietened their exuberance a little, showing respect in the house of the serrin.

Paths led past more courtyards, amidst which rose stone buildings that an eye trained in human structures could not precisely place. These were residences, and often kitchens, with underground storages—Errollyn had already given her the tour, though he still knew barely a fraction of the

Mahl'rhen's intricacies. Tracato's ever-present water courses ran through the complex, taking advantage of the gradual slope to fashion little streams. They passed a grand pool in which naked serrin children splashed and yelled, supervised by several adults with one eye on a board game, the other on the children. Sasha had never seen serrin children before. Amusingly, they were just as noisy and troublesome as human children, proving, perhaps, that serrin sophistication was more a question of nurture than nature.

Sasha recalled her way from her two previous visits, yet at an intersection where she knew to turn right, several serrin came past running the other way. Sasha heard a distant commotion, other nearby serrin stopping to look. She headed that way herself, the lads following.

Soon they came to another entrance to the Mahl'rhen, but this one filled with armed figures, mostly serrin. From outside came a lot of shouting. Daish approached an older serrin lady, and asked what was happening.

"There's been trouble at this gate for months," she told them. "The Civid Sein have been camping here, displacing the farmers' stalls and causing quarrels. I hear some have complained to the Blackboots, requesting the squatters be removed."

Sasha and the Nasi-Keth lads edged through the wall of cautious serrin at the gate, to observe the scene beyond. It was a courtyard like the one they'd entered through, yet this was a market of farmers selling produce. Amidst the stalls, makeshift tents had been erected, tanned hides over poles and rickety wooden frames. Defending the tents from perhaps thirty armed Blackboots was a mob of raggedly dressed rural folk, armed with hoes, scythes and other tools. So far it was merely pushing and shouting, as the Blackboots appeared to demand the makeshift settlements be taken down.

"Perhaps we should try to intervene?" one of the lads suggested.

"With this lot?" Daish said dubiously.

"We are the Nasi-Keth," said another, stubbornly. "It is our duty to maintain the peace."

Sasha shook her head. "Svaalverd is a sharp tool, only good for offence. We can kill whomever we choose, but we can't keep two sides apart who'd rather fight."

The Nasi-Keth boy ignored her and strode forward. Sasha watched, as he and two others joined the shouting. The Blackboots did not seem pleased to see them. Soon the three Nasi-Keth lads were arguing firmly in favour of the squatters, as stall owners guarded their produce and looked displeased with everyone.

Sasha was displeased too. "We're supposed to be impartial," she said crossly to Daish, who gave her a wary look.

At the courtyard's edge, Sasha saw a Blackboot lieutenant astride a horse, watching proceedings with a small personal guard. He looked angry.

She strode to him. His personal guard moved forward, hands on hilts, but Sasha simply extended her hand to them. Their distrust faded a little, and one accepted her handshake, then another. Sasha beckoned to the lieutenant on his horse. The lieutenant thought about it, then dismounted. Sasha shook his hand too.

"Sashandra Lenayin," she introduced herself in Torovan, hoping he spoke the same. "Uma to Kessligh Cronenverdt."

"Lieutenant Muline," said the Blackboot. He stood a great deal taller than her in his high leather boots, yet his eyes flicked warily to the sword hilt at Sasha's shoulder. Sasha had met men who disbelieved her martial prowess until it was demonstrated to them. Clearly this man had seen enough serrin women use the svaalverd that he was not one of those. "What brings the Nasi-Keth to this gate in force?"

Sasha repressed a smile. She could hear Kessligh's voice in her ear, chiding her to be polite. "It's my fault," she admitted. "I came to visit, and some new friends accompanied me. Purely a coincidence. What brings the Blackboots here?"

"Complaints from the farmers," said Lieutenant Muline, with irritation. He meant the stall owners, Sasha realised, not the Civid Sein. "This courtyard is for the selling of goods, yet the Civid Sein think they have a perfect right to camp here and disrupt the livelihood of hard-working country folk."

"The Civid Sein argue they *are* hard-working country folk," Sasha replied.

"I was raised in Varne," Muline said. "It's a little town in the east, not far from the Saalshen border. My father is a miller, my uncles farmers and tradesmen, and none of them loves the Civid Sein." Sasha was coming to suspect as much. "They are from the countryside, yet they take advantage of that status, as though it gives them special rights. They claim support of the farmers in this courtyard, and probably they did have some support a month or two ago when they first arrived. But now that support runs short, and the farmers ask us to come and clean up the mess . . . only for the Nasi-Keth to intervene on the Civid Sein's side, without asking questions."

He glowered at her. Sasha sighed. "I apologise for my friends," she said. "I'm new to Tracato. I'd like the Nasi-Keth to be more thoughtful about this than I've seen. But they dislike the nobility, and so assume the Civid Sein are their friends."

"Because they're poor and downtrodden," the lieutenant said sarcastically. "I was born as poor and downtrodden as any of this lot, yet I rose to this station because I believe in law, justice and the security of Rhodaan. Ask this lot what they believe in, they'll give you only complaints."

Sasha glanced back at the courtyard. The stall owners looked as displeased with the Civid Sein as with the Blackboots, perhaps more. And now, her Nasi-Keth lads were taking sides, perhaps the wrong one.

"I can't promise I can help much," Sasha told the lieutenant, "but I can get the boys out of it."

She walked toward the confusion, beckoning to Daish, who darted between stalls to reach her. "The tall lad is Palis, the younger Torine . . . who's the darker one?"

"Alfone," said Daish.

"Hey!" Sasha yelled. The squabbling was mostly about the Civid Sein's makeshift tents, which the Blackboots were attempting to take down. No one listened. Nearby was a wagon, doubling as a stall for sacks of grain. Sasha climbed up onto the sacks. "Hey! Palis, Torine and Alfone! Nasi-Keth!"

In amongst it, on the Civid Sein side, the three lads looked up at her.

"You get the hells out of there!" she yelled at them. And when they hesitated, "Now!"

Two of them moved. A third, Palis, stayed where he was, pushing Blackboots away from the tents.

Sasha leaped from the wagon and pushed through the crowd. She came up near Palis and grabbed him by the arm.

"If you won't use your ears," she snarled, "I'll cut them off and grant them to someone in need!" He moved, but several Civid Sein men saw and grabbed him back. Another grabbed Sasha. She twisted, and in the blink of an eye had a knife at the man's throat. He froze, and the others backed off. The nearby Blackboots also stopped.

"No grabbing!" Sasha insisted.

"You'd draw steel against sons of the soil?" exclaimed a Civid Sein man.

"These are the sons and daughters of the soil!" Sasha retorted, pointing angrily at the stall owners looking on. "*They're* the ones who asked for the Blackboots to come, to get you off their damn market so they can make a living!"

"Lies!" shouted the Civid Sein man. "The nobility are scum! They've been trying to get rid of us for weeks." The shouting and shoving along other parts of the line was lessening as attention turned to this new confrontation.

"What makes you think you have the right to camp before the Mahl'rhen gate for weeks anyhow?" Sasha replied. "Harass the serrin, deprive country-folk of their livelihood and locals of their peace?"

"We come to appeal to Saalshen!" shouted the man. "To resist the snivelling demands of the nobility! General Zulmaher, even now, marches at the head of our army in Elisse, befriending the noble families there rather than defeating them—"

"Have you talked to the serrin?" Sasha cut him off.

"They don't talk to us, they're bought and paid for by the nobility." There were angry shouts of agreement from other Civid Sein.

"Let me tell you one thing about the serrin, friend!" Sasha said firmly. "No man or woman, ever, has bought and paid for their opinions. I'll get you in." The man stared at her. The commotion had nearly stopped. "Don't just stand there, choose three men from amongst you, and I'll take you to see someone senior."

The man still stared at her, not knowing what to say. Sasha clapped her hands impatiently, and he jumped to choose his men. Sasha pointed firmly at the line of Blackboots, indicating that they should stay. They stayed. She turned on her heel and strode back to the Mahl'rhen gate.

"The commotion will stop if they get to speak to someone," she said to one of the serrin there. "I said I'll bring three of them inside."

"Must we?" said the serrin, drily. "Speak to them?"

Sasha was astonished. She'd finally found a group of people the serrinim found too tedious to muster any enthusiasm for debating. They had, she guessed, been putting up with this for years. Decades, even.

"Would you rather have blood spilt on the courtyard?"

The serrin actually appeared to think about it, and be uncertain of the answer. Then he sighed. "Bring your men. I shall select the lucky inter-locutor."

Someone else edged through the wall of armed serrin. It was Errollyn. He came to her side and looked out at the courtyard. "What happened?"

"Civid Sein trouble," Sasha explained. "I settled them down. I'm escorting three inside for talks."

Errollyn stared at her. "You!" he said with astonishment. "You broke up a commotion? You're certain you didn't *cause* this?"

Sasha punched at his arm. Errollyn dodged and laughed.

Four

RHILLIAN TORE ACROSS NEWLY PLOUGHED FIELDS, skirted a vegetable patch bordered by several peasant hovels, and leaped a fence. Ahead, the last of the bandits were galloping for the forest. No matter, she thought, leaning low in the saddle. That way was not a good way for them.

She pulled back on the reins to stop the grey mare from charging too far ahead of those riders fanning on her left. To the right, more riders formed their position by looking to her. Another fence, which she jumped, and then they were slowing further to ride amongst the trees.

She allowed the mare her head, weaving between trunks, supplying only a general direction while ducking the branches. The mare was not as large as some lowlands warhorses—she was *elur'uhd*, a Saalshen breed of stamina and swiftness combined. The *talmaad* did not fight as humans would, and had little use for animals built like battering rams of muscle and hide. It was dark under the canopy of leaves, and the gloom and speed combined to play tricks on her eyes . . . but if it was difficult for her, it would be doubly so for the bandits.

Rhillian tore through undergrowth, skirted an impenetrable tangle of roots and brush, and dug in her heels as the mare showed uncertainty, tossing her head. She turned onto what she decided was the straighter course, and heard a scream from ahead. Suddenly there was a horse and rider before her, a brown tunic and hood of smallfolk's dress over mail, a sword in hand. Left-handed, Rhillian saw, swinging her mare to the left and cutting past his weakside before he could adjust. Her backhand tore through mail on his back, and he fell with a scream, crashing into tree roots.

Now there were more horses ahead, plunging through the trees, rearing, wheeling in desperation. One man held a shield with two arrows in it, even as a third took his companion in the eye. Rhillian reined past another rider, slumped with a shaft in his throat, and galloped toward another yet unfeathered. He saw her and raised his shield and blade to greet her with a cry, and was promptly cut from the saddle by a third rider who flashed past his side. Rhillian paused and circled to look around, but it seemed to be over, the few remaining bandits yielding with desperate cries for mercy, throwing aside their blades. Rhillian did not need to give orders. Her *talmaad* knew what to do, and closed in on all sides to take prisoners.

She urged the mare to the side of the rider who had flashed by and deprived her of another victim. Aisha sat astride near where the prisoners were being herded and searched for weapons. Her naked blade remained in hand, ready to ride down any others who tried to run or fight. None looked likely to try. Clearly these understood the nature of their opposition, for there was terror in their eyes and cringing obedience in every posture.

"That was a lovely cut," Rhillian complimented her friend. "Your horsemanship remains superior to mine, despite my practice."

"City girl," Aisha said, which explained everything. "You'll not rid yourself of me that easily."

"More's the pity." Aisha had completed her journey from Enora to Elisse barely ten days ago, to retake her accustomed place at Rhillian's side. Rhillian was delighted to see her again, and even more delighted that her wounds suffered in Petrodor had healed so completely. But, in part, she still wished that Aisha had remained safely in Enora with her family, and had not come here to Rhodaani-occupied Elisse, and the newest front in the latest chapter of the never-ending series of wars that was the Bacosh.

Arendelle arrived at Rhillian's other side, his bow in hand. "Three escaped," he told her. "Gian and Leshelle are after them, I don't expect they'll get far."

"No," Rhillian agreed. Gian was the second-best archer Rhillian had ever seen. He alone would probably have done. "A good ambush."

Arendelle shrugged. "They rode straight into us. If all irregulars are this clueless, we shall be done with them in weeks."

Rhillian did not reply, lips pursed, watching her *talmaad* disarming the terrified prisoners. Men-at-arms in smallfolk clothes, she thought. Their armour gave them away, and their horse skills. Cavalry fighting was a rich man's sport in the Bacosh, or the sport of those in their pay. Someone was trying to scare the true smallfolk into not helping the invaders, again. It was a predictable horror, and she was growing thoroughly sick of it.

They escorted the prisoners the short distance back to the village, not bothering to tie more than their hands behind their backs. It was almost an invitation to any who might think to try to run. Prisoners were useful, but not essential, and Rhillian was certain she could do without whichever of their number might think to try the accuracy of mounted serrin archers. Half a year ago, such thinking might have disturbed her. That was before Petrodor, and the War of the King. Now, the fate of a few murdering bandit prisoners barely troubled her at all.

The countryside in spring was beautiful, with hills and pasture slopes alive with wildflowers. Ploughed fields made a patchwork of brown against the green, with little huts for shepherds and farmers clinging to the rickety fencelines, beneath the shade of grand oaks.

The village itself was not so beautiful. Little more than a huddled mass of tumbledown shanties, small mud walls clustered as if for warmth, thatched roofs in various states of disrepair. Some goats, roped to a stake, made a meal of garden refuse, and geese honked and waddled away from the massed hooves approaching. Even the village dogs looked dispirited, running away with tails low and without so much as a bark. This was the land of a certain Lord Crashuren, Rhillian had learned, and these villagers owned nothing. Not even their pathetic little homes.

Further along the main "street," muddy with recent rain, they came upon the scene of the bandits' work, before Rhillian's party had arrived. Truthfully, there wasn't much to destroy. But there were doors and window shutters broken, precious clay pots smashed on the ground, and equally precious white flour strewn across the mud. And other, equally senseless destruction.

In a small, muddy square fronting a little stone temple lay five human bodies. Three were men of fighting age, but one was a lad of perhaps twelve, and the other a girl several years older. About the little square, doors were opening, fearful folk peering out to see the strange, wild-haired serrin dismounting about a cluster of eight human prisoners. Ahead, the temple door was guarded by a rough, balding man with a hoe. But others were seeing it safe, and two women pushed the man aside, and rushed to the square to resume their sobbing over the bodies of the dead. More joined them, and suddenly there were perhaps fifty gathering about, some men armed with makeshift weapons.

Rhillian stepped forward and stared down at the bodies. Their throats had been cut. Even the youngsters. She looked up and beckoned the rough man with the hoe forward. He came, and she realised his anxiousness was not fear, but rather deference. His gait was bent and he did not look her in the eye, but placed the hoe on the mud before her and knelt. Rhillian refrained from exasperation, and took his arm, gently, pulling him back to his feet. He might have been fifty, she saw, with a rugged face and very few teeth. More likely, she knew, he was about thirty.

"Do you speak Larosan?" Rhillian asked him in that tongue. A nervous shake of the head. "Aisha."

Aisha came forward, small, blonde and pretty. The man bowed to her too. "What happened here?" Rhillian asked him, and Aisha repeated it in Elissian.

"A Rhodaani man came to ask what they'd seen, of soldiers and the like," Aisha translated his answer. A scout, then. "He thinks someone must have told Lord Crashuren, and that's why the bandits attacked them."

Whether they'd actually told the scout anything useful, Rhillian noted, the man had not said. All the countryside was like this, paralysed with fear, of either side. Of men with swords in general.

"Ask him how many men killed these villagers."

"One," Aisha translated the reply.

"Does he recognise that man among these prisoners?"

The man straightened, to stare past Rhillian's shoulder. But before he could approach the clustered prisoners, one of the women started screaming, pointing and wailing. Another man caught her, restraining, but another woman was now pointing at the same prisoner, yelling loudly in Elissian as commotion swept the gathering.

Rhillian indicated, and two *talmaad* brought the prisoner forward. He was an ordinary-looking man, with a big nose and dark brows. He looked very frightened now, his eyes darting, jaw tight. The women in their emotion were very certain, pointing and shouting and crying. Rhillian took a step for space, drew her blade and took off the man's head in a flashing stroke. The severed head hit the mud with a heavy smack, then the body, spurting blood. Commotion ceased. Villagers stood in shock. Perhaps they'd expected some kind of trial, or ceremonial punishment. Rhillian had neither time nor inclination. Dead was dead, and the time for subtleties was long passed.

"This is your land now," Rhillian told them, drawing a cleaning rag along her blade. Aisha translated to the silent onlookers. "Lord Crashuren has no more title here. We abolish it. The land you work, you now own. Soon, when there is peace, Saalshen and Rhodaan will send you some people who can teach you to grow better crops, and become prosperous like the farmers of Rhodaan or Enora. That may take a while, with the war on. Be patient. Saalshen and Rhodaan are your friends, and shall not harm you so long as you do not fight us."

There was no wild celebrating. There never was. Men and women stood and stared at her as though she'd promised to take them to the moon. Rhillian sighed, resheathed her sword, and mounted her horse.

"What of the prisoners?" Arendelle asked her.

"Give their mail and weapons to the villagers, so they might at least have some protection from the next band that tries to kill them. Escort them back in your own time, I'll take the horses ahead. I need to see General Zulmaher."

Arendelle set about organising that, and Rhillian rode out. "They'll more likely sell the armour for livestock and new roofs," said Aisha, riding at her side. "Long winters kill more peasants in these places than bandits." Raggedy children stared at them from doorways. The last snows of winter were barely a month melted, and none looked well fed or healthy.

"Things will be better once this is finished," Rhillian assured her. "General Zulmaher promised me no more than a month."

"I'll wager Regent Arrosh says much the same," Aisha replied. "They're cutting it awfully fine, Rhillian. Simply marching back to Rhodaan will take time, and we're being led further and further north in search of a decisive victory."

"Arrosh will take well over a month to mount an attack," Rhillian replied. "The Army of Lenayin won't arrive for nearly a month, and I doubt King Torvaal will consent to attack before Princess Sofy is married, and the alliance sealed."

"The Army of Torovan will come sooner," Aisha replied. "What if they decide to go early?"

"Without the Lenays? Would you throw yourself against the Steel with just Torovans for support?"

"Half the Steel," Aisha corrected. "The other half are up here in Elisse. It's the weakest Rhodaani line the Larosans have had a look at in over a century. You don't think he might risk it?"

"Not with the Enorans ready to take his southern flank if he puts all his force into the Rhodaani line." Aisha looked unconvinced. "I agree though," Rhillian admitted. "This war must be finished quickly. Time is limited."

It was only a short ride from the village to the war. Cresting a hill, it was all laid out before her—a castle ringed by a moat, surrounded on all sides by a glittering silver army. Flames engulfed one of the castle's towers, clinging to the walls so that the stone itself seemed to burn.

"The artillery's stopped," Aisha remarked as they began their descent across sloping paddocks.

"The third regiment is withdrawing," Rhillian added, pointing to the castle's far flank. She frowned. "Crashuren must have surrendered. That was fast."

"Rhodaani artillery will do that."

Rhillian was unconvinced. This was not merely a war between feudal lords, where peace terms could be arranged and victorious opponents bought off with gold, lands or marriage proposals. This was a war to abolish feudalism in Elisse, as it had been largely abolished in Rhodaan, and completely so in Enora and Ilduur. It was doubtful Family Crashuren would get to keep so much as their castle, and certainly not what surrounded it. The enforcement of feudal rights would become unlawful, punishable by fine, imprisonment or death depending on the nature of the crime. Past crimes would be punished before a trial of peasants and serfs.

Many such lords became very brave, in the face of overwhelming odds, when confronted by the scale of what they had to lose. Not merely their lives, but their entire noble family line of land rights, holdings and taxes. Some had fought to the bitter end, and the blackened ruins of their castles made a smoking line back to the Rhodaani border. Could Crashuren truly have surrendered? From what Rhillian had gathered, he didn't seem the surrendering type.

General Zulmaher's encampment was on the lower hillside, perhaps a hundred paces back from the artillery line. Ahead of that, men of the Rhodaani Steel were breaking camp, downing tents and loading wagons. They moved with all the speed and efficiency one came to expect of the Steel. In a short time the third and sixth regiments beneath General Zulmaher would be moving once more, in pursuit of the greater Elissian Army that continued its retreat to the north. A single regiment of the Steel possessed two thousand men. The third and sixth made four, plus another thousand of attached outriders, heavy cavalry and artillery. The logistical precision of it all was a marvel, and Rhillian watched the preparations for departure with a mixture of admiration and trepidation. No serrin could organise so efficiently. Serrin were vague. Humans were impeccably, ruthlessly precise.

Rhillian found General Zulmaher already ahorse, consulting with captains as soldiers took down his tent. Aisha and the rest of the serrin contingent halted to allow Rhillian to ride on alone. She was prepared to await Zulmaher's invitation to join in, as it was primarily a Rhodaani war, but Zulmaher saw her and waved her alongside.

Several triumphant battles against Rhodaan's ever-invading foes had made General Zulmaher a popular man with many, though most soldiers had others they favoured more. When the High Table had finally won the acrimonious debate in Council to invade Elisse, Zulmaher had somehow leapt over three of the soldiers' more popular choices to gain the command. He had many close ties to the Rhodaani feudalists, that elite and powerful group of old families who retained wealth and influence in Rhodaan even after Saalshen's invasion. Those families had been most reluctant to assault their feudal neighbours (despite their neighbours' apparent eagerness to assault them) and Zulmaher's appointment to lead the Rhodaani Steel in battle had been the price paid to overcome feudalist objections in Council. Some Rhodaanis found the appointment disquieting.

"M'Lady Rhillian," said the general as she reined to his side. "What do you have to report?"

"*Talmaad* forces on Crashuren lands now total perhaps a thousand," Rhillian told him. "Our last count of irregular forces is perhaps a hundred and twenty killed, another seventy captured. . . . I was just involved in an action to pursue another twenty who'd been terrorising the peasant village along the far side of this hill behind us. We killed twelve and captured the other eight."

"Bold little buggers, aren't they?" Zulmaher mused. "Well, keep at them. They've analysed our tactics quite well, they know we need to move fast, so there's an awful lot of irregulars harrying our supply lines and terrorising any of the locals who might like to help. Without Saalshen and your *talmaad*, our progress would be significantly slowed. You have my thanks."

"It's what we're best at."

"It is at that," Zulmaher conceded. "If only Saalshen had seen wisdom, and had put all of its evident martial talents to work over the last two centuries building some significant armies of its own, our current predicament might not seem so dire."

Rhillian smiled. It was an old debate, and one that she had no intention of resuming here. It was a point, in fact, that the serrin had never stopped debating. Two hundred years ago, King Leyvaan had asked Saalshen a question, and today the greatest serrin thinkers were still undecided on the answer. No wonder so many of Saalshen's human friends found serrin so exasperating.

"What happened here?" Rhillian asked, nodding to the castle and the preparations to march.

"Lord Crashuren came to terms," said Zulmaher.

"Terms? When did we start offering terms?"

"When we started running out of time," Zulmaher replied. "Crashuren is a small fish, and meanwhile the big fish escapes to the north. I do not have a day to waste bombarding yet another castle to wait for another pig-headed lord to come to his senses and surrender."

"What are the terms?"

"He keeps his castle and lands," said Zulmaher. "His minor lords will lower their banners and go home, his militia will do the same. In return, we won't burn him down."

Rhillian stared at him. Then at his surrounding captains. Several looked uncomfortable. One in particular appeared to be fuming, as though he could barely hold his tongue. Zulmaher, as ever, looked supremely unbothered.

"I just told a village of half-starved peasants, over the bodies of five villagers murdered by Lord Crashuren's goons, that the lands they worked now belonged to them."

"Best in future that you don't," said Zulmaher. "We don't want to upset them with unfulfilled promises."

"You intend to offer this deal to others?"

"It may prove necessary. If the Steel do not return to Rhodaan before the

Lenays are ready to start fighting, Rhodaan will be lost. This military assault was always contingent on timeliness. If we are to defeat the Elissian Army on the field, we have no choice but to start skipping castles, and if that means we must make terms with their lordships, that is what we shall do."

"We have received support from the peasantry," Rhillian pressed. "Their talk to us of numbers and locations of enemy forces has been invaluable. Some have taken up arms to keep law and order in those lands where the old lords were deposed—"

"Closer to the border," said Zulmaher, with a trace of impatience. Rhillian had the impression he was now speaking not just to her, but to his captains as well. Several of the captains were looking to her expectantly, as though wishing her to challenge further. Perhaps they'd not dared. Humans took rank so much more literally than serrin. "There were lots of friendly peasantry on the Rhodaani border, just as there were in the early days of Saalshen's invasion into Rhodaan two hundred years ago. Those borders are porous, there is traffic back and forth in the dead of night, and those folks know us for the civilised people we truly are.

"Here, we are far from the border, and people are poor, uneducated and superstitious. They have much less support to offer us, and many won't be too thrilled to see the only working system they've ever known abruptly pulled out from under them. Poor folk fear chaos as much or more than they fear their lords."

"And how do you think to ensure that these lords will hold to the terms once the Steel have moved on?" asked Rhillian, sharply. "What will keep you safe from an attack on your rear, and on your lines of supply?"

"Noble honour," said one of the captains, with heavy irony. Several smirked, finding that funny.

"No," said Zulmaher, looking straight at Rhillian, "you will." She stared back, a slight distance up for her—she was nearly as tall as the general, but her horse was not. There was a faint disconcertment in Zulmaher's eyes, to meet her stare. "You say a thousand *talmaad* are on Crashuren lands . . . and perhaps three thousand in all Elisse?"

"Perhaps."

"That is three thousand of the most formidable light cavalry ever fielded in battle. You can cover ground quickly between castles, remain alert of any uprisings, and carry word quickly should trouble arise. You can also harry, and gather quickly to put down any localised insurrection before it can gather pace."

"We are not armoured cavalry to put down such heavy forces as the lords can muster," Rhillian returned.

"When they muster in force, no," Zulmaher agreed. "But these will be isolated pockets, if any. Their armour may be strong, but even light cavalry, in the numbers you possess, should be sufficient."

Rhillian let out a snort, and stared at the castle. The flames on the tower showed no sign of abating. Large castles could withstand the hellfire for a greater time. Smaller castles like this one had little chance. Barely two days of bombardment, on the scale even a minor array of Steel artillery could deliver, would have towers ablaze and walls collapsing from the intense heat.

Serrin had given humans this power. Serrin oils, and serrin fires. Serrin steel, so formidable it had given the armies of the Saalshen Bacosh their name. Serrin bows had given human craftsmen ideas for new catapults, leading to advances in artillery that even without the hellfire were truly frightening. Human and serrin minds had combined to form a military of such killing power that it had no equal in all human lands. Thus far, the Steel had fought to protect Saalshen as much as human lands. But still, it was sometimes disquieting. Many great serrin thinkers, Rhillian knew, would look out at the Elissian battleground and wonder exactly what Saalshen had done to create this fire-breathing monster on its doorstep.

"Rhodaan had Saalshen's approval for this war," Rhillian said quietly, "on the understanding that the feudal nature of Elisse would be reversed. Feudalism is our death, General. It holds humanity in poverty, ignorance and powerlessness, leaving the masses of your people helpless to the predations of unchecked powerlust and fanatical religion—"

"It is not for Saalshen to tell humanity how to conduct our affairs with other humans," General Zulmaher interrupted.

"No," said Rhillian, "but it is for us to decide which of these actions we should support."

Zulmaher's grey eyes flashed dangerously. "Are you threatening to break your word to Rhodaan?"

"No more than you have broken your word to us."

"I gave no such word."

"You did. You said that you would liberate the Elissian people from their oppressors. We serrin have long memories, General. We know that a problem left unsolved will fester. This is our chance to solve the Elissian problem for good, and I feel you are squandering it."

Zulmaher looked back to his army. The artillery lines were preparing to move.

"I am in no mood," he said, "to have my commands dictated by the writ of Imperial Saalshen. You do what you will, M'Lady Rhillian. I shall do what I must, for Rhodaan." He pressed his heels to his horse and rode toward the head of the forming column. His captains followed, several with final, unhappy looks at Rhillian. She stared at the castle, intact despite the burning tower, and wondered how many hundreds of Elissian fighting men were left within those walls, armed, armoured and undefeated. Perhaps five hundred, including heavy cavalry. And of Lord Crashuren, his lands intact, his rights undisturbed . . . all from here to the northernmost tip of the Elissian Peninsula, there would be other lords left the same, if General Zulmaher had his way.

Aisha rode up, Arendelle with her. "Did you hear that?" Rhillian asked them. Both nodded.

"He's a feudalist," Aisha said glumly. "I'm not surprised."

"Why not?" Aisha was Enoran, born of a serrin mother and a human father. On matters of local motivations and politics, Rhillian trusted her judgement more than her own.

"His loyalties in Rhodaan lie with the old families," Aisha said. "They've been battling for the restoration of more feudal rights in Rhodaan for a century or longer. What did you think he was going to do—continue to isolate his supporting families by abolishing all feudalism in Elisse?"

"His captains did not appear happy," Arendelle remarked, watching the command party riding off. "There are some in Rhodaan who would call his position traitorous."

"Zulmaher is a proud Rhodaani," Aisha said. "He's fought and won many battles for his people, and suffered many wounds. He believes the feudal ways are the natural ways of humanity. . . . I doubt he'd wish them all restored to what they were—even he can't deny that things are so much better today than before the fall of Leyvaan. But the old families are wealthy, and in human lands, wealth creates power. It seems natural, to such men."

"And he resents the power that Saalshen has over Rhodaan," Rhillian added. "Did you hear him, 'the writ of Imperial Saalshen'?"

Aisha nodded. "He's very polite to us when it suits him, but most feudalists believe the current chaos in Tracato was Saalshen's plan to neuter Rhodaan and all the Saalshen Bacosh. It means little to him that Saalshen withdrew its last true imperial writ over a century ago. He believes Rhodaan needs a strong leader to be glorious, and the current system of council and High Table only combine to make a weak leadership. It's supposed to be a plan of Saalshen to divide and rule the Saalshen Bacosh, whatever their supposed independence."

"Of all the strange human concepts I've discovered," Rhillian said sourly, "I believe the one I like least may be 'nostalgia.'"

"Worse than 'war' or 'rape' or 'pillage'?" Arendelle asked her.

"Yes," said Rhillian, "because the one leads to the others so frequently."

"So do 'revolutions,'" Aisha said quietly. "Yet that is what we propose for Elisse."

"I know," Rhillian sighed. "You are Enoran, and you remember your history. But one bloody episode has led to two centuries of relative peace and prosperity, Aisha. Sometimes, the ends do justify the means."

"And other times," said Aisha, "blood is repaid with blood."

Five

ERROLLYN AWOKE TO THE SOUNDS OF THE COURTYARD CAMP beyond the windows. It was louder than previous mornings. Cattle were lowing. Hooves clopped on stone. Tent straps rattled, and there were voices, gruff with sleep. He could smell campfires. A rooster crowed.

"Sounds like the whole damn countryside moved in to town," Sasha murmured.

Errollyn knelt up in bed to peer through the shutters. The Tol'rhen courtyard was grey with smoke. Across its stones sprawled many campsites. The number had grown during the night.

There came a knocking at the door. Sasha groaned. "Go away," she said, burrowing back into her sheets.

"Enter!" Errollyn called. The door opened, and a serrin girl of no more than twelve entered. She had white hair, a slender face and pretty grey eyes. She wore pants rather than robes, identifying her as a *talmaad* in training. However, she wore no blade.

"Errollyn!" exclaimed the girl, coming to the bedside. "You must attend the Council of Ythemen this day at the lunch hour."

"Must I?"

"Yes." the girl insisted. She looked familiar, though Errollyn could not recall an introduction. "Ythemen is visiting all the way from Umal'ester'han, and she has much *ra'shi*!"

"And what shall Ythemen be doing at the Mahl'rhen today at the lunch hour," Errollyn asked with amusement, "that shall require my attendance? Juggle flaming balls? Swallow a whole cow? Perform some sexual trick with a candle?"

Beneath the sheets, Sasha whacked his leg.

Being serrin, and largely unshockable in such matters, the girl barely blinked. "But Errollyn, she came all the way from—"

"Umal'ester'han, yes, I know. Girl, have you ever been to Umal'ester'han?" The girl shook her head. "It's a series of boardwalks atop a muddy bog. You'll find greater native wisdom here."

"Lesthen requires your presence," said the girl, more sternly.

"Will Lesthen swallow a cow?" said Errollyn. "I'd turn up to see that."

"Spirits forbid he tries the trick with the candle," Sasha murmured. Errollyn grinned.

"Girl, I'm busy," he said. "Try another day."

The girl frowned at him. Serrin could never figure him out, whatever their age. Before she could leave, Sasha flung out her hand and grabbed the girl by the jacket. She pulled her closer, and slitted open her eyes.

"Serrin truly have no concept of privacy, do they?" Sasha said.

The girl blinked at her. "Should I have waited outside? It was not my intention to cause offence."

Sasha sighed. "No. No, of course not. Damn serrin. What's your name?"

"Letish."

"Letish. In some parts of Tracato, if you rush in on a man and woman abed, you'll be sorry for it. Be aware."

"I'm sorry," said Letish with a small bow, looking anything but. She was gazing at Sasha with intense curiosity.

"*I'm* not offended," Sasha said with exasperation. "Others might be. Where are your parents?"

"In Saalshen."

"How long since you've seen them?"

"Two years." As though nothing could be more normal.

Sasha smiled. "You go home now, and you tell Lesthen to stop pestering Errollyn." She gave the girl a kiss on the cheek, and burrowed back into her pillow. The girl began to leave, astonished and pleased. Halfway to the door, she dashed back, kissed Sasha on the cheek in kind, then left with a smile. Errollyn saw Sasha was smiling too.

"You've confused her," said Errollyn. "She thinks that's some kind of custom now."

"Perhaps it should be," said Sasha. "It never hurts to be nice." She closed her eyes. "I'm always nice to serrin, I can't help it. Maybe too nice."

"I'd never say that," said Errollyn. Sasha kicked him beneath the sheets, but gently.

Errollyn got up, stretched briefly and wrapped himself in a robe to visit the privy. The Mahl'rhen had been trying to lure him back since his arrival. Word had spread from Rhillian, on her passing through, of his odd behaviour in Petrodor. "Traitorous" was not a word serrin would naturally use. But he had them alarmed. Rather than deal with the problem directly, serrin did what they always did—they talked. Endless talking, endless councils, endless lectures and halfhearted attempts to understand. He'd given up trying by the end of the first day. Now, they sent messengers pleading with him to return to the fold.

Sasha appeared to have gone back to sleep. Errollyn stood and looked at her for a long moment. There was something vaguely wild and untamed in the muscles of her arms and shoulders, the way she sprawled on the mattress, the way her hair stuck up against the pillow. The sight of it set free something wild and untamed in him, too.

He crawled over her, and sat straddling upon her backside. Then he dug his fingers into her shoulders and neck, just the way she liked. Sasha smiled and winced. She worked hard at those muscles, perhaps harder than a man needed to. After some bad strains she could barely turn her head.

"You have classes today?" she asked him.

"I promised Ulenshaal Timar I'd take a Saalsi class," said Errollyn. "After that, I have Aemon to visit."

"You be careful with Aemon; the Tracato nobility may look very tame but underneath I'm certain they're no different from elsewhere."

"I know," Errollyn said mildly. He slid his hands down her back, then up her bare sides.

"That doesn't do my stiffness any good at all," she said, smiling.

"Does wonders for mine," said Errollyn. Sasha laughed. She threw off the sheets and rolled over.

"Come on then," she dared him, with her irresistible, mischievous smile. "Wake me up properly."

After morning training, and a wash, Errollyn walked to the Tol'rhen courtyard to see the camp. There had to be a thousand people, he guessed. Some made tents from wooden frames, others strung ropes between statues upon which to drape canvas, while others slept under carts. Now there were fires, and farm animals gathered amidst piles of hay. Banners hung, several draped over statues—the sickle-and-scythe flag of the Civid Sein.

Tol'rhen Nasi-Keth walked amongst them, handing out food and blankets. A cart was making the rounds, unloading firewood, also supervised by Nasi-Keth. Errollyn saw several youngsters he knew, talking amiably with rough-dressed rural folk. All the rural folk seemed to be armed, some with tools, some with genuine weapons. About the courtyard perimeter, Blackboots were watching, with grim expressions.

By the foot of a grand statue of some famous general, Errollyn spotted Ulenshaal Sevarien and Reynold Hein, in conversation with several Civid Sein men. He walked to them, and wondered what cityfolk would make of these outsiders using their historical statues for tent posts. Sevarien spotted him, and waved him over.

"Master Errollyn!" he boomed. "These are farmers Stefani and Dujane, leaders of our gathering."

Our gathering? Errollyn wondered to himself.

"Where is your satellite?" asked Reynold, looking around.

"Presently eclipsed in a class of Lenay history," said Errollyn, flexing a shoulder where Sasha had struck him at training.

"Ah, Sashandra would make an excellent Ulenshaal!" exclaimed Sevarien with a laugh. "It might help the meaningful discussion of Lenay history if she could do so without waving her sword around midlesson, mind you."

"Sasha believes that history should never be dull," Errollyn said, shaking his head. "The camp has grown considerably."

Farmer Stefani nodded. "Soon it will be bigger," he assured them. He was a large man, with a moustache, and smelled of animals. "We heard what General Zulmaher is doing in Elisse. This cannot be allowed—Elisse cannot become a stronghold for the Rhodaani nobility's feudalist allies."

Sevarien beamed, and slapped Stefani's shoulder. "And nor shall it be allowed. We'll show those nobility that Rhodaan belongs to the common folk, not the entitled wealthy."

Reynold excused himself and made off through the crowd.

"What kind of demonstration do you intend?" Errollyn asked. He made his tone conversational, betraying no concern.

"Whatever it takes," said Stefani, with dour certainty. "The nobility debate in council, how to restore taxation to the landed men. Maldereld made it illegal two hundred years ago, and now they try to bring it back. To remove the power of the Council, and replace it with the money of nobility and their paid men-at-arms." He glowered in the direction of the Blackboots. "In Enora they'd cut off their heads for daring to suggest it."

"My friends at the Mahl'rhen are certain it won't go that far," Errollyn offered. "They say the debate in council is more about relieving some over-burdened nobility from too much taxation, not about granting nobles the power of taxation."

"Dear Errollyn," said Sevarien, putting a hand on his shoulder. "You of all people should know better than to place much store in the analysis of the Mahl'rhen. Yours are a gentle people, they do not understand the viciousness and brutality of such folk as the nobility. Only a du'jannah such as yourself can understand."

Errollyn thought he understood quite well. Exactly *what* he understood, about gatherings like this one, and some of the Nasi-Keth's recent infatuation with them, he did not think wise to share.

Sasha was talking to Ulenshaal Martinesse when Reynold appeared at the door. The class had been overflowing, with students standing in alcoves and sitting against the stone walls to fit in. Martinesse had interrupted frequently, and the two women had argued for much of the class, to the delight of onlookers. Sasha had been quite alarmed at just how wrong Martinesse's interpretations were of the reasons for Verenthanism's spread through Lenayin. Now the silver-haired lady continued the debate, as perhaps twenty students clustered about to hear.

"Ladies, please excuse me," Reynold cut in, walking from the doorway. "Ulenshaal, could I borrow Sashandra for a moment? She is much in demand, I know."

The students looked disappointed. "We shall continue this at lunch," Martinesse told them.

"Assuredly," said Sasha.

"Come students!" Martinesse announced, clapping her hands. "I know you have other classes to get to." They departed, some with a final, appreciative thanks to Sasha.

"Martinesse is an excellent Ulenshaal, yes?" Reynold said.

"She's very smart," said Sasha, trying to be polite. That much was true at least, and she hated lying.

"But?"

"I don't know, some of the people in this place . . . I mean, they're very clever, but they have these favourite ideas. And instead of accepting that they're wrong when evidence proves their favourite ideas silly, they refuse to, and twist all evidence to try to make it fit their opinion."

"Ah," said Reynold. "But you cannot deny the passion for ideas in this place."

"Ideas, yes," said Sasha. "But ideas are not facts. Any fool can invent a crazy idea and be passionate about it, I don't see that counts as wisdom."

Reynold laughed. "Oh, come, surely we're not that bad?"

"Not all of you, no," Sasha conceded, stretching. She needed to get outside for a while, and clear her head. "Not most of you. I don't know. . . . I'm from a land of simple, straightforward people, Reynold; they say what they think and accept facts as they appear obvious. They're not as sophisticated as anyone here, but I don't think education and wisdom are necessarily the same thing."

"Or perhaps you're just homesick."

Sasha shrugged, and smiled at him. "A little," she admitted. "Did you wish to speak to me about something?"

Reynold thought for a moment. "I was wondering of your relationship with Errollyn."

Sasha gave a puzzled smile. Reynold would not be the first to be curious about that. Hells, she was curious herself. "Yes?"

"Do you foresee marriage?"

Sasha laughed. "To a serrin?"

"It does happen, in Tracato," Reynold insisted. "Initiated by the serrin themselves."

"I'd never thought that far. Foresight and planning aren't my strong points, as Kessligh's always telling me."

"So you don't foresee marriage?"

"Reynold, I honestly couldn't say."

"He is very handsome," Reynold pressed. "Most girls would be jealous of the chance to bed a man like him each night."

Sasha was amused, but didn't find the conversation reason enough to stay away from the sunlight. "Yes, well, the many jealous girls of Tracato will just have to deal with it. I have to get outside, I can't stay inside for long."

She headed for the door, expecting him to walk with her. Reynold stepped backward instead, facing her, partly blocking the way. "I mean, if I were bedding some stunningly beautiful girl," he continued, "then I might prolong that situation for as long as possible, even if I did not intend to marry her."

"Um, sure," said Sasha, slowing down.

"But such a relationship could not continue forever," he continued. "At some point, don't you think, the flesh might tire of such simple pleasures?"

He reached for her cheek. Sasha was astonished, but mostly at herself, for being so dense. She was so unaccustomed to being courted. In Lenayin, most men desired a picture of feminine domesticity, and she was certainly not that.

She took a step back. "Reynold, I'm truly flattered. But Errollyn is more than my bed partner, he's my best friend. Please understand." She tried a smile, and hoped that worked. Spirits knew what went on in the minds of men, in such situations.

"Oh, come, you're Lenay," Reynold said easily. "The women of Lenayin are adventurous, surely?"

"Passionate," Sasha corrected. "And loyal."

"Next you'll be trying to tell me that Errollyn is the only man you've bedded."

Sasha opened her mouth to reply in the affirmative, and stopped. None of his damn business anyway. Now she was getting frustrated.

"Reynold, look. You seem a nice man, but the answer is no. I'd like to go outside now." She gestured him out of the way. He advanced another step instead.

"Sashandra, you are an amazingly beautiful woman. I am not an inexperienced man, I am certain you'd not be disappointed."

Sasha realised that she was retreating. She stopped, and he drew very close. "Look," she began angrily, "let me make this very plain for you—"

Reynold tried to kiss her. Sasha sidestepped quickly. Reynold grinned, and pursued. In desperation Sasha threw a punch at him, and missed. He grabbed her arm and wrestled her close, and suddenly her arms were pinned, and his hands were on her, and there was no leverage at all. She couldn't reach her knife, let alone her sword, and he was pushing her against a wall—not an enormously large or strong man, but a swordsman all the same, and infuriatingly she'd missed her opening chance. How many times had Kessligh warned her never to let a man get this close? She was a strong girl but against fighting men it was not enough; with her it was blades or nothing.

He had her off balance against the wall. In a flash of inspiration, she kissed him hard. She could feel his surprise against her body, his momentary flutter of excitement and astonishment . . . he grabbed her and kissed her back harder. That freed her arm, and she grabbed his balls, and squeezed tighter than she'd ever squeezed anything.

His face contorted, his grip slackened. In sheer fury for the taste of his mouth in hers, she smashed him with her forehead. He fell to his knees, clutching his nose, and Sasha drew her sword in a flash and put it to his neck. She felt unsteady, seeing stars, and her head hurt. That had been stupid. What the hells was she going to do, kill him? This shining intellect of the Tol'rhen, who until now had been nothing but pleasant and civilised? This unarmed man, who had never drawn a blade against her?

She sheathed the blade, and resisted the temptation to kick Reynold senseless while she had the chance. She strode out into the hallway, putting a hand to her head to check for blood. She found none. Still she couldn't think straight, and doubted that was the blow to her head.

Who should she tell? Errollyn would kill him. Or not . . . but he'd finish what she'd started, and produce a lot more bleeding. Kessligh would . . . hells, she had no idea what Kessligh would do. Much of the Tol'rhen would undoubtedly side with Reynold. He was their man, their esteemed leader. She felt unclean. Damn him for doing this to her. What the hells had possessed him? The desperate need of a fuck? Surely not—Reynold was charming, not unattractive, and many women swooned after him. Why her?

The more she thought about it, the more furious she became. A few more strides down the hallway and she nearly reversed and drew her blade, to do what she should have done in the name of Lenay honour and cut his head off. But it was too late now—Lenay custom dictated that hot blood was fair and just, but now the moment was passed. Damn him.

She entered the great hall, one of Tracato's many architectural marvels. There was a commotion at the far end, amidst the usual student bustle. People had gathered in numbers and voices were raised. Sasha strode that way, in a perfect mood for trouble. Hopefully someone would need killing. Someone evil.

A group of students were booing. Sasha pushed through the crowd and saw a small cluster of well-dressed men in argument with several black-robed Ulenshaals. *Very* well-dressed men, Sasha corrected herself, eyeing the jewelled sword pommels, the intricate embroidery on their jackets and pants, the feather tufts in wide brimmed hats. Nobility.

High nobility, she corrected herself further, seeing the woman in the blue gown who accompanied them, with a pair of servants in close attendance. The gown was more understated than some Sasha had seen, yet tasselled and embroidered to an extravagant extent for a journey into territory beyond comfortable noble grounds. . . .

The beautiful young woman noted Sasha, and her eyes widened. "Sasha!" Sasha's jaw dropped.

"'Lyth?"

Alythia crossed to her with unladylike haste, and embraced her. Sasha hugged her back. Her sister smelled of perfumes beyond Sasha's experience to describe. Alythia pulled away and grinned at her.

"I *told* you I'd come!" she exclaimed, daring Sasha to contradict her.

She *had* told her. They'd exchanged letters, a ludicrous contrivance for two sisters living barely a morning's run away, but it had been the only way for more than two weeks now. Once within the fold of Family Renine, Alythia had vanished. Sasha had worried, and accosted several noble messengers to insist they delivered her concerns into important hands. Finally there had been a letter, in Alythia's script, insisting she was well, and happy, and of increasingly good fortune. Sasha had not been surprised, but suspicious. Further correspondence had convinced her that Alythia's words were genuine. They could not meet. Alythia was always "engaged," and nobility did not visit the Tol'rhen in these times.

"Dear Lord Elot," said Alythia, turning back to her group, "you do recall my sister Sashandra?"

"Indeed," said Lord Elot, and Sasha recalled the lord from the night of their arrival in Tracato. That had been the last time she'd seen Alythia, until now. "We meet again, Lady Sashandra."

Sasha returned his bow. "Lord Elot."

"And Master Alfriedo," said Alythia, taking Sasha's hand and walking her over. Sasha realised that she was addressing a boy of no more than fourteen—she had overlooked him entirely, his head came barely to Lord Elot's wide midriff. His young face was very fine and pale, he wore a small sword at his hip, and carried himself with lordly dignity.

Alfriedo, Alythia had said. This must be Alfriedo Renine. The rightful heir to the long dormant throne of Rhodaan. If one still believed in that nonsense.

Alythia curtseyed low. "Master Alfriedo, may I introduce my sister, Sashandra." She presented Sasha's hand to the boy. Alfriedo, with impeccable etiquette, took Sasha's hand and kissed it.

"Dear Lady," he said, his voice high and clear. His eyes were very blue. Sasha had heard a scandalous rumour that the boy king had serrin blood. Seeing him now, she wondered. "Is it true, as your sister tells me, that you prefer not to be addressed by the royal title of your birth?"

Sasha gave him a bow of respect, but no more. Behind the boy, several lords' faces darkened with displeasure. "I do," she said. "And more to the point, my father disapproves that anyone should use the title."

"Perhaps then we should start calling you Princess?" Alfriedo suggested. "It would not do to please the King of Lenayin." The nobles laughed. The surrounding gathering was largely silent, all shouldering each other to see. "I have come, at your sister's encouragement, to tour the Tol'rhen. I have always desired to, and now I have the opportunity."

Sasha was astonished. So were most of those around them. She spared a quick glance at Alythia, and found her sister's gaze trained very firmly upon her. Alythia was up to something.

"I see no reason why that should be a problem," Sasha recovered herself to say.

"I can think of several," said one of the Ulenshaals drily. Garen, Sasha recalled the man's name. "Feudalism is a disease of the mind; we exorcised it from Rhodaan two centuries ago. Feudalists and their ilk are not welcome in the Tol'rhen."

There was some loud agreement from the crowd. Lord Elot looked stonily unsurprised. As though, Sasha thought, he expected this exercise to fail, and was pleased with the prospect.

"Exactly what kind of intellectual are you?" Sasha asked Garen sharply.

"The discerning kind," said Garen, and several in the crowd tittered.

"You're a bigot," she told him.

Garen's eyes widened. "I beg your pardon?"

"Can you show me one passage in all written works of serrin philosophy that states that a person with an alternative point of view should be turned away, without engagement?"

"Feudalism is a plague upon the land!" Garen said angrily. "Everything that held humanity back for centuries was swept away when Maldereld abolished feudal powers in Rhodaan, and now these *characters* wish to bring it back!"

"Well, I think that's a fine argument!" Sasha said grandly. "Make it!" She indicated to the waiting nobles. "You call yourself Nasi-Keth, yet you refuse to debate! What have the serrin taught us if not to advance knowledge through congenial argument?" Garen's look was sullen. "Show them around your marvellous institution! How ridiculous is it that the highest nobility have rarely seen it with their own eyes. Here's your chance, show them what they're missing, or admit that you're either too feeble an intellect to make your case persuasively, or too cowardly a man to engage your foe upon the field of intellectual battle."

There was a silence in the hall. Then, an isolated applause. Another joined it, and another. There was little enthusiasm in it, but no one shouted the applauders down. Ulenshaal Garen took a deep breath, seeing that he'd lost. Lord Elot also looked displeased.

"Very well," said Garen. "People, guests, if you will follow me?" He gestured down the hall, and the crowd parted.

Young Alfriedo paused before following, and looked up at Sasha with respect. "Lady Sashandra. Your sister told me that you were formidable. I see that she has told me only the truth." He glanced at Alythia, who smiled and bowed her head gracefully.

"Smart kid?" Sasha suggested.

"Oh, you have no idea," said Alythia. "He is a proper little lord, Sasha, smart well beyond his years. More so than most of his elders, I think."

They sat at a study table on the balcony overlooking the Tol'rhen library. They had followed the guided tour as far as the library, before taking their leave to talk in private. The touring party had attracted quite a crowd, and were thus far all well mannered. Kessligh's arrival had ended any further chance of trouble, despite the continued displeasure of several Ulenshaals. The last Sasha had seen, Kessligh and Alfriedo had been engaged in an animated discussion on various points of Tol'rhen learning.

"What about his mother?" Sasha pressed. "I hear stories."

"Oh everyone in this city tells stories," Alythia scoffed. "Lady Renine is an amazing woman. She's well educated, she speaks five tongues and knows so much of the history of these lands, yet the Civid Sein speak of her as though she were stupid. She's the reason Alfriedo has had such a good education. She is a fine mother to her son."

"And what of you?" Sasha pressed. "What is your situation with them?"

"Family Renine have been very kind," said Alythia, with measured satisfaction. "I have been granted my own quarters, with a staff of five. I am a guest of the noble household."

"I can think of several other words for it."

"Such as?"

"Hostage. Bargaining piece."

"Sasha, all institutions shall seek power and leverage," Alythia said impatiently, "including this one. You don't think the Nasi-Keth seek similar advantage from you and Kessligh?"

Sasha opened her mouth to retort, then thought of Ulenshaal Sevarien and Reynold Hein, their efforts toward the Civid Sein and their attempts to drag her and Kessligh into it. She looked away in frustration.

Alythia frowned at her. "Sasha, is something the matter? You seem a little . . . tense."

"I'm all right." She was actually pleased that Alythia had noticed. "Unwanted male attention," she admitted.

Alythia smiled broadly. "Ah," she said wisely. "You can't kill them all, can you?" Sasha scowled at her. "It's someone of status, yes? Someone well regarded within the Nasi-Keth? Difficult when there are no clear lines of good and evil, isn't it?"

"I'm glad it amuses you."

Alythia clasped Sasha's hand. "I'm sorry. It's just that you're finally in my world. I cannot be the blunt instrument all the time that you are, Sasha. Or the sharp one, more correctly. I can't just fight people who offend me, there is too much etiquette at play, too many conflicting loyalties. If I have been short with you in the past, it is perhaps because you seemed to have so much success taking the easy way out, and fighting. I've had to tolerate fools, Sasha, and unwanted advances, and all kinds of demeaning nonsense. You never did, and I envied that."

Sasha smiled at her, and grasped her hand tightly in return. They had been enemies for so long, and now, they were friends. It was the discovery of long-lost family.

"So, how do you see it?" she asked. "What do Family Renine want from you?"

"It's difficult to say," Alythia said. "I'm not entirely certain they are themselves sure. But consider the options from their perspective. First, the Army of Lenayin wins, and marches on Tracato. They have me for a hostage, or at least for a negotiator, perhaps to put in a good word for them with our father."

"If you were wed to one of them . . ." Sasha added, and did not need to complete the sentence.

"There have been leading questions," Alythia admitted. "But no firm offers for now. Under Lenay law the marriage would not stand without the king's first prior approval . . ."

"Unlikely," Sasha agreed.

"But it bears thinking on. The second option is that the Army of Lenayin loses, in which case they may expect to see members of our family fall." Sasha nodded grimly. "In that case, there is no telling where *I* would stand within the succession—"

"Nowhere, as women cannot sit the throne."

"But if wedded, what of my husband?"

Sasha stared at her for a moment, thinking that over. "No no no," she said. "I'm not that far gone from noble circles that I don't know at least the basic rules of succession. Foreign husbands can't inherit, men have to be true born Lenays. It's Koenyg, then Wylfred—"

"Who has taken the oath of brotherhood and cannot stand," said Alythia.

"Then Damon and Myklas," Sasha finished. "You're older than Damon but he and Myklas still come before you as men . . ."

"And if they *all* fall?" Alythia said sombrely.

Sasha didn't like to think about that, but circumstance demanded she must. "I'm not sure anyone knows. Our family's only sat the throne for a hundred years. The circumstance has never arisen."

"This is the point, Sasha. I'm not sure that anyone knows."

"But surely . . . I mean, Great-Grandpa Soros must have written it down?"

"Oh, yes," said Alythia, "the rules of succession are set, as you said. But they're old, Sasha, and untested. You know Lenayin, you know the battle to get the lords to do anything the way it's supposed to happen. Lenayin today is a vastly different nation than Grandpa Soros thought it would be, a hundred years since the Liberation."

Sasha nodded. Alythia made a lot of sense. "If all our family's men fall, what's supposed to happen?"

"Sons of the oldest heir," said Alythia, "in descending order of course."

"Little nephew Dany," Sasha said distastefully. "A Hadryn inherits the throne."

"He's not actually Hadryn."

"His mother is. And if Koenyg were dead, she'd rule his choices, the Archbishop would control his education . . ."

"Yes," Alythia conceded with a shrug. "It would be like the Hadryn acquiring the throne of Lenayin, certainly. Which would upset so many Lenay lords, to say nothing of Lenay people, that likely war would result. Which is why I don't think the lords would allow it to happen, and Grandpa's rules of succession be damned."

"So who would have an equal competing claim? Surely not a son of yours with some Tracato noble?"

"Sasha, think about it." Alythia leaned forward, eyes deadly serious. "What has been the single greatest advantage our family has had in ruling Lenayin the last century? The reason why the lords don't just get rid of us, as they so easily could?"

"We don't get involved in lordly disputes."

"Exactly. Baen-Tar is not a true province, and the royal family has no provincial loyalty. We're independent. The lords abide by Father's decisions because they know he is impartial. However much they disagree with any decision he makes against them, they'd still rather keep the king on the throne because they know the one to replace him would be a provincial great lord, and that would be intolerable."

"Like having a Hadryn on the throne," Sasha said slowly.

"Exactly," said Alythia, knocking the table for emphasis. "Half of Lenayin would rather tear the land apart than see it happen, because they know the chances of impartiality from a Hadryn king are precisely nil. And the Hadryn know the same of them."

"You think that an outsider, born in Tracato . . ."

"As Grandpa Soros was educated in Petrodor," Alythia agreed, "to the extent that he was practically a Torovan when he ascended to the throne and barely spoke a native tongue . . ."

"Oh," said Sasha.

"It's not without precedent in Lenayin," Alythia concluded. "Most of the great lords would rather see a son of mine, raised in Tracato, ascend to the throne than any son of Koenyg's."

"Wait, there's Petryna, she's older than you."

"And her son is heir to the Great Lordship of Yethulyn, same problem as with Hadryn. And Marya's older than us all, but the chances that any in Lenayin would let sons of the new King Marlen of Torovan ascend are unlikely, given it would simply make Lenayin a province of Torovan, beneath the command of King Marlen Steiner."

"And a son of Sofy would be beholden to the commands of Larosan nobility," Sasha added.

"Besides which, I'm older," Alythia agreed. "But yes, the very advantage of it being a son of mine, if the Army of Lenayin lost its fight, is that Family Renine are relatively powerless outside of Rhodaan. If the Army of Lenayin had lost, it would certainly suggest the current order here would still stand, which precludes Family Renine from assuming any greater feudal power. Meaning a son of mine would be a true outsider, with no unwanted connections. Perfect for Lenayin."

"You've thought about this a lot," Sasha said warily.

"Aye, well you think about sword fighting, and I think about noble politics. It's our lot in life."

Sasha was unconvinced. She no longer hated Alythia, if she ever truly had, but some of her previous assessments of her sister, she did not doubt. Power drove Alythia. Obsessed her, in every waking moment. It was not necessarily a flaw; as Alythia said, Sasha knew what it was to be obsessive in competitive matters, and that it did not always equate with evil. And yet . . .

"Sasha, I'm thinking of Lenayin, as are you," Alythia said firmly, as though reading her mind. "The armies of the Steel have not been defeated in two hundred years. If Lenayin suffers a catastrophic loss, royal ranks could be decimated, and then Hadryn takes the throne. We need options."

"Who would you wed?"

"I haven't decided. It would take a long time to raise a son to rule, if the great lords agreed to his legitimate claim. There would need to be a caretaker. A regent, of sorts."

"All right, this has now become too hypothetical for me. 'Lyth, we have more short-term problems than Lenayin's succession. What's General Zulmaher doing in Elisse?"

"You're the soldier. You tell me."

"Many around here are saying he's a puppet of the Renines, that he's more interested in making noble friends in Elisse than destroying feudalism there."

Alythia sighed. "Sasha, I am a new guest in the Renine household. I have leverage there, but not yet trust. I know nothing of the Renines' schemes."

"Do you think that there *are* schemes?"

"It's a noble household, of course there are schemes. I know that everyone's quite alarmed at these Civid Sein fools suddenly pouring into town."

"The surest way to rouse the Civid Sein is to set up Elisse as a feudal ally to the north," Sasha said with certainty. "I don't know . . . why do the nobles want to tear down everything that's been built here? Had you ever imagined a city such as this, before you came here?"

"It's very impressive, yes," Alythia said wryly.

"It's the wealth, and the ideas!" Sasha was almost surprised at her own enthusiasm. "I've been thinking a lot since I've been here, and there are many ideas we could take back to Lenayin. I'd love to see a Tol'rhen like this in Baen-Tar."

Alythia smiled indulgently at her younger sister. "You forget yourself, Sasha," she said. "The Army of Lenayin is marching to burn this place down."

"No." Sasha shook her head. "I can't believe that. If our army wins, Father would never order all of this destroyed."

"He would not wish to, no," Alythia agreed. "But, Sasha, look at what's happened here. All these institutions, this learning and invention that impresses you so much, this is the nobility of Rhodia's worst nightmare. This is a vision of the world without them. What was that old tale, about the king whose death is foretold by the fortune teller, and he orders every fortune teller killed? Why do you think this place has been so endlessly attacked the last two hundred years?"

"So why do the Renines want to pull down everything that's made Rhodaan a success in that time?"

"They don't want to pull everything down!" Alythia insisted. "They're proud Rhodaanis, but . . . have you been following the council deliberations lately?" Sasha sighed, nodding reluctantly. "They bicker and bribe and betray. They call themselves the elected representatives, yet in truth barely one in five has earned his seat with a fair vote. Rhodaan shall fall if she does not have a firm hand. You're a soldier, you know that an army cannot win without firm leadership."

Sasha stretched back, hands in her hair. "It's so frustrating. Every side has a piece of the puzzle, yet they refuse to share."

"Sasha, you should meet with Lady Renine," Alythia insisted. "You have heard only ill of her since you have been here, where everyone hates her. You will be astonished, I promise you. She loves everything about Rhodaan that you do, as does Alfriedo. And she despairs at the inaction of the council."

"'Lyth," Sasha said, "I'm not about to take sides in this."

"I'm not asking you to. On the contrary, you could be the perfect neutral mediator. Someone who can bring the sides to talking, instead of fighting."

Sasha stared across the library. She could not help the terrible feeling that she would be betraying her nation. The Army of Lenayin was marching to war against Rhodaan, and here she would be trying to help Rhodaan put its house in order.

Lenayin and Rhodaan were not yet at war, she told herself. Sofy was yet to marry. Larosa and Lenayin were a poor match, anyone could see it, and if those two sides came to blows in a fit of mutual outrage at the other's appalling behaviour, Sasha would not be surprised. The die was not yet cast, and until then, her loyalties, and indeed her duty, lay with Kessligh.

The Torovan maps called it Panae Achi, or Harbourtown, but the locals called it Reninesenn, or Renine's Town, in Rhodaani. Errollyn walked the cobbled streets, past wagons loaded with cargo, and wholesalers crowded with buyers. The haggling spilled onto the streets.

Blackboots chatted easily with a barber before his shop, cleaning a razor on his smock. A tavern did a rowdy business of sailors and dockers. In front of a bakery, women piled fresh bread into a handcart.

The Civid Sein liked to paint Tracato's divisions as entirely of class, the wealthy against the poor, but Reninesenn showed otherwise. Noble families had always controlled the trade in Tracato. Today the old ties lingered, and the Dockside folk had not embraced the idea of a future without the nobility, preferring instead the old ties of patronage and wealth. Noble families owned most of the ships and nearly all of the warehouses, and any merchant or trader looking to move goods had to establish good connections.

Errollyn did not sense any hostility toward him but, equally, he knew he should be careful what he said.

Questions on the docks took him to a tavern opposite a grain warehouse, where carts crowded three deep, and men heaved heavy sacks onto waiting shoulders. Errollyn walked straight to the barkeeper, past tables of loud-talking men.

"I'm looking for *Duchess Teresa*," he said to the barkeep, who waved him toward a table by the windows. Errollyn saw a table of sailors, rough looking yet not quite as disreputable as popular myth. Some had good coats, though hard wearing, and many wore braids in the fashion of seafarers. All looked as though they'd bathed in the last day or two.

"Welcome, sir!" said one man in Torovan as Errollyn approached the table.

"I thank you," said Errollyn.

"And what can I do you for?" Conversation at the table ceased, yet Errollyn sensed no ill will. Serrin business on the docks was common and, for the most part, welcomed.

"I'm looking to buy raw silver and gemstone," said Errollyn, hooking his thumb into his belt by a money pouch. "I'd heard the *Duchess Teresa* was in the business this run?"

"Ah," said the man, "I was the quartermaster for that run, but I'm afraid we're all pledged to other customers; my apologies, sir."

"Not at all. Might I buy the table a drink and ask of the conditions of trade?"

"Absolutely!" beamed the quartermaster, and his mate pulled Errollyn a chair from a neighbouring table.

Errollyn asked the usual questions, of wind and currents, but also of Larosan naval activity and what news of ships lately sunk or in action.

"So you've been in Voscoraine then?" he asked the quartermaster.

"Oh no, sir," said the sailor, sipping the ale Errollyn's coin had bought. "Poscadi."

"I wasn't aware there was good silver and gemstone in Poscadi."

"A new mine," the sailor replied easily. "Up in the northern Ameryn hills."

"Council won't allow us in Telesian ports anyhow," said a second man. "There's a war on, you know."

"Telesia has not declared for one side or another, the last I'd heard," said Errollyn.

"And the Torovan army'll be marching straight through Telesia on their way to Larosa," said the sailor, waving to an acquaintance who entered the crowded inn. "Excuse me, I spy a friend. Thanks for the drink." He got up and left.

"I heard they charge a tariff to enter Poscadi these days," said Errollyn, edging his chair aside as more sailors crowded onto a neighbouring table. It was hard to hear above the din of conversation. "Three per cent of cargo value, what impact does that have on the silver trade there?"

"That's a terrible thing," the quartermaster said. "Damned inspectors, they overestimate our cargo value then pocket the extra for themselves. I've made barely enough to feed my children on this run, the next won't be any better."

Errollyn talked until the man's ale was nearly gone, then thanked him and his companions and left, to empty-mug salutes from the sailors. But he already knew what he wanted to know. The *Duchess Teresa* had been in Poscadi Port in Ameryn. He knew from many conversations with Petrodor sailors that the Poscadi Port harbour tax had recently gone up to five per cent, not three, giving the quartermaster another chance to whine about how high his expenses were, if he'd known about it. The quartermaster had definitely not been in Poscadi Port recently.

That left Voscoraine, in Telesia. Telesia remained an independent kingdom, having at various times been a part of Torovan or Algrasse. Now they attempted to maintain neutrality, being greatly dependent on Saalshen and Rhodaani trade, yet squeezed on land between neighbours determined to wrest the Saalshen Bacosh away from Saalshen's influence by force. Telesia's port of Voscoraine was not far by road from Larosa and Sherdaine. The Rhodaani Council had barred Rhodaani flagged vessels from berthing there, knowing the port to be full of Larosan agents, and fearing a trade of spies, or the loss of vessels. For the *Duchess Teresa* to have been in Voscoraine Port would have violated the Council's order. They must have remained there a long time, to simulate the time it would have taken to reach Ameryn.

Further questions directed him to a laneway, in search of the *Duchess Teresa*'s captain, the man the quartermaster had professed not to know. The building was clearly a brothel—red lanterns hung between cramped tenements. Errollyn entered, and pushed past several drunken sailors in the hall. It opened onto a main room, where girls dressed like noble ladies coiffed and preened—another of Tracato's strange tastes, every ale-drenched, salt-stained sailor wanted to bed a noble lady.

"My, my," said the madam, leaving another customer in female hands to come to Errollyn, looking him up and down. "Dear sir, welcome. Can I interest you in . . ."

"I'm looking for someone."

The madam sighed. She wore much jewellery, all fake. "I should have guessed, you serrin never did appreciate the business."

"That's because we fuck for free," Errollyn said drily. "I was told the captain of the *Duchess Teresa* might be here?"

"My customers' business is strictly confidential," said the madam airily. Errollyn pressed a large coin into her hand. "Second floor, the third room on the left," she said, pocketing the coin.

He walked up the cramped stairs, edging past customers and working girls. At the room, he rapped on the door. It swung open. Errollyn was fairly certain such doors were supposed to be locked. He pushed it wide, a hand straying to his belt knife—the walls were too close for swords, he could barely spread his elbows. On the bed he found a naked man, face down and unmoving. The sheets beneath his upper body were soaked in blood. Somehow, Errollyn was not entirely surprised.

The windows were closed, but the small room had a closet. Errollyn flung open the closet doors. Within huddled a girl, dressed like the others. Her hands were flecked with blood. Errollyn grabbed her, and slammed her against the wall.

"That's the captain of the *Duchess Teresa*, yes?" The girl remained mute, eyes flicking back to the bed. "Why kill him? What was the *Duchess Teresa* doing in Voscoraine Port?"

The girl tried to drive a knee into his groin, but Errollyn had played rough games with a far more dangerous girl than this. He blocked her with his leg, and slammed her harder back against the wall.

"An honourable serrin gentleman wouldn't hurt a girl, surely?" she taunted him. Errollyn was getting tired of humans who thought behavioural codes could excuse all evils, and hit her in the face. He picked her back up, her nose bloody, and slammed her back against the wall.

"Murderers don't get to plead delicacy," he told her. "Why kill him?" Her stare was defiant.

"Family Renine aren't playing fair," Aemon had told him. There had been a courier on the *Duchess Teresa,* heading for Voscoraine Port, bearing the Renine Family seal.

"There was someone on the ship, wasn't there? Someone carrying letters for people in Telesia?"

The nobility of Algrasse? Algrasse was an ally of Larosa, they had stood with the Regent Arrosh when he had been but a lord of Larosa, and assisted him in his rise to regent of all the Bacosh. Their position was strong, there was no chance they'd be scheming with the Renines against their sworn feudal lord. Which left just one serious option. "Lady Renine is negotiating with Regent Arosh, isn't she? Behind the Council's back?"

"I'll not say anything to foulblood scum like you!" the girl hissed. "Murderer!" she screamed. "Murderer, come quick! Save me!"

Shouts came from the neighbouring rooms. Then a scuffling under the bed itself. Errollyn spun, and saw a man scrambling from beneath the mattress, and cursed himself for a fool.

The door crashed in, and Errollyn flung the girl hard across the room. A man rushed him, knife in hand—a house guard, protection for the girls. Errollyn caught the man's thrusting arm, broke it, and threw him back into the face of the second guard. Behind him the windows crashed open and the man from under the bed leaped out. Errollyn sheathed his knife and leaned out the window. Below was a canvas awning, protecting the brothel's rear entry in a narrow lane. Beneath the awning, the jumping man was scrambling to his feet.

Errollyn got a foot out for leverage, and jumped. Somewhat heavier than the first man, he hit the awning hard and it tore . . . he crashed to the ground in a tangle of canvas, scrambling to extricate himself while thankful it had at least broken his fall.

Finally up, he ran after the other man in time to see him vanish around a corner. Errollyn dashed around it, struggling against the stiffness of a bruised thigh. Down the next lane, past an unloading cart and tethered horses, he saw the man run into a crowded main street.

Errollyn followed, sunlight suddenly bright to a serrin's sensitive vision. Errollyn shielded his eyes and peered up the street. Was that him? He had spots in his eyes, and nothing was clear. There were crowds around him, some looking at him, others evidently startled by the recent passage of a sprinting man. Even if he caught the man, what could he do, in this crowd? These were feudalists, some of them even royalists, or restorationists, or whatever fancy term the clever scholars in the Tol'rhen liked to apply. Serrin were welcome so long as they did not swim against the stream. A serrin accosting a local in the street would be mobbed.

Errollyn took a deep breath, wincing as the bruises from his fall began to hurt.

"Everything okay there, sir?" a local man asked him.

Errollyn shook his head. "A murder in the Fletcher Street brothel," he said loudly enough for others to hear. "The captain of the *Duchess Teresa*, a man of a noble family." He pointed after the escaped runner. "That man cut his throat. Pass the word and have him caught, I can't do it myself. *Reninesen shendevan soni Reninesen shendevan.* Renine's Town business is Renine's Town business," that was, in Rhodaani.

The local nodded warily, and rushed to tell others. Soon, the Blackboots would be summoned. Errollyn turned and walked down to the docks, figuring he could do little more here, and satisfied that whatever Family Renine thought to gain by killing the captain, they could lose in having killed one of their own.

Soon he found one of the few people in Renine's Town he could trust to give him a straight answer.

"Captain Aimer was a renowned drunk and gambler," a red-coat drily informed him, sipping tea outside his customs house. "Frankly I'm not surprised he's dead. In a brothel, did you say?"

Errollyn nodded.

The red-coat shrugged. "I've heard he was in debt, then out of debt, then in debt again. Possibly someone got tired of constantly bailing him out. Then again, he also had a very big mouth, which is never a good thing."

Errollyn recalled his conversation with the quartermaster at the inn, and the sailor who had risen from the table to go and talk to a "friend." Had that been the same man as had been hiding under the bed? He hadn't got a close enough look. Either way, he thought it reasonably clear what was going on.

"Thank you, sir," he told the red-coat. "I have to head back to the Mahl'rhen."

"What do *you* think is going on?" the red-coat asked him.

"Noble games, my friend," said Errollyn.

"Those are the least entertaining kind," the red-coat said, and sipped his tea.

When Errollyn returned to the Tol'rhen, he found Civid Sein rallies being held upon the square. Leading them were Tol'rhen Ulenshaals, black robed and shouting, to massed cries from the thousands-strong crowd. If the philosophies of his people spoke of anything, it was the supremacy of one person's rightness to think alone. Here on the square, before the walls of the institution dedicated to the teaching of serrin thought, thousands of individual minds concentrated as one, and yelled in unison. They yelled for justice, yet it was emotion that spoke, not reason.

He left the square before some well-meaning fool spotted him and tried to make him a part of their dangerous game. Tracato was supposed to be above such human nonsense, yet here he could feel it slipping toward a precipice. His own people were supposed to embody the final word in enlightened thought yet, too often, in their own gentle way, behaved just like the mobs outside.

He found Sasha in the training courtyard, blade in hand and covered in sweat. Spirits, she was beautiful. He watched her for a moment, the shapes her body and blade made in the air. To watch Sasha train was to observe the primal and the civilised, the thinking and the unthought, the beautiful and the ugly, all in one.

She was so human, and in her humanity, described a world he recognised far more intimately than his own people had ever managed.

He saw something else, too.

"Sasha!" he called at a pause in her strokes. She turned to him, and her eyes lit up. Even now, his heart leapt. "Something's bothering you?"

"How can you tell?" she asked. She was sensitive about her moods.

"You always train when you're angry."

"You've seen the mob outside?" Errollyn nodded. "Kessligh's trying to talk to them. I told him he should just tell them to fuck off, but he refuses."

Errollyn sighed, flexing his sore leg. "Kessligh has great hopes for this civilisation, Sasha. He's been in the wilds in Lenayin for a long time."

"What's wrong with the wilds of Lenayin?" Sasha said indignantly.

"I'm not certain he's sure what he's achieved. He comes to a place like this, and he wonders if he could have done more." Sasha stared at the pavings. Errollyn put his hands on her shoulders. "I've offended you."

"No. No, you're right. But damn it, he should be able to see where this is going! These people are lunatics, haven't we all had enough of lunatics after Petrodor?"

Errollyn searched her face. "That's not all that's bothering you."

Sasha's eyes didn't quite meet his own. That was *very* unusual. "I'd rather not say."

Errollyn frowned. He thought about it. Sasha was prickly over her Lenay honour, but could typically deal with such things, sometimes in ways he truly wished she hadn't. She was embarrassed by little—in that, they were alike. But here, she almost seemed . . .

He raised his eyebrows. "Some man asked to fuck you?" Sasha aimed a kick at him, and missed on purpose, scowling. Worse than that, then. "Some man *tried* to fuck you." She looked elsewhere, exasperated. Damn. "Does he live?"

"Yes!" Sasha retorted, angrily.

"Do you still have one of his ears?"

"Errollyn, this isn't funny!" Errollyn couldn't help smiling, against his better judgement. The look she gave him nearly made him fear for his safety. "It was Reynold Hein!"

"Oh," said Errollyn, not especially surprised.

"What do you mean 'Oh'?" Sasha fumed. "That's the *one* form of attack I can't raise a blade against! And if I can't raise a blade, I'm left with fists, and I can't beat up a man his size! Or *your* size!" She knocked his hands from her shoulders. Errollyn folded his arms.

"Sasha," he said calmly, "you know as well as I do that if he'd tried to rape you, you'd have stuck a knife in his throat."

"It's not honourable!" Sasha snapped. "He never raised a blade against me!"

Oh, thought Errollyn, realising. That was it. "Well, you can hardly just let him overpower you and take you, can you?"

"Rather than stick a blade in a man not wielding one?" Sasha retorted. "I can't cut a bare-handed man!"

Errollyn rolled his eyes. "It's hard living to a code of honour, yes?

"You wouldn't know, you could have beaten him up."

"I'm quite sure Reynold Hein would not have been trying to rape *me*."

"Good spirits," Sasha muttered, striding back toward the Tol'rhen. "Men!"

Errollyn grabbed her arm. "Don't use that on me. Of all the men in your life, exactly how many times has this happened?" Sasha stared at him. Then her gaze fell.

"I'm sorry," she said. Suddenly the anger was gone and she was sombre. Vulnerable, even. "I was scared for a moment, I couldn't think. That almost never happens. I . . . I couldn't think of how I'd explain it to you, or . . ."

Errollyn shook his head in exasperation. "Sasha, if you know anything about serrin, you know that we don't place *any* credence in this human notion of female sexual virtue. If he had succeeded, it would make absolutely no—"

"I know, I know." Sasha held up her hands. "It would make a difference to me, though."

Errollyn put a hand to her face. "And to him. I'd have killed him. And still may."

"Don't," Sasha said sombrely. "We can't afford it. Kessligh can't, Reynold's too important."

Errollyn smiled. "When did you get so mature? Not long ago you'd have been demanding the right to split him from nose to groin and devils take the consequences."

"I know," Sasha agreed, a smile ghosting upon her lips. "I can barely believe it myself. Now kiss me, because I've had that shit's smell in my mouth all day, and I'd rather yours."

Errollyn did as she asked. It occurred to him as he did so, that she rarely asked for anything more than this, and his company. It only made him want to give her more.

They walked back to the Tol'rhen, holding hands.

"You didn't seem very surprised when I said it was Reynold."

"Powerful men, Sasha. I've seen human men relish the thrill."

"But a man like Reynold could have any number of women."

"And that's the point. He only demonstrates his power to himself by conquering the most unlikely. The grander the dragon slain, the greater his glory."

"Lovely choice of metaphor," Sasha said, bumping him as they walked. "How did you hurt your leg?"

"Small encounter in a brothel." Sasha looked at him, eyebrows raised. Errollyn grinned. "Let me tell you about it."

"Really, Errollyn. I know I'm not as experienced as some women, but a brothel?"

He cuffed her lightly on the head. Sasha returned one of her own, and they scuffled and laughed toward the rising wall of the Tol'rhen.

Errollyn found Reynold at the Great Hall during the evening music recital. Five Tol'rhen students, two Ulenshaals and a pair of serrin were playing pipes, strings and drum in strange combination. Perhaps two hundred people gathered about the hall to hear, across dining tables soon to be filled for dinner.

Reynold sat to one side near the kitchens, munching from a bowl of nuts. His usual friends were seated about the table, discussing politics in low voices. Reynold seemed more interested in the music, casting the others only an occasional glance. He saw Errollyn coming and smiled.

"Errollyn!" he whispered, with no apparent trepidation. That did not surprise Errollyn either. "What do you think of this composition? Isn't it wonderful?"

"I like the larger strings," Errollyn said. "These smaller ones sound like a cat being strangled." Reynold's nose, he saw, seemed swollen, with a trace of dried blood at one nostril.

"Ah yes, but the fusion of rhythm and melody. Like the fusion of human and serrin thoughts in one."

"Are we melody, or are you?"

"I haven't decided yet," said Reynold, watching the musicians. "A question for my morning lecture, perhaps?" It was so like the man, Errollyn thought. So determined to demonstrate to all his intellectual fascination in all points of culture.

"Reynold, I need to speak with you," said Errollyn. He indicated to the kitchens. Reynold nodded, entirely unworried, and went with him. That was expected, too.

Behind the heavy door grand fires blazed, and cooks laboured over benches piled with food. Reynold turned to Errollyn expectantly. Errollyn punched him in the stomach, very hard.

Reynold doubled over, and fell to all fours. Above the shouts and commotion of dinner, cooks turned in astonishment to look.

"The only reason you're still alive," Errollyn said calmly, "is that Sasha's honour precludes her from killing you. She has the honour of a warrior—not of a woman, or you'd be dead. I'm trying to talk her into a new interpretation. If you try it again, you may discover if I've succeeded."

"What did she tell you?" Reynold's voice sounded odd, beyond the shortness of breath. He was laughing, Errollyn realised. "Not the truth, obviously. I have to say, I was surprised. I'd thought a virile man such as yourself could satisfy even her, but no, she threw herself at me like she hadn't been fucked in weeks. She was quite upset when I said no. I don't envy you her temper my friend."

"I dislike fighting Sasha's fights for her," Errollyn continued, unbothered, "but she can be stubborn in her Lenay honour. If she won't do it, I will. Stay away from her. Or better yet, next time, come at her with a weapon in hand, I dare you."

"Friend Errollyn," Reynold sighed, getting one foot carefully beneath him, and making to stand. "I can see why your people have disowned you. Truly, you leap to unfounded conclusions, and you come to violence as your first resort. How you must alarm the gentle serrinim."

"I'm a scholar, Reynold," said Errollyn. "Like you. I learn my subjects well. I learn how they respond, and what motivates them best. It is my scholarly judgement that if you touch Sasha again, one of us will gut you like a fish."

He kicked Reynold in the stomach, and the man went down again. Errollyn left him lying there, as cooks rushed to assist. Disconcertingly, despite the obvious pain, Reynold only seemed more amused.

Six

ON THE HILL ABOVE THE SHALLOW VALLEY, Rhillian sat ahorse and watched the prelude to battle. From here, behind the Rhodaani Steel's right flank, she could see nearly everything. A small river ran across the fields below, and in front of her, on the far side of the river, she saw a small castle on a hill. No more than a minor holding—it was held, she'd heard, by a lord named Herol, a bannerman to the northern Lord Arendt. Here, upon the long slope before the castle walls, the Army of Elisse, beneath Lord Arendt commanding, had chosen to make its stand.

The Elissian Army was enormous. Scouting *talmaad* with a better eye for such things estimated their numbers at between twenty-two and twenty-five thousand. They bristled across the hillside. Banners flew, denoting each minor formation's allegiances in the many colours of feudal heraldry.

Rhillian could see why Arendt had chosen this place to stop running. For one thing, it was barely north of the coastal city of Vethenel, and squarely on a major route of supply. If the Steel took these roads and lands, Vethenel would be blockaded and, more importantly, would no longer be able to resupply the army. Also, most of the lords remaining were of the northern peninsula, and to not make a stand here would be to abandon many castles to incineration. But, mostly, what made this a good place to fight was the terrain.

The Elissian Army occupied a slope, up which the Steel must advance, in heavy armour. The castle made a good vantage, from which the battle could be directed. And at the base of the slope ran the river, which the Steel would need to ford, directly into the teeth of Elissian archers and charging knights. The Rhodaani Steel numbered nine thousand, as the third battalion under Captain Pieron had been the first to encounter the Elissian position here, and send word to the first battalion under General Zulmaher. The fifth battalion under Captain Malisse had not yet arrived, but was known to be two days' march to the east. Rhillian headed barely more than six hundred of her three thousand *talmaad* in Elisse—the rest were scattered across the lands behind, guarding supply lines, making certain newly sworn lords kept their oaths, gathering supplies and putting down minor revolts.

Surely Lord Arendt was feeling as confident as was possible of any commander, facing an army of the Steel. He had the favour of numbers, by three to one. He had the favour of the land, particularly the river. General Zulmaher was attempting a quick victory, and could not waste days or weeks attempting to outflank the retreating Elissians in manoeuvre after manoeuvre, seeking a more suitable place for battle. Arendt could retreat all the way up the peninsula if he chose, never fighting a decisive battle, and cost the Rhodaani Steel another month at the least. If Zulmaher wished to defeat the Elissian resistance on the field, he had no choice but to do it here.

Trumpets rang across the valley, shouts followed, in unison, and the Rhodaani Steel began its advance. Rhillian could hear the armoured clatter, even from this distance. Six thousand infantry, arranged in three formations of two thousand each. Each two thousand comprised of twenty squares of a hundred, in two lines of ten, one thousand men per line. The formations were precise in their geometry. Rhillian wondered how many of those serrin scholars who insisted that nothing of war could ever be beautiful, had ever seen the Rhodaani Steel in battle.

"Here we are," said Arendelle, pointing across the river. "The cavalry musters." The Elissians had been holding back their cavalry, presumably to keep Zulmaher guessing, but there had been little doubt as to Arendt's intentions. The best Elissian cavalry was heavy, and Rhillian's guess was that a quarter of these cavalry were knights. Downslope, headlong into the centre of the Rhodaani formation, they could break even a line of the Steel. Flanking would serve no purpose, for the *talmaad* worked on the flanks, on faster horses mounted with serrin archers, who did unfair, unchivalrous things like shooting unarmoured horses from under the knights' steel backsides.

Now, as Rhillian watched, cavalry were pouring down the hillside between formations of footsoldiers. Before the front ranks, they were forming.

"Signalman," Rhillian called, "if you please. Call to our *talmaad* to prepare."

The trumpeter was a tall, skinny Rhodaani boy, lent to her for the occasion by General Zulmaher. The boy raised his long horn, and blew a clear, high melody.

"That's very pretty," Aisha remarked, steadying her anxious mount with one hand, her bow in the other.

"Thank you, M'Lady," said the nervous young man. He seemed far more nervous of serrin women than men, Rhillian thought. Well, perhaps she should have forbade Eli and Sairen from trying to get him drunk and bedded last night. To the best of her knowledge, the lad had not succumbed. Which was still a pity, she thought now, watching the army advance toward the river. It would not do for any man or woman to die a virgin, and this lad certainly looked it.

From the rear of the Rhodaani formation, Rhillian could see her *talmaad* now galloping in two groups, three hundred to each flank. Arendt would see that, and have his conviction to go through the centre reinforced. Rhillian wondered if he would also note the artillery line moving up behind the infantry, and grasp its significance. Most feudal commanders rarely did. The great crossbow arms of two-stack ballistas bounced as the carts upon which they rode trundled forward, pulled by horse or oxen.

Of the nine thousand assembled men, fully a thousand were artillerymen. Each of the infantry formations was backed by fifteen cart-mounted ballista, and five catapults—for forty-five ballista and fifteen catapults in all. Usually, in forces equipped with such weapons, the artillery remained behind with the command and reserve. Here, the artillery advanced, while the thousand-strong reserve, of eight hundred foot and two hundred cavalry, remained behind. It was a great risk if the battle turned against the Steel. But General Zulmaher did not expect to lose.

The right-flank formation reached the river a little before the centre and left, and waded in past the broken screen of trees. Serrin riders had already tested its depth, braving occasional arrowfire to gallop through the waters, returning to assure all that at its deepest, it would be barely above a soldier's waist. Before the front rank of Elissian infantry, the cavalry line appeared to be nearing completion.

"How many cavalry, do you think?" Rhillian asked Arendelle. There were ten of them here, atop the shallow hill, all serrin save for the signalman. Enough to guard against sneaking scouts and outriders who sought to flank them, and ambush in the rear.

"I think about four thousand," said Arendelle, staring hard across the battlefield. "One thousand knights."

Another trumpet call from the artillery line, which ceased its advance. Rhillian saw rounds being moved to the catapults from amongst piles of wet blankets. Small fires were lit, men swarming to prepare their enormous contraptions.

"They're in range," said Tessi with certainty, measuring the distance with her eyes. "How unbelievably stupid of them."

"Let's go," said Rhillian, and galloped down the slope, her *talmaad* in pursuit. She was nearly at eye level with the artillery when the first catapults fired. With a great, unwinding rush, they hurled flaming balls into the sky. For a moment, the air filled with streaking, burning projectiles. Already the catapult men were rearming, winding furiously at the handles that wound metal-toothed gears, pulling back the giant arms thrice as fast as conventional rope winches.

Ahead, flames erupted across the Elissian cavalry line with a horrid orange and blue glare. . . . Rhillian winced as she rode, to shield her sensitive eyes. Then the noise reached her above the thunder of horses' hooves—the *whump!* of successive bursts of flame, and the screams and cries of a thousand men and horses, who had not realised themselves within range of the Steel's most feared weapon. Conventional artillery was hard to aim. How the Steel artillerymen could achieve such accuracy on wheels was beyond even her.

Now the ballista were firing, forty-five at once and each one a double-stack, the cartsmen not even bothering to halt their advance. Ninety bolts shot skyward, and mechanisms were immediately winched back, even faster than the catapults.

Rhillian arrived at the head of her three hundred right flank cavalry, just short of the riverbank, and stopped. From here, through breaks in the trees, she could see the confusion of the Elissian forward line—horses milling and rearing, senior men waving swords and flags, trying to rearrange the formation. Smoke hung in the air in great palls, and sections of grass still burned.

The Rhodaani infantry line had now stopped, midstream. They simply stood in waist deep water, and watched. More horses fell, randomly, to streaking ballista bolts. Cavalrymen held shields above their heads, and hoped, waiting for their seniors to sort out the confusion and give the order to charge. Surely they still had some time left before the next fiery volley, as catapults took time to reload.

A new series of thuds and whistles overhead put the lie to that. Cavalrymen saw it coming, and screamed in panic. Whole sections of formation broke, hundreds of horses scattering. Some rode straight into an eruption of flame, and were engulfed. Rhillian closed her eyes to save her vision. When she opened them again, she saw scenes of utter horror, men and horses engulfed twenty and thirty at a time, rolling and running, screaming and falling. Ballista fire whistled continuously, felling animals and riders with steady, random rhythm.

Finally the trumpets blew, others taking up the cry. Broken sections of cavalry came galloping downslope, and others joined them, as much in hope of escaping the murderous artillery as attacking the midstream Rhodaanis. More trumpets blew, this time from behind, and with a thunder of their own, a thousand Rhodaani cavalry charged for the river, and the gaps between their infantry's formations.

Rhillian held her horse in check, watching the mass of mounted Rhodaanis plunging through the frothing waters. They were not so heavily armoured as Elissian knights, wearing segmented armour like the infantry, yet their shields and lances, and huge warhorses, made them imposing enough. They cleared the far bank, and aimed for the gaping holes the artillery had torn through the Elissian cavalry's ranks. The Elissian charge split, some falling back in swirling confusion upon the Rhodaani cavalry, others charging on toward the river.

Rhillian tore her sword clear, raised it, then swiped at the air. She needed no trumpeter, and the serrin gave no yell as they charged, crashing into the waters in a churn of white spray. Ahead, beyond the confusion of cavalry, new bursts of fire were blooming further upslope. The artillery had turned their attention upon the Elissian footsoldiers . . . and Verenthane gods help them.

Her *talmaad* rounded the Rhodaani right flank, and emerged from the waters to find what heavy cavalry had made it this far, plunging into the river to attack the Steel infantry. The water slowed their horses in leaping, splashing bounds, and took the weight off their charge. The Steel held firm, behind solid walls of shields, and returned with sword thrusts and thrown spears from within the protective formation squares.

Serrin riders fanned out, bows ready, firing wherever targets presented. Always they fired at horses, never at armoured riders, and animals toppled. Perhaps fifty mixed knights and cavalry charged them instead of the infantry, huge armoured suits atop equally huge horses, angling wicked steel lances as they came. Rhillian might have attacked, courageously, but instead wheeled, and galloped before them. More serrin did the same, wheeling for the flanks, firing as they went. Pursuing horses fell, and knights crashed tumbling on the ground. A cavalryman to Rhillian's left, in chain and helm, took an arrow in the neck as he charged at her flank. Serrin ran on, twisting in their saddles to shoot with accuracy known only to the *talmaad*.

Smart Elissians turned around and galloped away as fast as they could. Ten frustrated cavalrymen rode about in circles, yelling and swiping at any serrin who came close enough, demanding hand-to-hand combat. Serrin archers stayed calmly out of range, shooting one horse after another, and taking a rider in the neck where the opportunity presented. Rhillian rode down one fallen, horseless man with her sword, and took a mounted man from behind with a blade through the neck. When all had fallen, or galloped away, the serrin moved on.

Rhillian paused her mount on some open grass, and stood in the stirrups to take stock. Elissian cavalry were retreating in scattered bunches, pursued by Rhodaani horsemen, or serrin with bows. The Steel infantry were emerging from the river, like a dripping, moving wall. Fallen cavalrymen yielded before them, threw aside weapons, and were trampled over if they did not seek a gap between the advancing squares.

A great roar filled the air, and a rattling thunder. Rhillian turned to see, past the scattered remnants of retreating Elissian cavalry, the infantry were charging downslope. She wheeled, signalled those riders still around her, and rode hard for a gap between the Rhodaani squares. Past the first rank, then the second as they emerged from the river, she turned left and cantered, splashing through the shallows toward the right flank once more. Upon her left, the Steel's front rank were shifting, the squares unfolding into a series of unbroken lines, with no gaps between. Ahead of them, a mass charge was descending, thousands of screaming Elissians with mail, shield and sword.

The second and third Rhodaani ranks threw light spears into that charging mass—some of the attackers fell, others slowed to dodge, others took a spear through the shield, narrow points punching deep, the spear shaft then entangling as they ran. The first wave that crashed onto the Rhodaani shield line was uneven, yet it broke with the fury of a great wave upon a cliff.

The cliff held firm. Soldiers leaned into the force of it, like sailors into a howling gale, the men behind pressing on their armoured backs. Shields tilted aside just enough to admit the Rhodaani's short, stabbing swords through the gaps, and men across the attacking wave collapsed, shrieking and clutching their abdomens.

Rhillian finally galloped clear on the right flank, and found a milling confusion of her own cavalry and some Rhodaanis already there. A lieutenant was forming them up, and her *talmaad* were spotting her own snow-white hair, and galloping across at speed. Rhillian waited for the Rhodaanis to move first, and watched that the infantry on this side were not outflanked. The extreme-right flank formation were unengaged, and instead moved forward, swinging around to press on the Elissian flank. Lieutenants yelled, dressing the line, and men shouted encouragement over the roar of clashing steel. Mostly, they coordinated by reflex, as though moved by a single, steel will.

Flames continued to erupt further upslope, decimating the later ranks. Elissian archer fire was so sporadic, Rhillian was uncertain if they *had* any archers. But Bacosh lords always employed archers. These must have been in the middle ranks, so positioned to be at good range against the advancing infantry, whatever good it would do. Those archers were now squarely in Rhodaani artillery range.

The Steel line advanced. Men yelled and heaved, pushing onto their shields, stabbing then covering, push, stab, cover. Push, stab, cover. Elissian soldiers hammered desperately at that impenetrable wall, and fended the lightning thrusts with their smaller shields, but with so little space to move, their defences were limited. Inevitably, flashing Rhodaani blades found the gaps and they fell, as did the next behind them, as did the next. At a whistle, the front rank of Rhodaani soldiers abruptly faded back between the shields of those behind, who became the new front wall, while the front rank took a rest in the rear. The Steel pressed on, trampling over the bloodied corpses of enemies, the second rank finishing those wounded who resisted from underfoot, pushing that huge sea of foes inexorably back up the slope. Occasionally a Rhodaani man would fall, to be replaced immediately by the man behind.

Ahead, the re-formed Rhodaani cavalry gave a yell and charged once more, this time into the flank of the Elissian infantry . . . of Elissian cavalry there was nothing to be seen. It seemed they had fled, or regrouped in the far, far rear. Several hundred cavalry ploughed into the Elissian flank, hacking and wheeling as men began scattering before them. The scattering gathered pace, and within the blink of an eye, the entire Elissian flank was falling back in terrified confusion.

Rhillian found Arendelle, eyes alive like he wanted to go after them. Rhillian put a hand on his arm. "It's over," she told him. "Let them run. I want Lord Arendt."

Here on the right flank, a wide expanse of hillside, paddocks, farmhouses and small woods were all that stood between the *talmaad* and the hilltop castle. That, and several thousand panicking, milling, retreating cavalry and infantry.

Rhillian galloped to the head of her re-forming cavalry, at least two hundred, with the remainder gathering fast, sprinting from the river, or from entanglements further up the slope. Most had bows, a few like Rhillian only swords, and some alternated, as only serrin cavalry would. Once in position, Rhillian wheeled her mare, waved her sword, and cut the air.

Again the thunder of hooves, and a headlong sprint up the gentle incline. Rhillian could not see her friends around her, and could only trust that they were well, somewhere in the pursuing crowd. She leapt a low wall, skirted a small dam and watercourse, and saw arrows whip past from behind, smacking retreating cavalrymen squarely in the back. Two tumbled, and a third rode on, slumped and dying.

There were running, panicked infantry, serrin riders weaving amongst them like wolves through so many terrified sheep, putting arrows into any who looked likely to swing a weapon. Ballista fire fell near, random streaks thumping the turf with force audible even above the thunder of hooves. To the left, retreating infantry were hit, smashed into the ground like piglets beneath a charging boar spear. Rhillian signalled her riders further to the right, hoping the artillery captains retained their usual vigil, and saw her move up the flank.

More flashes of artillery to the left, level with their position . . . less devastating now, with Elissian formations spread out and running, but horrifying to see so close all the same. Rhillian galloped past burning circles of blackened grass, littered with scores of charred, skeletal corpses in armour. About their perimeters, some men still writhed and screamed, faces half burned away, an arm blackened and peeling, or trying to run on blistering feet. Rhillian tore past running, cowering men, ignoring those who had dropped or sheathed weapons, but now leaning from the saddle to slash one running man who still carried a large polearm. Arrowfire dropped others, murderously accurate, serrin bows having little trouble with chain mail from this close range.

She rounded a blackened oak, its branches burning, smouldering corpses scattered on the upslope, another man pinned to its trunk by a ballista bolt that had gone through shield, mail, flesh and wood. Infantry lines were forming ahead—militia, she saw with disbelief, small folk with poorer weapons and little armour, while the mass of Elissian footsoldiers, comprised of wealthier men and village folk, possessed many. They were standing, while others were running. In the battle of Tirone, in the early days of invasion, southern Lord Horase had thrown the militia in first, to soften up the Steel for heavier assaults to follow. The slaughter had been so horrible, and for so little result, that demoralised infantry and cavalry had been reluctant to attack. Here, Lord Arendt had wisely held the militia in reserve, but had made the folly of committing his main force too close to the Rhodaani artillery. The battle had been over from the moment the first catapult had fired. If not well before.

Serrin cavalry opened fire on the forming lines from range—less use against more well-armoured footsoldiers, but felling numerous militia. Still they held. Rhillian saw men running up and down the line, screaming at their fellows not to run. There were scythes, poles, spears and axes, only the occasional sword. Half had small wooden shields. Rhillian leaped the last small wall, rode over some running infantry who fell flat before her, and picked her spot in the line. Arrowfire felled more, a murderous buzz, serrin now aiming sideways across the line to take shields out of play. Perhaps fifty fell, the lines thinning dramatically as bodies tumbled and hands flailed.

A few archers were firing back, but without serrin longbows or serrin accuracy. . . . Rhillian stayed low as shafts whistled overhead, and the last serrin volleys cut past ahead, whipping left and right across her path. More carnage, Rhillian's intended target falling with a shaft through the face, and her second target, and the third. She plunged through the first rank, and took the head off an axeman in the second rank.

Ahead was the castle, and she galloped on, finding enough clear ground to glance behind. The militia lines were gone, like saplings before a spring flood, and all she could see were serrin on galloping horses. Most had blades in one hand, bows in the other, but were resheathing those blades even now to nock another arrow. The horrid totality of it took her breath away. She couldn't believe a bunch of peasants had stood and died for their feudal oppressors while their better-armed and armoured comrades fled shrieking all around them. Sometimes humans were simply beyond her comprehension.

Ahead to the left, Elissian artillery made a line across the crest of the hill. Another poor strategic choice—catapults were nearly impossible to fire on sloping ground, and despite the hill adding to their range, they were still out of range of the advancing Steel infantry. Far too much depth to the Elissian formation, not enough width, artillery deployed too far back . . . but no choice really, given the hill. It was a disaster, and Rhillian wondered if she'd find Lord Arendt before his own men killed him.

She signalled to her *talmaad* to take care of the artillery, and cavalry behind her swung that way, intent on doing that. Already artillerymen were running, leaving their weapons loaded but unfired, the Steel lines still perhaps a hundred paces from range downhill. These artillery held in their slings only stones, not hellfire, and only the Steel used ballistas. Their construction looked poor, crudely hacked from recently felled trees. Everyone tried to copy the Steel, but no one knew how.

Rhillian galloped toward the castle. Its dark stone walls were more a tribute to noble vanity than any serious attempt at defence. It was small, with a single tower, a moat that was little more than a dry ditch, and a portcullis facing onto some small buildings that one might have called a village, if one were generous. She rode over cultivated lands, weaving past farmhouses and jumping stone walls.

She searched the castle's battlements for archers, but saw none. The portcullis was open, and a group of knights and armoured horsemen clustered about the bridge across the moat, banners flying. Even now, squires were handing lances up to knights, and other armoured men were mounting with assistance. Some now stared, halting to point in her direction. Everyone else turned to look.

Rhillian charged, and now there were other horsemen emerging from the town, and crossbowmen running to form a firing line. But already there were serrin cavalry overtaking her, hooves flying, riders raising themselves a little from their lurching saddles to steady their balance as they hauled back on their bowstrings. Arrows flew, then a grasp at the reins to leap a low wall. Landing, to gallop on open grass, and more arrows were nocked.

A few Elissian horses had been hit with those opening shots from range. A crossbowman fell. Return fire came, a shot fizzed past Rhillian's ear, a serrin horse fell with a horrid crash. Armoured knights were charging, straight into the attack, seven, eight, nine . . . twelve of them, Rhillian counted fast, with another twelve cavalrymen behind.

Arrows peppered the knights' charging horses, bringing down several in crashing rolls of long legs and armoured limbs. Survivors ploughed through the serrin lines, but found no opponents, serrin simply pulling wide of their charge to shoot them as they passed. Several more crossbow bolts streaked past, but then the bowmen were running back into the village, knowing they could not reload before the *talmaad* were on them.

Perhaps twenty serrin were ahead of Rhillian now, and galloped hard after the departing foursome. Weighed down with armoured riders, and lacking the endurance of sleeker, smaller Saalshen horses, those four would not get far. Rhillian waved some riders into the village to clear it, and peered through the open castle portcullis as she rode past. She glimpsed movement.

She reined up fast, diverting into the shallow, dry moat so as not to cause a pile-up with charging riders behind. But many others were also pulling up, sensing that the four escaping riders did not need more than thirty pursuers, however high their rank. More rode about to cover the far side of town, while others turned to head back down the slope and assist in the final effort to clear the battlefield. Another twenty rode across the small bridge to the portcullis, and Rhillian went in their midst.

The first two riders to reach the entrance dismounted, and ran into the gate towers on either side. The others waited, fanning off the bridge into the dry moat, and close to the base of the walls, arrows nocked and pointing up at the battlements. It was the simplest trick, to lure enemy riders into open castle yards just bristling with bowmen, and stick them full of arrows. Rhillian waited on the bridge, watching fleeing infantry and militia scattering past, and galloping horsemen, some escaping Elissians, others Rhodaani or serrin.

A cry came down from one tower, then the other. Serrin riders urged their mounts into the castle courtyard, watching warily at the surrounding walls, hooves clattering on the pavings. There was bundled straw, scattered manure and abandoned carts, some empty buckets about a well, a mule tied by the forge beneath the wall . . . but no people. The guardhouse was shut, as were mainhold doors, and the wide stable doors also. But the doors were barred shut on the outside.

Two more serrin dismounted and heaved the heavy bar off the door, dragged it aside, then pulled them open. Rusty hinges squealed, and twenty serrin pulled back their bowstrings, aiming to the dark interior. Rhillian put a hand to her brow and squinted . . . one thing serrin eyes did not do well was contrast, light against dark. Within, shapes became clear. Men on horses, in heavy plate armour. Knights. She could not see their faces, but their manner showed dismay.

"Lord Arendt, I presume?" Rhillian called. "Your decoy might have worked, if there were fewer of us." But your lines collapsed rather faster than even we anticipated, she might have added.

An armoured figure on horseback clopped forward several strides. This horse wore metal barding, covering sides, chest and flanks. Rhillian blinked. That would have been interesting, if all the other horses had been so armoured. Arrows would be as little use against that as all the rest of a knight's armour, even serrin bows firing arrows tipped with serrin steel were as useful for piercing armourplate as hurled acorns. But it would have slowed the horses, and exhausted them fast. On open ground, against heavier cavalry, serrin could just evade until the opposing horses collapsed of exhaustion, and archers could shoot for the legs. Which was, of course, why serrin hated to fight in fixed formation. It suited none of their fighting styles, on horse or on foot. And against any fixed, weakly armoured formation, this man before her was death on four legs.

"I am Lord Arendt," said the man in fluent Larosan, his voice muffled behind the armoured visor. He did not raise it. No doubt he'd heard stories, of serrin archers and marksmanship. A pity Errollyn was not here, Rhillian thought sourly. From this range, that visor slit was probably not beyond him. "You have the appearance of the one they call Rhillian."

It was the hair, Rhillian knew. It gave her away every time. "I might be," she conceded.

"I wish to grant terms," said Arendt.

"You've been defeated," Rhillian replied, faintly incredulous. "Those of your army not slaughtered are running like frightened deer. Why would I need your terms?"

"Not you," Arendt replied. His big horse looked so weighed down, the poor thing barely twitched. "I will give terms to General Zulmaher." Rhillian had thought as much. "I am the Regent of the North. Not all the northern lords have committed full forces, yet I can grant terms on their behalf. Otherwise, it could take you months to finish them all."

"Weeks," Rhillian said. "Less, if their castles are all as pitiful as this."

"This castle is Lord Herol's," Arendt replied. "He's little more than a hedge knight, it was chosen merely for its strategic location. The greatest castles of Elisse are to the north, thrice in size than any you have so far conquered, and commanded by lords far more stubborn."

Rhillian sighed, and sheathed her sword over her shoulder. "Come forth then," she said tiredly, "and we shall parley." That was what the man wanted, after all. To parley, and waste time, until General Zulmaher arrived.

Lord Arendt might have nodded, but the armour hid the gesture. He touched great, roundel spurs to his beast's sides, and clomped forward from the stable gloom. Rhillian rode to meet him halfway. Within the stable, perhaps ten mounted knights watched, swords clasped in gauntleted hands. Arendt and Rhillian paused with their horses nose to nose. Rhillian's mare sniffed at the warhorse, warily, but the warhorse barely responded. Rhillian gave the northern lord her best gleaming smile. It frightened some human men, that smile, even as it stirred their lust. Most found the effect disconcerting.

It seemed to have some effect on Lord Arendt, for he flipped up his visor to regard her face to face. Rhillian's right hand went to her belt, produced a knife, and threw. It struck Lord Arendt in the eye, and he lurched in the saddle, then toppled to the pavings with an almighty metal crash. His warhorse danced aside, as though with relief. Rhillian had not even seen what Arendt looked like. Within the stable, his knights sat stunned.

"Finish the rest!" Rhillian announced. Arrows flew, and horses shrieked, flailing and wheeling. These wore no barding. The necessity always saddened Rhillian, but with the riders so invulnerable, there was no other choice. It would take a while to finish the knights, once dismounted, but they were painfully slow against unarmoured *talmaad*, and soon enough the serrin blades would find armour joints, draw blood, and slow the man enough for someone to knock him down and leave him flailing like a tortoise on its back. From there, it was simple knife work.

Once it was done, Rhillian remounted, rode back to the castle bridge, and waited. Soon enough, the first line of Steel infantry crested the hill—the rear rank, as they had begun the day, saved the initial fighting and left fresh to charge into what remained of the Elissian infantry, to prevent any chance of the enemy line re-forming. The green shields of the men were spattered red, as were their short, razor-tipped swords. They showed little emotion as they formed new positions about the town and castle, too well disciplined, and too accustomed to overwhelming victories for that. Most seemed barely out of breath, having run up that slope in full armour and shields.

The second rank—formerly the front rank—came after, in small groups, escorting a truly enormous number of prisoners. Rhillian guessed about five thousand. More than half the entire Rhodaani force, weapons and armour cast aside, some clad in little more than undergarments. They were mustered into great groups on open fields, guarded by lines of Steel infantry and sections of looming Rhodaani cavalry. A surreal sight, like so much in war—a lovely Elissian hilltop, scattered shady trees, paddocks filled with flowers . . . and five thousand shivering, frightened, defeated men, who should have been home tending their fields, animals and families.

Finally General Zulmaher arrived, with several captains and junior officers, two of whom were bloodstained and explaining recent actions. The retinue halted beside the large elm at the lip of the dry moat, where Rhillian had taken a seat with Gian and Via, to sip water and rest, while their horses grazed. The horses would need water soon, which would mean a trip down the hill, past all the corpses and wounded. Rhillian did not relish the prospect.

Zulmaher dismounted, as Rhillian climbed achingly to her feet. The general smiled, and offered her an embrace. Rhillian accepted—Rhodaani men were like that with each other, so there was no reason to refuse.

"A truly inspired run up the flank," Zulmaher told her with a hard smile, hands on her shoulders. "You secured their artillery before our lines came within range, and split any chance of a regrouping on their left flank. I did say the *talmaad* of Saalshen were the finest light cavalry in all Rhodia, and today you proved it for certain."

Rhillian did not begrudge the man his lack of sweat or blood—in this army, with all its lethal parts, such work was not his function. Zulmaher had done more than his share of sweating and bleeding as a younger man, and needed prove nothing to anyone.

"It was well done," she said simply. "Everything worked. Most battles are chaotic, but in this army, somehow everything works." It was as great a compliment as she could imagine, and Zulmaher seemed to take it as such. He knew how difficult a thing it was that she described.

"And where is Arendt?" he asked her expectantly, with a glance to the castle. "Did you find him?"

"We found him," Rhillian agreed, sadly. "His decoy ran off, expecting us to follow, but there were enough of us to cover all options and then some. I took twenty inside, and found Lord Arendt and ten knights, hoping for a clear escape. They tried to break through, but failed. They were remarkably brave and stubborn. We had no choice but to kill them all."

"All?" Zulmaher was displeased. He looked to the castle once more, and back again. "You're certain it was Arendt? Not some decoy?"

"Yes." Being in command of three thousand of Rhodia's finest light cavalry, currently spread in a great network across Elisse, gave Rhillian first access to the greatest source of news and gossip in all the land. She knew Lord Arendt's identifying marks, and she'd had his corpse checked after the fact. "It was him."

Zulmaher still looked puzzled, his broad forehead creased. He ran a hand through short, helmet-flattened hair. "My information suggested he may have attempted to yield, if defeated on the field. His family in marriage to other northern families had been threatened—apparently he spent many a coin of gratitude in assembling this army, and gaining its command. Had he yielded, he could have used the threat of Rhodaani force to keep his relatives safe."

Rhillian sighed, and shook her head. "He did not attempt to yield. I couldn't tell you why, I'm just a poor serrin in the land of the humans. You baffle me."

Zulmaher took a deep breath, clearly reassessing. He shrugged lightly, and patted Rhillian on the shoulder with a smile. "It isn't your fault. You and your *talmaad* fought valiantly, I'll be certain your names are mentioned in my next report to council."

Rhillian made a light bow, and Zulmaher strode off toward the castle, his retinue in tow. No doubt to check for himself. Rhillian sank back to the grass with a sigh, and took a swig from her waterskin.

"What if he suspects?" Gian asked. "The general is not a stupid man."

Rhillian leaned her head back against the tree. "He may well suspect, but he cannot prove. Most of the captains are with me anyhow."

"The war may take longer now," Via added, cleaning his blade with a cloth. "Arendt may have convinced other lords to yield as well."

"Just the problem," said Rhillian. "The greatest threat to Rhodaan's defence now lies with the feudalists. They will weaken Rhodaan from within, and strengthen their allegiances to powerful vassals in Elisse, who will do their bidding. The aim of this war was to end the threat to Rhodaan's northern flank, not to create a new one. It's worth a few extra days to make sure . . . and besides, after today, the war is fairly well won. So long as these lords remain our enemies and do not become the friends of Rhodaani feudalists."

Via made a face. "This was well done," he said, with a glance toward the battlefield and the clustered prisoners. "*That* was not." With a glance back to the castle.

The dissent did not bother Rhillian. Nor the hint of rebuke. They were serrin, and they shared *vel'ennar.* She understood him perfectly, and he her. So long as it were so, no serrin needed ever to fear another.

"I know," she said tiredly. She gazed out at the shallow valley and the drifting mists of smoke that smudged the far horizon. Below, the carnage was thankfully out of sight. But the memory of it burned as bright as any sun. "The things they make me do, Via," she murmured. "The longer I spend among them, the more I fear what I shall one day become."

Seven

DINNER WAS A PLEASANT ENOUGH AFFAIR, certainly more so than what the vast majority of Lenay soldiery were enjoying, out in the cold and wet. Sofy made occasional conversation with a local lord who spoke only Algrassian and Larosan. Her Larosan, Sofy thought, was no longer terrible. Tonight, it was merely very bad.

The rain on the great tent grew heavier, a muffled rush that forced men to raise their voices. The local lords had provided the food, as it was understood by all that the Army of Lenayin was travelling light, and relied on allies for provisions along the way.

King Torvaal sat at the table's end and made sombre conversation with Lord Elen, who was senior of those present, by some measure Sofy had not ascertained—wealth and lands, most likely. Sofy watched her father, and wished he would give her some kind of sign. Surely it affected him, one way or the other. He was leading his kingdom's army to war. Surely he worried, or wondered at events to come. But, as always, there was nothing . . . merely a stern, impassive gaze from a lean and bearded face.

Koenyg talked loudest, a broad, commanding presence at the king's right hand. It was all warfare, of course—horses and provisions and preferred formations of infantry. He'd learned a new word, "chivalry," and seemed fascinated by it. Sofy knew that several of her handmaidens were similarly intrigued, although for very different reasons.

Damon sat opposite Sofy, and seemed more interested in her questions regarding the food than Koenyg's regarding battles. Further down sat Myklas, with several younger lordlings. Of her three brothers, Sofy reckoned that Myklas was the one most enjoying this ride to war. In Baen-Tar, Myklas had found little interest in almost anything, rarely worked hard, and breezed through lessons on raw talent and intellect. Only tournaments had interested him. But lately, he'd seemed positively alive, gazing about at every new sight, and asking Koenyg questions of strategy, politics and logistics. He had even sought out his two-years-older sister on occasion, to ask her opinion of the towns they rode through, or on the artfulness of a temple spire, or the manner of the local townsfolk toward them. Sofy was pleased that her little brother had finally begun to take an interest in the world. She was only sad that it took a war to do it.

With the last meal finished, there came the stupid Bacosh tradition of excusing the women so that the men could talk on important matters. It was not a Lenay tradition at all, yet Koenyg and father insisted that while the Lenays were guests in the lowlands, they would obey some local customs as well. The entire table rose as Sofy excused herself, many of the Algrasse lords bowing to their future queen. A year ago, Sofy might have found it all very romantic and exciting. Now, it only depressed her.

She fetched Yasmyn from the secondary tables, and headed for the tent flap. Servants scurried, producing Sofy's and Yasmyn's cloaks, one darting into the rain to alert the Royal Guards.

"Was the food good?" Yasmyn asked her princess.

"Yes," said Sofy. Armour rattled as Royal Guards came running in the rain. "I don't wish to go back to the tent."

"We could walk the line once more," Yasmyn said with a sly grin. She enjoyed walking through the soldiers' camps with Sofy. With the princess, men were never less than proper, but a daughter of Isfayen nobility could be expected to flirt a little.

"Perhaps," said Sofy. "Lord Pclury says there's a lovely old temple atop the hill on the other side of the stream. It dates to Saint Telvierre's time; some say it was even constructed by Telvierre himself, sometime after the War of Three Rivers. All of the local nobility are baptised there, and they say it has many holy artefacts."

"I'm not very interested in temples," said Yasmyn.

"You could stay here."

There was little chance of that, though.

Sofy and Yasmyn walked with their guard toward the stream beside the camp. There was light enough to see by, as many campfires burned beyond the tents, soldiers having foraged plenty of wood in anticipation of a cold, wet night. They made great blazes now, too hot for rain alone to extinguish. The air was thick with smoke and conversation, and even some laughter and song.

At the camp's perimeter, several of the guards lit oil lamps, and walked to the fore. The stream sides were walled here, and a small stone bridge made an arc directly opposite. Crossing the stream, Sofy looked back down the road they had come. The army did not waste time contracting into fortified camps every night, soldiers merely camped and slept where they stopped. They were in friendly lands now, and no doubt the locals felt themselves in far greater danger from the army than vice versa.

"Your Highness!" came a call from behind. A cloaked man was running through rain toward them.

"Oh no," Yasmyn sighed. "I thought we'd lost him."

Sofy smiled. "Master Willem," she said pleasantly as the tall man came to a panting halt and bowed. "I swear you must have the eyes of a hawk and the nose of a hunting dog. I had thought to leave your writings undisturbed."

"Oh, but Your Highness, you must not trouble yourself for me! I am at your service for the duration of this journey! Where are you off to this evening?"

Master Willem was a scholar from a noble family of Algrassian scholars. The column had acquired him in the Algrasse capital of Tathilde seven days ago, when his services had been offered by his father, a noted scholar of Bacosh history. Since then he'd spent much time observing the Lenay Army, asking questions and writing in his carriage or tent.

"I had thought to take a brief walk to the Heronen Temple," said Sofy. "I'm assured it's not a long climb."

"But . . . but, Your Highness," Willem protested, "is it wise for the future Princess of the Bacosh to stray from camp with a mere eight guards?"

Captain Tyrel might have frowned at that. "I had not thought the lands of Algrasse so lawless," Sofy said innocently.

"Lawless? No, no, Your Highness . . . not lawless. But such an importance as yourself should surely not . . ."

"I'm tired of being an importance," Sofy declared, and resumed her walk. Her guards followed, and Yasmyn gave Willem a smug look as she whirled to Sofy's side. "If I'm to become princess of this land, I feel I should come to know its places and people, do you not think, Master Willem?"

"Oh, a fine, worthy sentiment, Your Highness." The tall man hurried to keep up. His earnest face was youngish—perhaps thirty-five, Sofy thought. Yet his jaw seemed to recede into his shapeless neck, and his posture was slightly hunched, in a way that was not fitting for a man his age. "Wobbly men," Yasmyn had declared most Algrassian men, disdainfully.

Sofy walked briskly up the muddy trail toward where a path began to climb the opposing hill. Clear of the smoke and fires of the camp, the hill was more visible now, a dark and looming forest with a light burning on top. That, Sofy supposed, would be the Heronen Temple.

The guards' lanterns lit gnarled, wet tree trunks and spreading canopy from below, to ghostly effect as shadows crawled and twisted through the wood. An owl hooted, and Yasmyn made the spirit sign to her forehead.

"Don't be silly," Sofy told her. "I think it's a perfectly nice little forest, there's nothing haunting here."

"Eastern Verenthanes are crazy," Yasmyn retorted. "Everywhere is haunted. You just can't feel it."

"There he is M'Lady," said the guard directly ahead, holding up his lantern and pointing downslope to the left. Two bright eyes caught the lamplight, glowing like yellow coals.

"*Narl yl amystrash*," Yasmyn called to the owl, in her native Telochi, making the spirit sign once more. The owl fluttered away on silent wings. Yasmyn grinned. "He heard me."

"What did you say to him?" Sofy asked.

"The owl spirit, he foretells the future," Yasmyn said. "In Isfayen, we say that the owl comes in the night to make a woman with child."

"In Valhanan, they say that of the town baker," Sofy replied. Guardsmen laughed. Sofy was very pleased. It wasn't often she'd think of a bawdy joke to make Lenay warriors laugh.

"I tell the owl *and* the baker to go away," said Yasmyn, also laughing. "I want no child tonight."

"Excuse me, if you please . . ." Willem interrupted in Torovan—they'd been speaking Lenay, of course, forgetting that one in their midst spoke none. "This is the spirit sign, yes?" He imitated Yasmyn's sign, poorly.

"It is," said Sofy, resuming the climb.

"Bad for Bacosh man make spirit sign," Yasmyn added brokenly in Torovan. "Lenay man make spirit sign, good. Bacosh man make spirit sign, cock drop off." Sofy giggled.

"Please forgive me," Willem continued, "but I was under the impression that there were no Goeren-yai nobility in Lenayin."

"Well yes," said Sofy. "But Yasmyn is from Isfayen, in the western mountains. The faith is practised differently there. Even Isfayen Verenthanes still believe in spirits."

"But . . . these are not the true gods," said Willem, uncertainly. "How is it possible that one can believe in both?"

"Gods is gods," Yasmyn said shortly. "Spirits is spirits. Different thing, yes? No problem."

"The scripture says that it is blasphemy to worship any other gods besides the true gods," Willem said firmly.

"They don't worship spirits in temple," Sofy said impatiently, trotting briskly up a flight of wet stone steps. "They're just folk tales, really."

"More," Yasmyn disagreed. "Spirits are the world. Gods are the reason."

"But . . ." Willem looked completely baffled now. "Surely the Archbishop of Lenayin does not consider such beliefs to be truly Verenthane?"

"It would take a very brave man, Master Willem," Sofy said with no little sarcasm, "to tell the Verenthanes of Isfayen that their beliefs are not true."

"But . . ." Willem protested once more.

From the front, Captain Tyrel finally lost his patience. "What's the Archbishop going to do, man?" he said sharply. "Excommunicate the western provinces? Demand they convert properly? Some Baen-Tar priests tried once, their body parts were sent back packed in little baskets. Half of the army you've invited into your precious Bacosh doesn't follow your gods *at all*. Best you get used to it."

Willem coughed, and thought better of reply. Bacosh nobility were not accustomed to rebukes from their lessers. In Lenayin, he was perhaps learning, a man might rebuke whomever he chose . . . if he had confidence enough in his swordplay to survive the honour duel that followed.

It was a fair climb to the hill's crown, but not greatly taxing—her days filled with riding and walking, Sofy had not been so fit in her life, and was rather enjoying the sensation. Another of those things Sasha had once assured her of, that she'd only now begun to appreciate.

The path made a switchback up the hillside, and then emerged on a small, wet courtyard that looked out over the little river beside which the Army of Lenayin had camped. Sofy could see a line of campfires, smothered in smoke and drifting rain, like a long line of flickering stars. Above was an old stone temple, with a bronze bell prominent between twin spires. Behind, a village of low, stone houses loomed dark in the rain, lit only by the glow from several windows. The temple might have been attractive were it not for the four long, iron cages suspended to one side of the courtyard from the branch of a huge, squat oak. Sofy had not seen such contraptions before, but she'd heard them described. Captain Tyrel, too, was darkly intrigued, and walked forward, raising his lantern. Each suspended cage was human shaped, and as the lantern light caught them, it became clear that each also contained a person.

"Dear gods," Sofy murmured in horror.

"Devil's fruit, they are called," explained Willem, quite unperturbed. "Do men not use them in Lenayin? They are quite common in Algrasse, for punishing blasphemers and the like. Not so much in Larosa though, the Larosans are quite inventive."

Two of the captives in the devil's fruit were female, a woman and a girl, dresses torn and filthy. One was an old man with a thick beard. The fourth was a child of perhaps ten, half naked and long haired—whether male or female, it was impossible to tell. They slumped against their confining bars yet could not lie down, knees buckled against the front, heads back, as though desperate for rest. Perhaps they drank the rain. Cutting through the pleasant smell of damp forest, earth and woodsmoke, Sofy smelled human filth.

"How long have they been up there, do you think?" she asked.

"Oh, over a rainy period like this one, it can take more than a week to die," said Willem, offhandedly. "Sometimes two. But come, Your Highness, since we are here, I shall explain to you the significance of this temple."

"This is no way to kill a man," Yasmyn said in Lenay. "There is honour in spilling blood. I see no blood here."

"What did she say?" Willem asked, with mild curiosity.

"She wonders why lowlanders call *us* barbarians," Sofy said coldly, striding to Captain Tyrel's side.

"Highness," said Tyrel, "these two are dead." Pointing to the old man and the woman. Sure enough, Sofy saw their limbs and fingers were stiff. "The girl still lives. I cannot say about the child."

What possible reason could anyone have for doing this to a child, Sofy wondered. Children had sometimes died in Lenay wars but, as Yasmyn said, those were deaths in hot blood, fuelled by ancient regional hatreds and motivated by the urge to destroy a blood enemy's line. Those killings, however horrible, were quick. This was planned and calculating. Whoever had done this wished these four to suffer.

And why in the world was she still standing around wondering what to do about it? Jaryd never would have. Jaryd would have cut them down in a flash.

"Captain, take them down."

"Aye, Highness," said Tyrel, and his men moved quickly. None of the guardsmen seemed interested in disputing the order.

"Your Highness," said Willem, "I'm really not so sure that's wise. . . ." Sofy ignored him, staring up at the girl Tyrel had insisted was alive. She looked lifeless to Sofy, but the captain was surely more practised in telling life from death than she. "Highness, these are clearly people guilty of some evil crime; the local people have every right to enforce their own justice in any way they—"

"They can argue with me once I'm queen," Sofy said coldly. "And just *pray* that I'll be as merciful."

The girl's cage came down with a clang, then the child's. The clamps that held both halves together were released, and guardsmen carefully lowered girl and child to the pavings. Each stank, and were limp, scrawny and filthy. The girl had a rope tied about her neck and between her teeth as a gag. Sofy guessed the townsfolk did not wish to listen to her sobbing while they prayed. She wondered how many days a person could sob for, fearing all the time, while thirsting, hungering and cramping, unable to so much as scratch an itch.

Guardsmen tried to pour each some water from their flasks. The child did not respond. "There is a pulse," Corporal Heyar said, feeling at the child's slim neck, listening close for a breath. "Very faint. Unsteady. This one will die unless we get some food into the child."

The girl gasped. Captain Tyrel patted her face, and sunken eyes fluttered open, beneath a fringe of straggly brown hair. "You're safe, child," said Tyrel, in Torovan. "Have some water." The girl sipped, desperately. And coughed.

"That's not right," a guardsman was muttering. Stoic and disciplined, Sofy hadn't known her guards to voice personal opinions. "Someone should be paying for this, this ain't right."

There were terrible sores on the girl's arms, where her limbs had been stuck, pressing for days against the metal. Weeks maybe, Willem had said. Then the temple bell began to clang. Sofy stared, and saw the pulley rope, leading somewhere inside, jerking it back and forward.

"Your Highness," Willem said with exasperation, "I was afraid something like this would happen. We've been seen, now there will be trouble."

"Get them up," Tyrel ordered his men. "We can't help them here anyhow, they need medicines before they can eat."

Up the town road, doors were opening, and villagers were emerging into the rain. Some were armed. Most came running. Sofy's concern mounted to alarm. Willem seemed almost frantic. "Your Highness, we must go now!"

"We're not running anywhere!" Sofy retorted. Even *she* knew how stupid that would be, tactically. "Captain!"

"Put them down!" Tyrel revised his last order. "We'll see off this mob first, we can't spare the hands. Highness, M'Lady, Master Willem, behind me if you please!"

The guardsmen fanned out fast, weapons drawn and shields unslung from their backs. Yasmyn pulled Sofy between herself and Willem, and from her belt pulled her darak. Heavy, curved and nearly the length of Sofy's forearm, it glinted dully in the dim light. Captain Tyrel had left the lanterns on the pavings beside the girl and child—Sofy scampered to pick one up and rejoin Yasmyn.

There were nearly fifty villagers, Sofy guessed, and even now, more came running. Most were men, perhaps half with weapons. Up the road behind, many women stood in doorways, clutching children as dogs barked and villagers shouted to each other in Algrassian. Still the bell clanged, summoning the town.

The temple doors opened as the crowd gathered, clustering four paces beyond the bare steel of the Royal Guard. A priest emerged, gaunt and balding, in a black robe. He stood on the stairs, eyes wide in alarm and fear. Still the bell clanged. So there were others in there.

The priest began shouting to the mob in Algrassian. Angry and fearful villagers looked at each other, then circled to see where two of the devil's fruit had been lowered and sprung open. Two guardsmen stepped away from the main formation, walking sideways to stay between those villagers and Sofy. Despite her thumping heart, Sofy was surprised to discover she was not terrified. Royal Guardsmen were amongst the most formidable warriors in Lenayin, and even six or seven to one, against common Bacosh villagers, would not trouble them. But more than that, she knew she was in the right. This predicament was neither her fault nor her mistake. Astonishing to realise that that simple fact alone dispelled half the fear.

She spared a glance at Yasmyn, and found her slightly crouched, her loose dress pulled up a little at the knees, darak held low and ready. Her eyes were eager, as though she wished the villagers to attack. Knowing Yasmyn, and the Isfayen in general, Sofy was hardly surprised.

Angry shouts began amongst the villagers as the priest finished speaking. Weapons were waved, dangerously. Sofy found herself more mesmerised by the guardsmen's swords. Huge, gleaming silver and wickedly sharp, it seemed unthinkable that someone might actually use them to strike another person.

"What's he saying?" Sofy demanded furiously to Willem of the priest.

"He . . . he says that you have desecrated a holy site . . . I . . . I can't make out the rest. . . ."

"You're Algrassian!" Sofy retorted incredulously. "Don't you know your own tongue?"

"The accent is very strong!" Willem protested, with moisture on his face that was not from the rain.

"Do something! Tell them who we are!"

"Your Highness, I don't think that will help!"

"Do it! That's an order!"

Willem shouted for attention, arms raised high. The crowd of villagers quieted a little. Willem continued, anxiously in Algrassian. When he finished, there was uproar. Willem looked at Sofy, and she could see "I told you so" in his eyes. An axe was thrown from the crowd, a guardsman leaping to interpose himself, taking the blow on his shield. Sofy was more astonished than frightened. She'd known Lenayin was poorly regarded in the Bacosh, but mostly, she'd thought the attitude one of disdain. This seemed like hatred.

Villagers moved wide, trying to flank the guardsmen's lines, the eight soldiers spreading sideways . . . they could not maintain a defensive perimeter about both her and the two unfortunates lying on the pavings, she realised. If the villagers waited until they were entirely encircled . . . but the thought vanished as several from the mob darted forward to attack. Sofy was nearly relieved.

One swung an axe at a guardsman, who fended with his shield. His fellow guardsman performed a simple overhead, his blade splitting the axeman through shoulder to midchest. Blood erupted in all directions, and the body hit the pavings like a slaughtered carcass. Another attacker lost his arm, fell to his knees screaming, then lost his head. To Sofy's right, a guardsman who was rushed by three at once knocked one off his feet with a shield charge, and hacked the second through the side. The third rushed past, a short sword in hand, but Yasmyn leaped into his path, slid inside his blade with a deflecting arm, and took the full impact of his rushing body. It knocked her back several steps, but then the man was falling, sliding from her arms, his guts spilling on the pavings where Yasmyn's darak had split his middle. Yasmyn danced back, her blade and right hand bloody, and hissed at the corpse with what sounded like pleasure.

The crowd reeled back, screaming and yelling. Four guardsmen pursued, while the other four re-formed the second line, with remarkable discipline. Two more villagers fell, and then the crowd was running in panic, flooding back up the main street or up the steps to the temple door.

"Willem!" Sofy commanded, still holding the lantern. "Carry the girl! Yasmyn, you and I will take the child! Let's go!"

They hurried to do that, as the final four guardsmen fell back, the first four fanning ahead, to discourage any attempt to re-form. No sooner had Sofy and Yasmyn grabbed the child than one of the guardsmen yelled "Crossbow!," and something buzzed the air. It didn't seem to hit anything. Then another yell, and this time there followed a thud on the shield of one of Sofy's protecting wall. That man cursed in pain, but did not waver.

"Move fast!" commanded Tyrel. "There could be more!" The path down the hillside would lead them past the first village houses, where the crossbow fire seemed to be coming from. The forward guardsmen were moving across to meet them and form a wall about their princess. But walking past those houses was just asking for someone to get shot.

Yasmyn saw it too. "I'll get them," she said happily, dumping the limp child entirely into Sofy's arms, and racing forward into the night.

"Yasmyn, no!" But Yasmyn was gone, cloaked and shadowed in the gloom. Sofy staggered forward, lantern in hand as the ten-year-old's limp weight dragged on her arms. Gods, the child was heavy. For the first time in her life, she wished she was as strong as her sister Sasha.

Another crossbow shot thumped and fizzed, but it seemed directed elsewhere. Yasmyn, Sofy thought fearfully, but there was no time to wait, and she staggered as best she could down the sloping path, with Willem coming behind. Guardsmen let her pass as she descended, holding shields above her head as they passed close beneath the house walls, then forming a rearguard behind once they were past. No further shots came.

Above, the bell was still clanging, and random, frightened shouts filled the air. One of the guardsmen slung his shield, then deprived Sofy of her burden. "Best you help Master Willem too," Sofy gasped, letting her aching arms droop as she jogged, for Willem seemed about to drop the half-conscious girl entirely.

A soldier did that, and when they reached the point where the path turned back on itself, they paused. Sofy saw then that one of the guardsmen —a tall Fyden redhead named Daryn—had taken that second-last crossbow bolt not only through his shield, but through the supporting forearm as well.

"Hold still, lad," Corporal Heyar said gruffly, pulling a knife while another man held the shield still. Heyar began sawing through the bolt beneath the metal head. No doubt it pulled the bolt back and forth within the wound something horrible. Daryn made barely a sound.

Sofy tore her eyes away to shine her lantern back up the path. Yasmyn was crazy, and now Yasmyn was going to drive *her* crazy by making her wait and worry, she just knew it. But it was barely a moment before a dark, cloaked shape came flitting down the path toward them. Sofy gasped with relief.

"Are you being followed?" Tyrel asked Yasmyn when she arrived.

"Maybe," she said, "but not by crossbow men." She reached into the pocket of her cloak with a devilish grin. "One crossbow man," she said and pulled from the pocket a severed ear. Then, "Two crossbow men!" pulling a second ear, triumphantly.

Sofy stared in horror. "Oh, Yasmyn. You didn't!"

"What?" said Yasmyn defensively. "My father tell me, never kill a man without proof. Or else, you have nothing to boast about."

Daryn hissed as Corporal Heyar yanked the headless crossbow bolt through shield and arm. "Bloody shields," someone muttered. "Never liked them anyway."

They resumed down the path, four guardsmen ahead, four behind, and Sofy, Yasmyn and Willem in the middle. "Arm!" Yasmyn demanded of Daryn, slashing a piece off his tunic with her darak. Daryn gave her his arm, and Yasmyn tied the cloth about the wound, then pressed it hard with both hands as they walked.

"You going to buy me another tunic?" Daryn asked her.

"Army has plenty of tunics," Yasmyn snorted. "You have only one left arm." He nearly stumbled, weak-kneed with pain, he tried to hide it. "Concentrate!" Yasmyn demanded, hauling him upright. "You stay awake, soldier-man. Maybe I visit you tonight. A bloody man is a sexy man, yes?"

Several men chortled. "Bloody Isfayen," one laughed.

"Say, those aren't left *and* right ears in your pocket, are they?" another suggested.

"No!" Yasmyn snapped, indignantly. "I kill *two* crossbow men. Not one. And the other one, on the courtyard."

"Aye, maybe you went back to him when we weren't there, and took *his* ears off."

"Stupid fucking fool, shut your fucking mouth or I cut your belly like a goat!" Howls of laughter from the men.

Gods save us, Sofy thought despairingly, we *are* barbarians. She turned her lantern to the child, hanging limp in the arms of the guardsman behind her. Barbarians yes, she amended the thought, but at least we don't do *that.*

Soldiers met them halfway up, alarmed to have heard the tolling bell. Tyrel turned them all around, cursing them for making a jam on the narrow path, as those at the rear kept running up while the princess and party were trying to go down.

Many men were gathered curiously about the bridge across the stream, a spread of dark figures against the smoky glow of the camp. Sofy headed for her tent.

She'd nearly made it when Koenyg intercepted her in a fast stride. "What happened?"

"I went up to the temple," Sofy said shortly, still walking. "There were four villagers there, strung up and left to die. This girl and child were still alive, I took them down. The villagers protested."

"And?"

"They attacked us. We killed six."

"Eight," Yasmyn protested. "You forget my crossbow men."

"You're an idiot," Koenyg pronounced.

"Spare me," Sofy shot back, pushing through her tent flaps. Koenyg followed, and Yasmyn, and the two guards carrying the girl and child. Hand-maidens leapt to their feet, tucking aside sewing, books and a game of dice.

"Medicines!" Yasmyn snapped at them. "Lemon water, honey and goats' milk, and heat some water! Poultice and salves, move quickly!" She clapped to hurry them along, as the guardsmen laid girl and child down on a bearskin rug. At least it was warm in the tent, Sofy thought, kneeling alongside the child. A boy, she decided, girlish only because of long hair, and undernour-ishment that highlighted the cheekbones. His shirt was in tatters, and his skin deathly cold to touch. It seemed that he barely breathed.

Lemon water arrived, and Therys, an older woman, took charge. She dipped a cloth into the jug and dripped lemon water onto the girl's lips, as Alyna did likewise with the child. The girl coughed, weakly, and in a tiny voice, asked for more.

Therys gazed at the girl's drawn face, and felt her throat. "I think she will live," she concluded. "I'll see to the child."

Koenyg took Therys's place, kneeling on the rug. "Ulynda," he commanded, and Sofy's grey-haired Larosan tutor limped to her prince's shoulder. "How good's your Algrassian?"

"Fair, Your Highness," said Ulynda.

"Ask her what crime she committed, to receive this sentence."

"What does it matter?" Sofy snapped. "Let her rest, Koenyg."

"Ask her," Koenyg repeated, ignoring his sister. Sofy fumed.

Ulynda knelt with difficulty, placed a hand on the girl's frail shoulder, and spoke in Algrassian. The girl's eyelids fluttered. She took several short breaths, then answered, in a barely audible whisper.

Ulynda frowned. "Witchcraft," she translated.

"Tosh," Sofy snorted. "What nonsense."

"We are guests on Algrassian lands," Koenyg replied. "We should respect their laws and customs."

Sofy glared at him. "You'd string her back up?"

"The Hadryn burn a hundred at the stake every year for blasphemy," Koenyg said impassively. "Women amongst them, and some barely older than the child over there. If the crown tried to stop it, we would have war in Lenayin."

"We do what we can, brother," Sofy said frostily. "What we can rather depends on how hard we try. *You* may not feel compelled to try very hard. *I*, on the other hand, feel resolved to make an effort."

"We are guests in foreign lands on their tolerance, dear sister," said Koenyg, with the first trace of hard temper. "You may have saved two lives, but you took another eight to do it. You may be an excellent student of arts and language, yet I fear your maths is lacking. Worse, our guest lords will surely hear of this very soon. The people will demand justice for those your men killed. What do you think I should say to them?"

"You know, Koenyg, I really don't care." She was suddenly feeling beyond all of this. "You figure it out. Instead of making constant excuses for doing the wrong thing, for once you can think of a good excuse to do something right."

Damon threw aside the flap to the royal tent. The dining tables had been cleared, replaced now by chairs, small tables and braziers to ward the cold. Lord Elen, their host, stood in animated conversation with Koenyg, while King Torvaal looked on. Willem Hoeshel hovered nearby, anxious and pale, offering possible translation. The conversation, of course, was in Torovan.

Lord Elen's two minor lords made way as Damon approached with the army's senior priest Father Syd . . . with a scuttling bow that made Damon's skin crawl. He did not like these people, with their furtive, darting glances and fearful manners. Lord Elen was a big man, as much fat as muscle, balding with long, black hair at the back, and thick whiskers down to where beefy neck met receding jaw. He dressed as lordly lowlands nobility would, house colours over armour and sword, all martial to impress the Lenay warriors.

"This man can swear to it," Elen was insisting, pointing to another. Only then did Damon notice the Algrassian priest, an ageing, scrawny man in a threadbare black robe, leaning on a staff and shivering. "This man, he sees, and he speaks with the authority of the gods!"

"The Royal Guards are honour-sworn to protect the princess under all circumstances," Koenyg replied flatly. "It would not matter if she were attacked by a mob of little girls wielding kitchen knives, they would kill to protect her from so little as a scratch. We'll not hand them over to your justice, it's impossible."

"But, but . . ." Elen spread his hands. "Your Highness, this is a crime! A crime has been committed, eight of my villagers are dead! Surely there must be justice?" He looked past Koenyg, to King Torvaal. Torvaal stood deathly silent, wrapped in his black robe. Dark eyes within an impassive, lean, bearded face. Damon had barely heard him speak five words on the ride so far. He did not expect that to change now.

"The justice you suggest is impossible," said Koenyg, folding his arms. Damon recognised that look, that stance. Had seen it too often through his childhood. It had been his torment then, but now, it heartened him. Koenyg would not give this man a hair from a Lenay guardsman's head. "The soldiers are honour-bound to protect and obey the princess. In truth, the fault is hers. She is young and soft of heart. She acted without understanding the grave insult she would cause to your people. I trust you do not suggest that *she* should be punished?"

Lord Elen seemed to find that amusing, in the manner of a man confronted by an obvious fact, denied by idiots. Yet he could not say so, and so comported himself with forced dignity, fighting back exasperation.

"Of course not, Prince Koenyg. I have nothing but love and admiration for the princess, our future queen. But . . . there must be some reparation. What do you suggest?"

"Lenayin is not a kingdom of paupers, Lord Elen," said Koenyg. "We can pay gold to the villagers for their loss. Name a suitable price."

Willem Hoeshel winced. Lord Elen looked uncomfortable, and coughed. "Prince Koenyg, it would be beneath us to discuss such unseemly matters so openly." Lords did not talk about money in the Bacosh, Damon recalled. To do so was . . . uncivilised. Meanwhile, peasants starved and lords dined on fine fare in opulent castles. But heavens no, gold was not discussed. "Furthermore, I fear that mere gold shall be insufficient. In the Bacosh—as, I am led to believe, in Lenayin—blood is repaid in blood, and . . ."

"Lord Elen," Koenyg said shortly, "what do you suggest? That I find some poor sop for you to behead at random? To appease your desire for revenge? In some few weeks, Lenayin's finest sons shall spill their blood upon your fields to reclaim that which all your armies have been unable to win in two centuries of trying. We have marched a very long way to do so, upon your invitation. That is gift enough, don't you think? Or would you ask more?"

There was no mistaking the dangerous edge to the prince's tone. Lord Elen's faint humour vanished and he inclined his head. "No, my Prince. Forgive me, this is a difficult situation. At least, allow us to reclaim the two criminals that the princess has freed, and restore our justice upon *them*."

"The boy died," said Damon. All present turned to look at him, and Father Syd. "His bones were showing, our healer thinks there was an infection too."

Lord Elen inclined his head once more, as though to acknowledge a good thing. "The other one, then," he requested.

"He was ten," Damon continued. Koenyg was staring at him, warningly. Damon did not care. "The girl is his sister. She is sixteen. Villagers accused their mother of laying with a man who had serrin blood. The mother was one of the two already dead. The older man was her father. I can't see how he is responsible for his daughter's bed partners. I suppose he was merely *available*."

"My good Prince," said Lord Elen, with a condescending, bitter smile, "I do not question your laws or customs. Please do not question that of your hosts."

"Witchcraft," Damon snorted. "The serrin are not witches, Lord Elen. Hate them you may, if you choose, but these charges against innocent villagers are nonsense."

"You show great concern for the welfare of my villagers, Prince Damon," Elen replied, "for one whose men have just murdered eight of them. What we choose to call the serrin is our business. They are unholy and ungodly, of that our priests assure us. They are a blight on this land, filling the minds of the corrupt with filth and decadence. Why, barely three years ago the forces of good made a great purge of all serrin influence and bloodlines in this region. There were fires, devil's fruit, nooses and impaling stakes across the hills and valleys, and it was indeed a beautiful sight."

The man's blue eyes were wide with defiance and anger. Damon stared, feeling cold. He'd heard of the purges. The slaughters. He'd thought some of the lords, at least, might have the humanity to feel embarrassed. Serrin had rarely even visited these lands; it was unlikely any of the several thousand killed had been guilty as accused.

"Nothing ungodly about the serrin," Father Syd growled. Lord Elen's wide blue eyes turned upon the big priest. "Serrin are gentle folk. Their only crime is words, while others who call themselves godly impale innocents with steel. The scripture of Saint Vestos says all evil is flowered in the souls of men. Gods have nothing to do with it, and serrin neither."

"And this is what passes for the faith in Lenayin, I presume?" Lord Elen asked the gathering.

"You will not presume to teach the faith to our lowlands guests," Koenyg told the priest, sharply.

"You speak for your armies, Your Highness," Syd retorted fiercely. He was a big man, looking more a warrior with cloak, beard and staff than a man of faith. "I speak for the faith in Lenayin, not you."

Lord Elen blinked in astonishment. He looked further astonished that Koenyg did not strike off Syd's head for the insolence. Koenyg merely ground his teeth and fumed. Lord Elen repressed a laugh, to see the fractious, uncivilised Lenays arguing so, priest against prince in the presence of others. The old, shivering Algrassian priest merely stared, uncomprehending. Not much Torovan spoken in these parts save amongst the nobility, Damon guessed.

"Highnesses," said Elen, swallowing his amusement with difficulty. "If you please, I would collect the remaining criminal and be gone. There will be angry families to answer to, and reparations to make."

Damon stared at the man, and at Koenyg, and his stern, silent father. They would marry his Sofy to the likes of *this*? For a moment, he felt almost sick with fury.

"You may take her," Koenyg said impassively. "I shall accompany you. There will be my sister and her guards to deal with." Lord Elen bowed.

Koenyg swept past Damon, with a glare that nearly made him flinch. Furious as he was, still a glare from Koenyg could make his knees tremble. Lord Elen and his cronies followed Koenyg, and Damon strode fast to confront his father.

"My Lord," said Damon, his voice trembling. "You will allow this?" His father's dark eyes bore into his own. "Is this the mercy of our gods?"

Within the tent, deathly silence, save the gentle rain that fell on the canvas above. The king looked away.

"Have you nothing to say?" Damon asked. "We march to make war on good people, in the name of murderers and thieves who would despoil all that is good in the Verenthane faith, who would slaughter thousands of innocents, to unite their lands and rally their people in terror of imaginary evils, and you say nothing? Thousands of Lenay families will lose fathers, brothers and sons to this cause, and your only reply is silence?"

"Lad," said Father Syd, laying a hand on his prince's shoulder. "That's enough."

"The path has been chosen," said King Torvaal. His voice sounded strained, as though roughened by lack of use. "The destiny of Lenayin is Verenthane. We fight for the Verenthane cause, the holiest of the holy causes. We reclaim the holy lands for the faith. The gods have ordained it."

"Are you certain?" Damon pressed, desperately. "Have you seen it? With your own eyes?" His father had spent so many days in prayer, since the death of his heir and Damon's eldest brother Krystoff, nearly thirteen years before.

Damon searched his father's face, for the consolation of knowing that the king, at least, knew this cause to be a just one. That he would not sacrifice so many lives without the certainty of righteous truth.

His father's dark eyes stared back. And again, he looked away. Damon no longer wanted to strike someone. He wanted to cry.

He turned and strode from the tent, out into the rain. Father Syd followed, and a pair of Royal Guardsmen joined to their flanks. Great Lord Ackryd of Taneryn nearly walked into him from another tent, reversing quickly.

"Bad?" Ackryd asked, watching Damon warily. Damon snorted furiously, glad the wetness of his eyes could be explained in part by the rain. Ackryd was the third new great lord to be appointed after the Udalyn Rebellion, following the deaths of Usyn Telgar of Hadryn and Cyan Asynth of Banneryd in battle. Taneryn's previous Great Lord Krayliss had lost his head at the order of the king for sedition. Ackryd had then been Captain Ackryd of the Red Swords, one of Taneryn's two standing companies, and had joined Sasha to fight for the Udalyn against the northern Hadryn and Banneryd. His role in that battle had gained him enough credit with Taneryn's various village leaders and great warriors to get him selected Krayliss's replacement at the last Taneryn Rrathynal.

"We march to Loth, Lord Ackryd," Damon snarled. "To Loth!"

"You'll not speak such words, lad," Father Syd cautioned, striding close behind.

"Your Highness," Ackryd pressed, "we Taneryn hear rumours that this incident with the princess was arranged by the northerners. Is it true?"

"I'm sure they'd love to have thought of it," Damon muttered.

"It is true, then?"

"No, it's not true man!" Damon snapped. "Pay your wits more attention and your rumours less! The northerners want this war most of all, they need Sofy married safely to Prince Balthaar, however much they dislike her."

"You accuse them of rational common sense," Ackryd growled. "Those fanatics are as stupid as they are evil—"

"If it please you, Lord of Taneryn, I've more important matters to hand than Taneryn's old wars with—" Damon broke off, as he heard screams from ahead. A woman's screams. They sounded frighteningly familiar.

Damon ran, Ackryd, Syd and their men running behind, toward the commotion. Royal Guardsmen held a gathering press of men back from the entrance to Sofy's tent, shouting angrily and threatening with weapons those who thought to push through.

Damon shoved others aside, and the guardsmen let him through. Inside, several men were shouting, but the broader entourage were silent. The servants' faces were shocked and pale. There was Sofy, in the arms of two of her maids, her face tear streaked. Before her stood Yasmyn Kraal, her darak drawn, warily guarding her princess.

The shouting men were Koenyg, and one of the Bacosh lords. Between them lay the rescued villagers. The boy, covered with a blanket, and his surviving sister . . . now impaled with Lord Elen's sword. Her eyes stared sightlessly at Lord Elen, her weatherworn dress drenched in blood. Lord Elen straightened his neck self-righteously, and withdrew his blade. The girl's body lurched as it came out, limp and bony. Sofy was sobbing. Those had been her screams.

"Upon the princess's own hearth!" Koenyg was yelling furiously. "Have you no honour?"

"Our lands, our justice!" the other lord yelled back. Lord Elen wiped his blade with his cloak, looking most unbothered by it all. Pale blue eyes met Damon's, and he gave a cold smile.

Damon drew his blade and strode forward. A Bacosh soldier saw Damon's intent, drew his own blade and interposed himself. Koenyg yelled, drawing his own blade, as others did likewise. Damon smashed through the soldier's weak defence, his edge driving into the man's shoulder, then sidestepped and cut through his middle. A second came at his left, Damon half step-faked, then dropped back as that man's blade whistled past, then tore through jaw and throat with his counter stroke.

There were yells and confusion, Lord Elen stumbling backward, sword raised to ward the impending attack as two surviving soldiers and two minor lords made a barrier between him and the enraged Lenay prince. Damon would have gone through them, but Koenyg was there on his right flank, weapon ready, yelling at him to stop. In all their years of rivalry, Damon had only bested Koenyg in a full sparring sequence once. Should he continue his attack, he would expose to Koenyg his flank. And he had no confidence that his brother would not take that available opening.

"A duel!" Damon yelled furiously at Elen, pointing his sword. "I'll have you to the death, here and now!"

"Enough!" Koenyg bellowed. "You've done enough!"

"This is an outrage!" Lord Elen was yelling, in fright and fury, his round face flushed bright red. "By what honour would you do murder on an invited guest?"

"The wound is deep," Damon snarled in Lenay, "and can only be salved with blood!"

"You don't know what you say!" Koenyg said furiously, also in Lenay. "You don't know what you say, and you shall retract . . ."

"The wound is deep and can only be salved with blood!" Damon insisted, his blade an unwavering pointer at Lord Elen. Koenyg hissed in exasperation. It was the traditional challenge, the one in hot blood, not the ceremonial. It was what was said in countless squares, fields and hearths across Lenayin, when tempers grew too great and insults thrust too deep, and two men's lives made a dissonance that could only be resolved with death.

"What is this barbarian garble you speak?" Lord Elen demanded in Torovan. "Don't you point that blade at me, or by the great gods you'll regret it!"

"He has the right," said Father Syd, also in Lenay, ignoring the Algrassians. The big priest pushed in behind, close between Damon and Koenyg, yet not so foolhardy as to stand directly between them.

"He has no right!" Koenyg declared. "We are guests on Algrassian lands. . . ."

"Don't you speak in tongues in my presence!" Lord Elen demanded. "Of what do you speak?"

"Your death!" Yasmyn Izlar said.

"I'll not be threatened by a scabby, slanty eyed, barbarian wench!" Elen roared. "I'll have your head, I tell you!" The Isfayen girl paid him little heed, her eyes only for Damon, alive and gleaming with admiration.

"He stepped past the talleryn stones," Father Syd continued, now in

Torovan. "He paid his respects. This is Lenay land, it is consecrated by our hearth, our food and our tents. We sleep upon the ground, we slay animals for our feast, and now, it has been further claimed with blood."

"What are you talking about, you babbling fool?" Elen retorted. "I have been attacked, one of my men has been slain!" The other, on the ground behind Damon, was now rising, with the assistance of guardsmen. "The regent shall hear of this outrage! I shall demand satisfaction, and punishment!"

"You are being offered satisfaction," Father Syd told him, an impassive rock in the face of the Algrassian's bluster. "A fair fight. A prince against a lord. The gods will decide."

"Don't be absurd! I'll not follow your barbarian customs! I am the Lord of Liside Vale, these are my lands, these are my ways, and I shall choose the reclaiming of my own honour!"

"I saw him pay respects at the stones!" Great Lord Ackryd cut in, from the back by the tent entrance. "He came upon our hearth, our camp, and he submitted himself to our ways. He has conducted himself without honour, he has slain innocents, he has offended a Lenay princess and made her grieve. If Prince Damon's challenge is rejected, I volunteer my own! He shall accept, or he shall die here, right now! *Ayalrach entyr dalan!*"

"*Ayalrach entyr dalan!*" came the reply, from surrounding Lenay men, nobles and soldiers alike. Even, Damon noted, from some of Sofy's maids, and not merely from Yasmyn. "Honour before gold," it meant, in Lenay. Gold was not at issue here, but the saying was understood by all in the highcountry. Honour was everything. Some matters, even the highest lords could not weasel their way out of. At the intonation, even Koenyg looked sullenly resigned.

Lord Elen was not a stupid man. He seemed to sense that something had changed. "I am an important man with the regent!" he declared. "The regent's sister is my cousin through marriage. I am not some lowly man-at-arms to be subjected to barbarian justice."

"We are the army without which the regent cannot win his war," Koenyg said darkly. "This is the future queen of all the Bacosh. You have offended her, and Lenay honour with it, and badly misjudged your own standing, Lord Elen. There is a reason why lowlanders tell fearful tales of the Lenay hoards. It would have been better had you recalled."

"I've heard enough!" Lord Elen declared. "I am leaving, and rest assured the regent shall hear of this outrage!" He did not move very far. All about the tent, Lenay warriors stood at the ready. Their stance was unyielding. Lord Elen's men would not advance into that threat, and Lord Elen remained fixed to the spot. He was breathing hard now, eyes wide with anger and defiance that Damon did not doubt was real. But so was the fear that it masked.

"You have been challenged to a duel by a prince of Lenayin," Koenyg said quietly. "One does not shirk such an honour." Koenyg could not stop it now, Damon knew, with a surge of satisfaction. In some matters, even the heir of Lenayin could not defy the common will. Not if he wished the men of Lenayin to follow him into battle.

"I do not accept!"

"Then you will die here," said Koenyg. "As will any who defend you." Koenyg raised his gloved fist, and guardsmen shifted the grip on their weapons. Lord Elen's defenders flinched backward.

"I accept!" Lord Elen retracted, just as fast. Koenyg lowered his fist, slowly. He gave a slight bow.

"We shall make preparations." He gave a signal, and guardsmen rushed from the tent to yell orders. "You have the right to await a morning duel. . . ."

"Now!" Damon snapped. "I would not do him the honour of a formal start."

"As you will," said Elen, haughtily. "However, I protest at this notion of Lenay honour. I was attacked, your brother meant to murder me in cold blood, and one of my men is dead. This was no honourable declaration."

"Conceded," Koenyg said. "Yet it happens even in Lenayin, when a man's honour is pushed too far. In Lenayin, men learn to be careful, Lord Elen."

"We're not *in* Lenayin!" Lord Elen fumed. "I demand advantage."

"Thought you might," someone muttered, in Lenay.

"I'll fight unarmoured," said Damon.

"Done!" Lord Elen declared. "See you outside!" Men stood aside as the furious lord and his entourage strode from the tent.

Damon sheathed his sword, and shrugged off his jacket, handing it to a guardsman. Another assisted him with the chain mail beneath.

"Damon," said Koenyg, but Damon ignored him. "Brother."

"I don't care for your strategies and politics, brother," Damon retorted, as the heavy mail vest came up over his head. "That man needs killing."

"Aye!" came the loud reply from angry Lenays about the tent. "That he does," Father Syd agreed. "The gods will strengthen your arm."

"Half the Bacosh nobility needs killing," one of Sofy's maids said coldly.

"He will die in agony, my Prince!" called another. The mail removed, Damon reclaimed his jacket. His eyes met Sofy's. She was standing small and huddled, wrapped in a fur coat. Her face was pale and drawn. Fearful and upset, yet not about to protest his actions.

"I'm not trying to . . . !" Koenyg began, and broke off in frustration. He took a deep breath. "Look, Damon." He grabbed his brother's arm, his grip ferocious. "Watch his shieldwork. All the Bacosh use shields better than we, it is an offensive weapon as much as defensive. He will crowd you, take away your space, your room to swing. Remember, the shield is his parry, his counterstroke will be fast. Don't look for easy openings. Be patient."

Damon stared at his eldest brother. There was concern in Koenyg's eyes. Not worry, never that. But it surprised him all the same. And maddened him. "You think that fat pig will trouble me? I'll give you his head!"

Damon strode from the tent. "Did I say that?" he heard Koenyg's plaintive question behind. "Did I say he'd lose? I swear, little brothers are the most . . ."

Damon lost the rest as guardsmen shouted approval . . . and here were several Baen-Tar lords, slapping their prince on the back and shoulders as Bacosh men would never have dared of their royalty. A crowd was gathering, and moved with him as he strode in Lord Elen's wake, down toward the river.

"*Damon! Damon! Damon!*" The chant grew louder, more bloodthirsty. Damon let it fuel his rage. He feared what would happen should his rage dissipate. He feared what might happen should his weakness be exposed, before all those who deferred to him as prince. He had always been a good swordsman, but never great, like Koenyg . . . or even Sasha. He had always been a good prince but never great, like Krystoff. He had always been somewhat well liked but never loved, like Sofy. Lenayin was not a land of the second best. Lenay men were either heroes or martyrs. That was why so many would willingly throw themselves into this meaningless, bloody war. They would be found worthy, or they would die. Either was acceptable, and indeed preferable to seeking neither.

A crowd was gathering, men running, calling for others. Best get this over fast, Damon decided, before they were overrun by onlookers. The officers, nobles and village heads would keep order, but not indefinitely. A prince of Lenayin had not participated in an honour-duel since . . . Gods, he could not think of when. Koenyg had threatened it several times, to provincial lordlings who tried his patience, and once to a southern lord who had been spreading rumours of infidelity. All had declined, wisely. For most Lenays, such a duel was unwinnable—to kill a prince of Lenayin in a duel would win no favours from anyone, the king least of all.

"Damon!" Myklas gasped, pushing through the crowd to walk at his side. He'd clearly been running. "Watch his shield, he'll try to bash you with it, get you offbalance—"

"I know!" Damon retorted. "Koenyg told me already."

"You'll get him," Myklas said fiercely. "He looks strong, but he's fat and slow too."

"I'll not underestimate him," Damon replied. His heart was pounding, more from rage than fear. "I seem to recall I've fought far more battles than you."

"I wish you'd let me do it," Myklas said. He walked not as tall as Damon, nor as broad, his limbs still slender with seventeen years' youth. Yet there was a swagger to his step that some old enough to remember said reminded them of Krystoff. "Why not just yield to me? I could use the experience, like everyone's always telling me . . ."

Damon knew it would be useless to shout at Myklas, and remind him that someone was about to die, and that none of it was any game.

"Myklas," he said instead, and put a rough arm about his younger brother's shoulders. "If anything should happen to me, tonight or any other night, I want you to swear you'll look after Sofy. Not only look after, but listen to her. She's wiser than all the men in this family combined, so you listen to her, you hear me?"

"What are you talking about? You'll kill this fat porker and play lagand with his head. . . ."

"Or any other night, Myk," Damon repeated. "We're marching to war, and this is only the first of many battles. Swear it to me."

"Of course I'll look after Sofy. What else would I do?" They clasped forearm to forearm.

"And listen to her," Damon repeated.

Masters Heldryn and Tyvenar pushed to Damon's side and grasped at his shoulder. Young men, the sons of lords on their way to their first war, and very excited.

Myklas grinned helplessly. "Brother, you know I don't listen to anyone."

"Your brother has the soul of a warrior," Heldryn told Myklas. "Yours is the pride, young Myklas!"

Past the camp periphery, Lord Elen and his entourage stopped on the wet grass ten strides from the river. There, in the misting rain, he took his position. Guardsmen flanked out, forming a circle, about which the crowd rushed in, some carrying torches or lamps, lighting rain and firesmoke in flickering yellow.

"Lad," said Father Syd, "do you wish the blessings?"

"No," said Damon, sword unsheathed, and testing its balance. "I'll not waste the gods' time." If he waited longer, the fear would come. He recalled the girl's body on the tent floor, impaled by Lord Elen's sword. It angered him, yet strangely, the rage seemed to fade a little. Fear threatened, until he recalled Sofy's face, stricken with horror. Then the rage came back.

He glared at Lord Elen, attended by his minor lords and several guards. A man came running with Lord Elen's shield. Elen slid his arm within the straps and hefted its weight with expert balance. Damon recalled Sasha's duel, against Farys Varan of Hadryn, more than a half year ago. He was not of Sasha's standard with a blade, he knew . . . but just as surely, Elen was not of Varan's. Varan, however, had followed the codes of Lenay honour. Elen would not. Best to remember.

Hefting his shield, and comforted by the weight of his mail, Lord Elen seemed to grow in confidence. He regarded Damon coldly above the rim of his shield, and smiled. The clustering crowd quietened, expectantly.

"How do these things begin, in the highlands?" Elen asked.

"A man is appointed adjudicator," said Father Syd, the only other man within the circle. "A priest, if available. Or a holy man, amongst Goeren-yai. When I am satisfied, I will give the word."

Elen nodded, sidling sideways a step. His balance, Damon noted, looked rather good despite his weight. "I have fought eight duels and won them all," he said smugly. "I'm sure I'll adapt." No doubt he thought this revelation a timely blow. Damon didn't care.

"Will you require the blessings?" asked Father Syd.

"Of a highlands priest?" Elen scoffed. "I think not."

"As you will," said Syd, and stepped back to the circle's edge. "Indicate your readiness."

Elen nodded. Damon took stance, two hands to his sword's hilt, and did the same. Syd said, "Begin!" and Damon lunged.

It was nearly over in four strokes. Damon crashed rapid blows onto Elen's shield, forcing the Bacosh lord back and then sideways, defending to his sword side while circling left, desperately, away from the strikes. Shields encouraged a defensive pattern Lenay warriors always scoffed. Those who wielded them would rather block with the shield than the sword, and so lost the latter art completely. Thus defending, Elen made no attempt to thrust his blade forward, but merely held it back, hoping for the counterstrike opening that never came.

Damon cut from high left, forcing a rapid back shift that caused Elen to slip on the wet grass . . . the shield wavered across, and Damon reversed to slash from the low forequarter. His sword tore into the rim of Elen's shield, far enough to strike his hip. Elen staggered and swung back desperately, Damon parrying and skipping back from range.

A roar from the crowd, and Damon caught a brief glimpse of Elen's entourage, faces fearful in the firelight, seeing their powerful, armoured lord so completely overwhelmed. Fear, too, on the face of Lord Elen, as perhaps the pain of his hip wound reached him, and he realised that now even his mobility would suffer.

Schooled in Lenay swordsmanship, Damon did not allow his opponent any chance to regroup, but immediately pressed his advantage. Elen blocked the crushing overhead and risked a sideways slash with his sword . . . desperation, and Damon had expected it. He parried close, spinning inward and ramming his shoulder into Elen's shield. The wounded man staggered at the impact, slipped, and the shield dropped once more. Raised just in time to meet Damon's second overhead with its rim, but the blow was powerful and sliced through the shield's edge, crashing it downward . . .

. . . and suddenly, it all stopped, Damon half surprised to find his blade buried in Elen's skull, nearly down to one eyebrow. Blood trickled into one horrified eye. He wasn't dead yet, and that was sickening. Damon pulled his blade clear, to the sound of cracking skull, but Elen collapsed before he could give the mercy of a beheading. He lay there on the grass, kicking and struggling, trying to speak. The crowd was yelling, a deafening roar of chants and triumph, blades and fists punching the air. Damon knew he should finish Elen, but suddenly, the rage was gone, and all he felt was . . . despair. It was not a clean kill. Why had the gods not granted him the mercy of a clean kill?

There were brains on his blade. He felt the sudden urge to throw it aside, to spin and hurl it ten strides and more into the dark river . . . but there was Koenyg watching, arms folded beside Myklas, and he could not do such a thing before Koenyg. Instead, Damon pulled his sword rag from a pocket, wiped once, threw the rag away and sheathed the blade. Only then, amidst the yells and exuberance, did he catch the look on Koenyg's firelit face. Relief. Sheer, undisguised relief. Damon wondered if he was seeing things.

Koenyg saluted, one warrior to another, a clenched fist to his chest. Damon returned it, and the yells and chants grew louder. They were chanting his name, warriors all. Lord Elen lay kicking on the ground and that excited them. Damon's despair grew, but he returned the salute anyway. Koenyg's face now seemed only impassive, hard and shadowed in the lamplight. Myklas, Damon noticed, looked a little pale. Good, he thought. At least something positive might have come from this.

The yelling crowd accompanied him back to Sofy's tent. This time, none of them touched him or tried to clasp his shoulder, or pat his back. To show the prince informality before a fight was one thing. A victorious warrior, however, required the dignity of respectful distance.

Sofy was there, at the entrance to her tent, not surprised to see him coming, but relieved all the same. Her face was tear streaked and pale, and her lip trembled as he approached. It would not be warrior-like, nor indeed manly, for the victorious prince to embrace his sister at such a time. Damon embraced her anyway, and held her tight.

"I wish you hadn't done that," Sofy told him. "But I'm not sad he's dead." Damon knew how she felt.

"I'd rather kill them all than let them take you from me," he replied.

Eight

RHILLIAN RODE UP THE BROAD STREET toward the Ushal Fortress in the bright sunshine, and wished she could feel happier. Crowds lined the road, cheering and throwing flowers. Ahead of her rode General Zulmaher, with captains Renard and Hauser at his flanks. Ahead of them, the banners flew, the great shield and sword of the third and sixth regiments.

The second row was for the serrin, but Rhillian did not mind. This was a human war—humans had suffered the greatest losses, and she would not have minded them taking all the credit were it not so. Aisha rode on her left side, and on her right, Kiel, recently returned from southern Elisse, where he had been helping the peasantry to organise in preparation for further Rhodaani and Saalshen assistance.

Behind them marched the Steel, rows of armoured soldiers in perfect formation. Infantry first, cavalry behind, and to little complaint from the cavalry, who counted themselves lucky not to be fighting "in the mud." The infantry protested against marching behind formations of horses. "Marching through the shit of our betters," a corporal had remarked ironically, within Rhillian's hearing.

"Almost enough to make one pleased to march to war, is it not?" Kiel suggested, surveying the cheering Tracatans who lined the road. His eyes were pale grey, so pale they were nearly colourless. His hair, unusually for a serrin, was jet black, making stark contrast against clear white skin. "Not that I actually got to see the war, of course."

"It is unbecoming to fish for an apology, Kiel," Rhillian replied. "I left you in the south precisely because you have the knack of command. The southern peasants were friendly, and ready to be commanded, and I had precious few options better than you."

"One does not complain," Kiel said mildly. "One merely observes."

"One might have thought you'd seen enough blood," Rhillian said, with an edge.

"Blood does not interest me," said Kiel. "Only survival."

"Survival lies in a stable Rhodaan and a stable Elisse. You also served, Kiel."

"*Mes'a rhan*," said Kiel with a faint smile. He put a hand to his heart and bowed. "I am convinced."

Rhillian snorted. Somehow, with Kiel, the smile never quite reached those pale grey eyes. She had not invited him to the war because she distrusted his methods. Kiel, of course, knew so. One knew such things, between serrin, where humans might keep secrets, or suspicions.

Not all the crowd seemed pleased to see General Zulmaher, Rhillian noted. They applauded stoically, as one must, if one was Rhodaani and confronted with the victorious Rhodaani Steel. Without the Steel, free Rhodaan was finished, and most Rhodaanis knew it. But there were grim stares at the general, riding erect in full colours and armour, save the helmet.

The serrin were received very differently. Some Tracatans gasped, pointed or cried out. Women in particular gave exclamations, and hoisted their little girls up to a seeing vantage. Rhillian smiled and waved back often, to enthusiastic reply. She wore her snow-white hair loose down her back, carefully washed and brushed of all the war's tangles. Her best jacket and riding pants, too, washed and pressed, and she even wore a silver chain with an emerald pendant for her neck. The pendant matched her eyes, brilliant green, particularly on a day like today when the sun would strike the jewel, and burn like green fire.

"The white one!" she heard them call. That, or "The white lady!" Rhillian supposed it was a vast improvement on "The White Death," as she'd been known by many in Petrodor. General Zulmaher, they had all seen before, but Rhillian's presence in Tracato was much more rare. They seemed intrigued.

"Unfair," Aisha declared. "I made at least as much effort to be well presented, yet they are not staring at me."

Rhillian smiled at her. "You look beautiful," she assured her friend, and it was true. Aisha wore an *in'sae* jacket, a serrin riding top of patterned green and brown, her leather riding boots were newly polished, and her mare gleamed as though she'd been polished too.

"I know," Aisha replied. "Yet even so, they stare as though I were a lump of coal beside a diamond. Which I fear is true."

"They stare because we are strange," said Kiel. "Humans are obsessed with uniformity. They strive for sameness, like wolves to the pack. Strangeness excites their senses, sometimes to pleasure, other times to fear."

"A double-edged sword, as are all things," Aisha declared.

"Perhaps," said Kiel. "But even in love and pleasure, humans are moved by fear. Fear is the constant emotion. The foundation to all. It is never absent."

Rhillian's eyes strayed to a mother holding her daughter in the crowd. The little girl was staring, eyes wide, mesmerised yet uncertain. What would a child choose? To fear the stranger with the strange looks? Or to love her? Surely it depended on what she was told. In Rhodaan, children were told good of serrin. Enora and Ilduur too, for the most part. Yet the Saalshen Bacosh was small, compared to what lay beyond.

"What is *our* foundation then, Kiel?" Rhillian asked. "The foundation to all in serrin thought?"

"Reason," said Kiel, without hesitation.

"There was once a man who reasoned that he knew the reason of reason. And, once reasoned, found it unreasonable."

"I had not heard that," Kiel admitted. "*Eternis?*"

"No. It's Lenay." Her smile faded. "Sasha told it to me, in Petrodor. She never believed in serrin reason."

"It showed," Kiel said drily.

"She never believed in serrin infallibility," Aisha reminded them both. "Best that we follow her example, in that."

"Aye," Rhillian said. Not infallible, no. Merely determined.

They rode into the city, where the buildings loomed tall and grand, like little else in all human or serrin lands. Great façades of arches and columns, and courtyards flanked by statues, watching like sentinels, mythical beasts and great Rhodaani heroes alike. Here, before the House of Justice, stood upon a pedestal the statue of a serrin woman, dressed in the formal robes of a Grand Justiciar. She held a book of law under one arm and raised a sword to the heavens with another, her hair free and loose as a true justiciar would never wear it.

It was Maldereld, Rhillian knew. Elsewhere in the Saalshen Bacosh, humans called her a general, yet in Tracato most recalled her for her contributions to law, in the years of occupation following the fall of King Leyvaan. Rhillian also knew that this particular statue was the third, and little more than ten years old, the previous two statues having been defaced. Not all Rhodaanis liked to be reminded of serrin overlordship, least of all by a woman. Particularly not here, in the wealthy centre, where every building spoke of commerce and power, and the clothes of the common cityfolk were rich indeed.

The crowds here were huge and rapturous without reservation. Black-boots lined the road, and some garrison soldiers in full armour, to hold back the cheering people, many of whom threw flowers or grain. No dark looks for General Zulmaher here, Rhillian noted. The wealthy folk loved their general.

Then they came upon a particularly grand courtyard, pressed against the eastern wall of the Ushal Fortress. A line of soldiers and Blackboots held the crowd back from the courtyard, for within were arrayed the various importances of Tracato—perhaps fifty people, mostly men: ten standing on a great platform and forty seated on a scaffold behind.

The flagbearers turned into the courtyard, followed by Zulmaher and the captains, then Rhillian and her two lieutenants. The marching Steel did not follow, but continued their way up the road, headed to the south edge of Tracato, and the barracks there. There would be barely a night's rest, before deployment to the western front, to face the invasion threat. No time at all, in truth.

Rhillian followed the officers about the central fountain, trying to keep her mare to a steady formation between Aisha and Kiel. She was not a natural rider, and serrin were not much given to formations anyhow. They all stopped before the platform and waited, while trumpets blew, and the crowd behind cheered some more, and a herald shouted a long announcement in Rhodaani that Rhillian caught only in part—something about glorious victories, and triumph in the name of the gods, and freedom for all humanity. Truly she was an appalling linguist, to not be fluent in Rhodaani. But then, she'd simply had more important matters on which to apply her mind.

More cheering, and then some young men in ceremonial gold came forward to hold the horses' halters, while the general and his entourage dismounted. The lad holding the halter of Rhillian's horse looked very nervous, and barely more than fourteen. Rhillian gave him a smile. He swallowed hard, and turned several shades paler.

Zulmaher stepped forward, and Rhillian followed, Aisha and Kiel having enough sense of human protocols to fall in behind. Zulmaher ascended three steps to the platform, where a priest gave him a holy book to place his palm upon, and a ring for him to kneel and kiss. Premier Chiron then placed a garland of leaves on his head, and Zulmaher rose and kissed Chiron on one cheek, and then the other.

Captains Renard and Hauser followed, to more cheering, as Zulmaher completed the circle of importances arrayed across the platform behind, clasping hands and kissing cheeks. Rhillian could not help but reflect how strange it was that Rhodaani men should kiss in public, while in Lenayin, a man could be killed for making the attempt.

Then it was Rhillian's turn, and the cheering was just as loud when the herald announced her name. That surprised her. The trumpets blew, and the priest hovered with his book and ring, as though in hope. Rhillian granted him a smile, and that was all. Some serrin, on occasion, had touched the book, and kissed the ring, not wishing to offend, and being serrin, having no strict belief that could in turn be offended. "What was the harm?" they'd asked.

The harm, Rhillian was certain, lay in encouraging human uniformity. In that, Kiel was correct—it was the most dangerous of all human instincts. If Rhodaan wished Saalshen's friendship, then it must accept Saalshen's strangeness. To accept such strangeness, without hatred, would surely do them good. Serrin, after all, had been doing the same for humans since humanity had first appeared in Rhodia.

She exchanged kisses with Premier Chiron, an unremarkable man of lesser height than she, balding and dark featured. His eyes held a certain confidence, however, that was neither arrogance nor power lust.

"You and all your *talmaad* have the thanks of all Rhodaan, Mistress Rhillian Resil'dyi," he told her in Torovan.

Rhillian repressed a wince at the last name. It was rare to meet a human who knew what serrin last names meant. "And the thanks of all Elisse one day, I should hope, Premier Chiron," she replied.

Chiron smiled grimly. "Quite, quite," he agreed. "One day I am sure, they shall erect statues in your honour in Vethenel, as we have for your glorious predecessor Maldereld. But for now, you have Tracato. The city is yours, Mistress Resil'dyi."

Rhillian wondered if the premier might soon regret he'd said that. "I thank you, Premier. Saalshen thanks you for your friendship."

She kissed cheeks and clasped hands with the others—there were councilmen and justiciars, wealthy merchants, senior civil officers, a general, an ambassador each of Enora and Ilduur and, of course, nobility. Some of those with appointed rank were nobility too. Some kissed too wetly, a few from lechery, and a few from that peculiar attitude of Rhodaani men in the presence of attractive women, part fatherliness and part lust.

"You'd make a good statue," Aisha told her in Haati dialect, so none would be likely to overhear. She took her place at Rhillian's side, looking amused.

"I'd rather be carved by a Petrodorian," Rhillian replied.

"Nude?" Rhillian shrugged. Aisha raised her eyebrows. "That would be an interesting addition to a Tracato courtyard."

"With a great python about my neck," Rhillian added. "Its tail about my thigh, and stroking it with one hand, like so."

"They stare at you as though you were a demon," said Kiel, taking his place on her other side. "If they could only understand what you say, they would be convinced of it." Rhillian grinned.

The courtyard's new arrivals were climbing the steps to the platform now, and Rhillian's smile faded. "I don't believe it," she murmured.

Lord Crashuren was first, a pale, tall man with a bald head save for great, grey whiskers. He was the first of the Elissian lords that General Zulmaher had made peace with. He took the knee before Premier Chiron, a palm upon the book, and kissed the priest's ring. And he remained on one knee, as a junior justiciar held a Tracato city flag at Chiron's side, a shield in blue and white checkers, and the words in Rhodaani—*Levas dei to mertas.* Live free or die.

Lord Crashuren kissed the flag. Premier Chiron asked for his allegiance, upon his word of honour. Lord Crashuren gave it, on behalf of all the lords of Yertan Province . . . that was a good chunk of middle Elisse, right up to the outskirts of Vethenel. There was no way the crowd about the courtyard's far perimeter could hear the words, yet when Crashuren rose, the trumpets sounded, and the crowd all cheered to see Crashuren and Chiron embrace. The Rhodaani leader of the people's office, selected by the general will of the Rho-daani population, and the feudal tyrant whose peasants Rhillian had found in pitiful condition, half starved despite the fertility of their lands, poorer than dirt, and brutalised by Crashuren's thugs. Rhillian recalled corpses in the mud of the little village square, a woman and child amongst them. She'd killed the man who'd slain them. She'd have gladly done the same to Crashuren.

On the steps, there were more Elissian lords awaiting their turn.

"I wasn't told this was going to happen," Rhillian said in a low voice.

"No surprise," said Kiel, sounding almost amused. Kiel usually expected the worst from humans. Today, his expectations were met.

Across the platform, at General Zulmaher's side, Captain Renard gave Rhillian a seething look. Several of the councilmen, too, looked uncomfortable. Rhillian returned Renard's stare for a long moment, pondering. Her stare moved to the general. Zulmaher stood oblivious, square shouldered and proud, watching as his accomplishments unfolded in all their glory. He did not spare her so much as a glance. Doubtless he knew what she thought. Equally doubtless, he cared not a bit.

The Mahl'rhen smelled of perfume and lavender. Errollyn walked the paths between courtyards, and saw coloured silk scarves blowing in the breeze, and heard windchimes and music. The *talmaad* had returned from Elisse— victorious, though the decoration would have remained even if otherwise. Serrin, not big on grand human ceremony, did enjoy their little celebrations.

In the northern complex, he found the baths. With a squeal of delight, a small, blonde woman leapt to her feet and ran to him bare footed. Aisha hugged him hard, and Errollyn hugged her back.

"Errollyn! Are you well? How is Sasha?"

"We're both well." Errollyn pulled back to look at her. There was no visible scar to the side of her head, beneath her hair. Aisha's loose robe afforded him the opportunity to examine her shoulder, and then her calf, where injuries he had previously treated seemed well healed.

"That's the most interest you've shown in my body for some time," Aisha teased. "There was a time you did show more."

"I'm with Sasha now," said Errollyn with a grin. "If not restrained by human custom, I assure you I'd take you aside for a good fuck."

"Oh poor Sasha," Aisha sighed, hugging him once more. "One day we should really broaden her horizons."

"She's human, Aisha. It's more complicated than that."

"I know, I know. I'm half human too, I do remember."

About nearby pools, conversation was fading. Serrin turned to look. Errollyn walked amongst them, removing an arm from Aisha's shoulders to hop across a joining stream. Once across, Aisha replaced his arm, defiant in the face of serrin stares.

Seated half submerged in the warm water, relaxed and disinterested, was Rhillian. Wet robes floated in the water, revealing bare skin on hard muscle. Errollyn could see no new scars, yet she looked changed. Hardened. Her face, when her green eyes found him, seemed to bear a grimmer expression than it could previously show. Although her skin bore as few lines as ever, she now seemed somehow weathered, her brilliant green eyes darkened in shadow.

Conversation ceased entirely. Rhillian looked at Errollyn.

"What do you want?"

"Many things," said Errollyn. "None of them brings me here."

In Saalsi, it was well said, dismissing selfish intentions and claiming broader purposes. Six months ago, Rhillian might have snorted at the clever words. Now, she did not bother even that. Emerald eyes flicked from him to Aisha and back.

"What does?" she said blandly.

"I have news of Lady Renine's intentions," said Errollyn. "Before I share them, I'd ask more of yours."

"Amusing," said Kiel from his seat from the poolside, "that you feel you have the right to ask." Errollyn ignored him. Rhillian just looked at him.

"I've not decided," she said. "General Zulmaher has made allies of our worst enemies in Elisse. They flock to him mostly for fear of us. He promises them retention of feudal powers. Should they use them to retain power in Elisse, they would in turn provide a safe haven for feudalism in Rhodaan. Wealth, marriage prospects, trade, all according to feudal custom, and with no concern for the Rhodaani Council. It would be as though Maldereld had never raised a sword against feudal power in Rhodaani."

"You can't just remove feudalism from Rhodaan, Rhillian," said Errollyn, his eyes narrowed. Had Rhillian learned nothing from Petrodor? "This cancer cannot be cut from the body, not without removing heart and lungs with it."

"Errollyn speaks sense," said an elderly serrin, seated on a cushioned chair in the wading pool. His skinny shins were half submerged in the water, his long hair white like Rhillian's, but with age. "Rhodaan is a three-legged stool. The feudalists and the Civid Sein make two legs, the majority uncommitted population the third. Remove one leg, and it shall fall."

"Saalshen makes a fourth leg, Lesthen," said Kiel. "We can hold up any stool."

"For a time," said Lesthen. "For a time, perhaps. But we are not the pillar of foundation in Rhodaan we once were. Human civilisation grows rapidly. Serrin civilisation, slowly. When I was a young man, Saalshen had great power here. Today, our power remains the same, but Rhodaani power has increased tenfold. Today we are small, the strong child whose younger siblings have grown to manhood, while we remain children still."

"I'm not planning to remove feudalism," said Rhillian. "But neither can it be allowed to sabotage Rhodaan from within. What news do you have for me, Errollyn?"

Errollyn examined her. Dare he tell her? Most serrin would have felt compelled by the *vel'ennar* to be here. Unlike them, he had a choice. If he granted her this information, it would not be for unreasoned compulsion, but for judgement, and logic. That, at least, was what he told himself. Or did he not truly fantasise that perhaps, one day, he would do something to demonstrate his love of Saalshen, and win them all back to him?

Maybe he was fooling himself to think that he had a choice. Saalshen's power here was a reality, as was Rhillian's control over it. He could not afford to see Family Renine's plans come to fruition any more than Rhillian could. Even if she chose a poor course of action, surely that was better than the alternative?

"There has been a courier. Between Lady Renine, and, I suspect, Regent Arosh of Larosa. I do not know how many messages. Perhaps several. Perhaps many, dating back years."

There was silence in the chamber. Rhillian stood up. She looked suspicious, though whether at him or the facts he revealed, Errollyn could not guess. "Treachery?" she asked.

"Assuredly. She may claim she was demanding his immediate surrender, but that is already the Council's demand. If she believed that, she'd simply support the Council. To go behind their back suggests other intentions."

Kiel was smiling more broadly by the moment. "Errollyn. This good turn you do us is most unexpected."

"I try to do what is right, Kiel," Errollyn said coldly. "What is right, and what serves your purposes, are not always the same thing." He looked at Rhillian. "What shall you do?"

Rhillian was gazing past him. Her emerald eyes were alive with possibility.

The amphitheatre was a marvel. Sasha sat cross-legged in her spot, midway up the slope, eating grapes and handcakes she'd bought from a vendor, and watched the play with intrigue. Daish, Beled and some other friends from the Tol'rhen sat on the stone seats, sharing food and exchanging murmured critiques of the dialogue. Occasionally Daish would murmur some important point of plot to Sasha, for the play was mostly in Rhodaani, with an occasional smattering of high-class Larosan. The theatre seated perhaps a thousand, mostly wealthy, fine evening clothes aflicker in the light of a hundred torches. The stage below was ringed with fire and lantern, to lend an unearthly texture to the actors' costumes, beneath a black and starry sky.

The atmosphere of the theatre amazed her. A thousand people, all gathered together to watch the telling of a story. In Lenayin, tales were told to friends and family by the hearthside, and acting was not a profession respected by the majority of Lenays. Yet here, it seemed a matter of some seriousness. Furthermore, the play was quite intricate, and very recent, in the time of its telling. A commentary on society. Sasha found the concept intriguing, and a little unsettling, especially when so many of the Tol'rhen's most precocious students insisted upon attending, and knew most of the playwrights' names, and argued frequently over the merits of each. Culture, in her experience, existed to affirm one's beliefs and values, not to challenge them.

A young woman in actor's guild robes, and a torch in hand, picked her way carefully from the theatre's steps, and along the ledge past audience members and trays of food. She paused at Sasha's shoulder, crouching to whisper, "There is a serrin lady to see you, Lady Sashandra," in Torovan.

Sasha frowned at her. Errollyn was at the Mahl'rhen, attending to Rhillian's return from Elisse. Sasha had wanted to attend, but hadn't been invited. She hadn't been happy about it, but Errollyn, Kessligh and others who ought to know insisted that Errollyn was safe there, and in all likelihood, the talks would take many days. Knowing how impatient Sasha became with such pontificating, Errollyn had suggested (rather forcefully, to her annoyance) that she go to the theatre with friends instead.

"Back soon," she told Daish and Beled, and left to follow the young woman. Steep steps led to a walkway around the rim of the theatre, guarded by a railing. Leaning on the railing a small, blonde woman watched the play with fascinated eyes. Sasha's breath caught in her throat. "Aisha?"

Aisha looked at her. Pretty, pale blue eyes within a softly rounded face, she'd always looked like a little girl. Save now, when she smiled, and the emotion in her eyes spoke of things no child had ever known. Sasha hugged her fiercely, and was relieved that Aisha's grip was just as strong. Some serrin had not forgiven her. Perhaps it was because Aisha was half-human herself. Or perhaps it was just that she was Aisha. When they pulled back to look at each other, both were crying.

"I'd heard you were well," Sasha told her. "You look well."

"You too. City life has not turned you into an old hag yet."

"Not yet!" Sasha laughed. "I went riding the other day. Spirits it was beautiful, I've missed horses so much. If I must spend another season away from them, I might just shrivel up and die."

"Me, I've been riding rather a lot lately."

Sasha nodded, wiping her eyes. "The war. How was it?"

"Victorious, happily. It was a war. They have their moments."

"They do."

They held hands, leaning on the railing and looking down at the stage.

"Oh it's been so long since I've attended a play," Aisha said wistfully. "Whose is this?"

"Some man named Deshirei," Sasha replied.

"Oh Deshirei. He's wonderful. A little tragic, though. I'm sure this will end badly."

"It does seem to be heading that way," Sasha agreed. "It began far too happily, and everything since has been a brewing storm."

"He does that," said Aisha. "It is rather the way of things, is it not?"

"Not always, surely?"

Aisha looked at her, and smiled. "Not always, no. Dear Sasha. I'm so glad you're well."

Sasha kissed her. "Why did you come tonight? I'd heard it was rather busy at the Mahl'rhen?"

Aisha looked back down at the stage. Evasively, Sasha thought. "Is your sister here tonight?"

"Alythia? No, with the company she keeps these days, I'd have noticed. Why?"

"How are your relations with her lately?"

"Good," said Sasha without hesitation. "Much to our mutual surprise. We've merely accepted our differences. It's amazing how much improves when you stop trying to convert other people to your own opinion."

Aisha nodded. "I think perhaps we should find her."

"Why?" And, in the cold trepidation that followed, "What, now?"

"Now."

They walked uphill from the amphitheatre. Daish had decided to join them, having more interest in meeting the Princess Alythia than watching a play. And probably, Sasha guessed by the young man's lively dark gaze, having more interest in Aisha, too. Perhaps he thought Aisha as young as she looked, and wondered if he were a chance. With serrin, provided one was somewhat good looking, well presented and agreeable, one was always a chance.

"Things are well with Errollyn?" Aisha asked.

"Oh not you too," Sasha groaned. "Everyone asks when we'll marry. It seems an alarming fashion amongst serrin in Tracato."

"Most serrin who live among humans for a long time do so from a sense of fascination."

"Born of horror," Sasha added.

"Perhaps. But *talmaad* in particular are always keen to try strange human customs. It's less alarming here because unlike in some other human lands, here divorce is also common."

"Oh it's still seen as a sin," Daish countered, "I wouldn't say it's common simply because the educated serrinim and the Tol'rhen think so. Ordinary folk are a different matter."

"Well, we educated serrinim can avail of it, at least," said Aisha. "But your relationship with Errollyn intrigues, it's no surprise everyone asks questions."

"Serrin and human bed all the time in the Saalshen Bacosh!" Sasha protested. "I'll bet no one asked *your* parents so many questions."

"Yes, but my father was a farmer, and my mother had no interest in politics. The uma of Kessligh Cronenverdt, the daughter of King Torvaal of Lenayin to boot, and Saalshen's most scandalous dissenter from the serrin unanimity, make rather more of a stir."

"Especially in Tracato," Daish added. "Everyone loves a scandal."

Sasha glared at him. "Exactly how are Errollyn and I scandalous?"

"You're not," Daish said. "You just seem like you ought to be."

"And what of you, Aisha? You're more familiar with humans than most serrin, yet I don't recall you ever claiming a human lover."

"Oh no," Aisha said adamantly, "serrin women don't do that nearly as much as men. Serrin men like to see themselves as virtuous knights rescuing poor human women from their misery . . . or like Errollyn, are drawn to the thrill of the wild and dangerous otherness. Women here are treated like doormats, I don't think many serrin women consider the prospect of tying their lives to human men particularly attractive. My father is a remarkable exception."

"But that's only to say that you've not yet found a human man to suit your taste," Daish cut in. "It's not to say that serrin women are not as adventurous as men, merely that you dislike what's on offer."

"That's very true," Aisha conceded, giving the young Tracatan a curious look. "Please elaborate."

"I mean," Daish continued, "what if you were to meet a particularly handsome human man, who was kind and courteous, and who found no difficulty in treating with . . . with beautiful serrin women who . . . who did not wish to be treated as doormats?"

"An interesting proposition," said Aisha, walking a little closer. "And where do you think I might meet such a man? They are in my experience quite rare. Even your master playwright Deshirei only considers romantic scenarios where the man courts, and the woman swoons."

"Well . . ." Daish was considering how far to push it. "I may happen to know such a man, in fact. I may indeed."

"*Would* you now?" said Aisha, walking closer still. "Sasha, is it not our blessing to be in the company of a man with such fortunate acquaintances?"

"Indeed!" said Sasha, and she whispered in his ear, "Careful lad, this one's nearly twice your age and can read every book in the Tol'rhen library in its original tongue." Daish, to his credit, did not look dissuaded, only intrigued. "Daish is currently studying the principle volumes of Giraud," she added more loudly.

"Oh Giraud!" Aisha exclaimed. "I love Giraud. Tell me, what do you think of his philosophy of original value?"

It was not a long walk from the amphitheatre to the walls of the Ushal Fortress. To Sasha's surprise, the guards at the fortress's main gate were not Family men but Steel, with their shields and full armour.

"Something's wrong," said Daish, as they approached across the lower Council House courtyard. "The Steel would not guard the fortress unless there were something wrong."

"I can get us through," Aisha reassured them.

"Aisha, what's going on? Why do we need to find Alythia right now?" Sasha's eyes swept the battlements above, but saw no sign of movement.

"I can tell you more when we're inside," Aisha replied calmly, leading them across a wooden drawbridge over an abbreviated trench that reached until the defensive wall began to climb the slope. She produced a medallion from her pocket, and presented it to a Steel lieutenant who stepped forward from his line. The man examined it, then nodded, and waved them through.

Sasha considered them as she passed. They were positioned not so much to guard as to defend.

Within the gate, there was a wide courtyard, stairs ascending the defensive wall, a broad stable and various buildings beyond. Perhaps twenty soldiers were pressed to a wall, all in silence and awaiting a signal. Ahead, past this courtyard and into the next, Sasha saw more moving silently, in orderly lines.

"Aisha?" she said warningly, and aside to Daish, "Don't touch your blade," as the young man moved to do so, in alarm. "We'll not pick a fight with the Steel if we can help it."

"Rhillian moves fast," Aisha said grimly. "Sasha, best you fetch your sister, quickly."

"Or what?" Sasha asked. Aisha did not reply. "Aisha? What does Rhillian do?"

"She moves against the nobility," Daish said quietly, staring about at the soldiers' preparations. "She'll need the Steel with her, and the Steel are angry at General Zulmaher. Speed will give her surprise."

"Surprise to do what?" Sasha hissed.

"Best you fetch your sister," Aisha repeated, quietly. "Before the soldiers do."

Sasha turned and ran, Daish and Aisha close behind. She'd only ventured within the Ushal Fortress once before, a quick tour with several Nasi-Keth who had had friends inside and knew the way. But she thought she could remember.

Yells and crashes split the night, as soldiers armed with small shields for the lesser space of hallways broke through the doors, and poured within. As she ran, Sasha wondered where all the fortress guards had gone, and recalled that while some were loyal family, most were merely paid. Surely Rhillian had offered a larger sum.

Across the second courtyard, soldiers were already clustered at the entrance to the grand hall. Sasha skirted them, heading toward where memory told her there should be . . . there, the kitchens. She ran down a narrow lane and found to little surprise that the rear opened onto the outer wall, beneath which were animal pens.

Sasha hammered on the kitchen doors, but received no answer. "Friends of the nobility!" she called. "We're friends! Let us in, I seek my sister the Princess of Lenayin!" A metal plate scraped aside, an old face peering out through lantern light. "I'm Sashandra Lenayin! I have to reach my sister before the soldiers do, let me in!"

"Gods help you if there's soldiers with you . . ." the old man muttered, and there came the clank of a latch withdrawn. The doors scraped open and Sasha squeezed within.

"Thank you!" she told the old cook, seeing commotion in the kitchen beyond, men rushing to hide things, others taking up carving knives as weapons. "Which way is fastest to her quarters?"

"Back stairs," said the cook, pointing. "They're too narrow for men in armour."

Sasha ran past the confusion in the room, Daish and Aisha at her heels. She'd seen enough royal kitchens to know the back stairs where maids could carry food directly to lordly quarters above, and sure enough the far kitchen wall had stairs cut into the stone in a tight spiral. She grabbed a lantern off a bench and scampered up it.

She passed the first level and kept climbing, recalling Alythia's claim in conversation that her quarters were on the same level as Alfriedo Renine's very own. Alfriedo's would be at the top, surely. She leapt stairs by lantern light two at a time, trusting that her fitness would not see her too exhausted to fight at the top.

She reached the final, fifth storey, and darted from the hole in the wall to find herself confronted by a nobleman in a hallway, his blade unsheathed, in an expensive gold-trimmed jacket and long hair in black curls.

"My sister Alythia!" she demanded of him as he readied his blade. "Where is she?"

"You are . . . ?" he ventured, blinking as Daish and Aisha arrived at her back.

"Yes, I am! Where is she?" The nobleman pointed, and Sasha ran about a bend in the hall, and found a pair of large, ornate doors thrown open, to reveal a grand expanse of lordly quarters within. Several huge rooms seemed to occupy most of this building's level. All now were crowded with nobility and servants, brandishing weapons, shouting instruction as they bustled to retrieve jewellery and coin from boxes, thrust family artefacts inside their jackets and collect sheafs of papers. Several now clustered about a fireplace, throwing many papers onto the flames.

Sasha thrust her way through, eyes searching, and finally found Alythia in conversation with Lord Elot. Alythia stared in astonishment as Sasha came running over.

"Sasha! Goodness gracious, what are you doing here?"

"I can get you out 'Lyth! There's no soldiers on the rear stairs. I can get you out through the kitchens, but you have to come now!"

Alythia blinked at her. "Sasha, I'm not running anywhere. I shall stay here with my friends."

Lord Elot bowed his head to her. "Your Highness's loyalty and honour are as great as her beauty."

"'Lythia, this is Rhillian's doing, you understand?" Sasha pressed desperately. "She's mad at General Zulmaher . . . hells, half of Tracato is mad at General Zulmaher—"

"And half are not," came a female voice. Sasha turned, and found an elegant woman in a blue dress, with refined features and neat, blonde hair, perhaps aged forty. Following to her side was the young Alfriedo Renine. "The Council shall not stand for this outrage and neither shall Tracatans. We shall go quietly to our dungeons if we must, for we cannot fight the Steel. The outrage of the city shall free us soon enough."

"Sasha," Alythia added, "this is the Lady Tathilde Renine, mother of Lord Alfriedo."

"There's not going to be a council for a while," Daish told them. "It will be suspended for sure."

Lady Renine looked at him with mild surprise. "My dear boy, why ever so?"

"Feudalists have taken over so much of the Council, they've made it a laughing stock," Daish replied. Sasha wondered if the enthusiastic youngster actually recalled to whom he was speaking. "And the Council appointed General Zulmaher. I'd guess they've arrested the general, and now they're after his supporters."

"Well if they do suspend the Council," Lady Renine countered, "it shall be a complete outrage, the first time that such a thing has happened in two centuries in Rhodaan! The people shall never stand for it."

"Actually," said Daish, "it was suspended three times between 682 and 690, when the serrin were . . ." Sasha jabbed him in the ribs.

"'Lyth, this isn't a good idea!" she pleaded. "If Rhillian's doing this it's because she thinks feudalists are a threat to Saalshen. We saw in Petrodor how she's come to deal with threats to Saalshen!"

"Tracato is not Petrodor, Sasha," Alythia said firmly, as shouting echoed near, and clattering armour. "Tracato is altogether more civilised, and we nobility have great support in the city. The powers are balanced here; Rhillian has less authority than she supposes."

Sasha looked to Aisha, who merely stood aside and watched, venturing nothing. Had she given this warning out of friendship? Had she gone against Rhillian's wishes? Certainly she did not completely disagree with Rhillian's actions. That alone gave Sasha pause. Rhillian's judgement she did not trust, but Aisha was another matter.

Soldiers burst into the grand chambers, shouting and lining men against the walls, but with no use of force save their tongues. Several pushed the men back from the fireplace, and retrieved those papers yet unburned. A captain emerged, and was confronted by the Lady Renine, all cool, unarmoured dignity before shield, breastplate, sword and crest.

"Dear Captain," she said graciously, "I welcome you to my home. May I have your name?"

The captain looked uncertain, as though suddenly unsure of his place. Sasha flicked a glance at Alythia, and found her attention rapt, eyes wide with adoration upon the Lady Renine. Ah, thought Sasha. Now she understood, this dangerous attraction to Rhodaan's most powerful noble family.

"M'Lady," the captain said gruffly, and removed his crested helmet. A big man, dusky and square jawed, he seemed unwilling to meet the Lady's gaze. "I am Mieren, Captain Mieren."

"Of the farmer Mierens of lower Pathan?"

"Related, M'Lady."

"Oh a delight, my dear Captain. Such a distinguished family, I hear the villagers of those lands speak ever so highly of them."

The captain took a deep breath. "M'Lady, I have orders to escort all residents of the Ushal Fortress to the Justiciary."

Lady Renine inclined her head, gracefully. "On what charge, Captain?"

"Treason, M'Lady."

There were outraged shouts from several noblemen, and soldiers' hands tightened on the hilts of their swords. Lady Renine held up her hands.

"Please, my dearest friends and family," she said soothingly, "your outrage is just, yet it is indeed pointless to direct it at our noble soldiers of the Steel. These are good and honourable men, merely obeying their orders, as all good Rhodaani soldiers will. If you please, Captain, we shall accompany you in just a moment. If we first might be allowed to gather some things?"

"No possessions, M'Lady," said Captain Mieren, uncomfortably. "I'm sorry, M'Lady."

"Indeed," said Lady Renine. "Come, Alfriedo, we shall go."

"Yes, Mother," said the young lord, walking to grasp his mother's hand, as cool and dignified as she.

"Fear not, my friends," said Lady Renine to those surrounding, "this thing has merely begun. Our serrin friends appear to have forgotten exactly whose land this truly is." With a cold stare at Aisha that had none of her previous, gracious warmth. And to Sasha, her charm quickly returning, "Dearest Sashandra, Alythia is fortunate to have such a dedicated and loving sister as you. Please give my regards to your noble uman; we have had the opportunity to meet on two occasions, and I hold his wisdom in the highest regard. Please ask him to consider the Nasi-Keth's position on this matter, and that of the Tol'rhen. That position could, I feel, become the pivot upon which rests the future of Rhodaan."

She walked to leave, accompanied by others, watched by wary soldiers. Alythia walked first to Sasha and embraced her. "Thank you for coming so fast," she said, with real emotion. She pulled back to look Sasha in the face, and her eyes were shining. "I'm very touched."

Sasha shrugged, and managed a wry grin. "You're my sister."

Alythia kissed her on the cheek. "And you're mine," she said proudly. "My little sister. Be well and look after yourself, yes? I think perhaps I shall be safer in a dungeon than you on the outside."

The streets of Tracato were deserted. In places there was debris on the cobbles, human items, lost pieces of clothing, a walking staff, an empty leather bag. The crowds and rioting mobs had rushed, and gone. From somewhere distant drifted yells and chants. The soldiers at Rhillian's flanks eyed the windows and alleys warily, shields ready, waiting for archers.

Nearer the Justiciary, the human traffic increased. Before its arches were milling cityfolk, horses, Blackboots, and a guard of Steel upon the steps. Above them all loomed Maldereld's statue, her sword raised to a cloudless sky. A familiar lieutenant saw Rhillian, and broke off his conversation with a Blackboot officer from the base of Maldereld's plinth.

"Lieutenant Raine," Rhillian greeted him as he matched her stride. "What progress?"

"Many arrests," said Raine, removing his helmet as they entered the building. "Someone is making lists inside, I've not seen the latest. I think we have half the councilmen we wanted. . . ."

"Renine?"

"Yes, all of them. But the law states we cannot hold them if we do not charge them."

"My, what a sophisticated city this has become."

"Do you wish the law suspended?" Raine asked her. It took Rhillian a moment to realise he was serious. She could, it occurred to her. Captain Renard was respected, but did not have the authority of a general. Zulmaher was under arrest, and alternative generals were at the western border. In Elisse, the Steel officers had come to respect Rhillian's command greatly, and had praised the *talmaad* for making the pacification of Elisse enormously more simple. That respect had spread to the men. That, and she spoke with the authority of Saalshen, perhaps even more, in the eyes of these men, than Lesthen. Until some other general was summoned back to Tracato, she was effectively in command of this rebellion. Lesthen agonised over the moral and ethical implications of what she'd helped to do. Rhillian felt entirely calm.

"No," she replied. "The Blackboots are unhappy as things stand, and I'll not make enemies of the justiciars entirely. The Steel cannot remain in Tracato for long, and once you're gone, true power shall flow from this building."

The entry stairs led into a long, wide hall, filled with activity. Justiciars in black cloaks argued, clerks hurried clutching immense rolls of parchment, Blackboots escorted hands-tied prisoners while other cityfolk protested and pleaded beneath the wary eye of local guards. Rhillian threaded her way through, with Lieutenant Raine as an escort.

She did not continue down to the rows of courts, but turned left instead, and was halfway down an adjoining hall when a page brought an old man out from a doorway ahead. Rhillian stopped before him, and bowed.

"Justice Sinidane," she said with respect. "I regret I have not had the opportunity to call on you since my return from the war. You look well."

Sinidane snorted. "One of the most irritating things about growing old," he replied, "is that every acquaintance must remark to my face their mounting surprise that I'm not yet dead. What have you gone and done now, silly girl?"

Sinidane had better than eighty years, yet looked well enough for that. He walked tall and unaided, though slowly, and spoke with an eccentricity that could seem to the unacquainted like absentmindedness. There were some Rhodaanis who opined that Sinidane, rather than Premier Chiron, was the true power in Tracato. As chief justiciar, his world was the law, and even premiers, High Table seats and councilmen must bow to the law. If only, Rhillian thought sadly, Maldereld had been more successful in removing the temples from the equation entirely. Sinidane's black robes bore the emblazoned silver of a great, Verenthane star. Rhodaani justice came from the gods, or else no citizen would respect it as true. And that, frustratingly, brought the priesthood into the equation.

"If you will accompany me downstairs, I believe I can demonstrate to you exactly what I've been doing, Justice Sinidane," Rhillian replied.

"Stairs, you say? Do I look like a sprightly young man to you?"

He followed her anyway, his page at his elbow, down some dark, stone steps, then, and into the bowels of the Justiciary dungeons.

A lantern hung outside Lady Tathilde Renine's cell, yet she blinked at the new light beyond its bars. She sat alone on a small stool . . . a lady of her breeding would never deign to sit on the stone floor, Rhillian judged. The lady's eyes narrowed in suspicion to see Rhillian, then widened as the Chief Justiciar shuffled into view, and leaned a steadying hand upon the bars.

"Your Justice," said Lady Renine. "You've come. I had feared this insurrection had claimed you too."

"The law is intact," Sinidane replied. "Merely somewhat taken aback."

Lady Renine came smoothly to her feet. "Your Justice, I would like to protest this appalling treatment, as it is clearly beneath a lady of my station.

Further, the laws of your beloved Justiciary clearly state that any so detained must be formally charged by an officer of Rhodaan, *not* on the whim or imperial writ of Saalshen." This last with a sharp glare at Rhillian.

"Captains of the Steel do qualify, Lady Renine," Sinidane said mildly.

"The Steel swore an oath before the gods to uphold the office of the Council, not to arrest them!" said Lady Renine. "I have seen many dear family friends and elected councilmen marched past these bars, men the Steel swore to serve and protect with their lives."

"You seem to confuse the nobility with the Council, Lady Renine," Rhillian observed. "They are not the same thing, whatever the nobility's attempts to purchase so many Council seats that it may appear so."

"I'll not stand here and be dictated to on matters of Rhodaani governance by a serrin! Just the other day, I was lunching with the serrin ambassador Lesthen, and he assured me that the days of Saalshen's interference in the affairs of Rhodaan were over. And now we see it happening all over again."

"Again?" Rhillian asked. "To my memory, we've never done this *before*. Unless you mean Maldereld. Do you mean Maldereld, Lady Renine?"

Lady Renine's jaw trembled. Sinidane watched her. It was a curious question for the leader of Rhodaan's feudalists to be asked, before such a man as Sinidane. Feudalists who decried the loss of old human ways, yet professed not to hate the new Council, the new Justiciary, the new laws, the divisions of human power, that had made Rhodaan everything that it was today. To regret the coming of Maldereld would be to regret all those things. To regret, indeed, that a man like Sinidane, practising the things he practised, should even exist.

"I wish to see my son," Lady Renine replied, her voice low and cold.

"He is in the Mahl'rhen," said Rhillian. "We do not lock up children, Lady Renine. He is well fed and looked after."

"Bring him to me!" Lady Renine shouted. Rhillian did not blink, the lady's furious stare struggled to hold her own, then flicked away.

"We have your correspondence with the Larosans," Rhillian continued. "The letters. The offers of conciliation, of marriage and alliance."

"Forgeries," said Lady Renine, recovering some of her imperious calm. "I was warned the serrin would try something like this. Do not believe them, Justice Sinidane, they are sly and full of tricks."

"I can prove otherwise. You would have offered the Larosans alliance, would you not? They already wed Sofy Lenayin. You would perhaps wed Alythia Lenayin to one of your allied nobles . . . perhaps even to your son Alfriedo? Or perhaps one of your new allies in Elisse? King Torvaal of Lenayin's honour would not then allow him to attack Rhodaan, but only if you could demonstrate true rulership over Rhodaan. To gain it, you could offer the people of Rhodaan peace, against the armies that threaten them.

"But that peace would come with terms, would it not? The Larosans have invoked a holy war to free Bacosh lands of ungodly serrin. If the Larosans cannot demonstrate Rhodaan to be free of serrin, then they cannot claim victory, and the priesthood that pays for much of their war shall be displeased. What would be your intent then, Lady Renine? To rouse a pogrom against all serrin and part-serrin in Rhodaan? To cleanse us from this place?"

"You speak in paranoid riddles!" Lady Renine laughed contemptuously. "We could not do such a thing if we tried. The Steel would not allow it, nor the Nasi-Keth. Saalshen has so many powerful friends in Rhodaan, yet the serrin claim fear of persecution to justify this new tyranny!"

"Or would you seek to use the support for the nobility that does exist within the Steel," Rhillian continued, "to undermine them? Already we have reports of desertions from amongst their ranks, and protests from some of General Zulmaher's friends at his arrest. Would you undermine them to the extent that you should encourage them to lose? If the Army of Larosa and their allies should march into Tracato and hand the Lordship of Rhodaan to young Alfriedo, that would solve all of your problems at once, would it not?"

"You fool," Lady Renine replied, "with your actions here, you make that all the more likely. *You* undermine the Steel, not us. Its soldiers desert because of *your* actions, not mine. You would leave us defenceless before the greatest army humanity has ever seen, and now you seek to lay the blame at my feet. Justice Sinidane, you cannot take these outrageous slurs seriously."

"I assure you, Lady Renine," said the old man, "I shall take no outrageous slurs seriously, should they be proven to be so. But quantified, proven accusations, I should take very seriously indeed. We shall see, in due course, which these are."

Sinidane warned Rhillian later, as they made their way slowly up the steps from the dungeon, "Do not think that you have convinced me of the woman's guilt, Lady Rhillian." The old man's grip was firm upon her offered arm, and she climbed slowly. "Nor that of her companions. I do agree to a likelihood, and in all my years I have never known serrin to produce false evidence, but the exact truth of such matters lies only in the laps of the gods. We mortals have only the law, and the law requires proof."

"If such exists, I shall present it to you."

"Furthermore, I do not like to see the Council suspended," said the old man. "The gods shall think it ill. I would ask that you allow it to sit in session as soon as possible."

"How is that possible, with half its members either arrested or under suspicion?"

"Lady Rhillian, I care not for your difficulties. This city's institutions have been all that holds us above the barbarian fray for two centuries now. I tell you, I will not see them suspended indefinitely. Instruct one of your people to look into finding replacements for those arrested, I will investigate the legality at this end. You may consider that my order."

"As you say," Rhillian agreed. She was not prepared to challenge the man's authority. They reached the top of the stairs, and Sinidane stopped, turning to face her.

"Is it you who commands?" he asked her, searching her face.

"By default, it appears so," Rhillian said carefully. "Until General Lucia is returned from the border. It was not of my choosing, but the captains insisted."

Sinidane sighed, and patted her arm. "I love this city," he conceded to her. "I love this land of Rhodaan, and Enora. Ilduur too, in my weaker moments."

"I too," said Rhillian. "I hope to save them from capitulation to the darkest forces humanity has known."

"I do not mean love in some woolly headed parochial sense, please understand. I mean that I love them for what they are. For the hope they represent, for all humanity. In fact, parochialism is my enemy. I fight it daily, and today, I see it running loose in my city. Beware the parochials, Lady Rhillian, for they believe in the conceit that Rhodaan's greatness stems purely from the greatness of the Rhodaani character. And I am well aware that it does not.

"It stems from institutions, such as my own. Institutions that work in *opposition* to the native Rhodaani character. To the native human character, if you will. People are cruel, Lady Rhillian. Humans, anyhow. We fight and we bicker, and if not for the firm hand of a higher authority, we would do each other such harm as could not be imagined by the cool minds of serrin. Beware what you have unleashed, dear girl. Do not trust it. I am glad, in truth, to see a serrin leading such an effort, however wary of the effort itself I may be. But you should never, ever trust the native instincts of the power-lusting mobs beneath you."

Rhillian nodded. "I understand."

"Do you?" Sinidane looked pained. "Sometimes I wonder if serrin truly do understand what they have done, here in the so-called Saalshen Bacosh. When Maldereld came to us, and brought with her the enlightenment of thousands of years of serrin wisdom, we were but savages, in truth. We believed in lies, we had eyes but could not see, we had minds but could not think, we murdered on a whim and felt naught for the consequences. Such savages threaten us today, from across the Steel border, and we look across that border and we are pleased to be so much more enlightened than them.

"But in truth, I do not think we are. This . . . this civilisation, that the serrin have helped us to construct, and the thinking that attends it . . . this is not the natural state of humankind. Or not, at least, from where we have just recently come. Left to our own devices, perhaps we could have achieved this sophistication in . . . oh, I would guess a thousand years?" Sinidane's fingers dug into her arm, with an almost painful grip from one so old. "Do you see what serrin have done here? You have accelerated us. You have taken a tribe of barbarians and dressed us up in pretty clothes, and taught us table manners and polite behaviour. And we are such good actors that when it works, it seems wonderful. Yet underneath, the barbarian still lurks . . . never doubt it! In some ways we have truly changed, yet in our hearts, we are not so advanced as serrin would like to have made us. We are children in adults' clothing, grown up before our time."

Rhillian took the old man's hand, gently. "I understand. This was our experiment, in human lands. But we have achieved it together, human and serrin, and now we must defend it together. Have no fear of my naivety, Chief Justiciar. I have seen Petrodor, and the War of the King. I trust no one." She smiled. "Not even you."

Sinidane smiled back, and patted her hand with a sigh. "Well enough. But, dear girl, know this. I would give my life for Saalshen. Coming from one so near the grave as I, that is perhaps no great offer, yet even so, I would throw myself upon the spears of Saalshen's enemies should it serve the purposes of Saalshen's survival. Everything that is good about Rhodaan, you have given us. You are humanity's greatest hope, and I despair that so many are ungrateful. I fear that we do not deserve you."

Rhillian recalled Master Deani, of Palopy House in Petrodor. He had said to her much the same, in those final, desperate moments of siege and fire. Palopy was now a ruin, and Deani was dead, with so many others. Only she and Kiel had survived. She would not see such a fate befall Sinidane and his beloved Justiciary. She understood human power so much better now, for the lessons she'd learned in Petrodor.

Rhillian kissed the old man's hand. "I am your servant, Chief Justiciar. Never doubt it."

She escorted Sinidane out to the Justiciary grand hall once more. His page walked with him back to chambers, while Rhillian cornered Lieutenant Raine.

"I need evidence of the feudalists' plot," she told him in a low voice. "The Chief Justice is well disposed to us in that he is ill disposed toward the feudalists, but he is a man of principle and will not deviate from the law. We need proof."

Raine ran a hand through his wavy blond hair. In the war in Elisse, he had proven to be one of the Steel's best. "I have all available men on the task, yet our powers to gather evidence are limited. I cannot trust the Blackboots, half are paid men of the feudalists, and the other half are scared of those who are. My men are soldiers, good at killing the enemy and little more. What you ask is Blackboot work, law and evidence. It may be beyond them."

"What of the city guard?"

"Hired soldiers, ordinary folk with ordinary values, neither good nor bad. Most are country folk though, so little sympathy for the feudalists there."

Rhillian nodded. "Use them more, to free up the Steel. Pay them more, if necessary. Find those sympathetic to our cause to help gather evidence. Make a list of the most troublesome Blackboots."

"I'd suggest we expand that list to red-coats and administrators, too. Feudalist money has bought powerful friends all through Tracato. I'd suggest a purge."

Rhillian did not like the way that sounded. And yet, she recalled what she'd only now insisted to Sinidane, of the lessons she'd learned in Petrodor, and the hardening of her heart. "Yes," she agreed. "Find me names first, and we'll move from there."

"What of the priesthood?"

"What of them?"

"Who do you think has been paying for all their holy trinkets and Saint Ciala's Day festivities?"

"Noble gold. I'm not at all certain I can purge the priesthood, Lieutenant. But some nasty gossip could work as well, I'm certainly not above blackmail."

"No shortage of that," said Raine, with an evil smile. "I used to be an altar boy."

"I'm sure you were charming. I'll also want to meet Kessligh Cronenverdt at the earliest." That nearly stuck in her throat, but she plunged on regardless. "I imagine he'll be speaking for the Tol'rhen, in time of crisis, and the Nasi-Keth will be looking to him on military matters."

"I would," Raine admitted. "But I doubt he'll speak for all the Tol'rhen Ulenshaals. Keeping that lot united is like herding cats."

"Well I'm quite sure I can't purge the Tol'rhen," Rhillian said firmly. "The priesthood at least can be embarrassed, but Ulenshaals have no shame. And I cannot make enemies of the Nasi-Keth. If we lose them, we lose the city."

"Agreed," said the lieutenant. He ticked off his fingers. "Justiciars, administrators, city guard, Blackboots, priesthood, Nasi-Keth . . . who did we miss?"

From back up the hall, there were shouts and cries. Both turned to look, and saw a gathering crowd of cityfolk, some waving colourful banners.

"The factions," Rhillian answered Raine's question. "Go to your duties, Lieutenant, I'll deal with these."

She walked up the hall to where the intruders were causing the commotion. Justiciary guards stood warily close, hand to their swords. *Civid Sein,* Rhillian read the Rhodaani scrawl upon their blue banners . . . such a love of banners through the Rhodaani factions, a colour for every ideology. And there at their front was an ageing, fat Ulenshaal in black robes, in animated discussion with a justiciar.

"Ulenshaal," said Rhillian. "Are you with these?" With a short nod to the rough-hewn men behind him. They looked too rustic for cityfolk, in truth. Farmers and village people, perhaps. Some held hoes or spades that could surely double as weapons.

"I am," said the man in a loud, deep voice. "I am Ulenshaal Sevarien. These members of the *Civid Sein* have come to appeal for justice to the traitors who would sell out Rhodaan to the beasts who threaten our borders!"

"I intend to see justice, Ulenshaal," Rhillian replied. "Be assured of it. In the meantime, you can demonstrate outside, the people of this institution are busy."

"It is well known that the institutions of Tracato are crawling with the feudalists' paid men," Sevarien bellowed. "As a serrin who does not suffer such impulses of greed, you should know the corrupting influence of wealth on men's morality and reason. We demand a purge of feudalists from the Justiciary and other institutions. We shall not leave until our demands are heard!"

Rhillian knew the *Civid Sein* well enough. They were the poor folk of the countryside, distrusting of cityfolk, of wealth, power and nobility. Many idolised neighbouring Enora, and hoped to implement a similar purge of nobility as Enora had done two hundred years before. As always, amidst humanity, there was no commonality. Even now, despite her many years' experience with humans, she had to remind herself of it. Where serrin shared the *vel'ennar*, humans felt nothing to bind one to the other, save that which they created in their religion and ideology. And could kill each other on a whim, and feel only justification.

"Your demands have been heard," Rhillian said sharply. "I hear them, we all hear them. Now leave, before I have you rounded up and thrown in the dungeons."

Ulenshaal Sevarien drew himself up, bristling. "And how do you propose to do that? We are the *people*! Should you arrest us all, a hundred times our number shall be on your doorstep by this evening!" Angry, defiant shouts echoed him. Rhillian was aware of justiciary guards closing on her flanks, protectively.

"You listen to me," she said icily to the big Ulenshaal. Beneath that stare, he paled, just a little. "The feudalists have tried to take control in Tracato, and for that, they shall pay. Now you tell me that *you* would take control in Tracato, through demands and threats of riot. For that, you shall pay. Now tell me again, do you threaten my authority?"

Somewhere behind her, Lieutenant Raine must have given a signal, for the blades of the justiciary guard came out all at once.

Ulenshaal Sevarien blinked at her. "You wouldn't dare!" he exclaimed. About the Justiciary hall, all movement, all conversation had stopped. From the entrance, more Steel *dharmi* came running.

"The voice of the *people* will be heard," Rhillian assured him. "You may make an application through the appropriate channels. The *arms* of the people, however, shall be mute. I have the Steel. Do not try me, or I shall crush you."

"Sevarien!" yelled a new voice, female and strangely familiar. Rhillian looked, and saw a Nasi-Keth girl, short haired in pants and jacket, walking close. Rhillian stared. "Sevarien, best you leave."

"Sashandra," Sevarien retorted, "you don't understand the gravity . . . !"

"Rhillian will deal with the feudalists!" came the angry reply. "Don't pick fights with your friends."

Sevarien took a deep breath and signalled for his party to withdraw. He may have bowed, or spoken something more, but Rhillian did not notice. She had eyes only for Sashandra. Aisha was with her, and a pair of Nasi-Keth lads Rhillian did not know.

"So," said Sashandra, as the *Civid Sein* departed. Her eyes flicked to register the guards' swords being sheathed, then refocused on Rhillian. They were dark, hard and beautiful. "You command Tracato now?"

"For the moment," said Rhillian. She recalled Halrhen, and Triana, dead upon the stern of their ship on Petrodor harbour, cut down by Sasha's blade. Recalled telling Arendele of Triana's death, upon coming to Tracato. Recalled holding him while he sobbed, and imagining crossing blades once more with the traitor whom she'd once been so foolish as to consider a friend. But humans made poor friends, she'd learned. Kiel had always insisted so—she hadn't believed him in Petrodor, for softheartedness, for wishful thinking, for misguided philosophies of coexistence between human and serrin. That night, on the ship in Petrodor harbour, had been the final stone on the tomb of her compassion, for this one in particular. "What brings you?"

"I'm here to see my sister."

"She plots with feudalists," said Rhillian, icily. "What of you?"

There was even less motion among those surrounding now than before.

The very air seemed deadly, frozen with hostility. Svaalverd warrior that she was, Rhillian could read posture like a book. Before her stood one of the very best, feet barely a half-breadth from the opening *tana* stance, hands free, muscles tense with expectation. One twitch could see a blade in her hand. Another could kill any within reach. Her own stance, Rhillian realised, was barely different.

"She probably does plot with feudalists," Sasha admitted, her voice hard. "She's a naïve fool with no clue how they would use her, despite my warnings. But I won't let you hurt my sister."

"You will submit to the law," said Rhillian. "The law is not in my hands."

"But it will be," said Sashandra, with certainty. "Just as in Petrodor, when the diversity is removed, there's only one faction left in power. Be it yours, or be it someone else's, the result is the same."

"The law resides in this building," Rhillian replied. "I defend it, as surely the feudalists would not, should they have attained the power they were plotting. I will submit to it, and you shall, and your sister shall, or there is nothing here to defend."

"*Anyone* but you," Sasha snapped, "and I might believe them. You're serrin, and this game you don't understand! How many cities will it take, Rhillian?"

Rhillian recalled the flames. Recalled the howling mobs, her friends hacked to pieces before her eyes. It wasn't her fault. It *couldn't* have been. "It was your game too. You're as responsible as I."

"You *gave* Maerler the Shereldin Star! You *wanted* the slaughter that followed! You killed *thousands*, with that one bloody act!"

"They threatened, Saalshen. They were weakened."

"Aye, you weakened them so much Patachi Steiner declared himself king, and now marches to war against us! With leadership like that, you don't need enemies, you'll be the end of the serrinim all by yourself!"

Rhillian could have killed her, right there. She struggled for breath, and fought to keep her hands from trembling. Sashandra must have seen the fury in her eyes, but unlike most, she did not flinch. Rhillian knew she could not draw, not against this one. As formidable as she was herself, against Sashandra, no fight was evenly matched.

"What proof do you have of Lady Renine's treason?" Sasha pressed. "It seems ambitious even for her."

"Go and ask Errollyn," Rhillian said. "He gave me the evidence. This is all his doing."

Sasha stared at her. And blinked. "Errollyn?"

Rhillian was surprised. Sasha hadn't known? "Yes, Errollyn. It's good to see that at least one of you has some idea of the nature of your new friends."

She stalked off, gesturing Lieutenant Raine to follow. Sasha stood in disbelief and watched them go.

Nine

SCHWEET, SPOKE YASMYN'S DARAK AGAINST A WHETSTONE. *Schweet*, in long strokes above the clatter of carriage wheels on pavings.

Sherdaine had walls. Sofy stared out the window of her carriage, and marvelled at the sight of them, sheer and gleaming grey in the bright, afternoon sunshine. It was said that in all the Bacosh wars, Sherdaine had only been sacked twice, and both of those a time long before the construction of these latest walls. The battlements stretched a long way, enclosing what was surely the largest city Sofy had ever seen.

The Army of Lenayin's vanguard rode about and before the carriage, senior lords from each province moved to the head of the column. They clattered across a small bridge, and here across the fields before Sherdaine's walls, Sofy could see an army encamped—white tents and drifting smoke, as far as the eye could see. Her heart nearly stopped, there were so many. The army of the united, "free Bacosh," the provinces of Algrasse, Tournea, Larosa, Meraine and Rakani, all together under the banner of the Regent Arosh of Larosa.

Riding alongside, Damon rapped the carriage door with an armoured fist. "Get your head back in. It won't do for the bride to ride into Sherdaine like a dog on a farmcart."

Sofy ignored him, wishing she could have ridden at her father's side in the vanguard. Koenyg had not even bothered to reply when she'd wistfully suggested it, he merely shook his head in disbelief and continued his conversation with someone else. Damon was now banished from the vanguard's head, appointed by Koenyg to be his sister's protector, since, Koenyg said acidly, he seemed so determined to kill any who offended her honour. Algrassian, and lately Larosan nobility, had shown a degree of respectful caution in their nightly feasts previously unseen, particularly toward Damon. Sofy thought their behaviour vastly improved since Lord Elen's slaying, and Yasmyn agreed. And Damon, truth be told, did not appear to resent his new duty as Koenyg might have hoped.

Sofy could now see a huge entourage awaiting across the road ahead. Knights, armoured head to toe, rowed lances pointing skyward and flying the coloured profusion of feudal heraldry. They parted as the vanguard arrived, and joined in the column's progress, flanking the road in great lines.

Damon kicked the carriage door. "Sofy, I mean it!"

She scowled at him and flung herself back on her seat. "They can't see sideways out of those helmets," she said, "I don't know what he's worried about."

On the seat opposite, Jeleny and Rhyana, two of Sofy's prettiest hand-maidens, sat in their finest, hair done up in ringlets laced with gold cord. Both looked apprehensively at Yasmyn, who continued to hone the edge of her darak.

"Oh Yasmyn," said Jeleny at last, "must you?"

"In Isfayen," said Yasmyn, "a bridesmaid must never be without two things—a sharp blade and clean undergarments."

"It does look very sharp already, Yasmyn," Sofy observed. "Though I cannot speak for your undergarments."

Yasmyn grinned, and sheathed the darak on the belt she wore beneath her blue waist sash. "We ride with many lobsters today," she said, peering out the window at the knights. "I wonder do they cook, when the sun is hot?"

Sofy found herself thinking of Jaryd. She'd been trying not to, for most of the ride. Occasionally, it was true, she'd ridden past the midportion of Val-hanan's part in the column, hoping to catch a glimpse, while at the same time pretending that it was merely coincidence that she should happen to be riding there.

It had been a mistake. If she were a truly devout Verenthane, surely she would fear for her soul . . . yet that was just the talk of priests, whose words of late she'd trusted less and less. Serrin did not believe such things, nor did Nasi-Keth . . . nor, in fact, most of the Lenay countryside, where few lads or ladies indeed were virgins on their wedding days, and the villagers loved nothing more than a gossip of the latest lascivious tales. Only Verenthane princesses were held to such standards, and oh how she'd grown to distrust the reasons for *that*. It was not about religion, she was quite sure. Sasha had always told her as much—the priests and the lords, she'd said, would use such beliefs to serve the ends of power. The righteousness of the faith itself was always a secondary consideration in such matters.

Perhaps her brother Wylfred was right, Sofy thought. Perhaps she had been corrupted by Sasha's influence over the years. Sofy knew there had been such hopes for her, the darling youngest princess, the apple of her father's eye. But now her father was marrying her off to a strange man for the cause of a foreign war she had no interest in fighting. What she'd done with Jaryd, that half year before on the return road from Algery, had felt good. And it had been *her* mistake, if mistake it had been. Something of her very own, that no one could now take from her. Soon, there would be few enough of those.

But it bothered her, now, that she had not made more of an effort to see him. It would have been impossible, of course, with so many eyes upon them, but that did not stop her from fretting. Did he think of her? It was foolish to hope so, the number of women bedded by Jaryd Nyvar was more worthy of a serrin than a Verenthane noble. And he was most certainly not of a type with her, with a head full of swords and horses, and rarely a care for the passions of Sofy's life—the arts, music, tongues and civil conversation. No, she thought—she was not bound for the hells, but it had been a mistake all the same. He was not for her, and was a landless no-name now, an impossible match for a princess. If the Larosans insisted on examining her virginity before marriage, well, she rode horses regularly and knew well enough (with more thanks to Sasha) that the activity rendered such examinations unreliable. A half year had passed, she was not with child, and none of it was any concern to her now—she was merely moping before her impending wedding, and wondering what might have been, at another time, in another life.

Yet still she thought of him, and remembered his smile.

Beyond the clustered horsemen of the vanguard, Sofy could see grand armies assembling to either side of the road. More feudal banners, rows and rows of horsemen, all the way to the gates of Sherdaine. Sofy could not tear her eyes away, a tightness growing in her throat. So many men. Such a powerful army. And all for her. The tightness in her throat was her old life dying. That carefree girl lay somewhere behind, in the distant hills of Lenayin. Sofy wished for her return, with all her heart, but that girl had no place here. That girl would be scared of this place. The Princess Sofy Lenayin could not afford to be scared with so much at stake.

Before her, the city gates opened wide, yawning black, beneath the portcullis's rows of metal teeth. Sofy felt her heart accelerate and her breath grew short. Yasmyn clasped her hand.

"Be not afraid," she murmured, "for all things shall end. Fear not the end, your friend and mine."

Tullamayne, she quoted. Sofy recalled the other places she'd heard Tullamayne recited, most recently upon battlefields, at great funerals for the many fallen, upon the lips of warriors gasping their final breath. She exhaled a deep breath and felt all fear leave her, as like the spirit leaving a dying man. She was Lenay, and this fate was not hers alone, but borne upon the shoulders of countless martyred generations. She squeezed Yasmyn's hand, as the carriage rattled on, and allowed the darkness to swallow her.

There was silver mist across the grassy fields as tens of thousands of men stirred in the morning. Jaryd finished his exercises, a mug of tea in his hand, steaming from the campfire. Baerlyn contingent, plus men of several neighbouring Valhanan villages, had claimed for a camp the land about a small farmhouse, including a track, some recently ploughed fields, and a small stream.

Lenay men greeted Jaryd as he walked to the paddock fence to see to the commotion there. He joined the men leaning on the fence and considered the cause of their amusement. Within the paddock, men were chasing an extremely large, ill-tempered bull. Or rather, the bull was chasing them. A warrior rolled aside as it charged, while two more jumped the fence, to catcalls and roars of laughter from the onlookers. The bull circled back on the man who had rolled—a magnificent animal, Jaryd thought, with huge, rippling shoulders and deadly horns, now lowered.

Jaryd's laughter was cut short at a sudden commotion to his side, and he spun to find that Gareth, a Baerlyn man, had grabbed another man from behind and had a knife to his throat.

"I don't recognise this one!" Gareth said suspiciously, peering at his captive's face. "He was approaching you to the rear, Jaryd, and I don't see him for no Valhanan man!"

The man held his hands clear. "I come with summons from Prince Damon," he said. "He requests the company of Jaryd Nyvar."

"I'm sorry about that," Jaryd told the man, riding on the spare mount that had been brought. "The Tyree and Valhanan nobility all want me dead, to say nothing of the northerners. My friends keep an eye out for me."

Prince Damon's man nodded. "There is danger in crowds. Your friends are wise." They rode along a road between fields crowded with the greatest encampment of soldiers Jaryd had ever seen. The ground before the walls of Sherdaine was a solid mass of tents, men and campfires. The air seethed with conversation, shouts, the clash of weapons practice, the whinny of horses and the rattle of armour. Cooking fires burned, and a mist of smoke smelled of equal parts bacon, green wood, and manure.

These were men of Larosa, Jaryd knew. Men-at-arms, for the most part—what Lenays would call militia, villagers and peasants sworn to regional lords, and pressed into service whatever their will. These men were poor, but they were gods-fearing Verenthanes, and did not relish the great numbers of pagan barbarians brought into their midst . . . though Jaryd thought they'd have been no happier if the Lenays had only brought Verenthane soldiers. Worse, the young Larosan Prince Balthaar was to be wed to the barbarians' princess.

Well, Jaryd thought sourly as he rode toward the gates, there were some Lenays none too impressed with the marriage either.

Prince Damon's man presented the guards at the gates with a Verenthane star from about his neck, which the guards examined, then returned with a wave through. Beneath the portcullis, and onto rattling paved roads, and the commotion of city life on a scale Jaryd had never seen before. There was a great courtyard to one side, fronted by a grand temple, all in the same pale stone as made for Sherdaine's walls. It seemed there was a market in progress in the courtyard, for crowded stalls did brisk business, and the cries of sellers competed with the bellows of a town crier for attention. The temple was spectacular, with soaring spires and coloured glass windows.

Past the courtyard, they rode between buildings of stone foundation, with wood-beamed walls and small, multipaned windows. The crowds were oppressive, housewives carrying food from the market, tradesmen hauling loads on donkeys, busy cityfolk of every description going about their daily lives, and clogging up the streets. Soldiers too, though they seemed more well dressed than most, and none were Lenay. Again, more stares at the two Lenays ahorse. Jaryd did not resist the impulse to ride straight and proud, and stare down at such men with disdain.

Damon's man led Jaryd around so many corners, and down enough crowded lanes that Jaryd soon found himself utterly lost, and without clear sight of Sherdaine's walls or towers. Eventually they stopped before a wide wooden gate, and the man rapped on a metal panel that slid aside. A brief conversation, then the gates were opened and they dismounted to lead both horses into a private courtyard surrounded by the facing windows of a wealthy residence. Here, it was peaceful.

Jaryd left the horse in the care of a servant and followed his guide beneath a small archway and into a second, more intimate courtyard. Here he found Lenays, nobility all to look at them, seated to catch the sun though shaded by the courtyard's central tree, eating good food and wine. None paid the new arrival particular mind, laughing and conversing with animation as Jaryd followed his guide to an open door. Within, he found Prince Damon, sitting with his back to an open window, reading.

"Ah," said Damon, looking up with a smile, and got up to embrace Jaryd. Jaryd was surprised, but returned it gladly. Damon had saved his life, in the hallways of Baen-Tar Palace, when the Tyree nobles had been about to kill him where he'd fallen. They had ridden together to northern Taneryn with Damon's sister Sashandra and Kessligh Cronenverdt, and Jaryd knew the prince to be no friend of his own enemies. He wondered what had inspired this invitation.

"You look well," Damon told him, seeming genuinely pleased at that. "And beringed." Touching the several rings in Jaryd's ear, with some amusement. "When your hair grows a little longer, you'll be a true Goeren-yai."

"You look well too," said Jaryd, not entirely truthfully. Damon looked well in that he seemed older than in Jaryd's memory, and there was a look to his lean face that was more manly than Jaryd recalled. Yet much of that new age was worry.

"We grow older," he admitted. "Koenyg assured me that it would happen, and I did not believe him. Please, sit."

Jaryd drew up a chair. The quarters seemed pleasant, far from princely, but they were comfortable.

"Why are you not at the palace?" Jaryd asked.

"Actually it's not a palace, just a castle." Damon shrugged. "Sofy prepares. I'm little use to her, she accuses me of brooding." His face fell, revealing a deep, troubled sobriety. "I'd thought as much beforehand. I sent men ahead to find me separate quarters. Being away from courtly intrigues can have its advantages, and Koenyg has tasked me with things that require a staff of my own."

"That man," Jaryd asked, gesturing to the door his guide had departed through. "Who was he?"

"Best you don't ask," said Damon. "He needs to go places and talk to people. If he is no one, that becomes easier." Jaryd frowned. "One of Koenyg's tasks was to help prepare the army for battle. He is concerned that for all our new equipment of shields and armour, our tactics vary from region to region, even from town to town. He warns that we need to introduce some uniformity to our battle plans, and I agree. The nobility are not such a problem, since most of them are cavalry, and cavalry tactics are more or less similar throughout Lenayin. It's the Goeren-yai and the villagers, as always, who make the problems."

Jaryd nodded. "I've been working with men of eastern Valhanan to improve our shieldwork and formations. I've tracked down any number of Bacosh men with experience of fighting the Steel. I think we've made improvements, but some men insist they don't see the point. Luckily the headmen of Baerlyn have influence with the other villages, so they don't argue too much, but not all regions are so lucky."

"I know," said Damon. "I need good men from amongst the Goeren-yai, men who know different styles of warfare. I need men I can trust, Jaryd, and who will be respected by those beneath them. I'd like you to be one of them."

Jaryd looked at him for a long moment. It was not a surprise, on the commonsense level of preparing for war. He was certainly qualified, and Damon knew that he was honest and loyal. But for politics . . .

"Have you any idea of the number of people who'd like me dead?" Jaryd asked the prince.

"A mark of honour, in this company," Damon said drily. Jaryd heard bitterness in his tone. "Northern fanatics, limp-wristed Tyree and Valhanan nobility, I've no care for them. Have you?"

Jaryd blinked, trying to think. Politics was not his strong suit. He had only recently come to learn, somewhat painfully, that direct assault was not always the best solution to his problems. Prince Damon challenged him to do what came naturally, expecting him to follow his instincts. It would be *smart* of the Dunce of Tyree, however, to consider his options first.

"Not *fear* of them, no," Jaryd said carefully. "But those men have great influence with Prince Koenyg, which shall surely be trouble for you."

Damon frowned. "I'm a prince of Lenayin," he replied, pointedly. "I make my own decisions. Your rank shall be captain. Militia captain, it's true, but it's about time we formalised the militia ranks, if only for sake of convenience."

"Are you fighting with him?"

"With who?"

"Your brother. Koenyg."

Damon stared at him. There was a darkness in his gaze. A power that Jaryd could not recall having been there before.

"Surely you hear rumours," Damon said then, gazing away, across the room.

"Highness, I've *walked* here from Lenayin," Jaryd replied, with sarcasm. "Blisters are my friends, I carry the tackle of a common soldier, and I've been as far from courtly rumours as is possible within this army."

"I have no issue with my brother. I have an issue with this war, Jaryd. I lack no courage for a fight, but look around you. Do you see Lenay interests here?"

Jaryd nodded, and gave a harsh laugh. "The people are truly friendly!" he quipped.

Damon leaned forward in his chair. "I am a Verenthane, Jaryd, but this faith that we serve is not something I recognise." His face was intent, his voice harsh. "They fear us, and loathe us, these people. It galls them that their failures against the Saalshen Bacosh have brought them to this—an allegiance with highland barbarians, and by *marriage* no less! One of those barbarians shall be their queen, once the regent dies. Father and Koenyg may see the greatness of allegiance to the Verenthane powers, but all I see is our own Lenay fanatics hoping to use such allegiance to spread the faith in Lenayin and convert all pagans. To say nothing of your old friends the lords, with dreams of a feudal Lenayin. We are all being fairly buggered for another's benefit, and I like it not."

Suddenly, Jaryd thought he understood. The seclusion of these quarters in Sherdaine. Armed men in the courtyard. A gathering of friendly supporters.

"Do you feel yourself threatened?" he asked.

"I do not choose this out of cowardice," Damon said warningly, and Jaryd held up a hand, shaking his head. Damon seemed placated. He smacked his leg in profound frustration. "Damn him! Koenyg thinks me a worrier, but I fear for my neck every night I sleep in castle quarters without my personal guard from the road. There are many discontents, Jaryd, and if something happened to me, they would have no one to speak for them."

Jaryd nodded slowly but he had no idea what to say.

"I would not choose to abandon Sofy so close to her wedding, but . . ." Damon grimaced, and glanced over his shoulder at the courtyard beyond the window. "This army may split, Jaryd, truly I fear it. Oh, the provinces are spoiling for a fight at the moment: Lenayin is a land of warriors and has never fought a united battle as a kingdom . . . hot-headed men think it's about damn time, and think nothing for the rightness of it. But when the Goeren-yai are tired of being used as fodder for foreign Verenthanes who care not a jot for them, and see all the rewards heaped upon northern fanatics who hate them worse than those we fight . . ."

He shook his head, despairingly. "I chided Sasha, once, for thinking to champion the cause of the Goeren-yai. Now I find myself realising as she did, that if we lose the Goeren-yai, we lose Lenayin."

"Ever think," said Jaryd, "that if we lost the nobility, we'd lose nothing at all?" Damon was silent. "Lenayin needs nobility like a bull needs tits."

"Now *you* sound like Sasha," Damon muttered. He gave Jaryd a dark look. "My sister. Did you fuck her?"

Jaryd coughed and managed, somewhat suicidally, a roguish grin. "Which one?"

"Surely not Sasha?" said Damon. Jaryd shrugged. Then shook his head, reluctantly, beneath that hard stare.

"Not Sasha," he admitted. "Though she did make very friendly with one of those serrin who came to help in the rebellion. Errollyn, that was his name."

"Sasha can fuck who she likes," Damon snorted, "it makes naught of an issue for anyone. Sofy is another matter."

"Why do you ask?"

"She was very different after she returned from her little adventure to Baerlyn. Only she didn't just travel to Baerlyn, did she? Or she tells me she didn't."

Jaryd blinked. "She told you?"

"I'm her friend, Jaryd. Not merely her brother. We tell each other things. It makes us a formidable pairing, one that some would love to see broken. I know she rode with you to Algery. What she would *not* tell me was if anything happened between the two of you. But I suspect. I may not have women's intuition, but I know my sister."

Jaryd felt a surge of anger. "Look, either state your accusation or don't!" he snapped. "Good gods, what do you want from me, an admission to something that should by law cost me my head?"

"'Good spirits,'" Damon corrected. Jaryd stared, not understanding. "You are supposed to be Goeren-yai now, you say 'Good spirits,' else someone take you for a fraud." Pointedly. Jaryd felt his face redden with anger. "Furthermore, I do not wish you to lose either honour or head. I merely wish to ask if you'd like to see Sofy once more. Before she weds, in private. I can make that happen."

"For the last time, I am not wearing that dress!" Princess Sofy Lenayin was not happy. She stood in the middle of a grand Larosan hall already decked out for the wedding, with great banners lining its walls. About her were Larosan priests, women of the Merciful Sisters, palace officials, numerous servants and an awful lot of dresses. The servants stood in a circle about her, each holding a dress, and struggling beneath their weight.

"Well then perhaps Your Highness could indicate precisely which wedding dress she *would* choose?" asked Master Hern, a portly, white-bearded man in an official's cloak and hat.

"None of them!" Sofy said angrily. "There must be *something* in this wedding that shall be Lenay!"

"There shall be yourself, my dear," the Princess Elora remarked, examining her nails on her seat nearby. "Surely that is adequate?"

Sofy struggled to control her temper. Princess Elora was soon to be her sister-in-law. She was a lean girl in her early twenties, and wore several times the jewellery that Sofy considered decent for a person of any station. Sofy thought she looked a little horsey. Perhaps she was overcompensating.

The *Maris Tere*, or "First Matron" of the Merciful Sisters was no longer present. On the first day, she had insisted that Sofy wear the white of Larosan maidenhood and that she cover her hair in the *torhes foud*, the pious shroud, of a girl to be wed. She had demanded that Sofy spend the next two days in the Sherdaine Temple "cleansing" herself in ritual prayer, presumably to remove the stain of a lifetime of barbarian practices.

When Sofy had refused, the First Matron had become angry, and slapped her. Yasmyn had struck her back, hard enough to drop the old woman to the ground, and drew her darak on the others who sought to retaliate. Blood had nearly been spilt, and Yasmyn plus Sofy's four-strong contingent of elite Royal Guards had escorted the bride-to-be to a deserted chambers and kept her there under guard until Koenyg, Princess Elora, and numerous lords and other importances had settled the misunderstanding.

Many of the Larosan court still demanded that Yasmyn be executed for her impudence, but were no longer demanding it so loudly after Koenyg had explained that executing the daughter of Isfayen's Great Lord Faras would be taken by the Isfayen as declaration of war, upon which event there was nothing any man of Lenayin could say to hold them. Now, Sofy caught Yasmyn staring at her. Her dark, slanted eyes beheld more knowledge of her princess than any other in the room.

"Your Highness is a nice girl," Yasmyn had said when they were alone, in the sarcastic tone of an Isfayen delivering a calculated insult. "She does not like to fight. People who do like to fight will see this, and challenge her with their blades until they back her up against a wall and there is nowhere left to run. Your Highness must realise that she cannot win a sword fight with a pretty smile and a silver tongue."

Sofy looked about at the dresses and took a deep breath. "None of these will do," she announced. "I shall decide my own attire for the wedding. I shall dress according to Lenay marital custom. I shall keep my own council only. Now thank you," and she made a dismissive gesture to the dress-wielding servants, "we have other matters to attend to."

Master Hern licked his lips nervously. "Your Highness, I do not think that it is wise—"

"Not wise?" Princess Elora challenged, rising to her feet in indignation. "It's improper! A wedding of Larosan royalty is not a matter of highland dresses and flower decorations, there is a grand tradition of many centuries—"

"As there is a grand tradition of millennia in Lenayin," Sofy said firmly. "I am *not* a Larosan, Princess Elora, I am a Lenay, and this marriage is a marriage *between* two peoples, not a subjugation of one to the other."

"There is no question of a Larosan bride attending such a wedding in improper attire!" Elora insisted as though she had not heard her. "The offence to the gods and the Larosan peoples, and indeed all the peoples of the free Bacosh, would be incalculable!"

"Then perhaps we could change these decorations?" Sofy suggested, indicating the feudal heraldry draping the surrounding walls. "To announce the rights of feudal nobility so loudly as this is surely offensive to many in Lenayin; I think some Rayen tapestries, and some flower garlands in the western style, would make a notable improvement . . ."

"Surely not!" said the Princess Elora.

"Your Highness," Master Hern attempted to intervene, "to remove the feudal heraldry would be a grave insult to the lords of Larosa and beyond. . . ."

"Then perhaps the timing of the ceremony," Sofy suggested reasonably, "according to the Lenay star charts instead of the Larosan tradition—"

"Impossible!"

"Thus I must again insist," said Sofy, her tone hardening, "that since so much of this wedding has been arranged without *prior consultation*, that those few remaining choices to be made must be resolved in favour of Lenayin!"

Master Hern glanced at Princess Elora. Elora sighed, and dismissed the servants with a wave of her hand.

"What does Your Highness request?" Master Hern asked.

"Dress," said Sofy, ticking a finger. "Music." Another finger.

"Not at the ceremony!" Elora protested.

Sofy smiled thinly. "We have no music at the ceremony," she said. "No pagan drumming to drown out the recitals, have no fear. But at the feast." Master Hern bit his lip. "Food," said Sofy, ticking a third finger.

"Dear sister," said Elora, "now would be a good time to ask . . . exactly what do Lenays like to eat?"

"Roasts," said Sofy, with a brightening smile. She could picture it now, the elements coming together in her head. "We'll build a great firepit in the centre hall, and roast steer or sheep or whatever you prefer. Great heat and cooking food, it should be quite a sight."

Elora and Hern looked at each other. "That does not sound impossible," Master Hern admitted. "But we should have Larosan dishes too from the kitchens."

"Of course!" said Sofy, unable to contain her building enthusiasm. She'd always loved to arrange such events. Now, she could build something of symbolic value. "We should seek to combine the best of Larosan and Lenay cultures together! Think of it as a mutual education in each other's lands and ways."

They made further progress, Sofy giving Master Hern the names of several Lenays whom she thought could help with food and music. Dresses, however, she would have to think on for herself. A servant arrived to inform them of lunch, and Sofy left the hall with Elora, Yasmyn, her Royal Guards, Elora's four sworn knights, and Elora's handmaidens. Dear lords, Sofy thought—it was a procession. Would her entire life be like this from now on? Could she never be alone?

"Dear Sofy," said Elora as they walked the hall, "it would be most appreciated if you could persuade your father the king to have audience with more of our lords. I hear he rarely stirs from the Sherdaine Temple since his arrival."

"Oh you must forgive him," Sofy sighed. "He's been like that a while, yet lately he grows worse." Elora waited, expecting more, but Sofy did not continue. She would not enumerate her suspicions of her father's doubts about the war, and the alliance with Larosa. She would not let slip her own, dawning frustration of a man who should have been leading his people in this trial, yet instead wallowed in self-indulgent prayer and moral uncertainty. Did he think he was the only one who doubted, or required reassurance? All that he achieved was to give the impression of a poor and uncertain leader. Thank the gods for Koenyg. "But I will speak with him," she added.

"He seems a vastly devout man," said Elora airily. "Such qualities are to be admired in a king." Sofy was not fooled. "I hear that you have a brother, too, who thinks to wear the black?"

"Wylfred," said Sofy with a nod. "He studies with our Archbishop Dalryn, with father's blessing."

"And he would forfeit his chance at the throne?"

"It is said that to be second behind Koenyg is like being last of a hundred siblings. The people do rather fancy him indestructible."

Elora laughed. "I can see from where they might gain the impression. Although one wonders if they ever thought the same of Prince Krystoff?"

"No," Sofy sighed. "I was young, but from what I gather, no one was particularly surprised that Prince Krystoff died young."

"Save for your father," Elora said shrewdly.

Sofy nodded. She was becoming accustomed to this probing by Larosan royalty. Such matters of family and succession were an obsession here. In Lenayin, the royal family was mostly unchallenged . . . though considering it had only held power for a hundred years, that was perhaps no great achievement. But Sofy had always thought nobility a vast and self-important thing in Lenayin. Gods knew, Sasha certainly did. Sasha would hate this place, Sofy thought glumly. Barely in Sherdaine for three days, and Sofy had been astonished at the utter self-possession of so many she had met. They lived their lives in palaces and castles, and knew barely a thing of what lay outside their walls, let alone beyond the borders of their lands. Sasha had occasionally made Sofy feel guilty that she obsessed on trivial royal matters more than they deserved. Here in Sherdaine, that guilt had vanished. The other evening, she'd been cornered by a noble girl who'd talked about her family's lineage for a full hour. If Yasmyn hadn't rescued her, she might have expired.

Now, the likes of Princess Elora were intrigued to know that Prince Wylfred, second in the line to the throne by birth, was effectively the ruler of Lenayin in the king's absence. The speculation, Sofy had gathered in mild shock, was that Wylfred was building a base of support in his father's absence, and would claim the kingdom for himself whether or not his father and Koenyg survived the war. Any protestations to the contrary were met with the pitying smile of an adult to a naive child. Sofy wondered what it said of a people that they did not understand even the simplest Lenay concept of family honour. In the Bacosh, there were many wars of succession. That meant brothers against brothers, sons against fathers, and sometimes even against mothers. It boggled the mind.

The Palace of Sherdaine was in truth a castle that had been rebuilt to a palatial standard once the newest city walls had risen, and saved the castle from its need for defensive intent. The dining hall was truly grand. Tall, narrow windows opened to let in the sun, overlooking palace courtyards and the tightly packed roofs of Sherdaine beyond. The hall's high walls were a many coloured profusion of coats of arms on shields, the mounted heads of animals and city pennants that Sofy had been told were battle trophies from past wars. There was room enough upon the polished flagstones for many tables and hundreds of nobles, but today there was but one table, set for lunch and aswarm with servants.

"Ah," said Yasmyn, sighting Jeleny waiting by a wall with an attending man, "your assistant has arrived." She spoke Lenay, and Elora frowned at her.

"Oh yes," Sofy sighed in Torovan. "Dear Elora, please excuse me, I should attend to this before lunch. A new assistant."

"Another? Whatever for?"

"I am informed that I must have a male assistant due to the necessity to liaise with the priesthood in preparation for the wedding." Not to mention the need to liaise with certain arrogant Bacosh lords and knights who would not listen to a woman, not even one with a darak.

Elora's eyes strayed to the man waiting with Jeleny. "He wears a sword. Have you no servants to attend to such matters?"

"The Army of Lenayin is an army of warriors," Sofy explained.

"Real men feed and clothe themselves," Yasmyn added unhelpfully. Her Torovan was improving, Sofy thought drily.

"Attend to it as you need," said Elora dismissively and slid away to greet others at the table.

"Really, Yasmyn," Sofy reproved her as they walked to Jeleny.

"This assistant looks very nice," Yasmyn observed, having forgotten Princess Elora already. The Isfayen considered themselves nearly a separate nation, and Yasmyn was the second daughter of that nation's king. She thought herself twice the princess that Elora would ever be, and found her utterly uninteresting. "Jeleny has chosen well."

Sofy looked, and found that Jeleny's man was indeed nicely proportioned in broad-shouldered Lenay leather, with midlength brown hair and several rings in one ear. He stood considering the rows of hanging shields on the wall, now turning to greet her with an insolently cheerful grin. Sofy stopped, utterly paralysed. It was Jaryd Nyvar.

"Your Highness," said Jaryd in Lenay, and bowed with a flourish. Yasmyn frowned at Sofy's response, and put a wary hand to her darak. "It is my great honour to serve you once more."

Sofy remained frozen, mouth partly open in shock. Jaryd only seemed to find that more amusing. "Highness?" Yasmyn asked. "Should I kill him?"

"You can try, lovely bloodwife," said Jaryd. "It would be a pleasure to dance with the daughter of Lord Isfayen."

"Not a pleasure," said Yasmyn, with a dangerous smile. "An honour."

"Aye, that also. Say, that is a lovely darak. Can you use it?"

"If the men it has killed could tell you, they would sing a grand chorus."

"Damon," Sofy breathed as it occurred to her. She stared accusingly at Jeleny. "Was it Damon's idea?" Damon being rather more in charge of the less martial aspects of the army. Aspects like food, shelter, politics . . . and weddings. Koenyg was too busy planning a war. Jeleny nodded mutely. "Oh what a *fool!*" Sofy exclaimed beneath her breath. She knew Damon occasionally petulant in his tempers, but the sheer stupidity of this took her breath away. "I shall have a word with Damon. Take him away."

"Take . . ." Jaryd looked to Sofy and back to Jeleny, confused. "Take me away?" Jeleny gestured for him to walk. Jaryd looked back at Sofy, temper rising. "Take me away?"

"Her Prin-cess," Yasmyn said slowly, in the manner of one speaking to the exceptionally stupid. "You com-mon man. Go away."

Jaryd stared daggers at her. And as Sofy turned to go, "Sofy . . . Sofy! You can't refuse your brother, he outranks you!"

"Can't?" Sofy rounded on him. "Can't? Jaryd, seriously, I cannot quite decide who is the bigger idiot, you or him. This is impossible, I must have another assistant. *Anyone* but you."

"Anyone?" Yasmyn interjected, with dawning fascination. "You are Jaryd Nyvar!"

"Ve-ry cle-ver," Jaryd pronounced to her. "What a smart little girl."

Yasmyn grinned. "Oh Highness, this is a perfect thing. You must allow him to stay."

"Perfect?" Sofy asked. Today she was surrounded by morons. "What in the name of all the . . . ?"

"But so romantic!" Yasmyn insisted. "The man who lusts for you but cannot have you, he comes to protect you! Oh this is like the ballad of Hershyl the Bride. . . ."

Sofy glared at her, with a glance back toward the table. There was only a servant or two within earshot, and both Jaryd and Yasmyn spoke Lenay with broad Tyree and Isfayen accents respectively, but it was not impossible that a servant might be fluent enough in Lenay to catch a condemning word or two.

"What's wrong with you two?" Sofy said harshly, her voice low. "Jaryd, I'm getting married!"

"And Prince Damon fears for your safety," Jaryd retorted. "He wishes you to have an assistant who is not of the lordly classes yet understands them, and mistrusts them, and can speak for both Goeren-yai and Verenthane custom in the wedding. Someone who cannot be intimidated, who knows your stubbornness and flightiness, and will not take any of your girly bossiness." Sofy bit her lip, fuming. "And, someone who would die in an instant to protect you."

"Oh very good!" Yasmyn exclaimed in admiration. "Your Highness, Prince Damon has chosen very well."

At the lunch table, people were looking her way. Sofy unclenched her fists, and took a deep breath. "Fine. Just . . . no more talking about it. Not even in Lenay, not even in Kytan or Telochi." (Those being the native tongues of Tyree and Isfayen.) "You never know who might understand."

"No more gossiping with, say, one's handmaidens, for instance?" Jaryd inquired, glancing at Yasmyn. Sofy rolled her eyes.

"She tells me everything," Yasmyn said with a smile. Her eyes trailed down Jaryd's body, to rest at his groin.

"I hope she told it well," Jaryd replied.

"Oh rest it, you two!" Sofy fumed. "Now if you'll just . . ." But Jaryd's eyes registered someone approaching, and Sofy turned to find that a man in rich, princely clothes was walking from the table. She regained her composure, forcing a pleased smile to her lips. The man was tall and dark, square jawed and wavy haired. His tunic was black silk with silver thread, white lace frilled at the cuffs, tight pants, tall boots and a silver pommelled sword swinging low on one hip. As he came near, Sofy gave a curtsey, and Jaryd a bow. Even Yasmyn curtseyed.

"My sweet," the Prince Balthaar Arosh greeted her with a smile, in Torovan. "Is there some issue?"

"Oh, my Prince," Sofy laughed, a hand to her chest, "you must forgive me. My brother has gone and done something stupid again, we Lenays are forever becoming animated in our little family quarrels. It is nothing, a personal item he has managed to misplace, my assistant tells me so."

"Ah," said Prince Balthaar, with a glance at Jaryd. "Please tell me, what nature of item? My lovely princess shall be showered with wedding gifts in just a few days time. If there is any item in particular that she would like to request, I shall see that she has hundreds of them."

"Oh no, my Prince, it is but a small personal item, a gift from my mother. Emotional value, nothing more." She had once been a poor liar. Lies had brought her guilt. Recently the guilt had gone, and she suspected her lying had improved accordingly.

Jeleny took Jaryd away, to Sofy's relief, as Balthaar escorted her to the table. At the table's end was a grand chair, like a wooden throne. Beside it, inviting her to sit, was the Regent Tamar Arosh, lord of all the free Bacosh. He was a tall man, with wisping hair at the front, but long and grey streaked at the back. His eyes were intelligent, yet his hands and manner seemed to Sofy somehow . . . soft. Not a martial man, was the word amongst the Lenay lords. Not a warrior. And she wondered at the changes in herself that while a year ago she might have considered such a thing a sign of sophistication in a king, today she felt an unmistakable . . . distaste.

She sat upon the regent's right hand, opposite her betrothed, with Yasmyn to her own right. Further down the table, others settled. Balthaar's sister Elora, and his younger brother Dafed. Aramande, the Lord of Algrasse, perhaps Larosa's closest ally. And Father Turen, the Archbishop of Sherdaine, and the holiest man in Larosa. The small table and isolated setting, here in the regent's private quarters, made Sofy nervous. The lady regent was absent, as were Balthaar's other sisters, and most of the grand provincial lords save Lord Aramande. In these great days of alliance building, a missed chance to dine with new allies and former enemies was an opportunity lost. Yet the regent chose to lunch with this select group.

"An issue with the new assistant, Princess Sofy?" asked the regent. He spoke with a curious detachment, and when he met a person's eyes, it was only fleeting. He was a man of elegance and refinement, who sometimes seemed to find the company of people . . . uninteresting. Sofy thought him one of the most puzzling men she'd met.

"No issue, Your Grace." It was the required form of address, she'd been informed, to the man who would be known as king if not for the ancient declaration of Elrude's Oath that no Bacosh man could name himself king until all the Bacosh had been reclaimed, and the throne of Leyvaan restored. "Rather an issue with my brother."

"Which one?" asked the regent, considering the soup that servants laid before them.

"Prince Damon. He is my dear friend, but sometimes forgetful."

"And unmarried," added Elora.

"Does the prospect interest you, sister?" Balthaar asked, teasingly.

"One merely observes," said Elora. They spoke Torovan, for Sofy's benefit. Her Larosan was approaching conversational standard, but not quite there yet. "Whom shall he marry, do you think, Sofy?"

"Oh dear," said Sofy. "With Damon, one is never certain. He is rather picky."

"I hear of considerable interest in Tournea," said Lord Aramande of Algrasse. He was a very handsome man, of no more than thirty summers, but short. Standing, Sofy reckoned he might not be too much taller than her. "Lady Sicilia is known to be asking questions on the prince's inclinations. He does prefer girls, does he not, Princess Sofy?"

Sofy did not resent the question, but rather the way it was asked. "Of the Lenay variety, assuredly," she said coolly. Balthaar chuckled. Sofy smiled at him. Lord Aramande made an unconvincing smile and blew on a spoonful of soup.

"What precisely is wrong with ladies of the Bacosh?" the Archbishop wanted to know.

"They wear wigs," Yasmyn replied. "Hair falls out. All bald beneath, like priest." The Archbishop whitened.

Balthaar laughed. "Lady Yasmyn, I swear, do all noble ladies of Isfayen have such sharp tongues as you?"

Yasmyn smiled. "And sharper knives."

"A pity there are not more of you on this ride. I should like to wed one of you to Dafed."

Elora giggled.

"Be nice," said Dafed. Balthaar's younger brother was broad, built like a young bull. Sofy thought he was the strongest warrior she'd met, amongst Bacosh nobility.

"No doubt an Isfayen marriage to the second son of the regent would alarm King Torvaal," said Lord Aramande. "The Isfayen being such a warlike people, he might consider it a play for power." Sofy thought the man determined to cause trouble. Many, she knew, did not like this marriage at all.

"No," said Yasmyn. "The gods chose Family Lenayin. There is honour to follow the king. The Isfayen are honourable."

"I have no doubt," Balthaar said easily. "Honourable and beautiful." Yasmyn smiled. "Yet not quite as beautiful as some," he added, with a smile at Sofy.

Sofy sighed. When she had first learned that she would be married to the son of the Larosan regent, she had been revolted. Then, when the consequences of resisting her father and Koenyg's plans had become clear, she had gritted her teeth, and resolved that if a man's service to his kingdom could involve dying on the battlefield, then a woman's fate of marriage and childbirth would not be such a bad thing, even were the man unlovable.

Balthaar Arosh was intelligent and gracious. He had a sense of humour, and a natural ease of command. Sofy knew that most women would think her irretrievably spoiled could she not be grateful for such a gift as this marriage had granted her.

After lunch, she took a brief walk with her future husband in the courtly gardens. Trimmed hedges made fascinating shapes, and about it all, the narrow windows of Sherdaine Palace looked down. Other couples strolled the maze, some knights in chain and surcoats. Many of the ladies wore long, silver wigs with curls and ornaments that glittered.

Yasmyn walked behind, with a black-clad woman of the Merciful Sisters, who had appeared from nowhere to keep an eye on the couple. No more than hand holding would be tolerated, Sofy had been told.

"I have invited your brothers to participate in the wedding tournament," Balthaar told her. "It has been too soon for a reply, however."

"Oh, Balthaar, *jousting*." Sofy made a face. "It does seem unnecessarily dangerous, with a war coming."

"Tournament lances, my dear," Balthaar assured her. "They are narrow things, and break easily upon contact with a shield or armour. Do you think they shall accept the invitation?"

"Oh, I'm certain you could not keep Koenyg away if you tried," Sofy said tiredly. "Myklas too. Lenay warriors have little use for lances or knightly armour, but I'm sure they'll prove fast learners."

"Not your brother Damon?" Balthaar asked. "I should warn you that there are rumours regarding Damon. They say that he is not a real Lenay man like your brother Koenyg."

"He was man enough for Lord Elen of Liside Vale."

Balthaar looked down at her with a little concern, and squeezed her hand. "I did not mean to cause offence."

"No, of course not. I'm sorry. I just . . . I recall what Lord Elen did, and it angers me. I never thought I could be proud of my brothers for killing a man in a duel, but I'm very proud of Damon for that."

"Dear Sofy," said Balthaar, and stopped. He turned her toward him, and took her other hand in his. "You have not yet inferred upon me a term of endearment. I am merely Balthaar."

"There shall be plenty of time for that once we are married, don't you think?"

Balthaar looked a little sad. "Of course. I merely hope that I shall not be plain and simple Balthaar forever."

"Dear Prince, I doubt that you have ever been 'plain and simple' anything." Balthaar smiled and kissed her hand. Sofy was relieved. Behind them, the Merciful Sister cleared her throat, loudly.

"Balthaar?" Sofy asked suddenly. "What would you have done with Lord Elen?"

Balthaar frowned. "It is not a prince's role to interfere with matters of law and punishment in a lord's own domain. Particularly not where those matters of law concern the faith. Lord Elen broke Lenay law within a Lenay camp, and I respect that your laws must be enforced. Prince Damon did what he must, and I hope that our fellow lords shall learn better from the lesson. But that is a separate matter from the first."

"And the killing of village folk accused of witchcraft?"

Balthaar shrugged, in that airy manner that reminded Sofy of his aloof, intellectual father. "The common folk believe and indulge in all manner of folly. Should princes or kings attempt to put an end to all of it, the kingdom should see war from one end to the other." Sofy thought that a somewhat hopeful answer.

"On the other hand," he continued, "to the extent that such silly superstitions keep our lands free from serrin, it is perhaps a worthwhile price to pay. Those evil filth should be killed wherever they are found, and I look forward to the day that we can rid Rhodia of the last of them. Perhaps in our glorious reign together, as king and queen." He smiled at her. "But come, let us continue, before the dragon lady at our backs orders us both beheaded for premarital indecency."

Ten

THE CELL WAS DEEPER IN THE DUNGEONS than most had cause to venture. Rhillian followed her guard through the low doorway, into a wide stone cell lit with torches. There, a man was chained to a slab of wood, wrists and ankles in manacles. On a chair to one side sat Kiel, morose, flipping his knife in one hand. One look, and Rhillian knew the captive had not talked.

She walked over, and considered the captive.

"You were seen at Voscoraine Port," she told him. "Reputable sailors swear so. Rhodaani vessels have been forbidden by the council from trading there during this time of war. Other honest sources have seen you in Lady Renine's company. There is much interest in the intrigue of secret messengers in Tracato. You have been followed."

"Ha!" was all the young man said, with great bravado. He gave the restraints a shake as though to break free with the sheer force of his disdain.

"He will not even tell his name," Kiel said. "He does not fear our methods. He knows we are gentle. It makes him brave."

Rhillian dismissed the guard, and waited for the door to close. "My patience runs thin," she told the young man, coldly. She leaned close, for the effect of her emerald stare. The man tossed his hair and stared at the ceiling. "You plot the downfall of Rhodaan, you and your mistress. I know of what you corresponded with the Larosans, I have so many pieces of knowledge from so many sources, but it does not yet add up to proof. I know there is more correspondence, hidden in the residences we now occupy. I wish to know where it is. I wish in particular to find a token of good will—a Verenthane Star of the ancient Saint Selene, that was granted Lady Renine as a gift from the Regent Arosh himself. Such are the things I desire. I wish you to grant them to me."

"You know what?" the man retorted. "I wish you to suck my cock!" He glared at her.

Rhillian placed her hands to either side of his restrained body, and leaned close. "My teeth are sharp," she said softly.

"You fucking serrin, you waste my time!" he exclaimed. And something else, in Rhodaani, that Rhillian did not catch. She looked askance at Kiel.

"Even less polite than the last," Kiel told her. "Something about your private parts."

"I think he would truly find me frightening," Rhillian observed to Kiel, still in Torovan, "if he truly believed I would hurt him."

"Serrin have been gentle for too long," Kiel said. "There is much at stake."

The prisoner stared at her. "You don't scare me with your talk!" he snarled. "It's all you serrin ever do! Words and words and words! I grow sick of your words!"

"I have made the same argument myself, to the councils, on occasions," Rhillian replied. She smiled. "So you see, my friend, we are in agreement. Kiel, show him."

Kiel flipped his knife, grasped its handle, and got to his feet. For the first time, the prisoner looked alarmed.

"No! No, wait, you cannot . . . !"

Kiel grabbed the man's left arm, and sliced off his thumb with a boney crunch. The man shrieked, and thrashed against the restraints, blood spurting over his hand. Rhillian stared in shock.

"That's one," Kiel observed. "There are nine more here. Serrin have little art for this kind of thing, so I'll start with the most obvious. It shall be a learning experience."

"Kiel!" Rhillian said sharply, barely hiding the shock from her voice. She beckoned him over, as the prisoner sobbed and wailed. Kiel, she was not surprised to note, appeared utterly calm. "I'd thought perhaps a cut, Kiel," Rhillian said coldly, in Saalsi. "Something that would heal."

"If he is as guilty as we seek to prove him, then more likely we'll cut his head off. Why should it matter if he heals?"

"Kiel, I'm warning you, this is not a path down which I intend to—"

"Rhillian," Kiel cut her short. "The fool is right. You talk words, but you do not mean what you say. This is the time for action. Let me show you something."

He turned and strode back to the sobbing prisoner. Grabbed the young man's other arm, and positioned the blade above the remaining thumb. "Are you now prepared to talk?"

"Yes, *yes!*" came the sobbing reply.

"I warn you," Kiel said mildly, "if you give me cause to believe that you lie, I shall take the other thumb and begin working through your fingers. Do you understand?"

"Yes! I understand, please, don't cut me again, please don't . . ."

"Kiel!" Rhillian snapped in Saalsi. "You go too far! He'll tell you anything he thinks you wish to hear!"

"We shall see," Kiel replied, with a note of intrigue to his voice. The intrigue of a scholar presented with an interesting puzzle. "We shall see."

The walk to the Ushal Fortress from the Justiciary was short and unsafe. Steel guarded the major buildings, and Rhillian and Kiel's escort was six strong, shields ready to lock into formation in case of archers. Two days since the arrest of Lady Renine and most senior feudalists, and the streets remained unnaturally deserted.

Central Tracato was feudalist territory, and though most residents were not nobility themselves, many worked for them, or owed loyalty by other means. Money bought not only loyalty, Rhillian had found, but Blackboots too, many of whom had been removed from service, some temporarily, others for good. Many other Blackboots were refusing to work, for sympathy with those dismissed. Night curfews became a necessity, to keep the thieves off the streets, and though some tradesmen had resumed work today, rumours abounded of retribution against those by the noble families who determined that to stop work was to protest. Only the markets were turning a regular trade, partly as people needed to eat, and partly because the markets were run by country folk who cared little for the nobility's problems.

Clashes had been frequent but isolated, with nothing large or co-ordinated as yet. Rhillian did not fool herself into thinking those would never come. The nobility had supporters and arms aplenty, they were merely biding their time, waiting until the Steel left for the western front. No, she needed to deal with the feudalists quickly, before the Steel departed. She needed to prove the leaders of this plot guilty, and dispose of them, with the consent of the Justiciary before the gods and all. Then, the nobility may well rise up, but they would have no moral weight. A countryside militia, led by the Civid Sein and perhaps the Nasi-Keth, and backed by her own *talmaad* back from Elisse, could account for any uprising then, even with the Steel away, and suffer no lasting enmity from anyone for it . . . save of course the remaining nobility, but in that course of events, they would hardly matter any more.

Across a wall, Rhillian saw, in red paint, scrawling letters that even her poor Rhodaani could read. *Kill the white witch.*

"I think that means you," Kiel said with amusement.

Rhodaan for humanity, read another. And, *Rhodaan for Verenthanes.*

"So the nobility claim to speak for all Verenthanes now," Kiel observed. "The Civid Sein will be intrigued to hear it."

Rhillian walked in silence, her expression grim.

The Ushal Fortress was as still as a tomb, save for wandering cats, Steel guards, and the occasional, furtive servant. Rhillian and Kiel left their guard downstairs, and climbed to the top floor of the Renines' quarters. Once there, Kiel walked to one window and bent to pull aside the heavy rug.

"Now," he said, "third stone from the wall." Rhillian watched from the doorway, arms folded. Kiel used his knife, and wiggled the stone until it came free. He reached into the hole, grasped, then pulled on something. From a neighbouring bookshelf came a loud clank. "Good," he said.

Rhillian watched him remove expensive vases from the shelf one at a time, and place them on the nearest table. She did not assist. "It proves nothing," she said.

"It proves everything," said Kiel, removing the last vase. The back of the bookshelf exposed, Kiel rapped on it, then pried one end up with his knife. The panel squeaked open and he peered inside. Rhillian found herself almost hoping that he found nothing within. Instead, Kiel reached inside and withdrew some light, cream squares of paper, fastened with a red wax seal and ribbon. "This seal looks *very* interesting. Ah the arrogant stupidity of nobles, having bought all the Blackboots and justiciars, and assuming no one would dare invade their sanctum."

Rhillian let out a long breath, and stared at the wall. Kiel gathered the last of the papers, and looked at her, seeming almost cheerful.

"Well," he ventured, "to borrow the human expression, this rather turns over a new leaf, wouldn't you say?"

"It does indeed," Rhillian said. "Let us hope that leaf does not become a forest."

Sasha strode down the Tol'rhen hall, still damp from her wash following morning training. Her muscles ached from working too hard, as happened when she lost her temper. Passing students gave her wary looks, and kept their distance.

She reached the class chamber, where twelve students sat at tables and made markings on parchment, faces screwed up with concentration. Errollyn walked slowly among them, observing their work. His hair was also damp, though Sasha had not seen him at training.

He leaned down now to indicate with a finger the line a student's quill should have been tracing on the parchment. The female student (more than half of them were) gazed up at him anxiously. Rapturously. Sasha's temper boiled once more.

"Errollyn," she snapped. All in the class looked up . . . save for Errollyn.

"It can wait," he said, and redirected the girl's attention to her quill work. It was *o'rhen*, the old serrin calligraphy that outdated most of their spoken tongues, yet remained the preferred style of writing for scholars and poets. Sasha had never known Errollyn to have a particular interest in the old penmanship, but the Tol'rhen had its way of bringing out a person's scholarly side.

"It can't fucking wait!" Sasha retorted in Lenay.

"I'll be back shortly," he informed the class, and walked to the door, grabbing Sasha none too gently along the way. Once in the hallway, she smacked his arm away.

"Where have you been?"

"In class," he said. His green eyes narrowed at her.

"Last night!" Sasha pressed. "I hear you shared a room with Emisile!"

"After you kicked me out of my own bed, yes," said Errollyn. "The alternative being to sleep in the hall."

"In her bed?"

"On her large, comfortable rug with some cushions," said Errollyn. "I *should* have fucked her. She wanted me to, it would have served you right."

He grabbed her once more and hustled her toward an empty room. Sasha struggled, and Errollyn simply pinned her arms and picked her up. She forgot sometimes just how much bigger he was than her.

Inside, he put her down and pressed her hard against a wall. "What right do you have to kick me out of my own bed, and then complain where I choose to sleep?"

"My sister's in a Justiciary dungeon because of you!" Sasha shouted.

"Your sister's in a dungeon because she allied herself with traitors," Errollyn said sharply. "I'm as sorry she's there as you are, but—"

"You fucking liar!" Sasha shoved him hard away. He backed up. "What possessed you to go to Rhillian before me?"

"I *did* go to you, I told you all about what I found—"

"Horse shit! You told me you found evidence of Lady Renine's treachery, you never told me the details! And I told *you* you'd be crazy to go to Rhillian, because she would overreact and turn Tracato upside down! And she has!"

"Who else then?" Errollyn demanded. "Kessligh's hands are tied because half of the Nasi-Keth are in love with the Civid Sein, and think this is just the excuse to kill all the feudalists. . . ."

"And they don't *now*?"

"Rhillian can stop them! She's the only balance in this city. Someone had to stop Lady Renine, and the only two forces that could were Rhillian backed by the Steel, or the Civid Sein! Which would you choose?"

Sasha stared at the ceiling, hands to her head.

"Sasha," Errollyn persisted, "I'm sorry Alythia got caught up in this, but Lady Renine has forces that can't be underestimated. What if she declared open rebellion when the Steel were at the front? A quarter of the Steel has feudalist loyalties, the army could split just on that declaration alone."

"Damn it, you didn't know that. You were guessing. If anything happens to Alythia because of this . . ."

She couldn't complete the sentence. Errollyn stepped back. He looked remote, in that way he sometimes had, when he pulled back, and trusted no one. He'd always been an outsider among his own people. Could he have been reaching out to them, seeking to prove himself with this act? Surely they must trust him now. Sasha knew how much it had hurt him to be cast out after Petrodor.

He shook his head, and walked for the door.

"Wait! You're just going to leave?"

He stopped. "I don't like arguing as much as you do," he said. "What else do you want?" Sasha stared at him. "Make up your mind. You can either be angry with me and thrust me away, or you can forgive me, and let me back in. You can't have both. And I'm not going to go chasing after you to beg for forgiveness. Lenays aren't the only ones with pride."

"Good for you, finally a serrin who understands the term."

She walked past him to leave. Errollyn grabbed her arm and pulled her back. She hit him in the chest, and he caught her and pulled her close. Suddenly they were kissing, frantically, hands grasping to burrow beneath each other's clothes. It had been a while since they'd gone a day without sex, Sasha managed to think as she sought purchase with her back against the wall. Perhaps that was all it was. Or perhaps it was fear. They'd argued before, but rarely as heatedly as this.

There was a storage closet at the room's end, which was cramped, but with the door pulled to, safe enough from immediate discovery. With no room to lie, and nothing to sit on, they stood, belts unfastening with fumbling hands as Sasha tried to think of something she could do to take charge, because she was still angry, and not about to just submit to his male attentions. But there was nothing but the obvious, and frantic lust compelled her to turn about, braced against a wall, and let Errollyn take her from behind until her legs threatened to give way from the shaking, and his fingers made bruise marks upon her waist and hip. Even now, he made sure she climaxed first. As she recovered, she found that funny, and nearly laughed.

There was a silence as they dressed. Sasha wondered what to say. It had never been a problem between them before. She still hadn't forgiven him. Was their relationship nothing more than this? Mutual need? No. Of course not, she was just angry, and thinking crazy things. And she'd never fucked angry before. Everything was confusing, and she had no idea what to make of it. Neither, it seemed, did Errollyn.

Finally she buckled her belt, and left the closet. Errollyn followed. They walked the hall in silence. Errollyn turned back into his class, and Sasha kept walking.

The Tol'rhen hallways were filled with running students and crowds of Civid Sein. Many farmers held pitchforks and other tools, while students bundled large banners, scrawled with Rhodaani script. Others piled torches against a wall, and smeared them with oil from earthen jars, ready to burn.

Sasha waved down a girl she recognised.

"Hala, what's going on?"

"Reynold is organising a march on the Tracato courthouse!" said Hala with enthusiasm, clutching a bundle of linen. "There should be several thousand people marching!"

"Marching for what?" Sasha asked. Hala shrugged. "What's with all the linen?"

"For bandages, in case there is trouble." Hala hurried on, apparently not worried by this prospect.

Frowning, Sasha pushed through the throng. The hall opened onto the grand courtyard, and there was indeed a great crowd gathering, some with makeshift weapons, others with banners or flags, or other symbols the significance of which Sasha did not know. Most of those gathered were Civid Sein from the courtyard encampment, but there were a lot of Nasi-Keth helping them.

She searched the confusion until she spotted Kessligh, arguing with Reynold, but she held back. She did not want to confront Reynold again, not in front of Kessligh. That would be awkward.

Then she realised what she was thinking, and what Reynold had reduced her to. Furious at herself, she thrust forward, pushing past bodies with determination.

". . . no Nasi-Keth involvement in this sort of thing!" Kessligh was insisting loudly to a young Nasi-Keth. It was Timoth Salo, a disciple of Reynold's. He was a blue blood himself, won over to Reynold's cause, and promoted, Sasha guessed, largely for the significance of his conversion.

"The Nasi-Keth tires of your neutrality, Kessligh!" Timoth replied with frustration. "Can't you see what's happening here? These brave men have come to take the fight directly to the feudalist oppressors, and they deserve our support."

Several more young students echoed loud agreement.

"Kid," said Kessligh, "you have no idea what you're doing. This isn't what the Tol'rhen is for."

"It's *exactly* what the Tol'rhen is for!" Timoth retorted. "To side with the weak against the powerful, to make right that which is wrong! If not for this, why have a Tol'rhen at all?"

"You're not the weak and powerless," Sasha snapped. All looked at her for the first time. "There's more Civid Sein than feudalists, and if the Nasi-Keth join it, there'll be a proper massacre, they won't scrub the blood off the pavings in Panae Achi for weeks."

"If that's what it takes!" said Timoth, eyes blazing. "Or would you rather that a small group continue to wield power over the majority forever, *Princess* Sashandra?"

"No," said Reynold, before Sasha could escalate things. "No, Kessligh is right. There should be no Nasi-Keth marching on the courthouse today."

Timoth gaped at him. "But Reynold . . ."

"Do as I say," Reynold instructed, with a level stare. There was a meaning in that stare Sasha could not guess. Timoth fumed, and stalked off. "Kessligh," said Reynold, with a faint bow to him, then, "Sasha," with a small smile.

Sasha's hand twitched toward her blade. But no more than that. Reynold turned away, into the crowd, and Sasha hated herself all over again.

"You should stop the whole thing," Sasha told Kessligh.

"I don't have that much sway with the Civid Sein."

"Nor with the Nasi-Keth, it seems," said Sasha. Kessligh's look was hard. "You've deliberately kept out of it."

"Maybe." Men in the crowd jostled past them. Somewhere, Nasi-Keth were shouting new orders. There were protests. "I recall giving you a lot of lectures, when you were younger. Lectures alone taught you little."

"I listened sometimes."

"Only after you'd had the substance of my lecture beaten into your thick skull with demonstration," said Kessligh. "I could lecture these people until I was blue in the face, I'd change very few minds. People need to learn by experience, Sasha. Otherwise, even should they heed my words, they would never entirely believe the truth of them."

Sasha recalled a line of Tullamayne. "Men only learn that swords are sharp when a thousand heads lie severed on the ground."

Kessligh nodded. "And even then, there remains some dispute. Lessons learned are nothing next to lessons earned."

Sasha looked about them, sourly. "You seem less enamoured of your grand learning institution today than last month."

Kessligh said nothing. He looked up and around at the statues towering over the courtyard and sighed. "Ideas made these men," he said. "Ideas carved this stone. I've always been a man of ideas."

"Ideas without morals are like knowledge without wisdom," said Sasha. "Any fool can shoot an arrow; it takes morals and wisdom to know what to aim it at."

"Is that Tullamayne too?"

"No," Sasha said wryly. "That's just me. But it's what you taught me."

Kessligh smiled at her. That didn't happen often. "Go and find what route this march intends to take. I'll find a Blackboots lieutenant and see if there can't be a force to accompany them. Some feudalists will take this for a provocation."

"I don't know what help the Blackboots would be then," said Sasha. "But I'll ask."

The people she found in the milling crowd knew little enough, everyone pointed to someone else. She received an evasive answer from one Civid Sein organiser, a pot-bellied pig farmer from the northern border regions, and then Daish emerged from nowhere to grab her arm.

"Justice Sinidane is here!" he shouted in her ear. "He's looking for Kessligh!"

"Sinidane?" Sasha was astonished, and let Daish drag her from the teeming courtyard. "He's here himself?"

"He has a palanquin!" Daish explained. Sasha saw the palanquin waiting by the Tol'rhen steps, the strong men who'd carried it resting while Sinidane stood on the third step, and peered at the crowd.

Sasha ran with Daish.

"Justice Sinidane!" she shouted to him. The old man saw her.

"Ah, the lovely barbarian herself!" Sasha did not often smile when someone used that word in front of her, but now she laughed. "Have you seen your wise and courageous uman?"

Sasha nodded vigorously. "Aye, he's about this high, grey hair, walks with a limp."

Sinidane scowled, but his eyes twinkled. They'd met twice before, at Tol'rhen functions. Sasha guessed he'd once been a skilled hand with the ladies, and liked to demonstrate that he had not entirely forgotten.

"Dear girl, are you a tease, or a fool?"

"Must I choose?" And to Daish, "Find Kessligh for me?" Daish nodded and rushed back into the crowd. Sasha climbed the steps to the old man's side. "Aside from flirting with me, what brings you here, Your Justice?"

"Oh, things." Sinidane's humour faded as he regarded the crowds. "I never tire of this city and its curious sights. Do you know what route they take?"

"Up High Road, as far as I can make out."

"Feudalist territory," said Sinidane. "But it could be worse, much of it is feudalist territory, around the Justiciary. When I was a young man, I recall dreaming of the day when all Tracato's lands would be merely lands and not defined by the loyalties of one group or another."

"I miss the countryside," Sasha said sombrely. "When I lived there I had wild, youthful ideals. The longer I stay in cities, the more my ideals choke and die."

Sinidane regarded her seriously. "I am sorry for it," he said. "Youthful idealism can be a curse, but without it, civilisations would perish."

"How many have perished *because* of it, I wonder?" Sasha replied, looking out at the courtyard.

"Do not despair yet," said Sinidane. "For as long as the Nasi-Keth have influence over the Civid Sein, I will not give up hope."

"Kessligh does not believe the Nasi-Keth in Tracato can be led," said Sasha. "He says their beliefs are too strong to be swayed by him, and they must learn for themselves."

"Reynold Hein, at least, seems an intelligent, reasonable sort," Sinidane offered.

"He tried to rape me," said Sasha. She did not look at him, but she felt his silence, pressing at her side. It was important that he knew. So much more important than her own wounded honour. When she did finally look at him, she saw something in the old man's eyes that chilled her.

Fear.

Kessligh climbed the steps to join them, with clacks of his staff. "Your Justice."

"Yuan Kessligh. Or would you prefer Ulenshaal?"

"The Nasi-Keth will not be marching with them," said Kessligh, ignoring the question. "Reynold Hein has forbidden it."

"That's something at least," said Sinidane.

"Something, yes. Good or bad, I don't know."

Sinidane look at Sasha, then at Kessligh. Wondering, perhaps, if Kessligh knew what Sasha had just told him. Sasha did not know herself. Perhaps Sinidane saw, or guessed.

"Something I wished to ask you," said Sinidane, skipping over the issue entirely. "Four of the seven senior justices have been dismissed by Lady Rhillian."

"Only four?" Kessligh did not appear particularly surprised. "Generous of her, I hadn't thought she liked even three of you."

"My own position with the feudalists is now somewhat difficult," Sinidane explained, "since I helped her to select the four dismissed."

At least half of the senior justices, it was common knowledge, and considerably more of the junior ones, were in the pay of the feudalists. Sinidane alone remained beyond reproach. No doubt the two others selected to stay were under Rhillian's duress . . . and probably Sinidane had helped to arrange that too. It was a bold move from a stubbornly principled man, who knew where many skeletons were buried.

"And now you'd like me to suggest men from the Nasi-Keth to fill some of the vacancies," said Kessligh. Sasha wondered if he and Sinidane had talked of this before. Perhaps not . . . where else were Sinidane and Rhillian going to find educated scholars of law, with independent hearts, to fill such seats?

"I'd ask for you yourself," Sinidane affirmed, "but you're needed here."

"For what good it will do. I will ask some of those best suited, but I can't promise you anything."

"Good enough."

"Your Justice, how is my sister?" Sasha asked.

"Dear girl," he said, "I'm afraid I cannot know. We justices are not to be directly involved in the affairs of prisoners in the Justiciary."

"I know that." Sasha scuffed at the steps with a boot, frustrated. "Just make sure she's looked after. You can at least ask someone to see to that."

"The Justiciary is independent, dear girl," said Justice Sinidane, sadly. "Would that I could intervene."

"You'll find that you can." Sasha gave him a deadly stare.

"Sasha," Kessligh warned her.

Sasha waved a hand in angry frustration, and strode back to the crowd.

News of the fighting arrived in the late afternoon, as Sasha struggled to take her class of Rhodaani youngsters through the works of Tullamayne in the Lenay tongue.

"Wait here!" she told them, jumping off her podium and snatching her sword. Out in the hall, many were running, shouts echoing off the high ceiling. In snatches of Rhodaani, and distant Torovan, she heard "High Road," and "Justiciary," several times. A fair run then.

She turned back to grab her waterskin, and found her way blocked by eager boys ignoring her instruction. "Where the crap are you lot going?" she asked them, pushing through to her podium. "You're not going outside."

"But, M'Lady!" Willem protested. Several more ignored her, and ran out into the hall. Others followed.

"Hey!" Sasha yelled, returning with her skin. "All right, get out, see what you can do and *obey your seniors!*"

They ran before her, all boys, for no Rhodaani girl thought the Lenay tongue a suitably feminine subject. Sometimes Sasha wondered if she were the only sane human woman in the world, or the least.

She ran from the hall, dodging traffic, and paused at the broad atrium to join the gathering who were filling waterskins at the basin.

"Sasha!" called Daish from nearby. "I hear there's fighting!" He looked excited at the prospect. She saw Reynold Hein nearby, with several Civid Sein friends, and scowled.

Errollyn came running, bow in hand but with no water. "Borrow mine," said Sasha. "Let's go."

They ran down the marble stairs. Sasha had no idea how the Tol'rhen remained so cool, for the air was stifling, despite the shade between buildings. The streets remained quieter than usual, a few clattering carts, some servants on errands, a running messenger. Elesther Road ran through the city and away from the bustling back alleys and courtyards of neighbouring districts. Working class folk did not venture so much here.

"Is it the march?" Errollyn asked as they ran.

"What the hells do you think?" Sasha snapped. "Of course it's the fucking march, they were spoiling for a fight from the moment they left. Reynold set this up."

Errollyn said nothing. Sasha knew she should not have snarled at him, but damned if she'd apologise. If Errollyn had kept his mouth shut, Rhillian might not have moved to take over the city at all.

"Spirits know what Rhillian thinks she's up to, giving the Civid Sein free rein like this," she muttered. "The marchers were all shouting for Civid Sein friendly justiciars to replace the ones Rhillian dismissed, and if she gives in, the Civid Sein will control the Justiciary . . . what the hells was she thinking?"

As fit as she was, Sasha was not accustomed to running in such heat, and as she and Errollyn reached the first of the Civid Sein column, she was dripping sweat and gasping. A crowd of men swarmed on the road, most retreating, many terrified. Some carried wounded, others tended to those who had collapsed by the side of the road, unable to run further. Sasha had seen victory and defeat on the battlefield, and this looked like defeat.

They passed carts piled with bodies, dripping streams of blood onto the cobbles. Some Civid Sein were crying, others rallying their comrades to rush back to the battle. But there was no momentum for it, and Sasha ran past without bothering to counsel them otherwise.

Errollyn led them onto High Road, a right turn upslope, following the trail of the rout. Sasha paused to drain some water, then resumed, finding her second wind on the toughest part of the run. Other Nasi-Keth were ahead of them now, as Errollyn held back to wait for her.

About a bend, and here rose the great Merley Inn, overlooking the Justiciary and Ushal Fortress both from atop a high hill. It was perhaps the highest point in Tracato, and a cool wind blew off the sea that chilled her sweat—a beautiful scene, were it not for all the blood.

The fighting had ceased, and bodies lay strewn about the courtyard, and along the road. Desperate men loaded wounded onto carts, then ran off to find a surgeon. Two sections of Steel had arrived, and a third was coming from the other direction at a run, ten men in tight formation, shields slung, labouring up the incline in heavy armour.

Most of the dead and wounded seemed well dressed, tailored shirts and sleek pants now torn and bloodied where they lay. Perhaps twenty dead, Sasha counted, and another twenty wounded . . . although more had been carried away.

She looked up at the rooftops, and saw crossbowmen surveying the scene. On the courtyard, more men were gathered, blood spattered and wild eyed, to confront the arriving Nasi-Keth. Feudalists all, and expecting more trouble.

Sasha strode forward, empty hands raised. They recognised her, and broke into fast, terse conversation amongst themselves. Sasha recognised Lord Elot, long blade in hand, his embroidered tunic slashed about its broad girth. Long hair plastered to a sweaty forehead beneath his bald dome, his eyes proud, his sword bloodied.

"Lord Elot," she said in greeting, and several feudalist men moved to her flank.

"Princess Sashandra," said Lord Elot. Those men around her paused, and made no more threatening move. Princess, he called her, and the men stopped. It was provocative, yet an offer of friendship all the same.

"What happened?" she asked.

"This was arranged," said Lord Elot, and spat. He seemed a man of cool temper, even in battle. Sasha could not help but admire it. "Your boys came right through our territory, shouting slogans of killing young Lord Alfriedo, and raping his mother."

"Not *my* boys."

"His," said Elot, and pointed with his sword. Sasha looked, and saw Reynold, surveying the scene. He did not seem shocked. Sasha felt her blood cool. Reynold had ordered the Nasi-Keth not to attend. The Civid Sein were little more than farmers and villagers, some with experience in the Steel, but not many. Feudalists, however, trained with swords for sport, and Elot's men were far better armed. Reynold must have known they'd be massacred.

"You've made them angry now," said Sasha.

"No doubt the intent," Elot said bitterly. "The White Lady sits on Council once more, and never mind that half its elected members languish in Justiciary cells. Civid Sein have numbers there now, and tomorrow they vote on the new justices. They'll be howling, all four appointments shall be Civid Sein or their cronies, you watch."

"All four." Sasha gulped more water, thinking fast. Seven justices. A majority vote was required to convict. There were clamours for Lady Renine's trial on treason . . . if the Civid Sein could muster four of the seven votes, they'd have her head. "Surely not. Justice Sinidane was just now at the Tol'rhen, asking Kessligh for help with the appointments."

"He seeks to present the White Lady with an alternative list," said Elot. "Sinidane is a good man, but Rhillian needs Lady Renine dead; it is the only way to control the mob."

"You think she'll fix the appointments?"

"I know it," said Elot. "Princess Sashandra, your sister is charged with complicity in treason. A Lenay king marches upon our northern border. There are far more who want Princess Alythia's head than Lady Renine's. Surely you've heard the talk?"

Sasha had heard the talk. Tol'rhen students who liked her had whispered it to her in the hallways, nasty things said by others. Apparently even some students were saying it, echoing what they'd heard demanded out in the courtyard, where angry farmers sharpened their hoes and scythes and called for royal blood. There had been writing on walls, and some effigies found hanging.

"Some are saying it's Alythia's plot, and that she is the one who led Lady Renine into treason."

Elot nodded. "I'd watch my back closely if I were you, Princess. If you wish to save your sister, come on your own at dusk to Shemon Square. It is the only way. Betray us you can, but Shemon Square is feudalist territory, and I know you love your sister well."

"I will," Sasha agreed.

Sasha was waiting in the alley when she heard a soft shuffle behind her, and spun. Errollyn was there, a shadow in the evening gloom.

"Damn you!" Sasha whispered, as her heart started again. Errollyn looked one way and the other, bow in hand. The air was hot and still, and there was barely a sound. Even here, on the feudalist midslope not far from the docks, people stayed indoors tonight. "I said I'd come alone!"

"You say a lot of things."

"They barely trust me!" Sasha insisted, back to the wall so as not to make a silhouette in the fading light. Errollyn leaned alongside. "They'll certainly not trust a serrin!"

"They will if I'm with you. Everyone knows I'm *du'jannah*."

"Aye, well *I* know that you're the reason Rhillian started this mess! If they've found out you're the one who spilled Lady Renine's plans to Rhillian . . ."

Errollyn reached across her, a hand on the wall by her head, his eyes intense and close. Even now, as well as she knew him, those startlingly bright eyes in the gloom gave Sasha an involuntary chill. "Sasha, Alythia's my friend too. I'm not sorry for what I did, but I am sorry for Alythia. If you think for a moment, you'll realise that you need me."

Need him? Abruptly Sasha recalled their passion in the Tol'rhen store room. She wondered if Errollyn might just take her here in the deserted alley, and did not mind the notion. But looking at his eyes, she realised that he meant his night vision.

She threw her head back in exasperation. "This is crazy. I don't know whether to fuck you or hit you."

"Can't you do both?"

Sasha glared, angry at him for daring to remind her why she loved him.

"Cover me," she told him, and slipped beneath his arm, edging toward the near corner.

Sasha crept about the courtyard, beneath the cover of arches. Errollyn followed, an arrow nocked to his bowstring, searching the darkness. Ahead, leaning against a column, there was a man in a cloak. A smoke stick flared orange, a gleam beneath his hood. Sasha left her blade sheathed . . . there was no advantage to feudalists in killing her, or taking her hostage now. But to recruit her to their cause . . .

"Sashandra," said the figure. Sasha came closer, and recognised Councillor Dhael.

"Councillor." She was surprised. She'd not seen Dhael since their voyage together, though she'd heard him spoken of. He was not a feudalist, nor was he said to have as many ties to them as some. "You are still free."

"Indeed," said Dhael, tapping his smoke. "There are those in Council who stand taller than I. I've long found that those who stick out their necks get their heads chopped off."

Sasha glanced back at Errollyn, who peered from the shadow of columns, searching the windows above.

"But you work with the feudalists now?" she pressed Dhael. She was here on Lord Elot's invitation. She did not want her time to be wasted. "I'd taken you for a friend of Saalshen. An idealist."

"A pacifist," said Dhael, with irony. "I know how you Lenays must dislike the word. Lord Elot asked me to speak to you."

"Because you once stood with Saalshen? I still stand with Saalshen. I just want my sister back. The way Rhillian's replacing high justices, she'll have the votes to take her head off. Spirits know the people are demanding it."

"Ah," said Dhael. "Well, there are no means here to help merely your sister."

"There's a plan to help them all escape?" Sasha guessed. "A breakout?"

Dhael regarded her warily. Then he looked at Errollyn. "A serrin working against Saalshen?"

"I told you," Sasha said impatiently, "we want Alythia. Nothing more."

"Such odd distinctions," said Dhael. "It is not an easy thing, Sashandra, to work for peace. Peace in this world is hard to find. Sometimes, its trail is confused."

"Kill your enemies," said Sasha. "Peace follows."

"Yes," said Dhael, amused. "Peace has followed you Lenays everywhere."

"I didn't say it would last. But that's your problem, Councillor, it never does. You seek the impossible; men like you search all their lives and find nothing."

"Saalshen, I think, has made a mistake." Dhael took a long breath of smoke. "Saalshen loves freedom. That is why serrin and Lenays have long enjoyed each other's company—you each have the love of freedom in common. But we humans . . . we know not what to do with serrin freedom. Rhillian now strives to preserve the order of freedom, by violence. I think perhaps Lady Renine has the best idea for the human future after all."

"Kesreligh warned me the pacifists would all side with the tyrants in the end—freedom is always violent, so tyranny must be for peace. I'm not interested in Lady Renine, Dhael, and I'm not interested in her plans to restore the throne of Rhodaan and put her son's skinny backside on it, and I'm quite certain it won't lead to a more peaceful world, just a world where the violence is more well controlled, and less inconvenient to the powerful. I only want to make sure that my sister's head stays attached to her shoulders. Now what is this plan of yours?"

It was cool underground. In the blackness, even Errollyn needed a lamp. Sasha walked behind, blade sheathed, fingers trailing the tunnel's stone wall. Behind them, five noblemen. She trusted none of them, and was uncomfortable to have them at her back, but reasoned well enough that if they wished to dispose of her, they'd surely wait until *after* she'd done them something useful.

They had entered the tunnel from the wall of a basement, downslope of the Justiciary, and Sasha figured that it would make a straight line for the dungeons. The basement had been part of an unremarkable house, owned by a family who owed allegiance. The tunnel had existed for quite some time, unbeknown to most, the Tracato nobility having long ago foreseen a day when such access to the Justiciary dungeons would prove useful. Certainly it was no rough-cut rabbit hole, its walls smooth stone, its floor paved, its ceiling a flat surface of timber planks.

After some distance walking hunched, the tunnel turned a bend, and stopped. Errollyn placed his lamp on the floor, handed his bow to Sasha (even in such tight quarters, he insisted on bringing it) and pushed on an overhead stone, uncovered by ceiling planks. The cell above was empty, they'd been told, courtesy of some inside source. That meant that it had been empty at the time the source had walked past it, most likely some time earlier today. A late transference of prisoners, or some newly captured person, would make things interesting.

The stone scraped as Errollyn heaved, then came free. He pushed it up, reached to set it aside, then heaved himself up on the lip to peer within. After a moment, he hauled up and disappeared, only to reach back down for his bow and lamp. Sasha followed, and rolled up onto a stone cell floor. The first of the nobles pulled himself through, unwrapped some keys from a bundled cloth and moved quietly to the door.

Sasha crouched beside him, and peered through the bars of the door's small port, listening intently. She heard nothing but the clacking of the key, then the slow squeal of the lock. The cell door opened, and Errollyn pushed past into the corridor, handing the lamp to Sasha and gesturing for the others to stay back. He moved with catlike grace beyond the lantern's dim light, past adjoining doors, and vanished in the dark. Sasha stood in the corridor, and could hear only her own breathing.

After a moment, Errollyn came back. "The first guards are not where they're supposed to be," he whispered. "They've gone."

"Then our way is clear," replied the senior nobleman—Torase was his name, and he was young, blond and brash. "Let's go, quickly!"

Errollyn led the way, Sasha this time bringing the lamp. The corridor turned, briefly right, then left, and then some stairs leading to an arch. That was where the guards would be, they'd been told. Errollyn had been confident that even with their illumination, he'd have been able to approach and disable them without killing, guard duty being dull at the best of times, and in a hole deep underground, even more so. There was no illumination now besides the lamp.

Errollyn gestured Sasha to stay at the arch, and walked alone to where his eyesight gave him the advantage, without illumination to give away his presence to any guards. He'd barely gone ten paces before he stopped, and cocked his head, listening. Sasha listened also—serrin hearing was no better than humans'.

There, she heard it. A distant yell, echoing. And another. More yells, a shouted conversation, somewhere up the corridor. A rattle of metal, an armoured man running. Sasha's hand moved to her blade, then stopped, as she realised the man was running away, sounds growing fainter.

She advanced on Errollyn. "An alarm?" Errollyn wondered.

"Guards won't leave their post for a mere alarm," Sasha muttered. "It's an attack."

"Conveniently timed," Errollyn said darkly.

Sasha nodded, and swore. The nobleman Torase approached, and Sasha had her blade at his neck before he could blink. "You told us nothing of an attack!"

Torase stared at her, his companions coming warily up behind, drawing weapons. He opened his mouth to lie, looked again at Sasha, and thought better of it. "It was necessary," he said. "We needed a diversion."

We're fools, Sasha thought bleakly. Naive fools, to have trusted them. But still, it could work.

"Dammit," she said. "Let's move fast before they suspect something."

Torase had the only keys, courtesy again of the inside source. Sasha moved with Errollyn to the head of the corridor, leaving the lamp with the noblemen. The light dimmed then brightened as cell doors were opened along the row behind, one after another, whispered words exchanged, footsteps scampering amid hushed cries and exclamations. Sasha peered up the steps from the dungeon, listening to the distant commotion. Errollyn had an arrow nocked to his bowstring, and he tested the tension.

Several loud, metallic blows, then, that echoed dangerously between walls. Someone was breaking chains. A hushed exclamation followed, as nearer doors creaked open. Then a fast approaching shuffle of footsteps.

"Sasha?" It was Alythia, barely visible in the dark. Her eyes were wide from several days without sunlight, her hair bedraggled. She hugged Sasha hard. "I knew you'd come! I knew it!"

"Lyth, you have to go with the others," Sasha begged. "Quickly, I'll be right behind you."

Alythia gave her a final, grateful kiss, and shuffled off, holding her dress up with both hands. Those retreating down the corridor were now carrying extra lamps, Sasha realised. At least the prisoners had not been left entirely without light. This row of cells now emptied, several of the noblemen were in dispute with a pair of newly released prisoners.

"My master Lord Hainel is not amongst these!" a furious ex-prisoner in dirty, once-expensive clothes whispered harshly, as Sasha retreated toward them. "There are more cells further along, we must empty them also! Hundreds of our noblest languish there!"

"We have the Lady Renine, and the Princess Alythia," Torase retorted. "If we try for more we may jeopardise the rescue for them. We do not take risks with the Lady Renine's freedom . . . !"

"And I say that my loyalty lies firstly with the Lord Hainel!" the ex-prisoner bristled. "I refuse to leave until—"

"You'll do as he says," Sasha told the man, "or we'll beat you bloody, throw you back in the cell and lock the door."

The man glared at her, but did not appear prepared to argue with the blade in her hand. Torase grabbed his arm and thrust him on down the corridor. Sasha and Errollyn followed, Errollyn turning constantly to watch the way behind, as the shadows advanced in their wake.

It was only when both she and Errollyn were back in the tunnel, and Errollyn was replacing the stone above their heads, that Sasha began daring to think that the entire exercise might actually work. She moved at a fast crouch, Errollyn behind, before meeting a queue as prisoners ahead climbed from the wall opening. Finally it was her turn, a short jump from the hole to the floor, behind shifted barrels of wine. Alythia was waiting for her by one barrel as other prisoners were ushered across the basement, and more men began shifting barrels back into place.

"Sasha, what now?" her sister asked breathlessly.

"'Lyth, did they hurt you?"

"No no," said Alythia impatiently, "I'm fine. What is the plan, do you have one?"

"Me? I'm just going along with your friends, 'Lyth. I was a bit rushed, I didn't have a choice."

"And their plan?" Alythia pressed.

"A boat, I think, for you and Lady Renine. To Larosa, or Elisse."

"I would rather stay! Feudalists are the majority in Tracato, we have money and weapons . . . we can win, Sasha! Why do they think to run away?"

"'Lyth . . . what's this 'we'?" Alythia frowned at her, not understanding. "I'm not on your side, 'Lyth! Or rather, I *am* on your side, but only yours!" She spared a fast look around, but those not leaving the basement were unlikely to understand Lenay. "They want me here because they think they can split me off from the Nasi-Keth, but . . ."

"Sasha, if the Nasi-Keth are to support hooligans and lawless murderers in taking over Tracato, what good are they for?"

"That doesn't make me a friend of feudalists, 'Lyth."

"Aren't you the one always telling me that sometimes, we have to take a side?" Alythia insisted.

Sasha rolled her eyes. Rhillian, again, had made a mess—she could oppress the feudalists for as long as the Steel were in Tracato, but the Steel were overdue for the western front. Leave the Nasi-Keth and Civid Sein in charge of the city?

"Sasha, Sasha," Alythia said soothingly, taking her hands. "It's all right, I understand. But I still don't see why they want to run away—we could stay and . . ."

"You don't want to be in a civil war in Tracato," Sasha said firmly. "The feudalists underestimate the Civid Sein, they're *everywhere*, they have sympathisers all across the countryside even amongst those who are not truly declared members. And they're coming, after today, I promise you that. Safer that you leave."

"We have to go," Errollyn broke in. "That fighting could spread downslope fast."

Sasha grabbed Alythia's arm and hurried her up the stairs . . . then froze halfway up as yells and shouting broke out above, and the crash of windows breaking. Sasha swore, whipped out her blade and ran to the top of the stairs to peer about. The room was wide, well furnished, and under assault. Noblemen grabbed tables and held them to the windows, piling behind to form barricades, blocking those attempting to enter. Sasha saw the broad shields and ridged helmets of Steel footsoldiers, a thrusting mass of oncoming armour.

"Up the stairs!" Sasha shouted at Alythia, pointing across the room to the next, upward flight. Alythia ran without question, clutching her skirts, Sasha and Errollyn having enough time to spin about, watching all sides as exprisoners ran in panic, and noblemen yelled for assistance, waving swords and gathering furniture to make further obstacles.

There was pandemonium on the stairs, Alythia stumbled, but Errollyn grabbed her as Sasha tried to clear the way. People were leaning from the windows of the second floor, dropping heavy objects onto the street below. No archers, Sasha had time to notice as Errollyn dragged Alythia around the bend and up the next flight. And none of those leaning out the window were under fire from below, as might usually be expected. It seemed the Steel, having been tipped off, were after prisoners. Had the whole thing been a setup, to recapture all the ex-prisoners along with their rescuers?

Two more flights, and they emerged into an attic. Set into the sloping roof on two sides were small windows, before which a number of nobility were now clustering, the men jumping onto the adjoining roof across a short gap. Sasha joined one cluster, and was astonished that several noticed Alythia and immediately made way, pulling others aside as they did.

"Oh dear lords!" Alythia exclaimed as she looked down at the gap. There was light enough from these windows to see the opposing roof clear enough, and the gap itself . . . but no light from below. Only a seemingly endless drop.

"'Lyth, let me go first, I'll guide you from the other side."

An arrow hissed and buzzed, and Sasha's heart nearly stopped. Errollyn pulled an arrow, nocked and drew impossibly fast, and scanned the direction it had come from with night-piercing eyes.

"We have crossbows in the windows of the adjoining property!" he announced for all to hear. "Time your jumps, and do not tarry!"

He released, a thump and twang like a heavy drumbeat, and quickly drew again, as Sasha began her slither down the tiles.

"Did you get him?" Alythia asked eagerly.

"Frightened, I think."

"But Sasha says you never miss!"

"Yes, but I *meant* to frighten him," said Errollyn, a touch sarcastically. "Not every target is clear."

Sasha gathered herself and leaped. An easy jump, for her, and she held enough momentum to scramble up and grab the window frame. Errollyn fired fractionally before a bolt whizzed past, barely an arm's length from Sasha's head.

"That one I hit," Errollyn announced, drawing again. "Though his helmet saved him."

"I'm beginning to think Sasha may have exaggerated," Alythia remarked. Not finding a target, Errollyn put away the arrow, and drew his sword instead.

"Hold still," he commanded, and drew the razor-edged blade quickly about Alythia's skirts, cutting effortlessly. He sheathed the blade, and knelt before her. "I've always wanted to do this to a princess," he remarked, and yanked at her skirts. With a great tear, they came away, revealing shapely legs in hose.

"Well, Master Errollyn, I never!" Alythia began positioning herself awkwardly to slither backward, Errollyn clutching her hand.

"Just slide," he told her, "I've got you." Another crossbow shot, and someone further along the gap was hit, on the verge of jumping, and toppled into the darkness. A thud from below.

"Let your foot reach the rim!" Sasha called. "A little lower!" She could hear crashes, armoured clattering and yells from lower windows as the Steel forced their way up the stairs. Alythia's foot strained, toes searching; Errollyn bore most of her weight one-armed, his bicep straining. Alythia's toes touched, and she wriggled around to a sitting position, most ridiculous with her bare legs hunched up, looking desperately across the gap.

Sasha was about to call more instruction when another crossbow shot whizzed by. In sudden panic Alythia stood and leaped, gracelessly, and crashed onto the sloping tiles before Sasha's secure window ledge. Sasha leaped forward, one hand clutching the window rail, one grasping Alythia's arm . . . the leap had dislodged tiles, which clattered down the slope and over the edge. Sasha's grip slipped, and Alythia slid, and screamed.

Errollyn slid straight down the opposite roof, planted feet on the edge and leaped, landing directly beside Alythia while hurling his bow through the window, and grasping the window ledge. His other hand grabbed Alythia, and pulled. With Sasha he bundled her through the window and followed her in.

He recovered his bow and led them across the attic room to another window, from where they could see a flat roof—a sungarden. This jump was shorter, and Alythia went last, with Errollyn and Sasha to catch her without falling.

They ran across the pavings, the half-moon giving enough light to see. Others also ran across the rooftop, or along adjoining roofs, and Errollyn paused to peer over an edge.

"I see no one," he said, rejoining the women as they ran.

"Doesn't mean they aren't there," said Sasha. "The Steel will follow, let's see how far we can get."

It was quite far, as it turned out. The adjoining floor was occupied by cityfolk who offered to hide them, but as Sasha told them, all of these buildings would surely be stormed and searched in short order. Another flight of stairs got them into the attic, out those small windows and up the side of the sloping roof. They balanced along the peak, Errollyn spotting the next sungarden and easiest jump well ahead. Alythia skinned her knee on that jump, and they were all now breathing hard and sweating profusely in the sultry night air.

There the easy routes ended. Sasha risked a trapdoor and stairs, which took them down through a common hall, and then more stairs. At the bottom of the stairs, Errollyn peered out into a small courtyard, an arrow to his string. Past her hard breathing, Sasha could hear distant yells, but no more.

"I wonder if Lady Renine got out?" Alythia wondered, a low whisper past laboured breathing.

"I'm sure she did," Sasha replied, calm and low. "She had a lot of people to help her, and she was ahead of us."

"And what of Alfriedo?"

"He's in the Mahl'rhen. It's too hard to rescue him there, the lords just wanted Lady Renine."

"With me," Errollyn whispered. "Alythia first, stay close to the wall, move in my footsteps."

He slid out the doorway and along the courtyard wall, Alythia following, Sasha next.

"Hold there!" came a yell, and Sasha and Errollyn spun. Several figures emerged from small doorways, bows drawn and aimed. Sasha looked up, and saw more archers appearing on the rooftops. Errollyn cursed.

"Nasi-Keth," said Sasha, with almost relief. "Nasi-Keth!" she said more loudly. "I'm Nasi-Keth, and he's *talmaad*, as you can see!"

"And who's that?" More figures were emerging, these with swords.

"That's my sister!" Sasha replied, on a flash of inspiration. "The Princess Alythia Lenayin! I'm reclaiming her for the Tol'rhen, she will increase Kessligh's bargaining power. We intercepted her during the escape just now!"

One figure came ahead of the others. Errollyn swore again, barely audible. Sasha could only guess that he knew the approaching figure in the gloom.

"We were watching your progress across the rooftops, Sashandra Lenayin!" the man said, and his voice was familiar. He came closer, and Sasha recognised the man—Timoth Salo, Reynold Hein's young ex-nobleman friend, and convert to the Civid Sein. "You have partaken in treason with feudalist wretches, and you shall be given directly to the justice of the Revolutionary Council."

"Revolutionary Council? What fucking nonsense are you talking now?"

"*The* Revolutionary Council, led by Mistress Rhillian, convened of revolutionary Rhodaani patriots and without those scum-sucking traitors whom you have come to call your friends!"

"Too many archers," said Errollyn in a low voice, looking about. "We'll be hit for sure."

"It is true then," Alythia said loudly, peering down her nose at their new captors. "Tracato and the Nasi-Keth are all going straight down the sewer."

Eleven

THE DAY AFTER THE WEDDING, Sofy awoke in her husband's bed and gazed at the ceiling. The bedchambers were enormous, and the bed wide. Its posts were decorated with sprigs of local herb, in the Larosan custom, and the sheets smelled of lavender. Her nightgown was silver lace, a scandalous thing that a year ago, a virgin girl, she might have giggled to behold. Morning sunlight fell across the wide flagstone floor, the carpets and wall hangings, the rich chairs, the cabinets, the breakfast table. Balthaar's shield, emblazoned with the Arosh coat of arms—a beast Balthaar had told her was called a griffin, and crossed lances. The mounted head of a buck he had once killed.

A bell hung from a stand by the bedside, awaiting her tinkle. Sofy refrained, wondering that her husband should have awakened so early, and left her in bed alone on her first morning as a wedded woman. Perhaps she'd made a mess of things already. Perhaps she'd been wrong. In the haze of the newly awakened, she wasn't certain of anything. It did not feel different, to be married. Perhaps she had been a fool to expect otherwise.

She recalled Sasha telling her of the first morning after her first battle. She'd killed a Cherrovan warrior in that battle, and had become a blooded warrior herself. In the Goeren-yai tradition, such an occasion was worthy of grim celebration, recognition not only of triumph and honour, but of duties fulfilled and responsibilities acquired. A warrior's honour was the foundation of Lenay society, and Sasha had expected to awaken the next morning feeling something, for good or ill. And yet, the sun had looked the same as it rose above the rugged Lenay hills, and the air had smelled as it always had, and Sasha was still Sasha; perhaps a little wiser, but no more than that. Relief, Sasha had said. That had been her main emotion. To have finally gotten it out of the way. Sofy thought she could empathise with that now.

She held up her right hand to examine the great, golden ring on her fourth finger. It held an emerald jewel, large and sparkling. In the Bacosh, green was the colour of royalty, and riches, and power. It felt odd upon her finger, cold and hard. It was going to distract her attention now, every time she used her right hand. Something about the thought annoyed her.

Thinking of Sasha annoyed her.

Sasha had sworn to be there, had sworn as though she would move heaven and earth to attend her little sister's wedding. Sofy had told her at the time that she should not promise that which she had no guarantee of delivering, yet a part of her had believed all the same. It had been a little girl's foolishness, believing her big sister could walk on water, and turn ale into honey at the wave of a hand. Now, she knew she had been silly, yet she felt annoyed at Sasha all the same. Betrayed, in fact, in her own small, petty, immature way.

Gods, she thought glumly. Perhaps I truly am cut out to be a spoiled, vain little princess after all.

She reached, and tinkled the bell. Ten maids entered the chambers in the blink of an eye, with trays for the breakfast table, new wood for the fireplace, and great, steaming jugs of water for her morning bath. Ten maids became twenty, and Sofy sat up, feeling slightly ridiculous in her lacy nightgown.

"Would Your Highness take her breakfast now?" asked the senior maid. "Or would she prefer to take breakfast with her bath?"

It sounded a little too decadent even for a princess of the Bacosh. "Breakfast first, if you please," said Sofy. And, spotting her Lenay girls amidst the others, "Hello Jeleny, hello Rhyana! Did you have a nice time last night?"

The girls paused, giving slightly pale looks at the head maid. Sofy frowned, abruptly understanding.

"I do recall stating that my Lenay handmaidens should take instruction only from me," she said coolly.

The head maid bowed. "Your Highness, these are the Larosan Royal quarters, and there are certain standards to which the Prince is accustomed in his chambers. . . ."

"I shall speak with him," Sofy said firmly. "Please, my girls, I will not have such stifling formality that you must ask permission before speaking with me."

"Of course, Highness," said Jeleny, finishing laying the table, and hurrying off. The senior maid continued about her business, expressionless. Clearly the old witch had frightened them. Well, Balthaar *was* occasionally short with the servants, and these were his chambers more than hers. Another annoyance on a very surreal morning.

"Someone fetch Yasmyn for me," she requested, standing to slip into the robe one girl held ready.

When Yasmyn arrived, the senior maid glowered at her, for Yasmyn wore only a scarlet morning gown, her hair still mussed from bed, her eyes squinted in the manner of one recovering from a heavy night.

"Some spiced tea for the noble Isfayen!" Sofy requested of the maids, as Yasmyn shuffled to the opposing chair and slumped. Headache or not, Yasmyn was smiling. "You look rather like the cat that got the milk, and was then beaten with the bowl," Sofy observed.

"A good wedding," said Yasmyn thickly. Tea arrived, and she took it, sipping deeply.

"Great Lord Faras will not have a new grandchild in nine months?" Sofy wondered.

Yasmyn grinned. "It was not *that* good a wedding," she said. "And what of the Regent Arosh?"

Sofy sighed. She glanced about, but most of the maids had gone, or were clustered by the far wardrobe chamber, arranging the princess's dress for the day. Yasmyn peered more closely. Sofy shook her head.

"He is not an ugly man," Yasmyn pointed out. "Or did you take the powder?"

"No, nothing like that," Sofy said tiredly. They spoke Lenay, though Sofy did not think that all the Larosan maids would be deaf to it. Surely the regent had spies. "It's just—"

"He could not perform? Oh the scandal!"

"Don't be crude, Yasmyn. I'm sure he could . . . perform."

"Did you not wish him to?"

Sofy opened her mouth to reply, then cut herself off. Exhaled hard. "We discussed matters. He was . . . kind. I . . . he . . ." Sofy took another breath. "We had argued. About the war, the serrin . . . I had asked him what he meant to do, or what his father meant to do, once his forces had invaded the Saalshen Bacosh."

Yasmyn looked very serious. It was clear she thought her princess had done a dangerous and possibly foolhardy thing.

"What did he say?"

"Oh, Yasmyn," Sofy scolded, keeping her tone light. "I'm not a fool, I didn't question the war itself. I merely expressed the opinion that I should not like to see every city and village burned to the ground. He thought it showed a soft heart, I think he found it sweet. But I did remind him that my sister is Nasi-Keth, and that surely not all serrin teachings are evil. . . ."

"Oh, Sofy," Yasmyn muttered.

". . . but he did not take it badly!" Sofy insisted. "He . . . we argued, and he was, well, condescending . . ." and her tone became a little dry. "But he was not upset. He merely suggested, after the wedding, that perhaps if I did not wish it so soon, that we should not make love until I felt that I truly wanted to." Yasmyn looked very unhappy. "I thought he was being sweet!"

"You did not consummate the marriage," Yasmyn retorted. "If anyone should find out . . ."

"What, you think it could be annulled?"

"No, worse. People will make rumours, and tell nasty tales, and you will be trapped in something hostile and dangerous. With all the suspicion between Lenays and lowlanders, our peoples do not need such a marriage. You make life dangerous for everyone."

Sofy gazed at her breakfast, no longer feeling hungry. Yasmyn finished her tea, and grasped her princess's hand.

"Sofy. No more weak little girl. You're lucky he is handsome, and nice to you. But even were he ugly and a brute, you'd still have to fuck him." Sofy rolled her eyes, but Yasmyn did not let go of her hand. "It's not so bad as dying in battle. I think it's much easier than a morning's hard work on a farm. It is your one royal hardship. Close your eyes if you must, but you must get it done." She leaned closer. "It's not Jaryd, is it?" she whispered.

"No! I know my duty, Yasmyn, and gods know he's bedded so many women that I've not the least problem with evening that score a little."

"And why would that matter to you if your head was not still full of Jaryd?"

"As though you can talk!" Sofy retorted. "You're the one who thought it such a wonderful idea to accept Jaryd into my staff in the first place!"

"In Isfayen," Yasmyn replied, "a woman can love one man, and fuck another. One is recreation. The other is duty."

Sofy paused to recover her hand and her temper. "I can too," she said firmly. "And I will. I don't love him anyway."

Yasmyn just looked at her.

Following the wedding, there was the tournament. With all grand weddings came grand tournaments, and this tournament promised to be the most grand in a generation. All the warriors were gathered, all the provinces of the "free Bacosh" come together with common purpose, for the first time in many years. Sofy rode with Princess Elora and several ladies-in-waiting. Sitting in the open-top carriage, with Larosan knights for escort, she had never felt so self-conscious. Cityfolk waved as the carriage passed, and called good wishes, and Sofy waved back.

All the lands before the Sherdaine walls, for as far as the eye could see, were covered with tents and campsites. Beyond the camp, atop a pretty hillside, rose Jacquey Castle. The tournament adorned the hillside like a jewelled necklace, a colourful profusion of stands, tents, stalls and yards. There was commotion as Sofy's carriage arrived, trumpeters scurrying to form a line, and knights ahorse to make an honour guard. These, Sofy was informed by a lord from Algrasse as she walked with Princess Elora down the line, were champions from across the free Bacosh. Everyone seemed excited to see how they performed against each other, in this rare peaceful gathering.

The tournament was intriguing. Sofy sat in the royal box in a wooden stand, with the regent, Princess Elora, a number of older lords now too grey to compete, and various ladies-in-waiting. Before them, a strip of grass had a rail down its centre, and mounted knights would charge each other, and attempt to break their light lances upon the other's shield or armour. Sofy did not think it much of a test of skill, for surely it was luck as much as anything . . . but her neighbours in the box sharply disagreed, and gossiped intently on the merits of various knights, techniques, styles of armour and horses. In the broader crowds surrounding the jousting strip, Sofy could see gambling, men with pouches of coin declaring their price, and taking bets by scribbling marks on parchment. She would have enjoyed the spectacle far more if she'd known where her new husband was. It was poor form for a man to compete in his own wedding tournament, so he was not being fitted into his armour, at least.

Dafed—Balthaar and Elora's brother—did particularly well in several passes, and was honoured with the colours of Lady Emore Turen, a daughter of one of Tournea's senior lords, and a dazzling beauty. All seemed greatly pleased at that, for tensions between Tournea and Larosa were never far from the surface. Sofy was then treated to a long gossip between Elora and several other ladies as to the prospects of Dafed's marriage to Family Turen . . . only that might risk war between Turen and Family Rigard, whose Lord Arjon was currently Lord of Tournea. The ease with which Bacosh-folk spoke of war astonished Sofy.

In Lenayin, war was serious, and fought over honour, insult or injury. In the Bacosh, it seemed a matter of formality and procedure, as regular as the seasons. Even now, she learned, many of the tournament's participant families were technically in a state of war. Bacosh wars did not seem so devastating as Lenay wars, however. Captured knights were ransomed, and while villages frequently swapped sides as feudal territories were rearranged, they were rarely slaughtered outright. Once, Sofy might have thought the Bacosh method more greatly civilised. But now, as she sat and watched the splendid knights charging in their gleaming armour, she wondered if the relative civility of Bacosh wars had caused the Bacosh people to come to love war too much.

There were no Lenays in the joust, Sofy was pleased to see. With no experience at this kind of warfare, it would not have been a good showing for her countrymen. However, there were Lenay-style swordwork contests elsewhere in the tournament grounds, she was told.

After several hours seated, she needed to stretch her legs. When one was princess regent, she discovered, one did not simply go for a stroll. By the time she was free of the stands and walking amidst the crowds, she had an escort of eight knights, a herald, Princess Elora, four ladies-in-waiting, and two servants. The crowds stared as the procession passed, and Elora chatted to her on the endless fascination of the Bacosh nobility—families, weddings, children, lines of succession and who was feuding with whom. Sofy had known it was complicated, but now she was beginning to feel dizzy. For the first time, she found herself wondering what would happen to her new family if the Enoran, Rhodaani and Ilduuri Steel held firm in the battles ahead. Almost certainly, she suspected, the regency would fall, and other families would begin fighting for the title. The boundaries of the Bacosh provinces would shift, and whether she or any of Family Arosh would still be alive at the end of it, she did not know.

The Lenay sword contests, which attracted nearly as large a crowd as the jousts, were held within a series of wide circles fenced for the occasion. Sofy stayed long enough to see several invited Bacosh knights, in padded bandas instead of clamshell armour, soundly defeated in flashing exchanges of wooden blades. Some of her female entourage ceased their excited gushing about the valiance of the knights, and began asking admiring questions of various Lenay warriors. All were astonished to learn that Sofy had no clue as to the identity of most of them, as they were not renowned nobles, but poor farmers or villagers from across Lenayin. Most were greatly discomforted when one such Goeren-yai farmer knocked a genuine noble lord to the ground . . . and astonished further that the nobleman's only reply was to grin, and acknowledge his opponent's superior move. Soon enough there were no more Bacosh knights contesting within the tachadar circles, and Sofy's contingent began to wonder loudly what was happening back at the jousts.

For lunch, the noble entourage was escorted back to Castle Jacquey, where a long table had been set in a grand hall. Still there was no sign of Balthaar. It took Yasmyn's approach, as Sofy sat to entree, to solve that mystery.

"He's in the high study," Yasmyn said over Sofy's shoulder in Lenay, as others frowned at the intrusion. "There is a gathering of Bacosh lords there. I think they argue."

"Over what?"

"These are men who love their tournaments. There is only one thing they love more." And when Sofy frowned, Yasmyn added, "War," clearly thinking her princess a little slow.

Sofy put her napkin on the table crossly, and stood up. "Sister dearest," said Elora in surprise, "does something bother you?"

"Yes something bothers me," Sofy declared. "I am a newly wedded woman, and I have not been attended by my husband all day. If he shall not attend to me, then I shall attend to him," she said, and left.

Knights scrambled from the table to pursue her, as the ladies looked at each other, astonished at the ill-decorum of it all.

"And where have you been all morning?" Sofy asked Yasmyn.

"Saving a marriage," Yasmyn said grimly. "It is not well that your husband should ignore you all day. If he were my husband, and he were in the wrong, I would strike him."

"And if you were in the wrong?"

"Suck him." Sofy blinked. "If you will not fuck him, you may consider it."

"Good lords, Yasmyn," Sofy muttered. "I've never had a friend quite so exasperating as you. Not even Sasha."

"I say what needs to be said."

The guards at the study doors did not prevent the princess regent from entering. Within, she found a room of tables, shelves and books, lit only by some narrow windows overlooking the tournament. There was nothing of calm discussion within, but rather a collection of lords in raiments and house colours, seated or standing in various small groups, arguing with animation. They barely looked at Sofy as she entered, Yasmyn at her side, and searched for her husband.

Balthaar sat at the table's end, head in hands, as several lords shouted and pointed fingers across him. He saw Sofy, and straightened, astonished. He climbed to his feet.

"My sweet," he said, taking her hands and kissing them. "You must forgive me, I have been a dreadful husband. Trust me that I should have rather been at your side than here, yet my duties have forbidden it."

Balthaar loved to ride, hunt and tourney. The study was gloomy, and he had looked bored as sin when Sofy entered. Her heart softened. "And what is this?" she asked.

"We discuss the order of battle. There is so much history in this room, families and feuds and old wars. There is great honour to marching one's standard at the vanguard of war. We contest for a place of prestige upon the field, and seek not to march upon the flank of some old foe. I fear it could take all day, and perhaps much of tomorrow." He kissed her hand once more. "Go back to the tourney, my sweet. This is not a matter for you."

"On the contrary," Sofy insisted. "I have heard little else besides such matters on the ride to Larosa. Lenayin knows as much of petty bloodfeuds as the Bacosh, I fear, yet we have seen them all resolved to this point. I am certain I can help."

"Your father and brother allowed your assistance to mediate between the Lenay provinces?"

"But of course," said Sofy. Koenyg was not so hard headed as to ignore his youngest sister's persuasive powers. He had coached her, of course, but where offers of possible marriages and royal gifts were concerned to seal an agreement, all knew that such things were far more readily accepted from her mouth than her brothers' or father's. And she recalled Myklas saying with affection, after she had persuaded Lord Iraskyn of Yethulyn to allow his son's standing unit, the Silver Eagles, to hold a rather less glamorous position on the inside flank, that he had no idea how they would run the kingdom without her. "Please, Balthaar, let me help," she continued. "It does not look good for the new princess regent to wander the tourney without her husband. I may not be able to wield a sword in our partnership, but I can certainly use my tongue."

Balthaar smiled at her. "One notices. As you will, then. Here, I shall fill you in on the details."

She had most of it resolved by midafternoon. Balthaar was not the only man impressed. All kissed her hand upon departing, and many bowed low. Sofy wondered how *any* of these fools, in the Bacosh or Lenayin, got anything done without her. Men blustered, made threats and were easily upset. She soothed their egos, made gentle flattery, and found the happy turn of every dark assignment. When that did not work, she bribed, but not crudely. Whatever the worst opinions of commonfolk and gossips, most noblemen in her experience did not desire simply wealth and power—it was rather status, and respect, that drove their craving for gold.

Following the night's banquet, Balthaar joined Sofy in their chambers, and dismissed the maids. He clasped her hands as they stood warm before the crackling fireplace, and Sofy's heart beat faster.

"You are not certain of this war," he said to her, softly. "Why then did you help today?"

For a long moment, Sofy did not know what to say. "The Bacosh is a grand place," she said at last. "I am the princess regent. I should try to do good while I have the opportunity. I see Lenays and Larosans sharing each other's cultures, forging friendships. Surely it cannot be a bad thing."

She said it firmly enough that she nearly believed it. Her instinct had always been to bring people together. She had never liked conflict. Peace between peoples was always good. She could make something good come of it, she was increasingly certain.

"I would like for many other things to be closer too," said Balthaar. He kissed her. Sofy thought it rather nice, and let him. He took her to the bed, and began removing her clothes. They made love, and Sofy thought that rather nice too. He seemed rather taken with her, and was ever so gentle. Too gentle, almost, when her own passion took her. As Yasmyn had said, he was a handsome man, and if this were her heaviest royal burden, then it was not a hard one to bear.

Later, she lay in his arms, and gazed at the fireplace. *Now* she felt different, as though married life had truly begun. Yasmyn would be pleased, she thought, and found herself smiling. And she'd only thought of Jaryd three or four times.

Or maybe five.

Elesther Road was in chaos. The Steel made formations across some alley exits, and cavalry clattered along the cobbles, but the riot continued. Bodies lay unclaimed in the street. Others hung from windows, tied at the neck with rope. The Civid Sein had been this way, and the revenge was spreading.

Lieutenant Raine rode at Rhillian's side, in full armour. Country folk watched them pass, roughly dressed and bearing all kind of rustic weapons. They roamed Elesther, near the Tol'rhen, and were working toward the Justiciary, while the Steel tried to keep armed mobs apart, with limited success.

"There's too many of them," Lieutenant Raine said darkly. "Hundreds more are pouring in every day. They make camp in the courtyards, and the homes of fled or murdered nobility. I need only a word, and I shall drive them back to the farms and villages from which they came."

"I cannot," Rhillian said. "Not until the Lady Renine and Alfriedo have been recaptured." The last was most galling; she had not expected so daring an assault upon the Mahl'rhen itself. Five serrin were dead, a friend amongst them, and the young Lord Alfriedo missing. Still, from the broader perspective, she was not too concerned. "This violence is the work of the feudalists. They were warned of the country folk's waning patience, and now they see the truth of it."

"M'Lady," said the lieutenant, "I am losing men to desertion. You know the Steel, you know the family that we are. The Steel *never* desert. Or rarely. But now I have noble-born enlisted and officers alike disappearing to see to their families, and I cannot in all honesty say that I blame them."

Rhillian repressed a grimace and looked across the street. A door had been caved in, and several Steel were rounding up looters, beating them with little mercy. Tracato, most civil and orderly of all human cities, was falling apart.

"Council sits today," she said. "What think the captains?"

"Council," Lieutenant Raine snorted. "That word used to mean something. These men are not elected. . . ."

"Neither were most of the old Council, in fairness."

"But at least there was an appearance," said Raine. "A pretence, no matter how they bought or bribed their way in. A Council without half its elected members, with all the nobility stripped away and replaced with Civid Sein cronies, is no Council at all worth the name."

"Yet the Steel are sworn to obey the Council," Rhillian said. "Will the captains do so? Captain Hauser does not give me a straight answer."

Raine's expression was bleak. His eyes lingered on a body, face down on the cobbles in a pool of dried blood. "I'm a country lad myself," he said, "but I'd cut these Civid Sein scum down like vermin given the nod. This is not civilisation, M'Lady, this is rule of the mob, and I like it not. Nor do a majority of country folk, I believe, nor a majority of the Steel. I'll not follow the orders of such people who now comprise the Council. But of course, I cannot speak for the captains."

"If not the Council, then who?"

"M'Lady, I would follow you. I believe most of the *dharmi* feel the same. The feudalists are traitors, and the Civid Sein are a barbarian lynch mob. You walk the path between, and are not concerned with factions. I believe that is exactly what Rhodaan needs."

"Lieutenant, you surprise me. Here I'd thought any expression of solidarity from a human would come with expressions of love and loyalty."

"My father once told me that if you filled up all the goodness ever done by the promises of councilmen, philosophers, lords and priests in your left hand, while shitting in your right, the right hand will be full much faster. I'll follow you precisely because you *don't* ask me to love you."

Rhillian looked at the young lieutenant for a long moment, then nodded. "I cannot in good conscience even ask you to trust me," she added. "Most of what I do here, I do not like, and much ill will be done before I am through."

"It was falling apart already, with what the feudalists were trying. There was little choice."

"I cannot move against the Civid Sein just yet, Lieutenant, whatever horrors they should perform in the meantime. But soon, I promise."

In the grand courtyard before the Tol'rhen, usually filled with factional and philosophical debate, there now camped a ragged army. There were many carts, mules and horses, amidst which country folk made makeshift camps. The smoke of cookfires filled the air, and an endless commotion of voices, animals, and from some quarters, shouted speeches.

Rhillian paused on the Elesther steps with Aisha to survey it all, and the Nasi-Keth who wandered through it, some talking and friendly with the new arrivals, others wary. She then pressed on through the main doors, guarded by Nasi-Keth, and into the dining hall. Here, familiar rowed benches had been rearranged crosswise, and crowded with people—perhaps half Nasi-Keth, and the other half not. At the far end, before the kitchens, a stage had been raised. Even above the roaring of the crowd, Rhillian could hear the booming voice of the speaker, in his black Tol'rhen robes. Only one man in the Tol'rhen possessed such a voice, and could rouse such a ruckus.

Rhillian made her way down the side of the hall, Lieutenant Raine at her back. ". . . and I say that we shall do unto them as they have done to us!" Ulenshaal Sevarien was roaring. "For so many centuries, the nobility have been a plague upon Rhodaan! They call it taxation, but in truth, it was theft! They are a gang of robber barons and thieves, and they have stolen wealth, and property, and the hard-earned labour of our sweaty and dirt-stained hands. . . ."

"Our?" Rhillian wondered sourly. Sevarien's hands were pink, plump and pale, like the rest of him. She doubted he'd ever pulled a plough, or raised a barn, or milked a cow in his life.

"We demand that the remaining feudal lands be redistributed amongst those who know and work it best!" A roar from the crowd. "We demand equality!" Another roar. "We demand the abolition of false titles and noble privilege!" Again. "We demand an end to the domination of Council by the wealthy few!"

"And what are you going to replace it all with, you fucking fool?" Aisha said loudly, above the din. Rhillian spared Aisha a glance, and saw the anger. For all her tongues, Aisha rarely swore. But Aisha was Enoran, and she recalled what form the Enoran purges had taken. Now, she saw them repeated on the streets of Tracato.

"And we demand the final punishment of those traitors who have plotted and schemed to enrich themselves on the blood and treasure of our great and noble Rhodaani brotherhood!"

This last, Sevarien delivered with a sweeping gesture, that ended on Rhillian, as she walked toward the stage. Many Civid Sein came to their feet, chanting and yelling. Some Nasi-Keth joined them. On the stage behind Sevarien, the Tol'rhen's other seniors were seated. Rhillian saw Kessligh, his chin in his hand. His expression was unreadable.

She climbed the steps, Aisha and Lieutenant Raine waiting below, and raised a hand to acknowledge the shouting. It amazed her that they should cheer for her. Perhaps a human might feel some emotional stirring and some common passion with the crowd. Rhillian stared out across the mob, and felt only an absence. She was serrin, and she had the *vel'ennar*. This was nothing. When the noise dimmed, she lowered her arm.

"You have come here for revolution," she told them. "I see no revolution in the town. I see lawlessness, murder, rape, theft and thuggery. If it continues, I shall send the Steel to this camp, and to all other such camps across the city, and have you all killed. Thank you for your attention, and good day."

She gestured to Kessligh, and he rose, in that stunned silence. Boos followed, as they moved from the stage, rising to a crescendo of yells and abuse. The Nasi-Keth drew weapons. Rhillian skipped off the stage amidst a rain of missiles, and walked with Kessligh to the kitchens, which were nearest.

"You'll only hold them with threats of violence for so long," Kessligh told her grimly. "After a while, they'll call your bluff, and then you'll really have to do it."

"You think I wouldn't?" Rhillian asked. Aisha and Lieutenant Raine followed them in, Aisha seating herself upon an abandoned cutting bench.

Kessligh leaned against another bench and exhaled hard. "This is fast spinning out of control. Again. You surely can't say you're surprised."

"How many are still with you?" Rhillian asked, ignoring the barb. Kessligh's stare lingered for a short moment. Unlike most, he never flinched beneath her gaze.

"Most of those not with the Civid Sein," he replied, finally. "I have more Nasi-Keth than Sevarien, perhaps twice as many. But he has the country mobs. I suspect I'll gain even more in this place shortly. There've been idealistic youngsters horrified at what they've seen, the last few days. Sevarien spins a grand and exciting tale of injustice and vengeful rebellion, but on the streets, it boils down to blood, rape and murder every time. I've been telling them so since I first arrived; only now do they see my point."

"Even after what Sasha tried, they'll still follow you?" Rhillian questioned warily. "Even most of those Nasi-Keth who do not love the Civid Sein have little love for the nobility. Very few nobility ever sent their children to study in the Tol'rhen. Sasha helped Lady Renine and Alfriedo escape, and you are not blamed for your uma's actions?"

"People here know Sasha," Kessligh said flatly. "They know she does as she will. I tell them I did not order it, and they believe me, because they know it is the truth. She has little interest in Lady Renine and her son, she was trying to save her sister. Whom you are still proposing to kill."

"I have no say in the workings of the Justiciary," Rhillian replied. Kessligh's expression was statement enough that he did not believe her. "Do you condemn Sasha's actions?"

"Seriously? In truth, she read my mind. Expulsion from Rhodaan was always the superior option for the Renines, and any other troublesome nobles. Sasha's own father did that to her, you'll recall. He's been a fool of late, King Torvaal, but he's been a wise man too, and sometimes that wisdom still shows. If he'd killed Sasha, all her supporters would have been mad. That makes for unpleasantness. You came here down Elesther Road. You've seen what I mean."

"I haven't killed any Renines yet."

"And so I wait for it all to get worse when you do," said Kessligh. "Yes, the Renines and all their allies were stupid. Yes, they are traitors, they collaborated with the enemies of Rhodaan in the hopes of regaining their old, feudal glory. But if you kill them, you lose the wealth of Tracato, and the only force to oppose the rage of the nobility is the Civid Sein. You need the Steel at the front, Rhillian, Sofy Lenayin's wedding is happening, and the Army of Lenayin will not rest idle forever. The Steel cannot make a strong front against the Larosans and Lenays while Rhodaan continues to burn at their backs. My advice—if you recapture Lady Renine and Alfriedo, let them go. Send them to Sherdaine, or Petrodor. Exile will remove them from the scene, without so much of the bloodshed."

"M'Lady, he's right," said Lieutenant Rainc. "In truth, the Steel should have left by now. In their heartland, the nobility can defend themselves, the Civid Sein have done much damage about the outskirts, but if we allow the nobles to arm and gather—as we have not been allowing—then the Civid Sein will soon take grave losses, and decide that settlement is best, whatever their talk today of total revolution. But the nobility will not accept a settlement that means the death of the Renines. Send them to exile, it is the best solution."

Rhillian gazed at the great ovens, black steel doors swung open, cold and empty. The air smelled of residual soot, and old vegetables. Then she nodded. "If I can find them, I will."

"Rhillian," said Kessligh, drawing her full attention. "I understand that Sasha has violated the law, and will remain confined. See that she is not harmed. Nor her sister, nor Errollyn."

Rhillian drew a deep breath. "As I said, the Justiciary's independence is two centuries old. I cannot be seen to tamper, or I will lose much of what support I currently hold, even with the Steel. Rhodaani justice is a matter for the gods. I cannot be seen to overrule their judgement. The priests have been quiet until now, but if I lose the priesthood, we have Petrodor all over again."

"I know," Kessligh said simply. "I merely warn you, for your sake and mine. You know me to be hard, but rational. If something happens to Sasha, I can assure you my rationality shall be tested. You'll be on the top of my list." The grip upon his staff, Rhillian noted, was white knuckled. His voice and face betrayed little emotion, yet the man was wound as tightly as a spring. Close as he stood, Rhillian could not help but feel a certain alarm. "Just so you know," Kessleigh said quietly.

They were returning to the Mahl'rhen when urgent word arrived in the form of a scout on horseback. Lieutenant Raine having returned to his unit, Rhillian and Aisha set off after the scout, their guard in pursuit. Deep into feudalist heartland they rode, as armed Steel stood aside, and the only others on the narrow, cobbled roads were armed nobility, in groups no larger than the proscribed five. Soon, Rhillian knew, given the size of the Civid Sein mobs, and the inability of the Steel to control them, she would have to give the order to allow the nobility to gather in whatever size force they liked. The nobility had good weapons, and good men. Then, it would be civil war.

Into a small cross street, between nondescript stone buildings halfway up the slope from the docks, there was a commotion of shouting men, wailing women, and armoured shields holding back the inconsolable crowd. They opened enough to allow Rhillian, Aisha and guards to pass, then closed once more. Rhillian dismounted, and entered through a door bashed off its hinges, then up steps to the first floor.

It was a simple room, unbefitting of nobility, perhaps, but then few of the feudalists of central Tracato were actually noble. A simple, wood-planked floor, some basic furnishings before the windows, and all now covered in the most appalling carnage. Bodies had been hacked, limbs removed, entrails strewn like depraved festival decorations. Rhillian had seen many such sights upon the battlefield, but somehow, the horror of this was far, far worse. This had been someone's home. Blood upon a simple tabletop, and gore dripping down the front of a small bookshelf, was somehow indecent in a way that even a thousand dead and wounded soldiers upon green or ploughed fields had never quite managed.

She stepped over a woman's body and saw a younger girl, a teenager, face down in her own blood and eyes wide, frozen in horror. Then the smaller child, a little boy, head partly severed from his . . .

Rhillian nearly wretched. Nearly broke down and cried. She had steeled herself to do these terrible things, and see these terrible sights, because if she did not, this fate would one day befall the people and children of Saalshen. Someone had to, and the *vel'ennar* had determined that that someone should be her. But she had rarely despised humanity more, at any moment, than she did right then.

Then she saw the Lady Tathilde Renine. The face was contorted, a grotesque shape of mouth and protruding tongue, from the rope that strangled about her neck. The rope was tied over an exposed ceiling beam, the lady's dress slashed and dripping blood, where men had cut her as she hung, and struggled, and kicked. Her once-beautiful eyes now beheld a dull finality.

Aisha saw the hanging body too, as she came in behind, and let out a small, sad sigh. "Oh no," she said. "Now there'll be trouble."

Sasha knew something was wrong the moment the cell door squealed open. She shielded her eyes against the lantern's glare, spying shapes that were not those of the regular Justiciary gaolers, but men with rough clothes and no armour. She tried to stand but could not raise beyond a crouch thanks to the manacles that bound her wrists, and then chained in turn to an iron ring at her feet. The man advancing on her was big, with bare arms and a nasty manner. This was going to hurt.

The first punch struck her in the side as she tensed, falling to her knees and covering, hoping to ride out the worst of it. Kicks thudded in as she covered her head with her arms, blindingly painful, but not so completely strange to a svaalverd warrior who had spent most of her youth being beaten with Kessligh's practice stanch, and falling off horses. She hissed and exhaled hard as she needed to; hard breathing always helped her svaalverd exercises, and it helped to deal with the pain.

Finally, as she ached in a fire of new bruises, a key was taken to her chains, and the chain released. Perhaps she was to be set free, she thought, as the men dragged her stumbling from the cell. Perhaps something had happened, perhaps politics had demanded her release, or Kessligh had held a blade to someone's neck—possibly Rhillian's. Perhaps this punishment was only the final, spiteful gift of those determined to get their shots in while they could.

She did not recognise the corridor down which they pulled her. It was not a part of the main row into which she had penetrated to try to save Alythia. She stumbled down some steps and into a larger dungeon, lit with flame. The air was warm here, and fire burned in an ironmonger's furnace at the far wall. Chains hung from the ceiling, and upon wooden tables were arrayed rows of grisly implements. Bloodstains spattered the floor, and there was a smell to the air that was not quite foulness, but far from pleasant.

It was fear, Sasha decided, as they dragged her to the hanging chains. It was her own fear. Her eyes would not leave the row of implements on the tabletop, however hard she tried to drag them away. Her heart was hammering. She had long ago confronted the prospect of disfiguring wounds in battle. Such a thing would happen quickly, before she could think on it. This would be slow. She wanted to cry, to scream and beg, and the Lenay warrior in her soul hated herself for it.

The chain between her wrist manacles was linked over a hook, two blows to her midriff ceasing her attempt to struggle. That hook was pulled high with the rattle of a winch, and soon she was nearly dangling, booted toes barely touching the ground. The big man took a sharp knife off the table and stood before her examining it as a farmer might examine his blade before slaughtering a sheep. Sasha tried to kick him, but her ankle chains had been secured to a floor ring, and she only succeeded in thrashing.

The man was bald, with a large belly and thick arms. Another man was handsome, with shoulder-length dark hair and a goatee. His eyes examined her with flat curiosity, and his accent, when he spoke, was that of an educated man.

"Who ordered you to rescue Lady Renine?" he asked her. "Was it Kessligh Cronenverdt?"

Sasha swallowed hard, for a moment not trusting herself to speak. A Lenay warrior did not show fear. "It was my decision," she said. "Kessligh was not consulted."

The handsome man nodded to the big one, who inserted the blade into Sasha's collar, and sliced the shirt neck to hem. He then walked around, and did the same behind, and tore the rest away. The light, serrin undershirt protected her modesty for a moment, but the big man cut that too, and left her topless. Perhaps they thought to humiliate her. Sasha had far worse concerns than that.

The big man then put the blade on the table, and punched her in the stomach. He was powerful, and the blow rocked her back in a jangle of chains, yet it was a relief. She was still too important for them to start cutting. Kessligh would kill them, and by far worse means than they might do to her. Kessligh led the majority of Tracato Nasi-Keth. Things were not that desperate yet.

Several blows later, and she half swung by her aching arms, struggling to breathe, reflecting that just because they weren't about to start cutting bits off, it didn't mean this was going to be anything other than hell. With her arms up, she had no way of defending herself. She just tensed hard, and hoped that her countless hours of training had built enough muscle to absorb the worst of it without permanent damage.

The handsome man asked her more questions. He wanted her to admit that she was a pawn of the feudalists, and that Kessligh, by association, was also a pawn. Probably, it occurred to her, Kessligh was not being helpful to the Civid Sein. He was caught between two groups of fanatics, each unwilling to admit the possibility of a third side. Holding the Nasi-Keth together, in the face of such one-eyed stupidity, would not be easy.

Soon her arms and shoulders began to hurt almost worse than her bruises. Her wrist manacles were agony, the chafing metal surely splitting the skin. Her boots were removed and her pants cut away, leaving her in only the thigh-length woollen underwear that she'd always favoured, good for both svaalverd and horsemanship. Strangely, they did not strip her completely naked. It seemed another line they were not prepared to cross. She wondered what was going on above ground that would make it so, and when that line would disappear. She answered the handsome man's questions truthfully, in part because no other answer would help her, and also because it was not what he wanted to hear. She did not scream or yell in fury, or make threats. She knew, as surely the men did, that if she survived, and were given an opportunity in the future, she would kill them, their comrades, and possibly their families, no matter how they screamed and begged. She would be patient, and wait. If these men knew her intent, though, it was unlikely they would let her live.

Through a haze of pain, she heard the dungeon door open, and a new voice spoke. It was familiar, and she half twisted on her chains to see Reynold Hein, in an expensive dark shirt and elegant boots, the ginger remnants of his hair impeccably trimmed, as was his goatee. He addressed the handsome man calmly, and they spoke in Rhodaani.

She was not surprised to see the man smile, and make an exasperated expression to Reynold's question. It seemed they were talking about her. Reynold explained himself. The handsome man gave a shrug and put a hand on Sasha's side, trailing it down her hip to her thigh. Sasha did not waste energy resisting, and calmed herself with visions of the handsome man screaming in agony, her blade twisting in his guts. Then he walked away, heading for the door.

Reynold adjusted his shoulder bandoleer and strolled before her. "Perone is disappointed that I have limited his freedoms here," he said. "Another woman of your looks might not have been so fortunate." Sasha said nothing. "You have a pretty face—I told him I would not like to see it scarred."

Sasha just looked at him, breathing hard, slowly twisting. It did not surprise her particularly that he should be capable of these things, nor that he could inflict them upon someone that he had at least occasionally, in the past, been friendly with.

"There is rather a mess outside," Reynold continued. He lifted a water-skin from his hip, and took a sip. Only then did Sasha realise how badly she wanted a drink. "The Lady Tathilde Renine is dead. Somehow, word got out to our Rhodaani patriots of her hiding place, and they stormed it in force. The feudalists are now rather upset, as you might imagine, and the Lady Rhillian has abruptly refused to use the Steel to contain their gatherings, as she had been. Upwards of hundreds at a time are now roaming to the west of Ushaal Fortress, and the fighting is fierce. It is all the Steel and Mahl'rhen can do to contain the warfare, and the Nasi-Keth of course, those who remain with Kessligh, are not much use at keeping the peace."

Sasha knew what he meant. The svaalverd, the ultimate offensive weapon, but useless for defending anything against mass attack. Those Nasi-Keth like Reynold, however, would be a deadly weapon against the feudalists. Slowly the picture was becoming clear to her.

"Thankfully," Reynold went on, as easily as he had ever discussed politics over a cup of wine, "new militias of rural patriots have entered the city from the east, and gained control of the Justiciary. It does afford us some opportunities, with the prisoners currently held here. We can ask some questions that the Lady Rhillian, for example, might have found distasteful. The Justiciary is currently surrounded by several thousand patriots, and separated from feudal heartlands by the Ushal Fortress, so it would seem that your rescue appears unlikely, in the short term at least. Best that you cooperate with us now."

"I've spoken nothing but the truth," Sasha replied, her voice low and strained.

"Ah yes." Reynold smiled indulgently. "A Lenay warrior's honour. But truly, I do not care particularly if Kessligh ordered you to do what you did or not. I could just as easily invent some statement from you, it would serve as well . . . and probably those who support you would not believe it, precisely because they know I could have invented it." He paused, appearing to expect her to question further. Sasha merely stared.

"No," Reynold continued, "the reason for this interrogation is much more that the supporters of the revolution expect such things, of the revolution's enemies. They ask what has been done to punish the traitorous Lenay Princess Nasi-Keth, and I say nothing, and they take it ill. Revolution is grievance, Sashandra." He tightened his fist, earnestly. "It is grievance, tightly focused. Just as the svaalverd is energy, the *mayen'rathal* of the serrin philosophy of motion, tightly focused, and controlled. One cannot break the momentum of energy, any more than one can check the swing of a svaalverd strike. Not without losing that momentum, and that energy. Dissipating it."

I'm being tortured to prove a point of philosophy, Sasha thought, somewhat drily despite the pain. That did not surprise her either. Kessligh had taught her too often of the nature of ideas, and their dangers.

"No, any information you could offer me would not serve the battle for Tracato, for that is well underway, and its path is now out of your hands or mine. But it would be remiss of me, as a Rhodaani patriot, not to ask you of the greater battle for the survival of Rhodaan. Our glorious Rhodaani Steel must defeat the Army of Lenayin in the field, or all is lost. I have asked you of Lenayin's tactics before."

"And I said you can go to hell," Sasha retorted through gritted teeth.

"And," said Reynold, holding up a finger, "you said that you did not know how a combined Army of Lenayin would choose to fight in the field. But come, you are a student of Lenay warfare, and your brother Koenyg will be in direct command. Surely a sister knows her brother."

"I've hated him since I could walk," Sasha snarled. "As he has hated me."

"Hatred does not preclude knowledge. I know the pampered, thieving lords of Rhodaan all too well, with their snobbish ways and presumption of godly entitlement." Reynold was a merchant's son, Sasha recalled.

"Koenyg likes to attack naked," Sasha told Reynold. "Great formations of Lenay warriors, with not a blade of grass to cover their arses. I've told him often of its ineffectiveness, but he does not listen."

Reynold snorted. "You appear to think this a game. This is no game to me, Sashandra Lenayin. The survival of my nation is at stake."

"Mine too."

Reynold nodded to the bald man, who retreated to the furnace and pulled on a thick glove. Sasha's heart began to race.

"Unlike Perone, I do not enjoy this, Sashandra," said Reynold, his blue eyes deeply serious. "But desperate times call for desperate measures. Making revolution is far harder than making cake, it requires far more than the breaking of a few eggs."

The bald man picked up a steel poker. Its end, resting within the coals, glowed bright orange. Sasha stared at it as the man approached and shook her head in shaking disbelief.

"Oh you're dead," she muttered. Her head felt as though it were about to burst, from the pounding in her ears. "I am going to so enjoy killing you."

"Tell me something useful," Reynold said reasonably, "and it need not be so."

"You're wrong," said Sasha shakily. "I'm going to kill you regardless."

The bald man waved the poker close, and Sasha flinched aside, desperately. The chains brought her swinging back, and that was when he laid it across her side.

Sasha screamed and thrashed. It hurt indescribably. The poker pulled away, but the pain did not go. It got worse, burning bone deep. She tried to lash out, reflexively, but only made herself swing some more.

"Tell me something useful, Sashandra. What state is the Lenay artillery in? About what proportion of the cavalry rides lowlands steeds, and what the native Lenay dussieh? What tactics has Prince Koenyg preferred in his previous, if limited Lenay campaigns? I have heard tales that the warriors of Isfayen province are particularly ferocious, shall Koenyg use them in the front, or in the reserve?"

"If you wait long enough," Sasha gasped, "maybe one of them will fuck you with his spear!"

The poker was applied to her other side. Sasha had no shame in screaming. Screaming helped. When the screaming passed, she reverted to Tullamayne. "*No sheth an sary, no sheth an sary, no sheth an sary.*" Over and over, eyes squeezed shut, sweat drenching her body as her muscles trembled uncontrollably.

"I know a little Lenay," said Reynold. "It means . . . 'blood on the steel,' yes?"

"*No sheth an sary, no sheth an sary.*" From the speech of Aldrynoth, at the Battle of Myldar. Danyth of Rayen had killed his brother. Aldrynoth had sought revenge. "No herb shall heal, like blood on the steel." She had never wanted love, nor sex, nor warmth, nor life itself, as badly as she wanted to kill Reynold Hein. It was a revelation to her.

Twelve

S ASHA'S LAMP WAS DYING when the cell door creaked open, and new light flooded the cool stone. She lay on her back on a pile of straw, trying to keep her breathing shallow. What was left of her clothes now made for a pillow. Her one relief was that underground, in the dark, the air was neither warm nor cool, and near nakedness suited the temperature. Despite that, her skin flushed hot and then cold, with the onset of what she suspected was fever. The pain was incredible. She wanted to pass out, but had no chance of sleep, and was too strong of constitution to faint. Suicide occurred to her, and was dismissed just as fast. Errollyn needed protecting, and Kessligh helping, and Lenayin saving. And enemies killing.

She closed her eyes against the new glare, trying to keep her wrists still. In the manacles, they chafed something awful, a pain nearly as bad as the burns. There were ten of those, two to each side, two on her back and two on each thigh. The cane had made cuts, and her stomach and ribs were bruised all over. Every breath was agony, though she did not think a rib was broken. Fury was the only thing that made it bearable.

The cell door shut. The owner of the lamp crouched nearby. Sasha slitted her eyes, rolled her head, and looked. Emerald eyes, beautiful and frightening beyond description. Snow white hair. Such unearthly, long-limbed beauty. Memories of loving friendship, all betrayed . . . fury surged, and she was lunging to her knees, lashing with manacled wrists, whipping the chain toward that long, shapely neck. . . . But it was pointless, and the chains pulled her short, an agony of severed skin, and wounds disturbed.

Rhillian barely moved. She watched as Sasha strained against the chains like a mad thing. And finally collapsed, frothing and gasping. She set the lamp aside.

"Sasha," she said coolly. "I've been to see Errollyn. They would not let me talk to him, but he is well. Alythia too. You are the only one I can talk to. Kessligh is demanding that someone gives him proof you are still alive." Sasha said nothing.

"Sasha, the Justiciary is heavily defended," Rhillian continued. "A thousand, I'd guess. I have not seen Sinidane, I don't know if he lives. There is open war in the city, I have not the forces to contain that and retake the Justiciary. I must prioritise. Council has fallen too. The Civid Sein hope to make a rallying cry, by claiming control of Tracato's institutions."

Sasha gave an exhausted, crazed, exasperated laugh. "What do you want me to do about it? Help? You make a fucking mess, Rhillian. You always make a fucking mess. Look at me. I'm a fucking mess."

The cell was spinning. It was too much, and she slid down on her side, and lay on the straw. Rhillian did not reply.

"I cannot be always attempting to justify myself to you," she said finally. Her voice was quiet. Strained, almost. "We shall all do what we will, for the best interests of all. It's all we can do. None of us is wise enough to know all ends."

"That's great, Rhillian," Sasha gasped. "A philosophical excuse. Sorry I fucked everything up, even the wise are fallible. How nice."

Another, longer pause. Rhillian got up abruptly, and strode to the cell door. Stopped just as abruptly. Came back, and squatted once more. Sasha struggled for focus, through slitted eyes.

"I cannot stop them from hurting you, Sasha," Rhillian whispered. Her voice trembled. "They are cruel. All sides are cruel. I play them against each other. I will defeat them soon, or they shall defeat themselves, but I cannot stop them from what they do here now. I have not the force."

"You said that already," Sasha managed. "What do you want from me? Forgiveness? You won't get it."

"There was a time you would have forgiven me anything."

Petrodor. Sadisi festival, dancing and cook fires on the dockside, reflections gleaming in dark waters. Rhillian, impossibly beautiful, taking a prawn from Sasha's plate. Laughing, avoiding the inquiries of forward young men, discussing the night with wonder in her eyes.

"Not anything," Sasha murmured. To her incredulity, there was a lump in her throat. Not now. Revenge required a steely heart, such softness appalled her. "Never anything."

"Do you recall," Rhillian said softly, "that once, I insisted you should sleep with Errollyn?"

"I didn't do it just to please you," Sasha croaked.

"No." Rhillian's lips pursed in a small smile. "I don't suppose you did. Had I known the trouble it would cause me, I would never have suggested it. Do you recall our discussions with Father Berin?" The North Pier temple on Dockside, near the great shipping docks. Berloni the painter, swathing beautiful, holy images across the ceiling. Spirits she wished she were back there now. "He insisted that if he could convince just one serrin of the holy teachings, he would die a happy man."

"You used to provoke him."

"I did. But he was a rare Verenthane, he enjoyed it. I truly think he was more interested in converting you than me."

Sasha managed a small, breathless laugh. "I'm even more the hopeless case than you."

"I did tell him," Rhillian agreed. "I also think he merely enjoyed the company of two pretty girls, whatever his priestly protestations." She gazed at Sasha in the lamplight, humour fading from her eyes. "Oh, Sasha." Regarding her wounds. "What have they done to you?"

"You protest yourself innocent of violence now?"

"Any serrin can kill for the cause of survival, Sasha, but . . ." she shook her head. "This is not in our vocabulary. To kill fast is one thing. To kill slow is entirely . . ."

"Kiel would," Sasha gasped. "I hear that Kiel has."

"Sasha, please, just tell them what they want to hear. The Army of Lenayin is powerful, it will make no difference if they know. . . ."

"I don't care. I don't care. I'll kill them."

"Sasha," Rhillian protested, in mounting desperation, "these people are crazy! They . . . some of them accuse the priesthood and refuse religion, but in truth, they remind me of the fanatics at Riverside. One truth, one belief, and it's repeated, over and over, as though by sheer force of will they can arrange truth and stone and blue sky above to suit their fancy. And Reynold Hein! The most intelligent man of the bunch, and the worst as well. Every opposing argument, he turns on its head, twists it, flips it, remoulds it to suit his preordained conclusion. It's the most incredible feat of intellectual self-blindedness. There are serrin in Saalshen who have not travelled in human lands who struggle to believe it when I explain it to them! How can I explain the likes of Reynold Hein to the wise and gentle souls of the Saalshen councils? Even Lesthen struggles, and he's travelled widely!"

"You forgot Sevarien."

"No, I never counted Sevarien amongst the most intelligent," Rhillian retorted. "He was always a big, blustering fool. Sasha, they have identified themselves as the victims, and in their victimhood, all manner of crime becomes acceptable. And worst of all, they *are* the victims of feudalist oppression, so their arguments appear valid to any without the patience to search more deeply!"

"Sounds familiar, doesn't it?"

"Sasha," she tried again, "just do what they say. Please. As the fighting grows more desperate, so will they. They believe blood can solve their ills." She looked again at Sasha's wounds. A tear rolled down her cheek.

"Don't," Sasha whispered. "You'll not get off that lightly. You got me into this. If anything happens to Errollyn or Alythia, I'll hold you responsible. I'm Lenay. You know what that means."

"You'll not scare me that easily. Serrin are a complex people, Sasha. We can hate and love at the same time."

Sasha could feel her steely resolve slipping. Through the agony, she felt a pain that had nothing to do with wounds. She swallowed hard, and tried to recapture the steel mask. She needed it. It sustained her.

"You're responsible," she whispered. "If the people I love die, I'll kill you."

"In the end," Rhillian said sadly, "we must all do what we must."

It did not seem like more than a few hours before Sasha was hauled from her cell once more down to the wide, hot dungeon. There, she was hung from the hook, grasping the chains with tight fists to try to keep the manacles from digging into her wrists. She did not see Reynold Hein, but the handsome, dark-haired man was there. Perone, she recalled his name.

She did not think much time had passed since the last session, however deceptive such perceptions could be underground. She thought perhaps the last session had been late afternoon, and now it would be night. Something about Perone's manner seemed hurried, perhaps distracted. From that, and Rhillian's visit, she guessed that the Civid Sein might think their time was limited. She didn't know if that made her less frightened, or more.

The grip on her chains began to slip. She felt beyond dizzy, nearly nauseous with pain. Any more treatment like the last time, and she knew she could die.

More footsteps entered the dungeon, and the sound of something heavy being dragged. Sasha twisted to look . . . and saw Errollyn, chained as she was, and dragged by two men. Her heart nearly stopped.

"Errollyn!" He twisted, and saw her. He had been beaten, his face swollen, but what he saw enraged him. He lashed at his captors, knocking one to the floor, but others grabbed him, kicking and beating him until he fell. It took four strong men to hoist his manacle chains over a ceiling hook, and winch until he hung nearly suspended, like her. "Errollyn, I'm all right!" she told him in Lenay, trying to be reassuring.

He did not look in quite as bad shape as her. He had taken blows to the head, which she had not, but his shirtless torso bore far fewer bruises, and no burns that she could see. His green eyes burned at his captors, beneath a wild, sweaty fringe. His breath came hard. Errollyn had no love of closed spaces, Sasha knew. He did not fear them, exactly . . . but he had lived most of his years before becoming *talmaad* in relative solitude in the foothills of Saalshen. Now, his eyes had that slightly crazed look, like a wolf backed into a corner.

"Your slut has not been particularly forthcoming to our questions," Perone said now, whistling a cane with expert flicks of his wrist. "She appears to enjoy pain . . . not surprising, for a Lenay bitch. I hear that lovemaking in Lenayin is little more than a violent beating followed by climax."

Laughter from one of the other men. Sasha made certain she got a good look at his face. She wanted to recall that laugh, when she killed him. It was with little surprise that she recognised the man—it was Timoth Salo, the young nobleman of the Tol'rhen, Reynold Hein's prized convert to the Civid Sein.

"Someone had the very clever idea," Perone continued, "that she might be more responsive to someone else's pain than her own." He shrugged. "I don't hold much hope, but I'm willing to give it a try."

He lashed with the cane, and a sharp, red line appeared across Errollyn's stomach. Errollyn made not a sound.

"Rhillian will kill you!" Sasha snarled. "All the serrin will kill you, you neither harm nor kill serrin without setting all of Saalshen at your throat!"

Perone smiled. "Oh, I think you exaggerate." He signalled to the big, bald man, who drove a fist hard into Errollyn's ribs. Errollyn barely grunted, swinging on his chains. "Rhillian could have demanded his release, but she did not. Besides, the serrin are fools to think they could rule Tracato. This city belongs to the true patriots of Rhodaan, and we rule here now. All who stand against us are traitors, human and serrin alike."

His stroll brought him to the horrid little table, picked up a nasty little blade, and examined it. Sasha's heart galloped. Another fist drove into Errollyn's midriff. "Stop it!" Sasha screamed at them. "Leave him alone!"

Errollyn's green eyes were fixed on her. "Sasha," he said hoarsely. "*No sheth an sary*. You tried to explain it to me once. Now I understand."

Perone strolled back to him, the blade in hand. Tears spilled in Sasha's eyes, sobs threatening to wrack her body.

"The only comfort," Errollyn told her, in Lenay, "is in the knowledge that you will kill these men. Concentrate on that, and do not fear for me. Your revenge shall sustain me."

Perone's knife flashed, and a new red line appeared, this one trickling blood. Pain flashed on Errollyn's face, yet he made no sound. Sasha thrashed against her chains, in desperation, crying. Perone slashed again. No one asked her any questions.

Later that night, if night it was, Sasha awoke. It had not been sleep, merely unconsciousness. She lay on dirty straw in her cell, mostly naked, in chains.

Her body bore no new injuries, but in her memory, she now carried her last sight of Errollyn as they'd unhooked him from the ceiling. There'd been a lot of blood, drenching his pants. A thin maze of scars across his torso. They'd used salt, which had finally made him scream. She'd never before in her life heard Errollyn scream. It did worse than make her cry, or make her stomach wretch—it robbed him of that strength of dignity he'd always carried.

But he'd been alive when they'd dragged him away. The cuts were shallow, designed more for pain than injury. She clung to that hope.

She wanted to think, but could not. Her mind was awash with pain, with fury, with exhaustion and fear. The fever she had feared had not advanced, yet still her skin flushed hot and cold. Her burns seemed to have come up in blisters. Her stomach muscles were bruised, her wrists badly strained beneath the chafing, but most of the injuries were no more than skin deep. Were she to get free, she was certain she could still move fast if she had to. If she could ignore the pain.

She closed her eyes, not wishing to see the dull, grey stone of the cell, lit by a single, yellow lantern. Not wishing the disorientation of feeling the walls and ceiling swinging around her. She would be all right. As would Errollyn.

She might have slept for a moment, she could not tell, but suddenly there was a rattle of keys, and the clank of the door's lock. The door squealed open. A thud as something was thrown into the cell, and then the door closed once more. Food maybe. One of those big, ugly loaves of stale bread. Sasha's stomach turned. She was not hungry, but she should try to eat.

She opened her eyes, and slowly focused on the object on the stones before her. It was a human head, facing her, eyes open. Long black hair. The eyes, the features, were Alythia's.

Sasha screamed.

A long time later, she was still screaming.

There was a commotion when they dragged her next from the cell. The first flight of steps did not go down, as before, but up. Dazed, Sasha realised she was being led out of the catacombs entirely. A cloak was thrown about her bare shoulders, covering her to the knees.

She registered a broad hall, filled with light, blinking and squinting as she was shuffled across the flagstones. Men were shouting, footsteps running, weapons clattering . . . and was it her imagination, or could she hear the distant sounds of battle? Yes, and then, clearly, there came a clash of weapons. The Justiciary was under assault. A thousand Civid Sein defenders, Rhillian had said. Who was assaulting? The feudalists? The Steel? Kessligh's Nasi-Keth? All three, she hoped.

She was pulled up more stairs, three flights in total . . . the Justiciary was no taller than four floors, surely? She could not recall. Despite the chains, the sleepless night, the lack of food, the horror, her head felt clear. The stairs seemed to help, as exercise always did . . . but mostly, she thought, it was the prospect of battle. It made her nostrils flare, like some old warhorse.

On the upper floor, her guards handed her to Perone, whose two Civid Sein companions dragged her down a corridor and into a small room that might have been a study. They threw her down on a chair beside a bookshelf, and one man stood by to guard her, his sword out. Perone gave that guard a harsh instruction in Rhodaani, then left, slamming the door behind. By the guard's stance, Sasha guessed those words had been to the effect of: "If she tries anything, kill her." Chained hand and foot, she did not fancy her chances.

There was an arched window nearby. With gritted teeth, she heaved herself from the chair and shuffled to the window, hunched like an old woman. The guard did not protest, but watched her all the way, his blade ready.

She had a view of the Ushal Fortress, across a jumble of tiled roofs. It was morning, she saw from the light. It had been just one night then, that the Civid Sein had occupied the Justiciary. Possibly Kessligh knew what that would mean, for her. Possibly that knowledge had forced his hand. She knew better than to assume so. Kessligh had far more on his plate than just concern for his wayward uma.

The sounds of battle were clear from this height. It was difficult to discern their location. Sasha guessed that was partly because the battle was all around. The Justiciary was being attacked from all sides. The feudalists would have the numbers for such an attack, but not access to the eastern approaches, which were away from feudalist heartland and currently strong with Civid Sein. The Nasi-Keth lacked the numbers, and were no good for massed combat anyway. It had to be the Steel. True to her word, Rhillian had lost patience.

The door crashed open and an angry-looking Perone strode back in. He paced across the room, apparently aimless, then reversed. Then kicked at a table, furiously, and snapped at the guard. Perone, Sasha noted, was wearing a swordbelt, good boots and a wide-collared leather jacket. The stylish attire of a wealthy Tracatan. Curious choice, for a Civid Sein revolutionary.

The argument with the guard continued. The guard looked a genuine country lad, tall and blond, freckled and missing some teeth. Sasha caught a few words, and knew enough of young men and warfare to guess that Perone had been told to stay here, and not to go out and fight. Guarding her, no less.

Perone saw her watching. He stopped and gave an exasperated laugh. "Look at her," he said, in Torovan. "Thinking this all so amusing." Abruptly he made toward her. Sasha backed away from the window, her ankle chains nearly overbalancing her. Perone caught at her wrist chain, and Sasha lashed back. Perone's blow struck her head, and suddenly she was on the floor, seeing stars.

Perone and the guard picked her up and dumped her on the table. "You should be grateful," Perone told her, unbuckling his sword belt, as the other man held her arms down over her head. "I am a great man of the revolution. If you are fortunate, you may die with my bastard in your belly."

They were going to kill her, Sasha realised, blinking her vision clear. Or at least, they had moved her upstairs so that no sudden breakthrough on the lower floors could liberate the dungeons.

"Pity to waste her," said the blond man above her. "Can I have a turn?"

"We'll invite the whole fucking movement," said Perone, placing his swordbelt aside, and unfastening his pants. "If they won't let me fight, they must at least let me fuck." He pulled a knife, inserted it into her underwear leg, and slashed.

Quite strangely, it occurred to Sasha that her hands, pulled back over her head, were close to the blond man's belt. Did he keep a knife there? Her hands reached and found a hilt. It seemed he did.

She pulled it hard and stuck it in his belly before he could notice what she'd done. The pressure on her arms ceased, and she flipped her legs up, wrapped her ankle chain about Perone's neck, and pulled as tight with her legs as humanly possible. Perone's hands grasped the chain, trying to pull it off. Sasha slammed her feet down on the tabletop, and took Perone's head down with them. His flailing arm struck her, reaching for her throat. Sasha stuck the other man's knife in it. Perone flung himself sideways, pulling her off the table. They hit the ground together, Sasha careful to brace her legs and not lose the tightness of that loop around his neck. Perone tried to roll away, and Sasha took the opportunity to make a second loop, hooking her ankle again around his head. Then she braced both feet on the floor, and tried to stretch out from the knees as hard as she could, pulling the chain tighter and tighter.

It was a big-link chain. A small-link chain would have been more supple, and cut more tightly. The big link chain took longer, and required more effort. Sasha thought that perfectly fine. Perone's horrid choking, his desperate agony, his flailing hands and spluttered attempts to beg, scream, cry for help, were all blissful music to her soul.

"I told you I would," she told him. She had never hated like this. It felt indescribably wonderful.

Perone died sooner than she'd hoped. She didn't trust it, and stuck the knife in his neck just to be sure. She got up, and found the other man slumped against the far wall, clutching a bloody wound just below his heart. She hadn't expected to have stuck him so well, but it seemed she was so good with blades these days that her hands knew what to do, even if the mind was elsewhere. He was sobbing and frightened, apparently in too much pain to risk inhaling, and cry out for help. Coward, Sasha thought, searching Perone's body for a key. She found a ring of them on his belt, dropped with his pants now about his feet. A few moments' searching found the right key, and she unlocked manacles from wrists and ankles.

No sooner had she done so than the door clanked open once more. Sasha was on her feet in a flash, taking Perone's sword from its sheath, and was onto the new arrival in quick strides just as he realised what had happened. The man's reach for his sword ended with Sasha's blade tearing his throat, the head nearly severed, blood jetting in violent sprays as he fell. It trickled down her face, warm and sticky, as she walked to where the wounded man sat, staring at her in helpless terror.

Sasha knew of no graceful stroke that would kill a seated man, or she would have done it then and there. There was a lot of blood on his hands. She'd driven the knife in almost to the hilt, and none of these Civid Sein wore armour. So close to the heart, there was no surviving such a wound. Better that he died slowly, anyhow.

She took his blade, a short sword like the Steel used, sheath and all. She also took Perone's coat, as it fitted her better than the big cloak, and would not impede her movement. The knife, she put in the coat's pocket. Then she padded lightly into the corridor, a naked midlength blade in her right hand, a sheathed short one in her left. Pain blazed with every motion, but it was a welcome price to pay. As against the joy of revenge, pain was nothing. She had tasted the blood of enemies, and like a drunkard sniffing the scent of a brew, she wanted more.

She moved quickly, bare feet soundless on stone, pausing to peer into open doorways before passing. Footsteps gave her warning to duck into one room, as several Civid Sein came into the corridor, then opened the door through which she'd last seen Reynold Hein disappear. She caught a glimpse within before it closed—it was a command room of some sort, perhaps it had a good view of the fighting. There could be quite a few men inside such a room. The thought brought her no pause, only cheer.

She strode calmly to the door, testing the balance of her blade. It had not the length of a svaalverd weapon, its hilt barely long enough for her accustomed two-handed grip, and the balance felt all wrong . . . but she knew enough one-handed svaalverd extensions to think she would manage. As for the rest, well, she had always liked to improvise. She changed the sword to her left hand, holding it and the sheathed short sword together, and opened the door. There were three high, arched windows on the right wall, before which four men were gathered, behind a large desk. Another three stood about a small table, poring over some parchments. None looked up immediately as she entered, gaining her several strides with which to close the range and take the knife from her pocket.

The first looked up—a Nasi-Keth, a man she recognised from the Tol'rhen. Jardine, she recalled the name. She hurled the knife, and he fell with it sticking from his throat. The second and third reached for their weapons in panic. Sasha killed the one nearest with a single slash, leaped onto the low tabletop to clear the third man's defence, and drove the point down through his shoulder, into the heart. She landed on light feet, rounded a chair and came at those by the windows. One, Reynold Hein, was yelling at the top of his lungs for assistance.

Sasha grabbed her short blade by the hilt and swung so that the sheath flew off, straight at the first man, who ducked. The big, bald man who had beaten her and Errollyn in the dungeon came around the big table at her, while Reynold drew a throwing knife. Sasha threw the short blade at Reynold, no great throw, but it made him duck. The big man swung hard from above . . . a stupid attack; Sasha just swayed aside and impaled him with his own momentum.

She pushed him back several steps, using his bulk as a shield from Reynold's knife. The man she'd thrown the sheath at was trying to come about on her left. As he raised his blade for a strike, Sasha pulled her sword free of the big man's gut, spun low and took the other's leg. He fell screaming, and Sasha grabbed up his fallen blade and hurled that at Reynold too. Reynold ducked aside again as the blade scythed by his head, and lost his knife as he rolled. The big man collapsed, face first, clutching his stomach.

Reynold's last standing companion was Timoth Salo. The young nobleman held his blade two-handed, Nasi-Keth style, staring incredulously at Sasha, then about at the carnage she'd wrought. The man she'd legged was still screaming, clutching the terrible wound. Sasha stuck her blade in his back to shut him up.

"What did you do?" Salo said with horror. And again, on the verge of hysterical tears, "*What did you do?*" As though it had not occurred to him that his friends could die so easily. As though it had not occurred to him that his own actions could lead to this end.

Sasha rose from her crouch and advanced slowly. "You thought this was a game?" The calm of her voice amazed her. Dripping fury, and cold as ice, yet steady. Revenge made her calm, when all about her was crazy. *No sheth an sary.* She had never felt more Lenay than she did at that moment. "Did you think I was joking when I said I'd kill you all?"

Salo looked ill with fear and horror, the sword trembling in his hands. Reynold was backing away, circling about, his own blade far steadier. No assistance had yet come through the doors. Sasha reckoned most would be busy with the defence of the Justiciary.

She paused to pick up the big man's blade. He had been Nasi-Keth too, it seemed, though she had not recognised the face . . . but most Tracato Nasi-Keth were ex-pupils of the Tol'rhen, not present ones. His blade presented her with a much better balance than the shorter one in her hand, so she exchanged them with several expert twirls.

Behind Salo, the room held something extraordinary—a great sphere on a stand. It was covered with the dark squiggles of map lines, and on one high corner, Sasha recognised the coastline of Rhodia. A map of the world. The serrin world, perfectly round, that the Verenthane priesthood considered sacrilege of the highest order. Only a little of the coastline seemed complete, the rest was mostly guesswork. There were banners in the room too, and parchment inscriptions in scrawling Rhodaani letters. A Verenthane star, prominent upon a shield in the Tracatan colours. Sasha realised whose chambers these had been.

"This is Chief Justiciar Sinidane's room," she said to Reynold. "Where is Sinidane?"

"I don't know," Reynold said, breathing hard. "Somewhere about."

"You arrested him, didn't you?"

"He was a traitor!" Salo screamed. "They were all traitors! All who cannot see that deserve to die!"

"You breed a calm and thoughtful disposition in your movement, I see," Sasha observed to Reynold. "In your search for justice, you've destroyed justice itself."

Salo panicked, attacking because he knew nothing else to do. Sasha had seen that before in youngsters and was not surprised, deflecting his first strike on pure reflex, and killed him with the counter before his follow-through had finished. Reynold ran.

Sasha tore after him, into a deserted hall. She was a good runner, but Reynold was taller, uninjured, and a man. As he flew away from her, Sasha felt her burns and wounds screaming in pain for the first time, and fancied she felt some skin on her leg tear. Still she ran, slowing a little, listening above the slap of her bare feet as Reynold disappeared about a corner, lest his footsteps abruptly stop, indicating ambush. But his boots pounded on and Sasha charged about the corner, onto a balcony above the wide floor of the Justiciary below, now awash with people and confusion.

Reynold flew down some stairs, faster again than Sasha, who plunged after, unconcerned of who he might rally against her—half of the crowds were women, hauling bloodied bodies of dead and wounded, crying for water, for bandages, for anything to cope with the flood of human catastrophe that now lay sprawled across the flagstones. She darted after Reynold, sighting a flash of movement ahead, a ducking figure there . . . she wove past hobbling wounded and skirted around a makeshift bed where a desperate surgeon cut crossbow bolts free from shrieking victims. The figure she'd thought was Reynold turned out to be a stranger, and she spun about, thinking perhaps he had tricked her, and was doubling back to surprise her from the crowd . . . but she saw only frightened men and women, and the same, panicked disbelief she'd seen on the face of Timoth Salo.

Sasha snarled, spinning back. Reynold could not run far—the Steel had the Justiciary surrounded, soon enough he would be forced back here, as the noose tightened. A young man she recognised from the Tol'rhen passed, supporting a bleeding, ashen-faced comrade. It was poor discipline, however much one cared for friends, for all to be abandoning the defence to carry their comrades back to shelter. The priorities were . . .

Priorities. Errollyn.

She turned away from the direction Reynold had run, and pushed her way back through the throng toward the dungeon entrance. To abandon her revenge on Reynold made her want to sob. But to abandon Errollyn would be worse.

The dungeons were unguarded, and she moved silently down the darkening stairs. Her wounds burned like murder now, and her legs felt unsteady, her balance suddenly dubious as the light slowly faded. She did not know how she had done what she'd just done, save that warriorhood was the truest nature of what she was, and came to her as naturally as a horse did to running. That, and pure, blood-lusting fury.

It was almost as though . . . almost as though . . . but she pushed the thought aside, for later contemplation.

Light from the Justiciary hall had nearly vanished, when a yellow lamp lit the way from below. The descending corridor bent, and suddenly, she saw the guard room and a man who looked to be Civid Sein holding a lamp, gazing up the stairs toward her. Sasha merely kept walking, as though she had every right to be there, as the man looked at her curiously, perhaps not making the connection between the girl who had been taken from these dungeons not long before in chains, and this one with a Nasi-Keth blade in her hand.

Suddenly his eyes widened, and he yelled a warning, a hand reaching to his sword. Sasha pressed on, unsurprised by the attack from her right by the second guard as she followed the retreating man into the room. One parry and a diagonal slash dropped his corpse to the flagstones. The first man dropped his lantern, a flash of flame as serrin oil erupted. Sasha ducked past it, and took the man's sword hand off at the wrist. He screamed and fell to his knees. Sasha stood over him, sword at his neck as he tried to stop the terrible bleeding, stuffing the stump under his armpit and squeezing.

"In which cell is the serrin? Or your head will be next."

She found her way down more stairs with another lantern from the guardroom, leaving the guard sprawled unconscious from a blow to the head. He might die from blood loss while asleep. Sasha didn't care—she hadn't cut his head off, so her honour was intact.

One door before the corner the guard had indicated, she stopped, and inserted the selected key from the great key ring. The door unlocked, and she pulled it squealing open and crept inside.

Errollyn lay on his back on dirty straw, his torso a criss-cross of cuts and dried blood. His wrists were free, his arms loose, only his ankles chained. His eyes slitted open to look at her, as she placed the lantern down, and knelt at his side.

"Errollyn." There was sanity in those eyes, blazing green in the lamplight. And pain. "Errollyn, can you move?"

"Did you take your revenge?" he asked her hoarsely.

Sasha nodded. "The big bald one from the dungeons," she said. "Perone. Timoth Salo. Some others too."

"Reynold?" Sasha shook her head, bitterly. "Then I have reason still to live. Let me out."

Sasha used the keys, and released his ankles. "The Steel are attacking," she told him as she worked. "It should be over very soon."

"It could be no other way," said Errollyn though gritted teeth. "This portion of humanity has become diseased. It must be cut out."

"Your wounds will turn bad," Sasha worried. "I have to get you to the Mahl'rhen, they can heal such things best."

"We have to fetch Alythia first," said Errollyn. "Do you know where she . . ."

"Alythia's dead," Sasha said shortly, as the last manacle released. She made to haul Errollyn to his feet. Errollyn clasped her hand, but did not move.

"You're certain?" he asked, shocked. Sasha nodded, unwilling to speak more. She tried to haul Errollyn upright once more, but again he resisted. "How do you know?"

"Errollyn, not now. She's gone, I must get you to the Mahl'rhen. If you get some disease of the blood it may already be too—"

"Sasha!" Errollyn insisted, with pain on his face that was not all from his wounds. "I cannot claim to know your loss, but she was my friend too, and I cannot leave without knowing for certain!"

Sasha could not meet his gaze. "I saw her head," she barely managed to force out. She was trembling. "They threw it into my cell." Errollyn looked stricken. "I spent . . . I spent half the night with it. . . ."

She curled over, straining as though with a new, physical agony, trying to contain the sobs. Errollyn grabbed her shoulders with chafed, bloody hands and pressed his face to hers. Sasha tried to breathe deep, tried to calm. Errollyn was here, and alive. The nightmare was passing. Somehow, she managed to straighten.

"Let's go."

By the time they'd limped to the guardroom, Sasha could hear that the sounds from the Justiciary hall had changed. She could hear armour rattling, and the yelling of orders, disciplined and purposeful. The Steel were here already, and the Civid Sein lines had collapsed.

As she stood listening, Errollyn's arm about her shoulders for support, a pair of lithe shapes came soundlessly down the stairs. Eyes blazed in the lamplight, one pair gold, another hazel. They paused, and shouted something back up the stairs in a Saalshen tongue Sasha did not recognise, then came to Errollyn and helped him up the stairs. Another serrin offered Sasha an arm, but she waved him away, and climbed up to the main floor while keeping to one side of the stairs, as more serrin came rushing down, swords in hand.

Soldiers of the Steel now guarded every doorway, stairway and archway of the Justiciary, Sasha saw, blinking in the light. There were some fresh corpses on the ground, blood pooling, and other soldiers dragged prisoners, arms twisted behind their backs. The chaos of wounded continued across the floor nearest the grand entrance, left undisturbed by the soldiers. Officers and some serrin now walked among the wounded, looking at faces, searching for certain individuals. They would find Reynold, if he were still hidden here.

Sasha shielded her eyes as she stepped out into the day. It was warm, the sky a cloudless blue, and the peaked rooftops of Tracato's elegant buildings seemed to mock her with their beauty. Upon the wide stairs lay more bodies, blood flowing as though down a series of waterfalls. There were soldiers everywhere, and horses, and already some horse-drawn wagons, with men to load the corpses into the back. The efficiency of the Steel amazed her.

A serrin came to them, leading another, smaller serrin in a wide hat, a bloodstained blade in her hand. Aisha. She met them at the base of the steps, and would have hugged Errollyn ferociously had his wounds not given her pause. She hugged Sasha instead, gently, with shock in her eyes. Fury quickly followed.

"Who was it?" she asked quietly. "I'll have them killed."

"Already done," said Sasha. "All save Reynold Hein. He got away, but he's mine if you find him."

"Mine," Errollyn said hoarsely.

"Oh merciful light," Aisha muttered, observing his cuts more closely. "I'll have you at the Mahl'rhen shortly, just let me commandeer one of these carts."

Errollyn eased himself down onto the lowest step, and Sasha sat alongside. Sitting hurt terribly. Every new position did. And every old one. She was certain Errollyn felt much worse. He looked up, to regard the blue sky. A serrin placed her hat upon his head, yet still he squinted fiercely beneath its broad brim.

"It's a beautiful day," he said. Soldiers dragged the bloodied corpses of young men away from the steps. One of them, Sasha saw, was a Nasi-Keth who had sometimes sat in her Lenay classes. A young man, happy, idealistic, passionate about his city and his people. He left a long, thick trail of blood as they dragged him away.

"Yes, it is," said Sasha. Thud, went the body, into the cart. She felt nothing at all.

Thirteen

ERROLLYN AWOKE TO A LOVELY DAY. It was not the same day as he recalled, leaving the Justiciary with Sasha, the day that freedom had returned. He knew because he thought of other times between—brief, blurred snatches of time, between sleep, between consciousness and waking, between night and day. He did not know how much time had passed. Through the blur of pain, it was a struggle to know anything.

The room could only have been in the Mahl'rhen. It was circular, and half exposed to a courtyard, save for silk curtains that drifted in the breeze. There was a jug and cups on the bedside table. He reached, gingerly, wincing at the pain of that movement. The cup held water, and he sipped with difficulty from flat on his back, relief in his parched mouth. From the courtyard, he could hear a fountain tinkling and children playing.

A little serrin boy pushed through the curtain and stared at him, then ran away, shouting for someone. Several more children came to the curtain, whispering amongst themselves. Errollyn stared at the ceiling, wishing for privacy. He'd always liked solitude. Fellow serrinim had always considered that odd. Most serrin loved company, and became lonely without conversation. But then, he was accustomed to other serrin considering him odd.

Soon Aisha arrived, with a tray of food, a small feast of fruits, bread, sliced cheese, condiments and spiced meats. She sat on the side of his bed, leaned over and looked him closely in the eyes.

"How long?" Errollyn murmured.

Aisha shook her head. "Not long. You were awake this morning, you probably don't remember." Errollyn shook his head, and that hurt too. "Helsen is treating you, his lore is vast." Her eyes flicked down to his torso, bare above the sheet. Errollyn looked too. There were bandages tied over the worst cuts. Lesser cuts were exposed, inflamed red and unpleasant to look at. "How do you feel?"

"Numb. Except for when I move. And my back is murder."

"You will have to roll over soon," said Aisha, nodding. "And spend some time sitting or standing, however bad you feel, those cuts need air. I'd recommend the pools."

Errollyn nodded. "How's Sasha?"

"Last I saw, she was fine," said Aisha. Her blue eyes held concern. "She will recover quickly enough. Three weeks, perhaps."

"Where is she? I want to see her."

Aisha took a deep breath. "She left, Errollyn."

"Left where? What do you mean . . . ?"

"She left." The concern in Aisha's eyes now mixed with sadness. "Her worst injuries are not physical. I've never seen her so . . . cold. There are serrin here who would detain her once more, they see only that she acted against Rhillian, and thus against Saalshen. I helped her to get out before a decision could be made, and after she'd received some treatment. She was very sad to leave you. She sat where I sit now, and kissed you and cried. But she could not stay. I saw something terrible in her eyes. I fear it drives her."

Errollyn's heart thumped. "I don't understand," he said. "She is at the Tol'rhen, surely? With Kessligh?"

"She intends to head for Larosa," Aisha said quietly. "She will join with the Army of Lenayin. But I do not repeat it loudly, else riders be dispatched to catch her."

"She's crazy." Errollyn squeezed his eyes shut, fighting back panic. "She's crazy, she'll be caught." He wanted to rise. To pull on clothes, grab a horse and ride after her. But the thought of even sitting upright made him nauseous.

"There are some she could ride with who would make a good escort," Aisha whispered. "They know the roads well, and have many helpers."

Of course. Errollyn let out a long, slow breath, and felt the tension fade. It made sense. Suddenly, it all made sense. He knew her that well, and she was not insane. Sasha's position in Tracato had become nearly impossible. She had acted against the serrin, and thus damaged the relationship between the Mal'rhen and Tol'rhen, between Rhillian and Kessligh. With the Civid Sein now largely defeated, Saalshen and Nasi-Keth in Tracato needed urgently to unite, to help restore the shaken foundation of Rhodaani society. It would be better, perhaps, were Sasha not here.

And Sasha had lost her sister. It meant things to a human, and a Lenay in particular, that even a *du'jannah* like Errollyn could not begin to comprehend. He feared for her, in her grief. A serrin in grief could at least feel the comfort of the serrinim. A human in grief would feel alone. Perhaps that was it, he realised. All serrin were one family. Perhaps this loss was a loss that, for Sasha, could only be borne with the help of family. It hurt that she did not consider him as such . . . but then, he had known Alythia only briefly, and could not know the depth of what it meant to lose her. It did not mean Sasha loved him any less. It merely meant that he could not understand.

He took another deep breath. "If I had not told Rhillian, then Alythia may still be . . ."

"No," Aisha insisted. "It was not you. Rhillian would have found out Lady Renine's plans, already she suspected, and then Alythia would have been detained anyhow. It wasn't your fault."

"Sasha may not feel that way."

"She did not want to leave. She was sad to leave you."

"Yet she did." Aisha said nothing. "I'll miss her," Errollyn said weakly.

"I too. But Sasha is a force of nature. She cannot be contained, and it will take more than a great war to stop her. You and she will meet again, I am certain." Aisha leaned and kissed him on the forehead. "Now eat. I'll see you fed if I need to stuff it down your throat."

Late that afternoon, Errollyn managed to limp as far as the pool in the courtyard. Helsen's uma, a lad named Irin, helped to remove his bandages, then left him to soak naked in the cool water. For a while, his wounds stung so badly it brought tears to his eyes. Then the pain faded, and he even managed to walk back and forth, confident at least that in the water, he could not lose balance and fall.

The afternoon's activity continued as high cloud turned to evening pink, and lamps began to illuminate the columns, paths and gardens. Some serrin looked at him in passing, and a few paused at the pool's edge, hoping to talk. Errollyn ignored them, and they went away. His wounds tugged at his skin in dozens of different ways. Like sharp, foreign objects, digging into him whenever he moved.

More footsteps approached, with the tapping of a cane. Errollyn looked up, walking in shoulder-depth water, and saw Kessligh, heading toward him. Kessligh pulled off his boots, rolled up his pants, and sat on the pool's edge beside Errollyn, feet dangling in the water.

"Kid," said Kessligh, looking down at his wounds, "you're a mess."

"I'll heal," said Errollyn. "And I won't require a cane."

"Sasha didn't want to leave you," said Kessligh, gazing across the courtyard. "That hurt her more than anything. But she couldn't wait either, and you're in far worse shape than her. Where she's going, you wouldn't be safe."

Errollyn nodded. "Larosa's not the friendliest, to serrin." He looked up at Kessligh. "You let her go?"

"Whenever someone asked me something like that, I used to just shrug, and say that with Sasha, it wasn't a matter of 'letting' her do anything." He cracked a knuckle, absently. "But yes. I let her go. Lenay honour declares that family must tell family of their losses in person. And she was an inconvenience for me here. Kiel's bunch want her dead."

"Kiel has a 'bunch' now?" Errollyn asked drily.

"His own *ra'shi*, no less," Kessligh said. "Pray that it does not come to rival Rhillian's."

"I come to fear Rhillian is no improvement."

"Never think so," said Kessligh firmly. "She visited Sasha in her cell. Sasha told me. Rhillian was upset at the torture. She did not mention the visit, last I spoke with her, so she did not do it merely to curry favour with me. Whatever her bloody methods, Rhillian's heart remains intact. Kiel is of the opinion that a heart is Saalshen's vulnerability. He strives to make a philosophical case that proves it."

Errollyn shook his head. "There was a time when I used to worry about the actions of my enemies," he said. "Now I learn that it's the actions of those we love that hurt us most."

"Hurt, perhaps," said Kessligh. "But we have both underestimated Rhillian. She knew she had to act against Lady Renine, and fully expected the Civid Sein to over reach once she did. She waited until they did, and disgusted any in the Steel who still sympathised, then used the Steel to crush them. Now the feudalists are chastened, and the Civid Sein decimated, their leadership killed or in hiding. Rhillian can depart for the front, with the Steel, and have less care for destabilising influences in Tracato."

"Hell of a way to do it," Errollyn muttered. "You're sure she didn't just get lucky?"

"You don't think I was ever lucky?" Kessligh replied. "The Tol'rhen is strangely quiet. We lost a lot of fools."

"Good," said Errollyn. "Fools are no use to anyone." Kessligh did not reply. He'd spent a long time since his arrival in Tracato, Errollyn realised, attempting to persuade the Nasi-Keth of his ideas. A strong Nasi-Keth, supporting Saalshen's forces. A bedrock of stability, to make a strong foundation for Rhodaan. Instead, the Nasi-Keth had split, as in Petrodor, and made arguably more trouble than it had solved. "It is the way, isn't it? With humans and free thought. They only learn through terrible mistakes. Free thought does not make wisdom. Instead it creates enough space for men to commit terrible folly, from which the survivors learn through disaster."

"I tried to tell them," Kessligh said tiredly. "I tried. Revolutionary ideals may be wonderful, but revolutions are nasty. You can't cure a headache by cutting off the patient's head. But they wouldn't listen. Only now do the survivors understand . . . and even now, some aren't convinced. They speak only of Rhillian's betrayal, not their own stupidity."

"Some people cannot be argued with," Errollyn said quietly. "Many serrin have argued that religion be banned in the Saalshen Bacosh, because most of those preaching death to all serrin were Verenthanes and priests. But

Maldereld argued that such teachings in religion were a symptom, not a cause. The thinking that gives birth to all the hatred is not born in religion, it merely finds a home there. Deprived of that home, it can find others."

"For all her cunning, Rhillian may have overdone it," said Kessligh. "She had no choice, the Civid Sein were getting out of hand, as is the nature of such things. But there was carnage at the Justiciary, the feudalists are regaining control of much of the city as surviving Civid Sein flee, and the Steel are marching for the west at last. After all that has happened, very little has changed, save a huge pile of corpses. Council will be reinstated soon, and probably the feudalists shall find friendly faces to replace those of their own who've been murdered. I will talk with the feudalists. Many are sensible, and seek only to focus now on defeating the Larosans. But many others recall Rhillian's initial betrayal, and that of the Steel. With the Steel departing, I fear for the safety of the Mahl'rhen, and all serrin in Tracato."

"They would be unwise to pick a fight with Saalshen in this city. The svaalverd is well suited to the streets and alleys."

"I come to talk with Lesthen," said Kessligh. "He promises more *talmaad* from Saalshen. I will see if he can bring some to Tracato."

"How many come shortly?"

"Perhaps five hundred. Some of Rhillian's force from Elisse are returning from those lands. Other serrin are arriving in southern Elisse, to help the peasants rebuild. It takes fewer numbers than they'd thought, since the lords continue to hold sway in the north, thanks to General Zulmaher."

"Zulmaher," said Errollyn, as it occurred to him. "What happened to him?"

"No one knows. Same with little Alfriedo. There is no sign of either."

Errollyn gave him a long look, however it hurt his neck. "Those two together . . ."

"They'll be deep in feudalist territory, and we have nothing like the force to do anything about it, with the Steel gone. But I wanted to ask you something. The *talmaad* will need commanders, any that Lesthen brings from Saalshen will have little enough experience in battle, and Sasha tells me you're one of the best horseback fighters she's seen."

"I'm out of practice," said Errollyn. "And by the time I heal, I'll be out of condition, too."

"I don't need you to kill all the enemy single-handedly," Kessligh said wryly. "But I'd like someone there whose head I can trust."

"It doesn't work that way. I may have experience, and that may gain me *ra'shi*, but to be commander, I must also gain *ra'shi* for my views. It's a long time since I've been active in such circles, in Tracato."

"So start," said Kessligh, an edge to his tone. "Lad, you love Sasha, I understand that. You feel estranged from your own people, I understand that too. But I think you've been too much the faithful puppy with Sasha, this past half-year. She's been your excuse to escape your own people, to throw their narrowness back in their faces. But following Sasha too blindly can be bad for your health, as you've discovered.

"Understand I don't say this out of some feeling of fatherly protectiveness— if Sasha were to have any man, I would rather he be you. But just occasionally, I think it would be good for her if you bossed *her* around for a change."

"Serrin don't boss."

"So start. You've changed a lot in the time you've been with her, as she's also changed. For the better, I think. Now it's time to use what you've learned. Don't keep running from your people, Errollyn. Confront them. Otherwise, all the path ahead shall be determined by Kiel and Rhillian, and while I trust Rhillian's heart, I do not trust the influences upon it. She must have alternatives, Errollyn. Alternatives that work. I think you can provide that. If you try."

He put a gentle hand on an unscarred part of Errollyn's shoulder. Then he rose, with the aid of his staff.

"And don't forget to stretch, however much it hurts," he added. "Just swing your arms and shoulders through full extension. Don't let the cuts heal too narrow or the scars will restrict you."

He left, a tapping of cane along the stone path between garden beds. Errollyn sank lower into the water, and watched the dancing reflection of lamplight on the pool's surface.

The day was too hot, Sasha thought. Or perhaps, the heat was her own. She could not tell any longer, as she dripped sweat beneath her broad-brimmed hat and squinted across the rolling fields to the nearest farmstead. They had been riding for days now. Three, she thought, although it was sometimes difficult to remember. There was only the next stretch of road, across country that would have been pretty were she in any condition to appreciate it, and the swaying backside of the horse in front.

Now the column stopped, and she sipped from a waterskin hung to her saddle. She'd been drinking too much water, and would soon have to pee. It was humiliating, as the only woman of the column, but there it was. Her condition was humiliating. She did not know where she was, nor which turn to take next, nor indeed that she was being taken in the direction she had asked. She only stayed ahorse and tried not to pass out, and hoped that the spirits would guide her to her people once more.

Ahead, Lord Elot was talking with a pair of outriders. Soldiers, Sasha saw, lightly armed and armoured. Men of the Rhodaani Steel but not of the main formations. These rode the trails nearer the border with Larosa and watched for infiltrators. Yesterday they had encountered the first such riders. This was the second time today. Surely the border drew closer.

The soldiers bid good day and came down the column, nodding to each man, and Sasha, in turn. Sasha tipped her hat so that it half hid her face, and neither soldier seemed to notice that she was a woman. She wore pants and jacket too large for her, with a man's tailoring to hide her figure. So far, she thought, her disguise was good.

A time later, the column ascended a forested hill until it arrived at a castle's walls. The drawbridge seemed permanently lowered, and the moat dry, overgrown with bracken. Maids and castlehands came running as they entered the grounds, and pulled up the horses before the stables. Sasha managed to dismount herself, yet her legs would have folded had not someone caught her under the armpits. She hurt so much, and her head now spun so she did not know one direction from another. She tried to walk, but that was futile. Someone picked her up and carried her like a helpless child, and she was too exhausted to even feel embarrassed.

Indoors then, within walls of cool stone, and up narrow stairs that echoed to men's boots. A room, and then a bed, and she was laid down. Men departed, voices fading, and then women were undressing her. They had the treatments Aisha had given her before she'd left the Mahl'rhen. They were kept in Sasha's saddlebags, and reapplied at each stop. She'd done this before. But first, she would have to survive a trip to the washroom, and a cold wash.

She awoke some time later in the room, lit now with a single lamp. Beyond the narrow window was darkness, wind in the trees, and insects chirping. Dear spirits, it was wilderness. The air had that smell to it of nearby forest, and the faint, musty scent of farm animals. Despite her pains, Sasha nearly smiled. So long she'd spent in cities, first in Petrodor, now in Tracato. Never again, she promised herself. And finally she did smile, for she knew the promise was a lie.

She heard laughter downstairs, and a snatch of song. A wafting scent of food cooking. Her stomach grumbled. She sighed, took a deep breath, and sat up slowly. Her arms and legs were quite a sight. The cane scars varied from short to long, with colours from pink to purple to deep, wine red. The deeper ones had scabbed over, and the whole mess pulled on her skin whenever she moved. Her stomach, sides and legs were purple and black with bruises. Her burns looked appalling. They scarred over now, with great blisters breaking the crust. Some blisters had burst, and now oozed. She hoped the skin would not heal badly, and restrict her svaalverd in the future.

On that thought, she got up, pressed her hands to a wall, and stretched her naked body upward until the scars began to scream in pain. She held it as long as she dared. Kessligh would tell her. She could hear his voice in her head, instructing her not to slacken off because of a few cuts and burns.

The only clothing in the chamber was a robe. Her fellow travellers, however, had not made the mistake of depriving her of her weapons. She tied the robe, took up her sheathed sword, and left the room. Her bare feet careful on cool stone steps, she descended into a common hall. Men and several women looked up from long tables, now stocked with steaming food. They hailed her, and gestured a seat on a bench. Sasha took it, alongside Lord Elot, and opposite young Torase, who had accompanied her and Errollyn on their rescue of Alythia and Lady Renine. Torase, Sasha had gathered, was Lord Elot's nephew. Lord Elot, in turn, was cousin-by-marriage of Family Renine.

These family connections had once been all important in Rhodaan. Such ties had compelled men to fight and die. Blood had been the law here. Now, Sasha surveyed the bare stone of the hall, the fireless hearth, and the simple wooden tables and benches, and saw the extent of nobility's fall. The banners and heralds on the walls seemed faded, and the cold, square stone was nothing like the grand, ornamental architecture of modern Tracato. These people were riding toward the past and would take all of Rhodaan with them if they could. Once, Sasha had considered that a terrible thing. Now, having seen what she'd seen, she wondered.

"Apologies for not waking you," said Lord Elot, "but you seem to wake yourself when hungry, I'd thought to let you rest."

Sasha managed a faint, acknowledging smile, putting meat and vegetables onto her plate. A maid came with wine, but Sasha took only water—Rhodaani wine was very good, and she did not think this bout of clear-headedness would last long if she indulged.

"What castle is this?" she asked quietly.

"This is the holding of Family Ciren," said Lord Elot. "These forested hills were once farmed, with a clear view of surrounding lands. The serrin took them away, when they came. All the family lands. Gave them to the peasants. Now, all that remains is what you see." He gestured about. "A simple place, yet it is home to some, and hospitable to all friends beneath its roof."

"We shall win it back," said Torase defiantly, his young face proud. "The serrin and the peasants do not understand, they think this was merely a *system*. They do not understand the power of family, and of blood. Family Ciren has ruled these lands for more than fifteen generations. We were enemies with them mostly, in that time, yet we respect their name. Today, we stand with them as brothers, to reclaim what is ours. And reclaim it we shall."

Sasha could think of nothing but Alythia. How beautiful she'd looked, gracing noble halls much like this. Such halls had been her element, and even those as drab as this one would have brightened with her presence. These were Alythia's people, in style if not in blood. These men's enemies had cut off her head, and left it lying on the cold stones of Sasha's cell, but an arm's length from her manacled feet. Sasha had once felt sorry for all who suffered beneath feudalist oppression. Now, she could not care.

"How far are we from the border?" she asked.

"Another four days' ride," said Lord Elot. "Soldiers here do not seem to be aware that you may be riding this way. Tracato is in confusion, possibly no one has sought to send word. Or if word comes, it should be days behind."

They meant to fight with the Army of Lenayin, Sasha knew. Or with the Army of Larosa, or whichever would have them. Tracato, to these men, was now under a foreign occupation. The Larosa, they'd decided, were the liberators. And the Army of Lenayin would find its morale much boosted by the return of one princess, and its soldiers much angered by news of the other's death. Angry Lenays would surely prove more formidable in battle. It was with such motivations that these noble men of Rhodaan now smuggled Sasha toward the border.

Sasha stayed only long enough to eat her meal. Upon returning to her chamber, she found by the lamplight that a red rose had been placed on her bed. For a moment she was puzzled, and sat on the bed, smelling the rose, and wondering why it seemed familiar. And then she recalled . . . it was a tale her friend Daish of the Tol'rhen had told her, about a castle that had been cursed by a wicked witch. About the castle's grounds, nothing would grow, all the crops had died and the gardens withered. The peasants had gone hungry, winter had settled upon the land, and all the castle's noble family had fallen into a deep sleep.

One day, an orphan girl from a neighbouring village had crept into the cursed castle. Wherever the orphan girl went, winter receded, the snows melted, and all the flowers bloomed. The curse was broken, and all knew that this orphan girl was in fact the lost daughter of the land's king, stolen away by the very same wicked witch who had cast the evil spell. In much of the Bacosh, princesses were frequently represented in illustration by flowers, and presumed blessed with the special powers of fertility. Now, this castle's maids placed a rose upon Sasha's bed, and considered her presence a blessing upon the land.

Well. She wondered.

And recalled, suddenly, another part of the tale. She got up gingerly, and walked to the window sill. There on the stone, she found a sprinkling of salt, to ward away witches and other evil things. Errollyn had spoken of travelling to less enlightened parts of Rhodaan, and having salt cast at him by village folk who could ill afford its waste. In the Larosan telling of the tale, of course, the wicked witch was serrin.

Sasha sat back on her bed, rose in hand, and felt suddenly, desperately sad. She wanted to see her sister Sofy once more. She wanted it so badly it hurt.

Fourteen

SASHA STOOD BEFORE HER HORSE IN THE UNDERGROWTH, and gazed across the river. Hills rose to either side in the moonlight, shrouded in forest. Across the moonlit water was Larosa. The enemy. But the ally of her nation, and the current location of its army. She had to get across.

After a moment, a man returned to the small column and signalled that they move further along. All twelve riders remained dismounted, in undergrowth too thick to make for easy riding. Much of the border was like this, farmlands left fallow over two centuries for the forest to reclaim. In some cases, the Rhodaanis had even replanted the trees themselves. It made for easier infiltration across the divide, but small infiltrations were not as worrisome to the Rhodaani Steel as large invasions. Through such forests, it was difficult to move large formations, and since the Steel was purely defensive, the only force troubled by these forests were the invading feudals on the other side.

Infiltrations, too, could work both ways. Rhodaani woodsmen and scouts for the Steel scoured these forests. So did the *talmaad*, on both sides of the border. The latter in particular made certain that Larosan scouts did not risk the trees lightly, especially at night. Many insisted the forests were haunted, as many Larosan scouts who ventured in, never ventured out.

After a while of picking a tangled path along the riverbank, another halt was indicated. Sasha waited. She glanced at Lord Elot's grim, bearded face, half-awash in a patch of moonlight, and wondered what it was to betray one's nation. She'd been accused of that herself, once. Perhaps betrayal meant different things to different people. And perhaps nations, too.

There was a commotion ahead, and some shouts. Men pressed forward, leading their horses. Sasha came finally to a spot amidst the trees where several Rhodaanis surrounded five ragged-looking peasants. Men and boys, the eldest having perhaps thirty summers. Several held sickles as weapons, warding those confronting them. Another held a spear. From their movements, Sasha guessed they had little more than basic weapon skills. Rhodaani militia were granted far better training, and were usually commanded by retired Steel officers.

Lord Elot strode forward, and growled at the men in Larosan. Sasha recognised the tongue well enough, but understood barely a word. Some things, however, she did not need words to understand. There was fear in the peasants' eyes, yet also defiance. The older man gesticulated grandly as he explained himself, and asked Lord Elot to do the same. And seemed incredulous at the reply.

A brief conversation followed between Lord Elot and another lord. Elot grunted assent to a request, looking disgusted. The other man drew his blade, with several others.

"No," said Sasha, loudly enough for all to hear. "Let them go."

"M'Lady, they are Larosan peasants, come to help the Rhodaani Steel. They will report to them, and we shall be known."

"That was your choice when you chose to come this way," Sasha replied. "Those in Tracato will figure it out anyway, if they have not already. These men seek only to do the reverse of what you do—to cross the border, and fight for the other side. Let them go."

"These are our enemies now!" another, younger man protested angrily. He took a step, sword raised.

Sasha put a hand to her hip, where she now wore her blade in unaccustomed position, and half drew from its sheath. "Let them go," she repeated.

Everyone stopped. Two days ago, she had felt the worst, shivering and aching in fever, and barely able to stay on her horse, or hold down anything she ate. Yesterday, she had come to feel better, her head clear and appetite strong. Today, she had managed some basic taka-dans, in full view of all. All knew the fate of Reynold's men in the Justiciary, having asked after them. Sasha had told them. None had seemed to disbelieve her.

Now, Lord Elot put hands on his hips and kicked at the dirt. Then gave a rough order, and the men's swords were sheathed once more. They parted, and the Larosan peasants moved warily forward, staring at Sasha. They inclined heads to her, in thanks.

"Nasi-Keth?" one asked, looking dubiously at the sword on her hip.

Sasha moved her hand from sword to shoulder, where it would normally be were her shoulder not such a mess, and nodded. "Nasi-Keth. Does anyone speak Torovan?"

More wary looks. One nodded. "A little," he said in that tongue. About them, the Rhodaanis were making to move on once more. "You go . . . Larosa?"

Sasha nodded. "I am Lenay. I go to my people." Ah, the man seemed to say, his mouth forming that silent word. "Why do you go to Rhodaan?"

"Some Larosan . . ." he searched for the right word. "Frighten? Yes, frighten of Rhodaan. Frighten of serrin. But we?" He pointed at his comrades. "We not frighten. We know serrin good. Rhodaani good. Larosan lord, bad. Bad men, they beat us, they kill us. They take our woman. We fight for Rhodaan."

"You fight with the Steel?" Sasha asked dubiously, looking at their makeshift weapons.

"No," said the Larosan, a little sheepishly. "Steel great warrior. We not great warrior. But we know Larosan land, Larosan lord, Larosan men, Larosan horses . . ." he ticked off his fingers, eyebrows raised at her, inviting comprehension.

"Ah," said Sasha. Not long ago, she would have wished him luck. Now, she only wanted to be with her people. She nodded, and stood aside. The men bowed again, and made their way into the undergrowth.

Soon, at another pause along the riverbank, Lord Elot brought his horse to her side. "The border has long been crossed by the likes of them," he said darkly. "Some serrin make contact with peasants nearby, and buy their loyalty with medicines and the such."

It was the same two centuries ago, Sasha knew, across the border between Saalshen and Rhodaan. As the peasants had come to like the serrin better than their own lords, the lords had become more and more fearful. That had led to more hateful speeches against the serrin by the priesthood, and so on, and so forth. Hatred and fear, the two sides of the coin of power.

"Why don't more Larosan peasants come to Rhodaan?" she asked.

"Like he said, most believe the priesthood," Elot replied. "Others will not come if they cannot bring their entire families, for those remaining will be treated badly. And in truth, few Rhodaanis encourage contact with Larosa. Some serrin doing so have got into trouble. It makes instability, like the last time, between Rhodaan and Saalshen. Most Rhodaanis want fewer wars, not more. So they leave most Larosan peasants to their superstitions of serrin demons and corrupted souls across the border, in the hope the lords and priests will not get too upset, and start another war."

"Didn't work," Sasha observed. Lord Elot said nothing.

Finally arriving at a suitable location, they crossed the river with no further troubles. By midnight, they had emerged from the forest and were riding across moonlit fields. This is Larosa, Sasha thought, gazing about. At first, it did not look particularly different.

Then, as they found a narrow trail between fields, they passed a small village tucked between a narrow strip of trees and a lake. There were no pretty stone walls and painted window shutters here. This village huddled close, with mud walls and thatched roofs, surrounded by small animal enclosures. Beneath a full moon on a warm late spring night, all seemed well enough. But Sasha wondered at the winters, when the ground turned to mud and those narrow walls struggled to hold the chill winds at bay. About the village, lands lay unused, perfect for villagers to expand their animal pens or plant a new patch of greens. Sasha knew very well what fate awaited them should they try.

Soon, a castle came into view. There was a village nearby, and sheep in the fields beside the road. Even from this distance, Sasha could see banners hanging above the main gate. It seemed somehow sinister, a hulking stone block upon the Larosan fields. Years of warfare in Lenayin had led to some walled cities, yet castles remained unknown. Now, more strongly than at any time since she'd left Lenayin eight months ago, Sasha truly felt that she had arrived in a strange and alien land.

Kessligh and Rhillian walked down a moonlit street in the heart of wealthy, feudalist Tracato. Five more Nasi-Keth walked with them, but it was little more than show. If the feudalists wanted them dead, so it would be. They walked at the heels of a pair of armed city men, and took some relief in the night's normality. From the nearby docks came the clanging of a bell.

"Thank you for not sending pursuit after Sasha," Kessligh said to Rhillian.

"She was too long gone when I found out," Rhillian replied. "I could not have caught her." There was no accusation in her tone.

"Thank you all the same."

"I am unhappy about it," Rhillian continued. "She is only one blade, but she has skills in generalship, and a following amongst some of the Goeren-yai. If she rallies them, Lenayin could grow stronger."

"There was nothing I could do," Kessligh said quietly. Rhillian flicked him a sideways stare that suggested she disagreed. "I have never seen her like this."

"I saw her," said Rhillian. "She suffered."

"It's not just the pain." The harbour came into view, down the road between rows of buildings. "She doubts."

"You fear you have lost her. You brought her here to see your vaunted Nasi-Keth, and the grand future of humanity that you promised. Neither has made a good impression. Her foundation is gone, her hope for the cause, her belief in you. She runs to her people because they are her last remaining foundation. Save for Errollyn." That last with an unpleasant, dry irony.

"She leaves Errollyn because she won't force him to fight his own people," Kessligh replied, edgily. "He would have followed her. He follows her too much, she knows that. She will find it difficult enough herself, to fight on that side, she would not inflict it upon Errollyn."

"Human emotion is a fickle thing. Humans change on a whim."

"Serrin too," said Kessligh. "You used to be a nice girl."

"Petrodor changed that," Rhillian said bitterly. "You did not mind your tongue on my failings there. Now you play precious."

The guiding pair of cityfolk turned down a dark, narrow lane. Soon they came to a nondescript door, and knocked a rhythm on the wood. A panel slid back, a password was given, and the door creaked open. The corridor beyond was narrow and gloomy, leading to a ramshackle courtyard beneath an open sky. Beyond the courtyard, a wide door led to a kitchen, grain and flour scattered about, signs of breadmaking, trails leading to a clay oven in the courtyard.

Two more city men awaited in the kitchen, blades drawn. Kessligh judged from their posture that they were ex-Steel, probably officers. A further door opened, and a small figure was ushered into the kitchen. There came barely enough moonlight through the windows for Kessligh to see his plain city clothes and longish hair about a slim, fine-featured face. The boy came forward on his own, to stand between the two big guards. Kessligh's five Nasi-Keth remained in the courtyard, all armed, as were he and Rhillian. It would not matter. Rhillian's upward glances told him that her serrin eyes had found archers in the courtyard windows. Crossbowmen, no doubt, and numerous. The corridors were too narrow for great swordplay, swinging the advantage back in the favour of Steel-trained men with no need for flourishing strokes. This was a death trap, should their invitees wish it to be.

"You came," observed the boy Alfriedo Renine. His high voice was calm. Regal, Kessligh thought. Though not in a manner anyone familiar with the Lenay royal family might recognise.

"Alfriedo," said Rhillian, and made a faint bow. "You seem well. I am pleased." Kessligh stood with both hands on his staff. The boy seemed to frown, as though displeased that he did not bow as well.

Behind Alfriedo, one of several shadows scoffed loudly. "Be silent, Aleis," said Alfriedo. And to Rhillian, "I do believe you, Lady Rhillian. I was not mistreated at the Mahl'rhen, quite the contrary. I was unhappy that some of your serrin comrades were killed in my rescue. I would have preferred a negotiated settlement. You have my condolences."

Again, Rhillian inclined her head. "I accept them. In truth, my comrades were sloppy. Serrin are not known for great defence. We do not build in high walls, as we do not think in straight lines. It is offence to which our minds are most adapted."

"You do not make threats here!" said the shadow by the kitchen bench behind. Kessligh strained his eyes, but could not make out the face. No doubt Rhillian could observe every feature. "You come because the power swings our way, and you have no choice, you do not make threats!"

"Aleis!" said Alfriedo in annoyance, turning fully about. "Am I the child, or are you? Hold your tongue like a man." Kessligh was impressed. Alfriedo turned back to Rhillian. "Again, my apologies. Much has occurred, and many tempers raised."

"I was not making a threat," Rhillian said calmly. "Merely an observation. The time for threats has passed. I come to talk peace, for the sake of Rhodaan, in the light of the most terrible threat Rhodaan has yet faced."

"You have finished your collaboration with the Civid Sein?"

"There was no collaboration," said Rhillian. "They are opportunists. When your mother's actions forced me to act and suspend the Council, the Civid Sein took the chance to flex their arm."

"And my mother is dead because of it," said Alfriedo. For the first time, his voice betrayed emotion.

"A great many people are dead," Rhillian replied. "A majority of them Civid Sein. If my actions against the Civid Sein at the Justiciary are not sufficient proof that I do not side with their kind, I do not know what is."

"Son," Kessligh said tiredly, leaning on his staff, "you must understand the serrin motivation. Serrin do not act on spite. Rhillian was amongst the first to discover your mother's death, and was sad about it. She sought to maintain an equilibrium. A balance, to the powers of Tracato. She saw your mother's faction grow too strong, which in turn caused a backlash from the rural folk, most notably in the form of the Civid Sein—"

"You blame *us* for their rise?" Alfriedo interrupted, his high voice quavering.

"I'm a military strategist, primarily," said Kessligh. "To every act on the battlefield, there is a response. As general, I am responsible for my enemy's actions too, for everything I do, my opponent will counter. A clever general can use this to manipulate his enemy. Do you wish to be a clever general, Alfriedo? Or merely a boy protesting that his opponent did not play by the rules?"

Alfriedo did not reply. His thin shoulders heaved in the silence, as he struggled for calm.

"Your mother had groomed you to rule," said Kessligh, leaning more closely. "Had proclaimed that yours is the birthright of kings. To rule, you must be a general, and accept that *nothing* is beyond your control. Some in Lenayin call me the greatest swordsman of that land, and think it a gift granted by the gods or spirits. But in truth, I achieved this merely because I refused to accept that my opponent could best me. I controlled the battle, not him. And if he killed me, it would be my failure, not his success.

"Do not take your losses and griefs as insults inflicted by others, young Alfriedo. If you were truly born to rule, you would accept them as failings of your own, and resolve to learn better."

Alfriedo gazed at him for a long moment. Kessligh wondered if he had indeed judged the boy rightly, or if this would only push him over the edge.

"You do not believe in the rule of kings," Alfriedo observed finally. "How do you then claim to know so much of their kind?"

"It is because I know so much of their kind that I do not believe in them. And I speak not merely of kings, but of men. Of leaders of all stripes. A true leader knows that knowledge and wisdom are all, but wisdom tells that not all men possess it. Thus, it would be folly to leave the ruling of lands entirely to kings."

"Even should that king be you?"

"Suppose it was," said Kessligh. "Suppose I ruled well. But who would follow?"

"My mother ruled well," Alfriedo said stubbornly. "As did my ancestors, when Rhodaan was a true kingdom. I would follow."

"Your ancestors were murderers, thieves and tyrants," said Kessligh. "The serrin document it well. If you wished I have no doubt they would lend you many writings that say so, writings by reliable humans of the period, not merely by serrin. Your mother attempted to steal the Rhodaani people's voice in Council from under their noses. She bred hatred among the common folk, and destabilised Rhodaan so that Saalshen felt it had no choice but to step in. She is now dead, you are orphaned, there is blood all over the Justiciary steps, the grand institutions of Rhodaan that have served so well for two centuries are in turmoil, and the Steel is less well prepared for the greatest challenge of its existence than it should be.

"I have hope that you may lead your people well, young Alfriedo. But have no illusions that should you do so, you would be the first."

There was a bristling of anger in the kitchen, but this time, no outbursts. Alfriedo remained silent for a moment. Then he looked at Rhillian.

"Our differences remain," he said to her, "yet our greatest threat is a common one, and marches upon our border from the west. I will make a pledge with you, Lady Rhillian, that all who follow me shall refrain from any violent acts against serrin, Nasi-Keth, or any institution of Rhodaan that we may consider moved against us. In return, you shall allow the Blackboots to re-form, and reinstate all senior city officials dismissed from their institutions. That includes the Council and their councillors, of course. Those who are still alive."

"I accept your truce offer," Rhillian said calmly, "and I return it. The Blackboots shall be re-formed with no penalties to those who cast off uniforms and fought in militia. Any who committed crimes against innocents, however, may be brought to justice should witnesses come forward."

"The only innocents against whom crimes were committed were our women and children at the hands of Civid Sein thugs!" came a snarl from behind. Alfriedo, Rhillian and Kessligh ignored it.

"We will discuss the reinstatement of city officials," Rhillian continued. "Some, you may recall, have been implicated in treason. Trials for such matters can obviously wait until after the war in the west is resolved, but we must come to an agreement on interim appointees in the meantime."

"Agreed," said Alfriedo, frowning in thought. "How?"

"A sitting of the High Table," said Rhillian. "But first, we must resolve the High Table and Council. At our count, we have lost seven of our hundred councillors dead, with another three unaccounted for. Of those absent ten, six are known to be feudalists."

"We count six and five," came the first helpful interjection from behind.

"We shall compare our names and numbers later," said Alfriedo. "These people must be replaced before Council sits. I believe two of the missing are on the High Table."

"Indeed. This shall be our first order of business, but there are others on both sides who should attend such discussions. We must agree on a location for a meeting tomorrow, and on who should attend. Once we have made those appointments, we can have the High Table sit, and begin deciding which city officials should be reinstated, and which should be replaced. Agreed?"

"Yes," said Alfriedo. "Let's begin."

"That's a damn smart kid," Kessligh remarked as they walked up from the docks some time later, in the company of their Nasi-Keth guards.

"He is," Rhillian said sombrely. "But intelligence is guarantee of nothing. He is still his mother's son."

"We shall see."

"And they're all fools to trust a fourteen-year-old to do their negotiating anyway, no matter how smart," Rhillian sighed. "Fancy entrusting leadership of any group to a person determined by lineage alone. No serrin had believed such an anachronism could possibly still exist two centuries after King Leyvaan."

"Human ideals die hard," said Kessligh. "Logic plays little role."

"Do you think it will hold?" Rhillian asked him. The truce, she meant.

"We can try. The strength of the Steel is a great blessing, but a minor curse too. No one has taken seriously the prospect that they might actually lose. And so, even confronted by a common threat as immense as this one, it fails to unite Rhodaanis in its face."

"I must soon leave," said Rhillian. "I am ordering the last significant force of *talmaad* in Tracato to go in support of the Steel, they shall need all the help they can get."

"Must you command them?"

"I have experience," said Rhillian. "It is expected."

"If the Steel are defeated," said Kessligh, "all Rhodaani forces as can muster should depart for Enora immediately. We must continue the fight from there."

"You think a defeat is likely?"

"Not likely. But where the Army of Lenayin is in play, anything is possible. I am stuck here in Tracato, so I have nothing better to do than make contingencies. The Steel is vastly experienced, but the one thing they have never experienced is defeat. I do not think it shall be pretty. They are a complex, structured force, and rely upon total control of the battlefield to maintain that structure. In defeat and withdrawal, that structure shall disappear and will be nearly impossible to regain, in the face of what numbers are arrayed against them. I predict either victory or rout. In the event of a rout, the Steel's commanders shall march as fast as possible to Enora. Retreating to Tracato shall make no sense, it would be just asking for encirclement."

"And given the Steel's strength, Tracato has allowed its own defensive walls to fall into disrepair, and the city to expand well beyond them."

"You see the problem. The border is defensible. Tracato is not."

"And Saalshen's border shall be open to its enemies for the first time in two hundred years."

There was fear in Rhillian's voice. Rhodaan's people too would be at great risk of the predations of invading Larosans, but Kessligh did not think her fear selfish. Rhodaanis were human, and invaders would expect to return them to the status of vassals beneath a feudal overlord. Serrin, to the Larosans and others, were demons and deserved death to the last child.

"They must deal with the entire Saalshen Bacosh before attempting Saalshen itself," said Kessligh, with more confidence than he felt. "That will be no easy thing, even if Rhodaan were to fall."

"But they'll never have so many forces mustered for the task as now," Rhillian said quietly. "They'll not waste the opportunity, no matter what their casualties. They'll take the plains as far as the Telesil foothills, as Leyvaan did last time, only they won't repeat his mistake and march into the forests. Those they'll take piece by piece, clearing with axes as they go. It may take decades, but Saalshen will die a slow death. We cannot defeat such massed armour on our own."

If only, Kessligh was tempted to say, Saalshen had built heavy, armoured armies of its own. If only they had been willing to reorganise their society to

258

accommodate such a militaristic change. With serrin, "if only" solved nothing. They were what they were, and change came to them with the utmost difficulty. And perhaps, he had often pondered, in changing to face such a threat, the serrin would lose that very thing that made them so worth defending in the first place.

"I tried my best," Rhillian said, her voice small. "I tried to keep Rhodaan stable. I do not have a good record of achieving in human society that which I attempt to achieve, but . . . but I do not see what else I could have done."

For a moment, Rhillian appeared as Kessligh had rarely seen her—lonely and vulnerable.

"I do not believe you could have done much differently," Kessligh told her. "Lady Renine and her followers saw the coming war as a chance to retake control of Rhodaan for the feudalists. To place one's own group above the defence of all Rhodaan is traitorous to say the least, and she got what she deserved. Had you done nothing, the Steel would never have stood for it, and *their* intervention would likely have placed some general in charge with a far less balanced attitude than yours. The Civid Sein were a nasty complication, and as much a failing of the Tol'rhen and supposedly civilised thinking as anything else. Even I did not see the extent of that problem until it was on top of us. You dealt with each problem in turn, and released the Steel in time to confront the Larosans, with the issue at least temporarily settled. I don't think you did such a bad job."

Rhillian gave him a sideways look. "And what do you think to do now?"

"Reorganise what's left of the Nasi-Keth. Try to keep the peace here in your absence. Hope for the best, and plan for the worst. We shall not let Saalshen fall, Rhillian. Serrin civilisation is the greatest asset that we humans possess. We must save it for our own sake, not merely for yours."

"A man named Deani was of the same opinion in Petrodor," Rhillian said sadly. "He was killed when Palopy House was attacked. Justice Sinidane thought much the same. We found him in the cells beneath his Justiciary, tortured and dead of shock. Those who hold such opinions do not live for long, in human lands. And now one of you whom I have loved has run away to the other side."

"Sasha has not stopped caring," Kessligh said quietly. "She cares too much. She struggles to decide whom she loves more."

Sasha sat on a wet stone by the roadside, and waited in the rain. After a while, she heard a single set of hooves approaching. Then, about a bend in the road, a small horse came galloping, ridden by a man in a long cloak. Sasha's horse looked up at the approach, ears pricked. She seemed to accept Sasha's calm, and was not unduly alarmed.

The small horse stopped before her, stamping and frothing, and the rider pushed wet hair and hood from his eyes. The left side of his face was tattooed, in a perfect dividing line down brow, nose and chin.

"Identify yourself!" the man demanded, in thickly accented Larosan. Those were amongst the few Larosan words Sasha knew—probably it was the same for this man.

"I am as welcome here as you," Sasha replied in Lenay, and pulled from her cloak a crimson-and-yellow striped flag. It was the flag of the local House of Neishure, whose riders had escorted her to this point in the morning, proclaiming it the most obvious route to approach Rhodaan.

The outrider stared at her more closely. "Who are you? Have you a name?"

"I do," said Sasha. "But it is not for you."

"The King of Lenayin rides this way!" snapped the rider. His accent marked him a southerner. Neysh, perhaps. "I'll have your name!"

"Come and take it from me," Sasha suggested. Her face remained hidden beneath the hood. The rider peered further, his horse edging closer. Surely he suspected. But his suspicions would make no sense. He glared at her, and tore off up the crossroad, leaving Sasha alone in the falling rain. After a moment of silence, he came galloping back, having checked that reach and not found an ambush. He waited opposite her, looking back up the road. Soon another rider appeared and the first signalled to him. That man signalled back, plunged his horse into the stream, up the far embankment, and into the forest. Checking for ambush there, too. In case she were a lone spotter. Or a distraction of some kind. Or a lure.

Sasha waited. Two more riders came galloping, and talked to the first, who pointed to Sasha, and the crossroad, his words inaudible. Then he galloped on, and the remaining two split, one up the crossroad, the other across the stream and into the forest at Sasha's back. Again, she was alone.

After a long while, the rain eased to a drizzle. More riders arrived, and she was similarly challenged. She gave them no more than she had the others. One seemed about to take it further, but another persuaded him otherwise, in furious whispers. They galloped on, save one, who retreated as far as the approaching bend, and awaited the column.

Finally, there came the sound of many soft hooves, horses walking. But many horses. A chink and rattle of armour and equipment, and a squeal of leather. The sound hung in the air long past the moment when it seemed that surely the vanguard would appear about the bend.

At last, the vanguard's banners appeared, colours of royalty, of Lenayin, and of each of the eleven Lenay provinces. There was a Verenthane star, too, mounted on a pole. Sasha frowned, and thought dark thoughts. The vanguard soldiers were of the provincial companies, Lenayin's most well equipped soldiers, riding tall on fine horses. Unusually, she saw they all carried shields. Some things, it seemed, were changing.

Behind the vanguard rode a contingent of Royal Guard, resplendent in red and gold. The nobility followed, many wearing fine, unfamiliar cloaks over Lenay armour and leathers. The outrider who had waited back now singled out one man from the group, riding alongside while pointing ahead. As the vanguard passed, that man came off the road and stopped before Sasha, several Royal Guards and lords at his back.

The lead rider came before them all, upon a great, roan warhorse. Broad, powerful, and oh-so-familiar. "Do you await anyone in particular?" asked her brother Prince Koenyg with amusement. The lords behind him laughed.

"I don't know," Sasha replied. "Are you anyone in particular?"

Koenyg frowned, and opened his mouth to retort. Then paused. And stared. "Is it . . . ?" He edged his warhorse forward several more steps, peering closely.

"Easy Your Highness!" called one of the Royal Guardsmen. "It could be assassins!"

"Sasha?" Koenyg whispered. "Is that Sasha?" Slowly, achingly, Sasha slid off her rock, and pulled back her hood. And looked up at her brother.

Koenyg swung down from his saddle in such a hurry that Sasha's hand twitched toward the blade within her cloak. But Koenyg made no move for his weapon, strode forward and embraced her. The pain of it nearly made her scream. Koenyg seemed to realise something was wrong, and released her.

"Sasha? Are you hurt?"

"A few cuts," she gasped, and swallowed hard. "Flesh wounds. I'm fine."

He seemed about to ask further but stopped. And to Sasha's further astonishment, he cupped her face in his hands. "Sister," he said, smiling. "You came back to us! All of Lenayin is united in this quest for the first time in history! This is a great time for healing old wounds, and building a new Lenayin. I'm so pleased you're here. So pleased."

He kissed her on the forehead. Sasha was too stunned to speak. She had not expected this at all. Koenyg seemed as she had only rarely seen him before—happy, and content with the world. Riding off to war, at the head of a united Army of Lenayin. It began to come clear in Sasha's head, precisely what Koenyg saw in this whole adventure. An opportunity to meld together all the fractious regions and beliefs of Lenayin by the only forge all Lenays would respect—the fire of battle. She did not like his methods, but she had to admit, it was certainly a plan. Perhaps it would even work.

"Where is Kessligh?" Koenyg pressed. "I heard that you and he fought to defend Dockside in the War of the King. You must tell me your tales. It's rare that a sibling should have grander tales of battle to tell than I. And I heard that Alythia had joined you after House Halmady fell. . . . I suppose you've been in Tracato, yes?"

There were more riders passing by, looking curiously to see this dismounted gathering by the roadside. She could hear exclamations, and men calling to others. Soon the news would spread along the column like fire through grass.

Before she could answer Koenyg, more horses arrived and riders leaped off. Damon pressed through those surrounding, and Myklas. Koenyg had to tackle them to restrain them from smothering her. "She's hurt you fools! Be gentle!"

Damon pushed his elder brother away, fighting off an idiot grin. "Sasha, are you . . . ?"

"I'm all right," she said, with tears in her eyes. She hugged him, and he replied with gentle pressure. Then Myklas, whose idiot grin was unrestrained. "You've grown," Sasha observed.

"You've shrunk," Myklas retorted, and kissed her roughly.

"Sasha, where have you been?" Damon asked. "Was it Tracato?"

"Aye. Kessligh's still there."

"And Alythia?"

"How did she cope living as a pauper on Dockside for half a year?" Myklas asked joyfully. "I would have given anything to see that!" Koenyg cuffed him on the head.

Sasha looked at the sodden grass. She'd almost been hoping for a frosty reception, she realised. From Koenyg at least. Now, they were all together, and almost a family, for the first time in . . . spirits, she couldn't think of when. She wanted to enjoy it. Wanted to talk with her brothers and tell all her tales, and listen to theirs, and laugh, and eat and perhaps even down a cup of wine in their presence, where no priest would see her. But it had to be done. It was a duty of blood, that she be here. That they hear it from her own mouth.

"Alythia's dead," she said softly. "I saw the body." For a moment, there was no sound but the great passing of the column. Koenyg looked pale. Damon, aghast. Myklas, disbelieving.

"No!" Myklas insisted. Then he stamped in fury, his eyes spilling. "No! You're wrong! She's not dead!"

Koenyg grabbed him, a hard immobilising arm about the younger man's shoulders. Myklas tried to fight him off, but Damon grabbed him and Myklas collapsed against Damon's shoulder, sobbing. Sasha's own tears escaped her, and she was drawn into the four-sided embrace. Her brothers' arms about her hurt, but that was well. Everything hurt. They grieved together, a small circle of pain by the roadside. And Sasha wondered what it said about her family that pain and war should unite them at last, where so little else had worked.

The siblings took lunch in the same carriage that had carried Sofy from Baen-Tar to Sherdaine. It was a shameful thing for a Lenay prince to travel by carriage, but it was the only way all four could converse together without halting. The king rode further back in the column today. Word was travelling to him of Sasha's arrival. Sasha did not look forward to that inevitable meeting.

She told her brothers the story from the beginning. Her time in Petrodor, Kessligh's struggles to unite the Nasi-Keth, her friendship with Rhillian, and the trials that followed. Then Tracato. Koenyg listened grimly to hear of the troubles there. Damon looked wearily resigned. And Myklas, completely impatient with any politics, wishing only to hear of Alythia's end. When she finished, none of them spoke. The carriage wheels clattered and bounced on the road, jolting Sasha's wounds. She'd felt altogether more comfortable in a saddle.

"That is quite a tale," Koenyg said finally. "You and I shall talk some more on affairs in Tracato, and Saalshen's moves for power there. We shall talk on the Steel's formations and tactics, also. But I must know . . . you say the Steel have left Tracato?"

"Those formations that had been fighting in Elisse, yes," said Sasha. "It has taken me ten days to get here. The Steel moves more slowly, but are remarkably fast for such a heavy formation. They are all in position now, I am certain."

"And the Enorans?" Koenyg pressed.

"I have not been in Enora, I could not say. But rumour was that the Enorans were quite unnerved by Tracato's troubles. Some rumours suggested there may have been Enoran formations readying to march into Rhodaan to restore order, should the feudalists grasp control. But even if true, I suspect they too would be in position by now. You're late."

"The Torovans are late," Koenyg corrected. "And weddings between nations take an obscene amount of time. But it's true, it would have been nice to get here a week earlier."

"And Ilduur?" Damon asked.

"Ilduur is mountainous," Sasha replied. "Most Rhodaanis don't trust them, from feudals to Civid Sein. Ilduur has natural fortifications, there is no way through for any invading army, save through narrow passes that would be death against far lesser forces than the Ilduuri can muster. So the Ilduuri tend to sit in their mountain strongholds and wait. They are sworn by oath to defend their blood brothers of Enora and Rhodaan, but they show little enthusiasm for it. Their posture is defensive, and they will not launch a flanking thrust to threaten Enora's attackers, as Enora will and has for Rhodaan." She looked at Koenyg. "What's the plan?"

"It was to be a two-pronged attack, against Rhodaan and Enora. But this news of Tracato's troubles continues to mount, I now think it would best be focused upon the Rhodaanis . . . if the Rhodaani Steel has been suffering some desertions, and some of their soldiers have been fighting in Elisse, Tracato, and now to the border, they'll be tired, and perhaps disillusioned. A breakthrough against Rhodaan would seem more likely now than Enora."

It seemed very hopeful, but Sasha held her tongue. Any advantage against the Steel was a good thing. "So you'll be thinking a feint against the Enorans?" she asked.

"Perhaps a third of the total force. Or perhaps a quarter made to look like a third, if we think we can get away with it. Enough to hold the Enorans from a flanking sweep, and focus our maximum force upon the Rhodaanis."

"They're not that strong, surely!" Myklas scoffed. "Rhodaan and Enora have maybe thirty thousand each, but even with Torovan understrength, we number a hundred and forty. There's never been an army of this scale in all the history of Rhodia!"

"You'll need all of them," Sasha told Koenyg, not bothering to answer her youngest brother. "Focusing strength is good. Even if successful, it will be a close run thing."

Koenyg nodded, not contesting her assessment. Sasha was relieved at least to see that he had a clear idea of what they were up against.

Koenyg leaned forward, and looked her hard in the eyes. "Sasha. I will not lie to you. You are useful to me, and to this war. You have great standing amongst the central and eastern Goeren-yai, and many of them are still not too keen on the fight. Damon has been attempting to drum some sense into their thick skulls about the need to change their fighting styles, with some limited success. Your own words, from Kessligh's student, could convince them.

"But I must know. Kessligh is still in Tracato. He shall perhaps not assist the Steel directly, but he most certainly assists the defence of Rhodaan more broadly. As does your friend Errollyn. As do many others of your former friends and comrades. Now you choose to ride here with us. Tell me truly—when the horns are sounded and men start dying, where shall your loyalties lie?"

Sasha's gaze was expressionless. "With Lenayin," she said flatly. "Always."

Koenyg nodded. Convinced, perhaps, but . . . "Have you lost faith?" he wondered. "Kessligh had great hopes for the Nasi-Keth. He had great hopes for you, as a leader of the Nasi-Keth. What of those dreams, Sasha? Where do they lie?"

"Aside," said Sasha. There was no emotion in her voice, because she did not feel any. She felt . . . empty. "I cannot say that I have abandoned them entirely. But they lie far aside all the same. They were cast aside not by me, but by the factions of Tracato, Nasi-Keth amongst them. I saw that the civilisation they had built was but a thin shroud over barbarism. I saw Nasi-Keth themselves, who should have known better, casting their lot in with a mob who were little better than the frothing Riverside mobs in Petrodor, only better dressed and led by intellectuals. I gave them my best, I gave them a fair chance, and they betrayed all my dreams, tortured me and Errollyn, and murdered my sister.

"I am here because one dream lies shattered. I cannot stand to see my nation shattered as well. I have come to defend the most important thing I have left, the thing I still believe in with all my heart and soul—my people, and my family. I may be only one person, but I am duty bound to help however I can. Lenayin will need every asset at its disposal."

Koenyg nodded. His look was one of firm approval. Sasha reflected that it was perhaps the only time she could recall him looking at her in that way.

"I will find you a role," he said, "never fear about that. You have done well for Lenayin. Welcome home."

He opened the carriage door and got out, walking to where a Royal Guardsman trailed his horse to one side.

"How good are they?" Damon asked when he was gone. "The Steel, I mean?" Sasha saw from his sombre look that he had grasped something that perhaps Koenyg had not.

"Good," she said. "Surely you've been speaking with Bacosh veterans of past wars?"

Damon nodded. "But they cannot give a full picture. Usually their fights were too brief, and consisted of everyone dying or running away."

"That's been the pattern for two hundred years," she admitted.

"What will it be like?" asked Myklas. He would be expected to participate in the attack, Sasha knew. At seventeen summers now, he was well and truly grown. Oh Myk.

"Hell," said Sasha. For the first time in memory, she thought she spied a flicker of fear in Myklas's eyes. It seemed a time for such firsts, among siblings. "Damon, we must think of some tactic to reduce the effectiveness of their artillery. Their infantry lines are tough enough, their tactics negate the primary Lenay strength, which is swordsmanship. We fight as individuals, they fight as a single entity. But even so, if we get that close, we can win, because it is what we're best at, and Lenay warriors will never lose their nerve.

"But I've spoken with Steel soldiers, I befriended the commander of the Tracato school for Steel officers, and I spoke at length with my serrin friend

Aisha, of her experiences in the war in Elisse. And my biggest fear now is that Lenay warriors may be *too* brave. Previous armies have survived encounters with the Steel because their nerve broke, and they ran away to fight another day. Lenay warriors do not retreat easily. And I worry that should we stay too long, under that kind of artillery fire, there will be no Army of Lenayin left."

Damon nodded slowly. "It will be cavalry," he said. "It is where we are most evenly matched. We must use cavalry to flank their infantry and disrupt their artillery."

"It's been tried before," said Sasha. "By two centuries of military thinkers. None worked."

"Why not?" asked Myklas.

"Because we are the attackers," said Damon, "which means they get to choose the ground on which they fight. They know their border very well, and have altered the landscape in many places to suit possible encounters. There are many fortresses and walls, channelling attackers through awkward approaches and limiting the room on the flanks for cavalry. They force the attackers to charge infantry straight up a selected approach, with little cavalry support, and the Steel artillery scythes them down like wheat. What's left, the Steel infantry are vastly overmatched for."

"And they've *talmaad*," Sasha added. "Lenay cavalry may be a match for Steel cavalry if we can find enough open ground to fight on, but no one can match the *talmaad* on horseback. Mounted archery is a terrible skill in the right hands. I wonder we've never tried it ourselves."

"There're many useful ideas Lenayin has never tried," Damon said darkly.

Myklas gave him an unimpressed look. "That becomes tiresome, Damon."

"Defeat will seem more so," Damon muttered.

The column halted for the evening by another castle, where local lords hosted all Lenay nobility and royalty in a feast. At Damon's insistence Sasha was ushered upstairs to the lord and lady's chambers, where maids assisted her to wash, and apply her ointments. Soon Damon and Myklas entered, ignoring the protests of the maids.

"It's all right!" Sasha announced tiredly as she lay face down, naked but for a towel over her buttocks. A maid tried to hide the rest of her with a robe, but Sasha shoved it aside, and waved impatiently for them to continue pressing the ointment-soaked cloths to her worst injuries, the burns in particular.

"Great fucking gods on a horse," Myklas muttered. "How in all the hells did you ride here from Tracato like that?" He walked around her, as though examining some strange fish washed up on the riverbank.

"I'm sure I don't know," Sasha murmured into the bedsheets.

Damon sat on the bed alongside. He grasped her hand. "This Reynold Hein," he said quietly. "If we find him, when we reach Tracato, may I have him?"

Sasha laughed, humourlessly. "There's a queue."

"Does it hurt very badly?" Myklas asked.

"Less than it did. It looks so bad now because of all the scabbing. When they peel it will be better. Perhaps a week." She turned her head to look at Myklas. "Did you come to see that I wasn't exaggerating?"

"They're shit," said Myklas. "I knew you weren't lying."

"Who's shit?"

"Oh the usual noble cow pats. They say you're exaggerating your injuries to make yourself a martyr for Lenayin."

"When I'm actually a traitor," Sasha concluded. It didn't upset her. She'd expected nothing better.

"Sasha, I need to warn you," Damon said. "Be careful. You're truly no safer here than you were in Tracato. Probably less."

"I didn't come here to be safe."

"The northern provinces all want you dead, of course," Damon continued. "Much of the nobility of all provinces, too. I don't think you can ride with the vanguard, too many high nobility ride there, and will take it ill."

"That's shit," Myklas snorted, lounging into a chair beside the bed. "She's our sister, she should ride with her brothers."

"It is not our decision to make," Damon said firmly. "We can't start a fight with the lords now just before a war, not even for Sasha."

"I agree," said Sasha. "Where do you want me?"

"Valhanan would not work," said Damon, and Sasha's heart sank. "They march too far back in the column, I'd like you nearer the front. And Koenyg is right, it would sow division. It is well known that the Goeren-yai of Valhanan have doubts about this war, having a former leader such as yourself ride amongst them would only remind them of the things that divide them from the Lenay nobility, and all the reasons they should not fight. You must ride with nobility, to show them you are no threat, and will not agitate the Goeren-yai."

"Well no one north, east or probably south will have me," Sasha pointed out. "Taneryn would, but you don't want to ignite *that* again. You're not going to dump me with the bloody west?"

"I have an idea," said Damon. "Tomorrow we shall see."

Sasha buried her face against the mattress, as the maids continued to soak and apply their cloths. In all her haste to return to her people, she'd forgotten how terrible Lenay politicking could be. Only now did it truly occur to her just how few of her people would be as pleased to see her as she was to see them.

Fifteen

SIDESADDLE, SOFY DECIDED, WAS NOT MERELY LUDICROUS, but dangerous. Several times when her mare lurched unexpectedly, she thought she might topple. She would have felt so much safer on her little Dary, but the travelling court had been scandalised enough that she would wish to ride on horseback to greet her sister Sasha, and to have the princess regent riding on a scruffy little Lenay dussieh would have been too much to ask.

She sat instead upon an elegant white mare lent to her for the occasion, alongside her husband on a tall black stallion. About them rode knights in full armour, and lords in less taxing mail and formalwear. The banners of the regency swung in the midmorning sun. They numbered nearly a hundred strong, with servants and squires, heralds and scouts. The Army of Larosa, and the Army of Lenayin, marched on parallel paths, not more than a quarter-day's ride apart, to save the roads from churning to muddy bogs beneath many thousands of boots, hooves and wagon wheels in the late-spring rains.

Balthaar seemed in good humour, laughing with his lords and knights, and admiring the sunny morning. He complimented Sofy often on how lovely she looked, and how well she rode, and missed no opportunity to reach for her hand and exchange a smile. Sofy did not know what she felt. She tried simply to ride, and enjoy the freedom away from the royal procession at the Larosan Army's head, and to appreciate the morning as her husband did.

Soon enough, the Larosan party arrived at the head of the great Lenay column, and Sofy exchanged greetings all over again with her father and brothers, while insisting that the army should not stop simply to observe the formality. All seemed very subdued, and her father in particular, deadly grim. That was no surprise, King Torvaal Lenayin was usually grim. And it had only been a week since leaving Sherdaine, so the sight of her was no great astonishment to any. But Sofy gained the distinct impression that something was very wrong, and no one wanted to be the one to tell her. Was it Sasha, she suddenly feared?

She left most of the Larosan contingent with the Lenay vanguard, and rode with a small party of knights in single file along the roadside. The

Isfayen rode forth in the column, and it took some time to reach them. Lenay warriors cheered as she passed, and she waved, smiling, and trying to be happier than she felt. It was all confusing. She wanted to see Sasha again so badly. Sasha had that way of making things clear and simple to her.

When she reached the Isfayen place in the Lenay column, her first sight was of Yasmyn, riding at her father the Great Lord Faras's side. The two of them talked and laughed, and Yasmyn's eyes shone with happiness. Sofy wondered what it would be like, to share a relationship like that with her own father. Sasha rode at Yasmyn's side, evidently expecting Sofy's arrival. Upon seeing her, Sasha rode forward, and dismounted. Sofy did likewise, and embraced her tearfully. She could not hug hard, for her brothers had told her of Sasha's injuries. She could not hug long, either, for the column marched on, oblivious to the concerns of sisters who had not seen each other in far too long, and wanted only a moment's pause to catch up. It felt awkward, and not at all the heartfelt reunion Sofy had dreamed of. When they parted, Sasha seemed reluctant to meet her eyes.

"Sasha, what's wrong?" Sofy asked, wiping tears from her cheeks. Sasha's eyes were dry. Somehow, that disappointed her.

"Did they tell you?" Sasha asked quietly. "About Alythia?"

"No." And with growing alarm, "Sasha, what about Alythia?"

Sasha made a muttered curse, and stared off across neighbouring woods. "She's dead, Sofy. The great Tracatan enlightenment killed her."

Sasha and Sofy rode and talked together at the Isfayen contingent's head for a long time. Sasha insisted that Sofy tell of her adventures first, from her ride to Baerlyn to assist in the revenge of Jaryd Nyvar, to the assembly of the army, and the subsequent ride to Larosa, and the wedding to follow. Sofy found it difficult to talk, so soon after learning Alythia's fate, yet she tried, and was not interrupted by floods of tears too frequently.

Sasha then told her own tale, and Sofy listened with mixed horror and concern to hear of Sasha's trials in Petrodor, and the War of the King, and her most recent horrors in Tracato. Sasha's tone was flat, lacking its usual expression. She skipped details, and did not embellish as she usually would. Sofy had always loved to hear Sasha's tales before, as her eyes would come alive with boisterous enthusiasm and carry her listeners along with the tale. Now, the words seemed as dry as Sasha's eyes, and her telling did not invite any response. Sofy tried interrupting, seeking further detail that might shed more light on what she suspected Sasha of hiding, but there was no joy in the discovery. When Sasha reached Alythia's death, she skipped very quickly to the end, and waited for Sofy's latest tears to end.

Sasha took Sofy's hand, and her grip at least was firm. "How's Balthaar?" she asked.

"Well," said Sofy, and paused to find a stronger voice. "He's hopelessly in love, Sasha." She managed a weak smile at her sister. Sasha just studied her, curiously. "It's rather sweet, actually. He's such a model of Larosan nobility. He's very refined, very educated, quite arrogant yet not at all mean. . . . I had not thought that such a man could fall in love with a girl like me. And a Lenay savage at that. Although I think for him that is a part of the attraction, he's fascinated that such a savage culture could produce someone like me."

"Are you happy?"

"Happy?" Sofy stared at her. Something about the question, so bluntly put, made her anxious. "I'm not sure what happy has to do with anything."

Sasha seemed as though more impressed with the answer than she'd expected. She rode very upright, Sofy noted, shoulders back, with none of her usual ease. Surely her wounds hurt her. "Do you love him?" Sasha asked.

Sofy shrugged. "I don't know."

"Then you don't love him."

Sofy opened her mouth to protest, but realised that Sasha's conclusion was obvious. "I barely know him," she said instead.

"But he's good in bed," Sasha persisted. Sofy frowned at her. "And tall and handsome. I hear the talk."

"He is very tall and handsome," Sofy agreed, still frowning. "But I'm not a naive little girl any more, Sasha. Tall and handsome is not why I married him."

"Do you hate him then?"

"Hate him? Why . . ." She shook her head, flustered. "Sasha, why are you saying these things? It sounds like you're accusing me of something."

"I hear you've been helpful," Sasha said flatly. "Helping the lords with their squabbles. Diplomacy was always your strongpoint."

"I *am* the princess regent now," Sofy retorted. "Such things are my responsibility."

"Your responsibility to help the Larosa murder half-caste serrin and invade Saalshen?"

Sofy stared at her, disbelievingly. Anger followed. "And you're here too! What does that make you, that you now ride against the armies of the Saalshen Bacosh?"

"A fool," Sasha said bitterly. "A fool, but not a traitor."

"And I am?"

"No, Sofy. Just a fool, like me. We're all fools."

They rode together in silence, amidst the great creak and sway of saddles and hooves. Peasants gathered on the hillside near their village, in huddled brown cloth, and stared fearfully at the passing army. Sofy swallowed her emotion.

"I don't know what you want of me, Sasha," Sofy said quietly. "I do the best I can for my people, as you do. My new family is not evil, they are just people, neither more perfect nor more flawed than most. I feel that perhaps I can do some good here. I'm good at diplomacy, as you say. Perhaps I can . . . perhaps I can moderate, or attempt to talk some reason to those who would not otherwise . . ."

"If they win," Sasha said bleakly, "they'll slaughter everyone. Serrin and half-castes they'll torture first. Artists, craftsmen, philosophers, all these people are dangerous because they have dangerous ideas, they'll be killed first. You can't reason with it, Sofy, because reason is not at issue. Reason is never at issue. In that, Rhillian was right. Only blood will stop it, one way or the other."

It was too much. Sofy felt her composure slipping, the tears resuming once more. "What would you have me do?"

"There's nothing any of us can do. Serve the path of honour: family, nation, faith. When all's said and done, it's all any of us have."

"And what about right and wrong?"

"A luxury I once believed in." Sasha's eyes were distant. "A fool's dream. No more."

In the early afternoon, word spread down the column that the city of Nithele lay ahead, and there a council of war would be held between the Bacosh and Lenay armies. The Isfayen lords, Sasha, Sofy and Yasmyn all rode forward to arrive at the city in good time.

Nithele was a great walled city on the fork of land between two joining rivers. The Isfayen party halted along one riverbank, and now observed the high city walls. Many small boats sat on the bank, and cityfolk walked there, to gawp at the Army of Lenayin, or to throw nets, or to gather driftwood. Planks made a path on the bank to form a low wharf. Men, bare feet slipping, pants rolled to their knees, carried cargo from riverboats dragged bow-first onto the grass.

"How do men live in such places?" Great Lord Faras wondered darkly, observing the stark walls. The red cloth about his brow denoted him as a bloodwarrior, a sacred title in Isfayen, marked by many trials of manhood, and codes of conduct rigorous even by Lenay standards.

"The lowlanders like stone," his daughter observed. "They live in stone cages, and fear the sky."

"Do men live as this in the Saalshen Bacosh?" Faras asked Sasha.

"No," she said. "Their cities are open. They have no internal enemies, and the Steel have not lost a battle in two hundred years, so they do not need these great walls."

"Never trust a man with no enemies," said Yasmyn, as they dismounted. Ahead, on the opposite side of the river from the looming Nithele walls, sat a small fishing village, with boats drawn up to the muddy riverbank. About it was a gathering of Lenay vanguard, with many banners and horses.

"The Saalshen Bacosh are surrounded by enemies," Lord Faras countered his daughter. "Not only have they the mainland Bacosh, they had the Elissian Peninsula to their north, and made short work of them just now. The Steel have won so many glorious victories outnumbered and surrounded, I have no doubt we do not fight for the side of greater honour in this contest."

The observation did not surprise Sasha. For the Isfayen, even more than in most of Lenayin, victory in battle brought honour, and honour was currency far richer than gold. When King Soros had liberated Lenayin from the Cherrovan a century before, the Isfayen had taken more convincing than most. Many Isfayen blood chiefs had challenged the new king to arms, and fought bloody battles against chieftains who converted to the new faith, be they Isfayen or from neighbouring Yethulyn or Neysh. Many Isfayen had never considered themselves to be Lenay at all, and had taken the liberation as an opportunity to fight for a separate kingdom . . . or indeed, for rulership of the greater Lenay kingdom. Thankfully, that prospect had so horrified the rest of Lenayin that they had banded together to ensure it never happened, and the resisting Isfayen chieftains had been crushed. That crushing had gained King Soros the respect of the rest, and Isfayen had submitted to rule from Baen-Tar, after the limited, uniquely Lenay fashion.

Yet the Isfayen had remained remote from the rest of Lenayin, their lands high, rugged and cold, their manners hostile, their justice crude. Even the Isfayen practice of the new faith was unique, a strange crossbreed of old traditions and new civilisation, their temples adorned with colours and flags, their holy stars inscribed with the spirit script of their ancient ways. And yet it was the faith, Kessligh had assured Sasha, that had brought the Isfayen into the Lenay fold to their current extent . . . which was not to say that they were brothers in the grand Lenay family, but merely that they did not kill the king's taxmen on principle, or raid the neighbouring villages without at least a warning, or seek marriage with the daughter of prominent lords by galloping into town and throwing the girl over a saddlehorn. With the Isfayen, that was considered progress. Many in the priesthood had taken on the role of educators in wild Isfayen, and had thus attained an importance far beyond the worship of gods. Such men had brought the outside world to Isfayen, and given its inhabitants a reason to care about what lay beyond for the first time in their history.

The Great Lord Faras, Sasha well knew, was considered the best and brightest leader that Isfayen had ever had. Faras's father had insisted he receive a Baen-Tar education, and now, the breeding showed. Faras had in turn insisted that his son Markan, and daughter Yasmyn, attend Baen-Tar, to learn the ways of the *kulemran*, or the "non-Isfayen." That meant everyone from fellow Lenays to lowlanders to serrin. Now, Markan rode with the column, and was rumoured to have befriended Prince Damon, while Yasmyn had become the Princess Sofy's closest confidante and protector. Many such ties were being forged on this ride, between leaders of lands with far longer history of mutual slaughter than friendship. Some of the credit for that lay with men like Lord Faras—a new kind of Lenay lord, educated and curious in a way that his predecessors had never been. And part of the credit, Sasha reluctantly conceded, lay with her big brother Koenyg. This had been his intention, to forge a nation on the road to war.

The hitch, of course, was that for it all to work, the army had to win.

Sasha stretched carefully as men dismounted. A galloping horse turned her head, knights moving to protect the dismounting princess regent as the new arrival came to a halt nearby. Jaryd Nyvar jumped from his horse and strode to Sasha, grinning ear to ear. He hugged her gently, having evidently heard to do that, and Sasha hugged him hard.

"The rabble have been giving you a hard time, huh?" Jaryd said affectionately.

"You've no idea," said Sasha. She pulled back to look at him. "Is that a ring I see? Two rings?" She fingered the metal in his ear.

"What do you think?"

"I think your hair looks better longer." Jaryd's hair had grown long enough to have curls. "You're nearly handsome now."

Jaryd laughed. "No tattoos though. Not even for you, Sasha."

"I've got one!" Sasha said brightly. "I got it in Petrodor, want to see?"

"Of course! I hope it's somewhere exciting."

"Just my arm, I'll show you later. Still trying to get my clothes off, huh Jaryd?"

Jaryd put a hand to her face. "No offence, Sasha, but you look like you could use a good fuck."

Sasha laughed outright, the first time she'd laughed since Tracato, and hugged him again. Spirits she was glad to see him. She hadn't quite expected to be this glad. Seeing her siblings again was wonderful, but hard, too. She knew they did not blame her for Alythia's death, but she felt responsible anyway. And Sofy was married, and Koenyg was on the warpath, and Damon was angry, and Myklas was . . . well, Myklas, and not someone with whom she could discuss anything important. Perhaps Jaryd had been the same once, but he'd changed. He knew loss and pain. He knew what it was to feel alone. And he was one of the few men in Rhodia who'd dare flirt with her so outrageously. She needed that.

"Well," she said, "right now I'm covered in scabs and bruises."

Jaryd made a face. "Some men are more easily deterred than others."

"You mean some men will fuck anything."

Jaryd grinned, and gave her a kiss on the forehead that was far more brotherly than his banter would suggest.

About them, a camp of sorts was unfolding, as men at the head of the Lenay column sought the sheltered places to lay their gear. Most made do with a simple patch of ground, and set about making camp. Given that the Army of Lenayin marched without tents and slept on the open ground, that was a relatively simple affair of dumping gear and making a fire. Soon the firewood carts would come clattering, their men having spent the day's march foraging for wood. The bedding cart would follow, with extra blankets for the footsoldiers with no horses to carry such heavy, unwieldy things.

Sasha, Sofy, Jaryd and Yasmyn walked with Great Lord Faras and the Isfayen lords through the gathering commotion of camp toward the fishing village. Here at the vanguard, tents were being erected, for royalty and lords. Already boats were crossing the river from the walls of Nithele, loaded with produce, and men who shouted to the soldiers ashore of things for sale. Sasha saw chickens held aloft, and fish, and baskets of eggs. Soldiers and merchants alike clustered toward the river.

Sofy walked further from Sasha, and talked with Yasmyn and Great Lord Faras. Jaryd noticed.

"She's not talking to you either?" he asked wryly.

"We've each been in very different places," Sasha explained, flexing one shoulder. Her taka-dans were becoming more strenuous, and her underworked muscles were protesting. Then, in Torovan, which she knew the Isfayen spoke only a little, "Did you fuck her?" Jaryd scowled at her. "Damon told me. Don't worry, I'm not about to take your head for it." And she smiled. "She could use a good fuck too. Better you take her virginity than that Larosan ass."

"It wasn't like that," Jaryd said shortly. Sasha watched him, with great curiosity. He wasn't joking now.

"How was it like?"

"I'm not sure," said Jaryd. "Perhaps you should ask her."

"I love her dearly, Jaryd, but she is a breathless young girl at times. I'm sure you've made more difficult conquests . . ."

"I told you, it wasn't like that." Jaryd's voice betrayed impatience now.

"I believe you. Do you love her?"

Jaryd sighed, and ran a hand through his lengthening hair. "Would it matter?"

"It would to you. And it would to her, I'm sure."

"That's the trouble," said Jaryd. "Best drop it."

He indicated ahead, to a gathering of flags by the village outskirts. Flags of the Larosan royalty, Sasha saw.

"Do they know?" Sasha asked.

"Probably. But rumour here is even worse than Baen-Tar. Sofy's rumoured to have slept with half the army, so I'm lost in the crowd. Yasmyn's been spreading the best rumours, she always rumours Sofy to be secretly in love with the best Lenay swordsmen, and makes it known to the Larosans that those swordsmen will demand an honour duel if accused. And the Larosans don't know Lenayin well enough to know which rumours are possible, and which are horse shit."

"I'm sure the priesthood isn't amused," said Sasha, as they skirted preparations for a large tent to be erected.

"The Larosan priesthood is amused by nothing," Jaryd agreed. "It's a curious thing. Bawdy lords and even some ladies at the feasts and weddings, and some behaviour that would even make a Lenay blush. The priests don't bother with that. They're concerned about the serrin, and purity. You'd be in far greater danger with your bed partners, by the sound of it."

Evidently he wanted to hear more of Errollyn, having heard the rumours. It was only fair, as she'd grilled him on his affair with Sofy. But she could not speak of Errollyn, and had to gaze toward the river to hold her composure. Jaryd saw her pain, and put a hand on her shoulder.

"He must be an impressive man," he said quietly. "To have won the heart of Sashandra Lenayin."

"The most impressive."

It was Prince Balthaar Arosh himself who greeted them at the outskirts of the village. He made a great show of noble courtesy, shaking the hands of the Isfayen lords, complimenting them on their warrior reputation, and then kissing Sasha's hand. He was not slimy like some lowlands nobility, Sasha conceded reluctantly. Tall and handsome, yes, with thick brows and a composed demeanour. Educated, with a straight bearing and an effortless grasp of comportment and manners. And he called her "sister," and walked with her through the outskirts of the fishing village, as though he had arrived here with the intention of doing precisely that.

"Tell me," he said in nicely accented Torovan, "how do the Isfayen regard you? I had heard that you'd had a confrontation with the Great Lord Faras before." In the Udalyn Valley, when Faras had ridden with King Torvaal to help put an end to Sasha's little rebellion. Balthaar had done some research.

"Great Lord Faras is loyal to his king," said Sasha. "He viewed my actions as disloyal, and thought ill of me. But his daughter Yasmyn has been riding with my sister, and Prince Damon informed me that the Isfayen opinion of me had been improving. The Isfayen respect warriors."

Sasha made certain to walk between the prince regent and Jaryd. Balthaar did not look at the younger man, but that might have been the simple arrogance of royalty. Sasha wondered.

The village houses were of squat stone walls and thatched roofs, wealthier than most Larosan villages, yet still unattractive to Sasha's eye. A woman walking toward them with a laden basket and two children in tow fell to one knee in horror as she realised who approached. The prince's knights swaggered past her, hands on sword belts, regarding her as a big dog might regard a small one grovelling at its paws. Sasha's mood, recently brightened, darkened once more.

"I do confess to being somewhat astonished," Prince Balthaar continued, "that such formidably masculine peoples as the Lenays should accept a woman with a sword into their midst on the road to war."

"The warriors of Lenayin respect skill with a sword," Sasha replied. She extended a hand to ruffle the hair of the kneeling woman's little boy in passing, but the woman drew him fearfully back from the nobility's path. The little boy stared, his face dirty, fingers in his mouth. "There is a saying in Valhanan, that should the mouse best the wolf, then give the mouse a chieftain's staff and let him rule in the land of wolves."

"It is not common though, surely, for the mouse to best the wolf?"

"Not common, no," said Sasha. "But should it occur, then should the wolves not show respect?"

"There is a tale of mice chasing cats in the Bacosh," said Balthaar. His manner was so languid and airy, it was difficult to tell what, if anything, he was truly thinking. "Not the same thing, but close enough, for the purposes of tales. This occurred following the murder of a king by a commoner. The natural order was upset, and the mice chased the cats, and the cats chased the dogs, and the women beat the men."

"Is it then an established order of the Bacosh that the men should beat the women?" Sasha asked coolly.

"Not the *good* men, dear sister. Be assured that you should never fear for your Sofy, I do love her most dearly."

"I have heard so," said Sasha. Jaryd, Sasha knew, spoke reasonable Torovan. She did not look at him, and he remained silent.

"Perhaps it would be wise of you, sister, to not wear your blade so prominently upon your back," Balthaar said then. "I fear that there are some in these lands who might take it ill."

"Where then should I wear it?"

"A hip would suffice," said Balthaar, with certainty.

"I do not like the scabbard to bang against my leg," said Sasha, nervelessly. "I have never seen a swordbelt that well fits a woman's hips. And I have always drawn over the shoulder. One does not toy with ingrained reflexes."

"I fear you miss my point," said Balthaar. "To wear a blade as such is to announce one's self Nasi-Keth. For centuries in these lands, the Nasi-Keth have been put to the sword."

"I am Nasi-Keth," said Sasha. "And if any would like to put me to the sword, they'll find that mine is sharper."

"M'Lady," said Balthaar, with the first trace of temper, "you are a guest in these lands."

"I'm not," said Sasha. "I'm an ally, and family to you by marriage. A guest is one who requires hospitality. Lenayin requires nothing from you, Prince Balthaar. You require *us*. We come to fight and die at your request, and we shall not now demean ourselves in bowing to your sense of decorum."

To Sasha's surprise, Balthaar raised his eyebrows and fought back a smile. "The tales I hear of you are true. You will not bow to anyone."

"You'll find it a common trait amongst Lenays," Sasha said.

Balthaar laughed. "That must be why you're always fighting and killing each other."

"Not nearly so much as here," Sasha replied. Balthaar's amusement faded. "Furthermore, Your Highness, if we fight and kill those who attempt to make us bow on this ride, it will not be other Lenays who do the dying. One should not invite the Army of Lenayin into one's lands if one does not understand that."

In the centre of the village there was a small temple in a courtyard. About it crowded many lords of Lenayin and the Bacosh. They milled in small discrete groups, and conversed as though waiting for something. Men saw Balthaar at the head of his party and bowed at his approach. Before the temple's steps, men in odd robes had gathered. Sasha left Balthaar's side to step through the throng of armed and armoured men, to catch a closer look.

From the edge of the crowd she could see the gathered formation, of men in black robes emblazoned with green, Verenthane stars. The men wore tall and pointed hoods, their faces covered with holes cut for the eyes. Several carried tall Verenthane stars on poles. To their side, prominent among the surrounding men, stood King Torvaal Lenayin, and Regent Arosh, side by side. All were waiting, and men stood clear of the path before them. Someone, or something, was coming.

Jaryd and Yasmyn pushed in at Sasha's sides. "Looks like the oddest wedding I've ever seen," Jaryd joked.

"They do more than marry people in the temples around here," Yasmyn said grimly. Sasha looked about, and found that they were alone amongst Bacosh lords and knights, many of whom gave them long looks. A moment later she saw Sofy, standing with Balthaar, her hand in his as he guided her behind the line of hooded men to stand by his father's side.

"Who are these idiots?" Sasha asked, confident that none immediately surrounding would be able to understand Lenay.

"The *elwon vaar*," said Yasmyn. "It means 'Black Order,' in Larosan."

"Original," Sasha said. She did not like the look of them. She had not heard of the Black Order, but she knew of the extremes to which some in the Bacosh took their beliefs. Any group so assembled, in uniform costume, beneath Verenthane symbols, would arouse her wariness. "Who are they?"

"Men," said Yasmyn. "All sorts of men. High men, low men, city men and country men. No peasants, but all other sorts of men. The priesthood selects them, but they do not say who they are. They are the silent arm of the priesthood."

Sasha thought she understood. "Informants."

"Yes. They tell the priests of blasphemy, witchcraft, all those things. Much better for the priests if no one knows who they are. So they wear hoods."

"Sofy says Lenayin has too many stupid old traditions," Jaryd muttered. "I'm quite certain I prefer our stupid old traditions to these."

"Not an old tradition," said Yasmyn, shaking her head. "Less than fifty years old."

"About the time the priesthood became impatient with the lords' failure to reclaim the Saalshen Bacosh, and set about turning it into a holy crusade," Sasha surmised.

"Yes. Here, faith is politics." Yasmyn sounded disgusted. "The priests make new beliefs, to suit their king. The king lets them, as it suits his interest. They make a travesty of the gods, and priests and king rule the land together, two hands about the peoples' throat."

"He's not a king, he's a regent," said Jaryd.

"Bah," said Yasmyn. "A king is a king. He only says 'regent' to make it impossible for anyone to disagree that he should attack the Saalshen Bacosh. That's new too. The last regent, Elrude, started that by saying no one could call themselves 'king' until the Saalshen Bacosh was reclaimed. They call it 'Elrude's Oath.' His son was killed in battle against serrin scouts, and he vowed no one could call themselves king until all serrin were driven from the Bacosh. Until then it was just more squabbling Bacosh kings, even with the Saalshen Bacosh in serrin hands."

Sasha looked at the Isfayen girl's grim expression. "You know a lot."

"Princess Sofy, she knows language better than me, she learns a people's ways, and listens to the music of their soul. I leave that to her. My father taught me blood, knives and politics. I try to keep her alive."

"And do so with my thanks," said Sasha.

"Thank me or not, it is my duty. My father told me a woman could defend her best, because a woman can go places and ask things a man cannot. Prince Damon agreed."

"Damon's quite smart," Sasha agreed. "For a man."

"Hey," said Jaryd.

"You have studied under Kessligh Cronenverdt," said Yasmyn, her dark, slanted eyes on Sasha.

"And?"

"He is the greatest man of Lenayin. I would share his bed and bear his child, should he ask."

"You're not the first to offer."

"I would share *your* bed, should you ask."

Sasha blinked. "I don't lean that way."

Yasmyn smiled broadly. "Me neither. But even so."

Hooves clattered nearby, and trumpets rang out. Sasha winced. She was beginning to dislike trumpets. They seemed indicative of everything brash, loud and arrogant that she disliked in the lowlands. Doubtless the Lenay lords would love them, and take them back to Lenayin to deafen guests at hall feasts.

Horsemen entered the courtyard, and rode in formation through the crowd. These were Torovan, Sasha saw, their steel helms pointed, their coats and sleeves longer than the Bacosh preference for vests. A mass of bannermen led the way, proclaiming house crests, and holding eight-pointed stars aloft. Sasha recognised the crest of House Steiner.

"The Torovan column must be catching up," said Jaryd, studying the riders. "Torovan cavalry ride well, I hear."

"Fine horses," Sasha agreed. "Many Lenay-bred. I might have raised one of these myself."

And here rode Symon Steiner, the king's heir. Prince Steiner. His horse was white, and he rode poorly, a slim man of no great stature in a great, golden cloak and a golden crown on his head. Good spirits, Sasha thought. Big, fat old Patachi Steiner bought his little boy a crown. How positively preposterous.

"I might be ill," she remarked as Prince Symon rode by, flanked by guards. The Bacosh lords raised a cheer.

"He is your brother, yes?" Yasmyn asked.

"No," Sasha said coldly. "Just another fucking in-law. I've killed his men and I'd do the same to him in a heartbeat. After Steiner became king, they sent assassins to Dockside to kill the remaining disloyal priests, and then they started after lower-slope families they thought had been too close to the Dockside. We had to kill upper slope Patachis and their sons until they stopped. Pity we never got close enough to get *him*."

"Sometimes I wonder if there are any truly honourable men in Rhodia save the Lenays," said Jaryd.

"Yes," Sasha said quietly. "There's the serrin."

Behind Symon and his entourage, there rode a priest. Sasha frowned, having never seen a priest on horseback before. She did not recognise this one, except that he wore black robes, and a stern haircut, and was doubtless one of Steiner's cronies. She knew what was coming now, and why all the leaders of the various allied armies had been gathered here in the village outside of Nithele.

The priest got off his horse to stand beside Symon Steiner, before the assembled ranks of the Black Order. The Black Order parted, and escorted the men to the steps of the temple. They climbed, and there waited another man in black robes, enormously fat and entirely bald.

"Archbishop Turen," said Jaryd. "The Archbishop of Larosa and the 'free Bacosh.' I had to negotiate with him to get as much Lenay tradition into the wedding as we did. He's a stupid fat shit."

"You think they're all stupid fat shits," Yasmyn replied.

"Which is why it was such a good idea to let me do the negotiations," Jaryd said. "I gave them nothing. Besides, they all *are* stupid fat shits. In Lenayin I knew many good priests. Here, I think the good men are disqualified."

"I knew good priests in Petrodor too," Sasha muttered. "Stupid fat shits tried to kill them all."

The Torovan priest withdrew a bundle from his robes, and unwrapped it, with careful ceremony. When the package lay exposed, Archbishop Turen blessed it, and sprinkled holy water on it. Sasha sensed the men about holding their breaths, eyes transfixed in silent reverence. For herself, she felt dread. She knew this object. In Petrodor, it had caused her, and people she loved, much grief.

The archbishop carefully took the object's chain, and raised a golden medallion the size of his palm. It glistened with jewels. Then he turned to the crowd and announced something in Larosan. Sasha heard the word "Shereldin." This was the Shereldin Star, holiest of holy Verenthane objects. The stars were forged upon the commission of something sacred to the priesthood, whether the elevation of common priests to higher status, or the founding of a new temple. This was forged on the founding of the Enoran High Temple. Two centuries ago, the serrin had come, and the star had been "saved," eventually to find its way to Petrodor, recently the centre of the Verenthane world. There, it had become the symbol of the priesthood's desire to reunify the Verenthane lands, and the rallying flag for the armies assembled for the task.

The archbishop raised the star with a final pronouncement, and all across the courtyard, men dropped to one knee and bowed their heads. Sasha remained standing. So did Jaryd. Yasmyn half-dropped, then paused in confusion. Sasha put a hand on her head and pushed her down properly. She could not see anyone else standing, across the entire courtyard, which meant that Yasmyn's father Lord Faras had knelt. Best that his daughter did not cause him trouble.

The archbishop did not notice the two still standing, and resumed his speech, but the priest at his elbow noticed, and put a hand on his arm. He pointed, straight at Sasha and Jaryd.

"How many do you think we could take?" Jaryd wondered aloud, eyeing the faces that were now turning their way.

"Hundreds," said Sasha. Jaryd smiled, and flexed his sword hand.

The archbishop stopped speaking. There was confusion, some in the crowd looking about, instructions, pointing and hand waving among the Black Order. Then several men in black hoods came running along the cleared path the horses had taken. Sasha did not feel any alarm. She knew where she stood. The prospect of killing these men did not particularly trouble her . . . if they asked her to kneel.

Four of the black-robed and hooded men stopped before Sasha and Jaryd, and threw their robes back to reveal swords at their belts. Sasha smiled. She did not think the Black Order would be the best of the Bacosh's warriors, and *those* were no match for Lenay swordsmen like Jaryd. She herself was better again. Perhaps these fools required a demonstration of the fact.

Yasmyn stood up. Sasha frowned at her, but Yasmyn ignored her, and put a hand to her darak. Perhaps twenty paces away, Great Lord Faras of Isfayen also emerged from the sea of kneeling bodies, giving his daughter a long, displeased look. About him, the rest of the Isfayen contingent stood in solidarity with their lord. Several more Lenays followed. Then some more, like new shoots sprouting from a fertile soil. A priest came striding to them and stood before Sasha and Jaryd.

"Kneel!" he said in Torovan. "Kneel at once!"

"No," said Sasha.

"We ride to war on a holy crusade!" snarled the priest. "If you will not kneel for this, what then do you fight for?"

"The warriors of Lenayin," Sasha shouted in Torovan, "shall kneel to whom and what they choose! It is not for any man here to instruct a *Lenay* man on to what, or to whom, he must or must not kneel!"

It was a *kayesar*, and she knew it. A pronouncement of righteous truth. About the courtyard, more Lenays stood. Most of the lords remained kneeling, but Sasha saw with satisfaction that many of their guards and company captains were standing. More long-haired and slant-eyed lords also stood . . . Yethulyn, Sasha saw, the Isfayen's western neighbours, and unwilling to be shown up by their hated rivals on a point of Lenay honour. And what was some golden trinket to a lord of Yethulyn? They were Verenthanes, but not in any fashion a lowlander would recognise. The thing in the archbishop's hands looked like jewellery, a thing of great value, with which to stoke a man's greed. The Lenays of the western highlands liked gold as well as anyone, yet few Lenays anywhere would fight and die for it. To suggest that a man might was to suggest that his honour could be bought. To suggest such a thing, anywhere in Lenayin, was a dangerous matter.

The angry priest seemed to take a breath, eyes darting, as he reassessed his situation. Clearly it had not occurred to anyone, in organising this ceremony, that something like this might happen.

"That is the Shereldin Star," he explained. "It is the founding star of the Enoran High Temple, the holiest temple in all Verenthane lands, the place where the gods did pass down the Scrolls of Ulessis to Saint Tristen, and to all human kind. It is surely most blessed by the gods, and should you not kneel before their audience, then you do blaspheme most grievously to their very faces!"

"I see no gods here," said Sasha. "Only men. Any god who would demand that a Lenay man kneel to a golden trinket is no true god of Lenays."

"You must kneel!" the priest yelled, tendons straining in his neck.

Sasha just stared at him, contemptuously.

"We Lenays," Jaryd said loudly, "have very stiff knees." There was laughter from Lenays about the courtyard. More rose to their feet, even the lords. To blaspheme was one thing, but even for devout Verenthanes, this was now about far more than faith.

Behind the priest, a dark-cloaked figure came walking. To Sasha's astonishment, it was her father, solemn and unsmiling as always. He stopped beside the priest.

"It was a mistake," he told the priest, in Torovan, "to hold this ceremony before the Goeren-yai. I would have told you that this would happen, but I was not consulted. That oversight now leaves us in an unfortunate predicament."

"This is your daughter," said the priest. "Make her obey."

"She is Goeren-yai," the king said simply, "and I cannot."

The priest stared at him. Sasha stared too, in greater shock than the priest. Her father had admitted the unsayable. She had lived much of her life in fear of what might happen should she state the fact so publicly. Now, her father did it for her, in front of a lowlands priest and his flock.

"Your Highness," said the priest, between gritted teeth, "Lenayin must decide whether it is a Verenthane kingdom or not. The moment for deciding is now."

"In Lenayin," said the king, "the chasm between what the kingdom is, and what its nobility may aspire to make it, is often vast indeed. I urge you not to press this matter. I know my people. A Lenay will bow only to whom he chooses, and should you seek to deny him that right, then this alliance is ended, and the holy lands shall remain in the hands of Saalshen. Worse, I think it likely this courtyard shall be drowned with holy blood. I urge you to consider your priorities, Father."

Torvaal Lenayin did not look at his daughter. He had not spoken with her since her return to the Lenay fold. Word was that he grieved for Alythia. Sasha had wondered if he blamed her and decided that she did not care what he thought. But now, she wondered again.

The priest stormed back toward the archbishop.

"Father," said Sasha. And felt a sudden, inexplicable yearning. For what, she did not know. "Father . . ."

Torvaal Lenayin turned on his heel and followed the priest, his black cloak flowing out behind. Sasha felt a pain in her throat. She wanted to run after him and grab him by the arms, and yell into his face. But she did not know what she would say.

There was dark, earnest discussion between priests, Archbishop Turen, King Torvaal and Regent Arosh. They took their places again, and the command was given to rise. The ceremony resumed with all now standing. Sasha could not see much over the tall heads of the men around her, but she did not care. Bacosh men standing nearby gave her very dark looks, but Jaryd and

Yasmyn kept guard of her flanks. She could not see Sofy, nor her brothers, from this position, but she could see the Black Order, pointed hoods in rows, like sharp black teeth before the temple steps.

Sasha trained with the officers and yuans that Damon had selected, discussing tactics, and the new use to which Lenay warriors were being instructed to put their shields. There were even several knights, one from Merraine, the other from Tournea, adding their expertise at Damon's request. They discussed, demonstrated, and made small formations on the riverbank a little upstream from the Nithele walls. Even here, Lenay soldiers intruded upon their practice, filling pots with water, leading horses to drink, bathing, or bartering with the boats that rowed upstream from the city. Those were everywhere, a mass of narrow vessels hugging the shore where the high waters moved with less force, men aboard shouting their wares to all ashore. In others, city girls lifted their dresses to show pale legs, as men ashore hollered and laughed, and asked after the price.

"Perhaps if our cavalry cannot win through the Steel lines," one powerful yuan said at a pause in training, "we could send our army of whores at them."

Men laughed. There were hundreds trailing the Army of Lenayin, it was said, though Sasha had not visited the tail of the column to see. Many had children with them, and some, husbands. It was even said that parents were offering daughters for a price. Sasha was astonished at the utter pridelessness of the Bacosh peasantry. She had never considered that a people might discard their honour so wantonly. Perhaps, it occurred to her, honour was not a necessity of human life, but rather a luxury. Her Lenay soul rebelled at the thought.

Mostly she watched as the men discussed and considered the battle to come, contributing occasionally, but not joining in directly. This was men's fighting, with heavy armour and heavy blows, and no room for finesse. Svaalverd technique counted for little in such an environment. Without technique, she would be just a woman surrounded by men, and no use to anyone. Ahorse, however, she fancied she might have a contribution to make.

One of the young men present was a new arrival, from Torovan. Duke Carlito Rochel, the Lord of Pazira province, son of Sasha's old friend Alexanda Rochel. He had ridden in with the advance party bearing the Shereldin Star, and said now that the main Torovan column was but two days' march behind. Sasha was pleased to meet Carlito, yet sad too, for his father had tried his best to prevent Pazira's participation in this war. He would be very sad to know that his son now rode to fight in the greatest battle the Bacosh had ever known. Sasha wondered if Alexanda had died in vain. And wondered if she would ever again see a day where every new thought did not make her sad.

As she sat on a riverside log, watching the men discussing the collision of two shield lines, she heard a rattle of armoured footsteps. A knight approached, in neck-to-ankles chain mail, and carrying a sack.

"Sashandra Lenayin!" he called, as though pleased to see her. Sasha stood up. Over the mail, the knight wore a surcoat of family colours that Sasha did not recognise. Four more knights walked with him, and there was something to their manner that she did not like. Sasha heard the discussion and clash of practice stanch on shield behind her cease.

The man before her was broad and dark haired. "Aren't you going to ask who I am?" he asked her after a pause.

"If I cared, I'd ask," said Sasha.

"I am Sir Eskwith, Lord of Assineth. Cousin to the prince regent. Your relation, I suppose."

"Great," said Sasha, expressionlessly. "Welcome to the family."

"I saw your little performance today, before the temple," Eskwith continued. "It has caused many of the good lords to wonder exactly whose side you're on."

"Lenayin's," said Sasha, with certainty.

"Pagan Lenayin's," said Sir Eskwith.

"Lowlanders make that distinction. Lenays don't."

"My new friends in the Lenay north certainly do."

"I've killed plenty," said Sasha. "I don't care what they think." She could hear her friends approaching, wondering at the intrusion on the Lenay camp.

"I hear you have a serrin lover," he said. "I wonder if he looks anything like this?" He upended the sack and a severed head fell on the rough grass at Sasha's feet. The hair was silver tingeing toward pale blue and tied with several long braids. The eyes, and features, were serrin. Sasha's heart nearly stopped. For an instant, she saw the head as Errollyn's. Then, as Alythia's, as it had lain at her feet in her Tracato cell. "This one was a scout, moving by night. We caught him, and I assure you, he did not die quickly. That is what we do to demon spawn and their friends in these lands." He paused for effect. "And to their whores."

Sasha drew her sword and cut off Sir Eskwith's head. The body toppled, fountaining blood. The head rolled to join the serrin's at Sasha's feet. "Is that a fact?" she said.

She advanced on Eskwith's companions as they fumbled for their swords in shock, holding her blade low, the fourth *en'alan* commencement, a wrist cocked behind one hip and inviting the obvious attack. One knight swung at her, and she swayed aside and took his hand off in the follow through. Swung back fast to deflect the second knight's attack, the second motion of which became a new strike that took off the handless man's head. She spun about the falling body to impale the third in the shoulder in mid-backswing, ducking away from the second as he came at her, spinning her blade through easy wrist twirls.

"Run away or yield!" she could hear Jaryd yelling from nearby. "I'm warning you, run away or yield, or you're dead!" He was not yelling at her, she knew very well. There were two healthy ones left, and the wounded one. They were powerful, but their chain mail and heavy swords made them slow.

One advanced on Sasha as she skipped backward on the grass. She invited his feint, swaying one way and then the other, only bringing her sword into play at the last moment to take his forearm as he lunged, then reverse into a cut up under the armpit, severing weak armour and most of the shoulder.

The last had been coming after her, but now stopped, looking scared. His companion, with a stab wound through one shoulder, was wavering on his feet, clutching the bloody slice through his mail. The man whose shoulder she'd severed was noisily dying amid great spurts of blood.

"Best let them yield, Sasha," Jaryd warned her, still from a respectful distance. Her comrades were all watching, making no attempt to intervene on her behalf. They knew she wasn't the one needing help. "I know this one man here, he assisted on the wedding. He's not a bad man, Sasha."

Sasha looked at him blandly. "Why should that matter?"

Jaryd looked back, warily, hand to his sword. Duke Carlito stood nearby, with wide-eyed disbelief. And Great Lord Faras, his dark eyes gleaming with admiration.

"Do you yield?" Jaryd asked the surviving two men. "There is no shame in it. She is the greatest swordsman in Lenayin."

"No," said Lord Faras, loudly. "She is the Synnich. You should bow before her, and be proud that your friends have had the honour to taste her blade."

"What did they say?" Koenyg asked his sister as she stood before him in the royal tent. Beyond the canvas walls, there were crowds. Royal Guards stood at the entrance, leaving the heir and his sister to privacy.

"The leader threw a severed serrin head at my feet," said Sasha. Her eyes seemed almost dull, devoid of feeling. Koenyg had never seen her like this before. It unnerved him, in a way that countless boasting, chest-thumping Lenay warriors had never managed before. "It was a threat, to my head, and to the heads of those I care for. He called me a whore to the serrin."

"Did you feel yourself personally threatened?"

"Only my honour," said Sasha. "In Lenayin, men die for less."

"Did you give warning?"

"It was a threat. The codes say an accusation must be tested in honourable combat, but a threat may warrant an immediate reply. There were five of them."

"You had support," Koenyg replied.

"Not immediately to hand. I was not favoured by numbers. They threatened me five-against-one. It was dishonourable, and they deserved to die."

"That's brutal, Sasha," Koenyg said. "Even for you." Sasha's eyes registered nothing. "I'd have expected such an interpretation of the codes from Lord Krayliss, or maybe Lord Heryd."

Sasha met his stare for the first time. The old temper was still there, burning deep. Somehow, Koenyg found that comforting. "Lenayin did not march to Larosa to be buggered by swinging dicks in chain mail," Sasha said loudly. "Are we an equal partner in this marriage, or do they get liberties? First they ask us to kneel. Do they next ask us to bend over?"

Koenyg shook his head in faint disbelief. "Don't attempt to excuse each of your personal tantrums as a grand act of patriotism. You're a mess, Sasha. You and I have rarely agreed, but I admit I did find some affection for the lively girl who rode horses and skinned her knees. That girl loved life, and often laughed. The girl I see now loves only death, and she never smiles."

"She was a fool," Sasha said bitterly. "She did not understand the world. She knows better now, and she knows that freedom must be fought for, or lost."

"And for whose freedom do you fight?"

"The freedom for Lenays to be Lenays!"

"Or the freedom to kill people you don't like," Koenyg suggested. Sasha folded her arms, and looked aside.

"If you wish to punish me," she said shortly, "then do so. I've better things to do than listen to lectures."

"I'm not going to punish you, Sasha. You've caused a mess, but it has its uses. I did warn our Larosan allies that they should tread carefully upon Lenay honour, and that lords should not presume to rub their lessers' noses in the mud, as they do amongst their own kind. I also warned them to accept that half of our army are not even Verenthanes, and not to provoke that half with the fact. But first they make a mess with the Shereldin Star, and now this. Best that they learn *their* place, with us."

He took a waterskin from its hanging peg upon the tent's central pole, and poured them each a cup.

Sasha took a sip, her eyes upon him, and frowning. She'd expected him to be angry, clearly.

"Sasha, you're an idiot. You've never understood my motivations. You're like all these stupid Goeren-yai gossipers. You think I'm putting Lenayin in the pockets of lowlands Verenthanes. No, Sasha." He leaned forward. "I am a Lenay patriot. I wish to make Lenayin strong. This war shall secure our strength, forging ties to the most powerful lowlands kingdoms, and proving our worth to all. It shall unite our peoples, as nothing else has managed before. And if you cutting the heads off a few lowlanders helps them to learn respect and fear of us, then so much the better. A little fear can be a good thing, Sasha. I do not mind that you frighten them, and I do not wish for any of us to kneel."

He smiled at her grimly. Sasha looked a little dazed. Perhaps she had not expected him to be honest.

"I saw Alythia's head," she said quietly. "When he tossed that head from the sack, I saw Alythia's head instead. I just killed him. I mean . . . I just killed him."

She looked shaken. Gods, Koenyg thought, she did the strangest things to him sometimes. There was a time when he'd hated her for being Krystoff's collaborator, for causing father and the kingdom such trouble, and for being so selfish. But she had much to admire about her too, like bravery, skill and leadership. Her presence here united the most troublesome factions of the Lenay Army firmly beneath his command—the eastern Goeren-yai, the ones who had followed her on her northern rebellion, and had never liked this war. If she followed him, then they would too. And now, it was clear that she'd truly loved Alythia, whatever their earlier differences. Sasha did not hold grudges, Sofy had insisted to him once. Sasha could change her mind about people. Perhaps there was yet hope for them, as siblings.

Koenyg put a hand to her shoulder. "I miss Alythia too."

"Do you ever get scared that one day, you'll do something really terrible?" The look in Sasha's eyes was haunted. "That one day, you'll just lose control, and be responsible for something that will eat at your soul for the rest of your life?"

"No," said Koenyg. "I worry that one day there'll be something I *didn't* do, that led to something terrible. Inaction is the worst sin of leaders, Sasha. If your cause is just, then the greatest sin in all the world is to sit and do nothing."

Sasha nodded uncertainly. It was the only time Koenyg could recall her seeming so vulnerable in his presence.

"Sasha, you killed Eskwith because he killed a serrin. Yes, he challenged your honour, but that was not the primary matter. Yet we ride against serrin. Doubtless there will be many, fighting against us in days to come. If you fight with us, you may even kill some yourself. Perhaps, if you are unlucky, even a friend of yours."

"Errollyn is too ill," Sasha replied, her voice barely audible.

"But you have other friends. And they have friends, and perhaps family, in the *talmaad* or the Steel. I know how serrin and human intermix in the Saalshen Bacosh." He tried to search her face, but she was looking down. Koenyg put gentle fingers under her chin, and lifted.

Sasha's eyes spilled tears. Her gaze was desperate. Pleading. Koenyg considered her for a long moment and nodded. Now he knew. What effect it would have, when the time came, he could not know. But he would be ready for all eventualities.

"Very well," he said softly. "No more questions. Do not think on it. Go back to your friends, and rest. I shall deal with the angry in-laws."

Sofy sat in the hot bath, and gazed at the roof of her tent. Outside, she could hear the sounds of the camp. Not for the first time, she wondered why she was here in the field, and not back in the palace in Sherdaine.

She knew that there were some in Sherdaine who did not appreciate the fact that the new princess regent was a barbarian Lenay, but she doubted that it was that simple. The Bacosh Army was not merely a temporary allegiance of Larosa, Tournea, Meraine, Algrasse and Rakani, it was an allegiance of all the families, properties, lineages and minor allegiances *within* those provinces. Much like Lenayin in that each province was shared by many conflicting interests . . . except that in Lenayin, the nobility were largely united, a necessity given how badly outnumbered they were, and how poorly respected among the nonnobility, both Verenthane and Goeren-yai.

In the Bacosh, those not noble were dismissed as "peasants," and used as little more than tools of power. All true power rested with the nobility, and noble families, it seemed to Sofy, had no true friends. The borders of the provinces were only temporary things. Sofy had seen maps of the Bacosh covering the last two hundred years, and further back still, before King Leyvaan and the creation of the Saalshen Bacosh. The borders changed every decade or so, it seemed, and the smaller boundaries of noble lands that split each province in a ragged patchwork of lines were constantly clustering, uniting, splitting and shifting. On those maps, the boundaries of noble lands remained drawn on the Saalshen Bacosh side of the border, where such things had long since ceased to hold any meaning. She had noticed, from decade to decade, that those lines never shifted, preserving the holdings as they'd stood, as though the coming of the serrin had been a great winter chill, freezing the territories as they'd stood in King Leyvaan's time.

There were some families marching in the army who claimed ancient ancestral rights on those territories, primarily in Enora where no surviving claimants remained. In Rhodaan and Ilduur, many thought to reinstate surviving claimants and thus gain powerful allegiances, or perhaps to have those claimants found unworthy once the lands were conquered, and struck out by ruling of the new Bacosh king. Some of the Rhodaani nobility had arrived in the army at the same time as Sasha. Men from Tracato, who now declared their rights to old Rhodaani territories, and registered their claims with old maps before the regent. Sofy had spoken with a Lord Elot from Tracato who had been displeased that instead of a joyful welcome from his noble allies, he had received cold hostility from some who felt that his claims were overstated, and impinged upon their own entitlements. Others, Lord Elot had said with frustration, were demanding land concessions as compensation for losses that would be incurred in battles to come. Sofy had tried to be understanding, yet she wondered if the Tracato nobility had ever truly considered the nature of civilisation they now sought to rejoin. It was power hungry and competitive, and wanted advancement to the detriment of others. To hear Sasha speak of it, the Rhodaani nobility had thought themselves to be fighting an ideological battle for the restoration of ancient justice. They had forgotten that to the nobility of the "free Bacosh," such sentiments meant nothing. They wanted land, and gathered beneath the priests' holy banners not for the gods, but like hounds behind their masters' horses on a hunt, hoping for the reward of fresh prey, and blood.

Balthaar and his father, the regent, had brought Sofy on this march simply for the safety and continuity of the family line, she was increasingly certain. She would not be safe from the family's rivals in Sherdaine, particularly were the war to be lost. In that case, there would follow a quick ride to the family holdings in Ashane, seventeen leagues from Sherdaine, and a mustering of allies there to ward off further challenge. Family Arosh risked a lot in this venture. But the potential rewards were phenomenal.

Sofy heard a commotion at the entrance to her tent, then a striking sound. Yells followed, and the noise of fighting, barefisted. She thought to leap from her bath, her heart pounding in sudden fear, yet mailed, angry men were coming into the tent even now, two holding between them one of the guards, his sword missing, arms immobilised.

"You!" said a man, and strode to Sofy's bath in fury. She recognised Sir Elias Assineth, Balthaar's cousin. Sofy barely had time to snatch at a bathside gown before he had her by the arm, and yanked her dripping to her feet, then onto the grassy tent floor.

"What is the meaning of this?" Sofy shouted, struggling to free herself and protect her modesty. "Let me go!"

"Speak Larosan like a true Larosan Queen, you pagan bitch!" snarled Sir

Elias, and backhanded her to the face. Sofy fell to her knees, her gown fallen. Elias's hand dragged her upright once more as her head continued to spin. She'd never been struck in the face before in her life. Far worse than the pain, she could not believe how helpless it rendered her. Her vision swam, and she could not think.

"You shall denounce your pagan sister!" Elias yelled. "You shall instruct your father to hand her to us for godly Larosan justice!"

Sofy's Larosan was adequate now to understand him. And yet, she felt utterly uncomprehending. "My . . . my sister?" Sasha. Oh gods, not again. "What did she do?"

"She murdered my brother!"

A blood-chilling cry from outside spun Elias and his companions about, one nearest the tent's entrance fending desperately with a mailed arm as a dark-haired girl with a wicked short blade tried to gut him like a fish.

"Yasmyn, no!" Sofy cried, as the first knight danced back, drawing his blade. Yasmyn spun to confront a second to her side, her slash deflecting harmlessly from his weapon. The first knight simply threw himself on her, heavy weight of mailed man crashing her down, then pinning her effortlessly beneath. They pulled her back up, deprived of her darak as she fought like a wild thing. The knights laughed, and hit her, again and again.

"Stop it!" Sofy yelled, tears flowing, but they paid her no mind. Sasha, she thought desperately, would have killed them all, but she was just a slim, naked girl. She struggled, trying to twist free, but Sir Elias wrenched her arm back and she fell to her knees. "Leave her alone, she was only protecting me!"

When Yasmyn was no longer fighting, the knights dragged her to a table, cleared it of cups and teapot with a sweep of an arm, and dumped her onto it, her head lolling and face bloody. One held her arms above her head, while another hiked up her dress, and yanked down her under garments. Yasmyn regained enough sense to kick him, and he and his companion punched her in the stomach with brutal force, laughing all the while.

Sofy screamed for help, but no one came. In the tales, the heroic knight always arrived in time to save the lady in distress. But although the tent was in the centre of the Larosan camp, and surrounded by those who could surely hear her cries, no one came. One knight took his turn with Yasmyn, and then the other. Yasmyn regained consciousness but she no longer fought. As a third knight unbuckled his pants, Yasmyn turned her head upon the table and fixed her princess with a stare of furious intensity, although one eye was already swollen nearly shut.

"Crying solves nothing!" she hissed at her in Lenay. "Be a woman, little girl!"

Sofy was so shocked, she swallowed her tears. Oddly, as soon as she did so, she felt something else, that the tears had perhaps obscured. Pure, molten fury. In her protected palace life, she had often wondered how Lenay warriors, or even her otherwise kind and wonderful sister Sasha, could hate a man enough to want to sever his limbs with sharpened steel. Now, finally, she understood.

While the third knight was taking his turn, Balthaar arrived, many armed men at his back.

"Unhand her!"

"Your Highness," said the man holding Yasmyn's arms, "at least let the poor man finish his turn!"

"Stop now," said Balthaar, "or I'll cut him so that he never has a turn again." The knights looked aggrieved, but not alarmed. They abandoned Yasmyn, the last knight regathering his pants. Yasmyn got off the table, straightened down her dress, and limped awkwardly across the grass to where Sofy was kneeling, Lord Elias still grasping her arm. Sofy feared Yasmyn might do something rash, yet she merely knelt, and recovered Sofy's fallen robe, and placed it about her princess's shoulders.

"Let her go," Balthaar said. He did not look at Sofy. Neither did he call her Princess Regent, or attempt to remind Sir Elias of his duty of respect to one above his station. Sofy wondered if she had ever truly been more than a Lenay barbarian to these people. And if her husband's seemingly loving gaze had been any more than the fascination of a wealthy man with an enchanting new bauble.

Sir Elias released Sofy's arm, and Yasmyn helped her to her feet. Sofy felt a rush of shame. Yasmyn had been beaten and raped, yet now stood with dignity and assisted her weak, pathetic princess shakily to her feet. Sofy stood, and put an arm around Yasmyn to offer a support Yasmyn did not seem to need. Hugging her was out of the question. Nothing in Yasmyn's manner invited it. Sofy knew enough of the Isfayen to know what that meant.

Balthaar said nothing more, nor asked it of Sir Elias. He merely stared, dark and foreboding.

"Her rabid sister killed my brother!"

"One person does you harm, and so you attack others," Balthaar observed mildly. "Very clever."

"They're all the same!"

"And our allies," said Balthaar, "by allegiance that Family Assineth agreed to. Do you not understand the concept of allegiance, Sir Elias?"

"These allies have done us murder upon our lands!" Elias yelled, spittle flying. "Unless they pay us reparation, this allegiance lies broken! I demand the bitch's head!"

"By Lenay tradition, and indeed our own," Balthaar replied, "the lands upon which an army is encamped are to be considered beholden to their own laws. Your brother very foolishly stepped onto the Lenay camp uninvited, and overstepped the bounds of Lenay honour. I have spoken with Prince Koenyg, and all Lenays seem agreed on the matter, even those who have no love of Sashandra Lenayin. So long as the Army of Lenayin abides by its own laws upon their own encampment, no one has any matter to complain about."

"Your Highness," Elias tried again, struggling for control, "we are cousins. Our families have strong ties over many long years. In the name of our families, I ask you only for justice. Grant me justice, for my brother. Or I shall be forced to take it."

"And sever an allegiance that promises to regain us the Saalshen Bacosh?" Balthaar replied, unperturbed. "The archbishops would view it ill. Perhaps you would like to argue the point with them?"

Elias hung his head, teeth grinding in frustration.

"Furthermore." Balthaar walked slowly forward. "I would advise against any further action against the Lenays. I have spent part of the morning sparring against Prince Koenyg, and I will reluctantly confess that he bested me quite handily . . . something that you, Sir Elias, have found elusive. They have an even greater love of honourable combat than we, and would challenge any who so grievously insult them until there are none such left alive. Best that you stay off their lands for now. We have other uses for our Lenay allies."

Elias opened his mouth, then paused, frowning.

Balthaar stopped before him, and put a hand on his cousin's shoulder. "Prince Koenyg tells me that the Army of Lenayin shall take the southern, Enoran flank. Alone, save for some Torovan reinforcement. Against the Enoran Steel, their numbers should be matched quite evenly."

Elias stared. "A feint?"

"To keep the Enoran Steel from sweeping onto our flank, yes," Balthaar confirmed. "The Army of Lenayin has pride at stake, and we learn today all about Lenay pride. They shall not retreat easily, no matter their losses."

Elias's eyes registered a dawning realisation. A delight. "One needs four-to-one odds at least against the Steel. They'll be annihilated!"

Balthaar shrugged. "Prince Koenyg thinks not. We shall see, indeed, to what all the tales of Lenayin's martial prowess amount." He shook Elias's shoulder, affectionately. "Cousin, I grieve for Eskwith. But be at peace, there shall be blood enough for all purposes before this is through. Come, we shall drink to Eskwith's memory, and of glories in battles to come."

He escorted Sir Elias and his men from the tent, without a backward glance. There would be no further reprimand, Sofy realised. No punishment to Yasmyn's attackers. When all had left the tent, she escorted Yasmyn to a chair and eased her into it, so she could better examine her injuries.

"Not blood enough for *all* purposes, dear husband," she said blackly.

The service for Sir Eskwith, Sir Temploi and Sir Ancheve was concluded upon sundown. The evening meal was more lively than Prince Balthaar had expected, however, enlivened by much talk of the terrible fate awaiting the Army of Lenayin at the hands of the Enoran Steel. The Lenays, it was generally agreed, were mindless fools who did not take seriously the many lessons of the Saalshen Bacosh's military prowess. Such talk was far freer of late, since it had been agreed by all that under the circumstances, the usual joint feast of Lenay and Bacosh lords was probably not a good idea.

As Balthaar trudged back to the royal tent, he wondered what would truly happen if they won. His father was confident that they would, but his father, like his wife, placed far too much faith in the good opinion of the gods. Balthaar knew that all of history's attempted liberators of the Saalshen Bacosh had believed the gods on their side too, yet defeat had claimed them all the same. Perhaps it was not enough to claim that the gods were on one's side. Perhaps the gods were waiting for an army, and a future king, to prove himself worthy of their blessing. Balthaar wondered if those who had died at the hands of the Steel were now happily ensconced in the heavens, or had been cast down to Loth, having been found unworthy, whatever their valiant efforts. Were the gods that vindictive? He fervently hoped not.

The matter with Sofy troubled him too. He did not like how Sir Elias had treated her, yet Elias was old family, while Sofy was very new. He thought that he certainly must love her, because she was so very pretty and full of warmth, and so fascinating in her foreign ways and exotic accent. Yet truly, his father was right—an event like this could only serve to show her her place, among the Larosans. He had to make her see that she must abandon her old world entirely, if she were to be truly happy in the new. And he did wish her to be happy, very much so. He would make love to her tonight, he decided, and apologise to her not in words, but in the warmth of his kisses and the lust of his loins. He would make clear to her all that she had to gain, and for so little a sacrifice, indeed, in what she would leave behind.

A man came running, a rattle of armour between the tents, interrupting Balthaar's thoughts. Balthaar stopped, not recognising the young man but noting that he seemed pale and alarmed. Something had happened.

"Your Highness. Best that you come and see."

Not far away, a farmhouse had been consumed by the sea of tents, and appropriated for noble use. Torches and lanterns now clustered about one wall near some bushes, where a pair of newly headless bodies lay. Both were knights, in chain and family colours.

"Sir Diarmond and Sir Felesh," said a man-at-arms, grimly. "Sir Elias found them. No one heard or saw a thing."

Balthaar stared at the bodies. The wounds were clean and swiftly made, the mark of an expert swordsman. "Elias, you say?"

"Yes, Your Highness."

"And where is Sir Elias now?"

"Under guard, by your leave, Your Highness. These two are his friends, I figured whoever did it might be after Sir Elias next."

"Soldier, your name?"

"Sarno, Your Highness. Alaine Sarno."

"You're Tournean?"

"I am, Highness."

"I shall pass on a commendation to your lord, Alaine Sarno."

"I thank you, Your Highness." The man bowed low.

Balthaar strode back to his tent, as the crowd about the bodies continued to gather. Sir Diarmond and Sir Felesh . . . they had been with Sir Elias in Sofy's tent this afternoon. They had taken liberties with that pagan Isfayen girl . . . could that be it? Surely even the mad, bloodcrazed Lenays would not go to such lengths to avenge the honour of a fool like her? Besides, honourable combat was the preferred Lenay method. But yet another duel, in the midst of this deteriorating relationship between Lenays and Bacosh men, would be surely refused by the Lenay king. Certainly his father the regent would refuse it, as was his right, in his camp. Perhaps the murderers knew that. Or perhaps, when a Lenay was angry enough, proper form ceased to matter.

He pushed through the tent flaps. There was not a maid in sight, only a small table on which dinner could perhaps have been served. Sofy sat in a comfortable chair, a book on her lap, lit by a lantern on another table between two glowing coal braziers. She looked up at him, serenely.

"Dear husband, is something the matter?"

"Where is your Isfayen maid tonight, dearest?"

"She's not my maid. She is back with her Isfayen family in the Army of Lenayin, I believe. Why do you wonder?"

"Two of Sir Elias's friends are dead," said Balthaar. "You met them earlier this afternoon. Their heads are missing."

"Oh," said Sofy. She resumed reading her book. "The Isfayen have not played lagand with real heads for years. I hear there will be a game tomorrow, though. Would you like to go and see?"

Sixteen

ERROLLYN ENTERED THE *RESH'ULAN*, and surveyed the scene. There were serrin present, gathered about the lower stage, which stood alone before rows of amphitheatre seating and surrounded by a small moat. The serrin were asking questions of a man who sat at the centre of the stage, his wrists manacled together.

It was Reynold Hein.

Errollyn walked gingerly down the steps. He no longer hurt like he once did, but efforts to rebuild his strength met resistance from bruised flesh and strained muscle. Lesthen stood by the moat, speaking at length, his long white hair spilling on blue, formal robes. He saw Errollyn and pointed serrin to face him, without breaking sentence. Two serrin rose to confront him, expressions apologetic but firm. Errollyn abandoned his first plan, to draw his blade and strike off Reynold's head. And he was in no physical condition yet to charge past his people, and execute their prisoner.

Aisha emerged from the group, took his arm, and guided him to a bench. Errollyn counted nearly thirty serrin present, many of the Mahl'rhen's most prominent remaining names among them.

"It's a formal *etoth'teyen*," he muttered to Aisha as Lesthen droned on, and the two serrin who had opposed him returned to their seats, but kept a careful eye upon him. "Why does he warrant the formalities?"

"It's the way, Errollyn," Aisha told him. Her words lacked conviction. Errollyn was not entirely certain why she was still in Tracato. Rhillian had gone, and taken the Steel with her. Aisha had remained, ostensibly because she was Rhillian's trusted lieutenant and would carry out her preferences, and make certain that the new peace with the feudalists would hold. Also, Errollyn knew, she'd been keeping an eye on him. But others could have performed either task as well.

"It's not the way," Errollyn retorted. "We *have* no way for this, we only use our formalities and debates because that's all we have."

"Well the human courts can't take him," Aisha said. "We're all there is for law and order in Tracato right now."

"Maybe we always were," said Errollyn.

He stared at Reynold, hoping that certain peasant superstitions were true, and the weight of a hateful stare alone could bring misfortune upon a person. Reynold did not look particularly troubled. He sat serenely, with excellent posture, and listened to Lesthen's droning—in Saalsi, too, for Reynold spoke excellent Saalsi, like any Nasi-Keth scholar. This was not a man who expected to die, not even given what he'd done. Reynold was a persuasive talker, and could think just like a serrin—round and round in circles. It had taken some time for Errollyn to ride here, after he'd heard, from out on the practice fields. This session had surely been progressing for more than an hour so far.

"Where was he caught?" Errollyn asked. Lesthen was talking about the philosophy of Mereshin, who had been dead fifteen hundred years. Gods help them all.

"Elisse," said Aisha. "Some Civid Sein went that way, amongst the villages we liberated in the south. They were talking revolution."

"What did the peasants say?"

"They expressed a preference for bread," Aisha said drily. "Several heard of a reward and alerted the *talmaad*."

"They'll eat well on that reward," said Errollyn. "Reynold finally achieves something for the poor." Aisha gave him a faint smile, and put a hand on his arm.

Lesthen's recital on the life of Mereshin moved into the phase of Mereshin's realisations on *usden'ehrl*, the acceptance of loss, and the uselessness of vengeance. Errollyn wondered if all the serrinim were mad, that he were the only one to find the whole scene utterly preposterous.

"I interrupt," came a new voice, and Lesthen paused. Not the *only* one, then. Across the stage, Kiel rose to his feet. "My apologies for the indelicate rupture," Kiel continued, in florid Saalsi, "yet my point is pressing, and none too far removed. This man has done us a great crime and he should die. If none disagree, and I feel the point is indisputable among reasonable serrin, then we should proceed with the obvious resolution and return to more important matters."

"I second the learned serrinim!" Errollyn called in reply. Kiel seemed a little surprised at his support and accepted it with a graceful bow.

"Third!" called Aisha. Seven more voices followed in support. Ten, from thirty. Errollyn rolled his eyes to the high ceiling. One of these days, the serrinim would realise that taking necessary action was more important than the pursuit of interesting debates. He only hoped that those serrin who reached that realisation would not be the small, huddled handful remaining after the rest had been slaughtered by foes who cared nothing for clever argument.

"Ten is insufficient," said Lesthen. "I believe that I continue to hold the floor."

"Horse shit you do," Errollyn muttered, and got to his feet. The two serrin opposing him also stood. Errollyn unbuckled his bandoleer, and handed it to them, sword and all. They waited for his knives, too.

"Errollyn," Lesthen said tiredly, "you do not have the floor. It would interest the impartial debate for you to remain seated, and follow the—"

"I've no time for that," said Errollyn, walking down to the stage side. "None of us has time for that. I am required at training for the new *talmaad* sent from Saalshen, they have little experience in battle and my presence here may deprive them of the one vital lesson they need to keep them alive. I submit to you that the life of Reynold Hein is not worth the small finger of a serrin *talmaad*, let alone his life."

"Much agreed," said Kiel. It disturbed Errollyn only a little, to have found a point of agreement with Kiel. Kiel seemed to find it amusing.

"Do you then suppose that we should abandon our learned debate?" Lesthen asked. "Abandon the one facet of serrin life that has served us best in all times, our search for truth?"

"You do not offer truth, Lesthen," said Errollyn, putting a foot upon a raised stone so he could lean on a knee. "You offer procedure."

"One finds truth by searching. The simple or brief thought is usually wrong, driven by emotion, by desires and wants of the heart. And so we have procedures, to serve as the filter for our thoughts."

"Lesthen." Errollyn looked at him, attempting patience. "We stand here in human lands. Some humans may care for our debates, but their society does not function by it. Human society functions by rules. They do not persuade each other as to the wrongness of their ways, they simply kill them, as necessary. We seek now to rule in human lands, yet we do not learn to follow the methods that work."

"We seek to elevate humanity," Lesthen replied. "In Tracato, humanity has reached a level of civilisation unmatched elsewhere in all human lands. Do you dispute this achievement?"

"For everything, there is a time," said Errollyn. "Not now, Lesthen. Not here, and not in this. A very simple rule was broken, and this man attempted to unbalance everything that you, and all serrin, have worked so hard to create, and that you now laud as a great achievement. We kill him not from vengeance but because to fail to do so will cause all right-minded humans to lose faith in us, or to view us as helplessly weak."

"And quite rightly too," Kiel interjected, "should we fail in something so obvious."

"And what should we become, if we kill this man?" Lesthen looked at Reynold. Reynold watched, with more trepidation now than before. The intelligence was there, in his blue eyes. The charm. At another time, Errollyn might have wondered how it were possible for a man who possessed so many admirable qualities to be so evil. Now, he only remembered the pain of blades and shackles, and the scars on Sasha's body.

"Should we become like our very worst enemies?" Lesthen continued. "Should we kill any who oppose us? Should we seek the sword before the word? Can truth be found in blood?"

"Yes," said Errollyn. "The poets write of a mystical balance in nature, yet I grew up in the wilds, and I see nothing like what they describe. Nature's creatures do not seek harmonious relations, they would all grow to a plague if allowed, and rape all the land. But they don't, because first, the food runs out, and second, the predators kill them. That is the truth of blood, Lesthen, that we serrin have forgotten. All the way of the world is blood, and the harmonious balance of the poets is nothing more than an equal measure of death. We forgot it for a thousand years and more, and now, the humans remind us. Yet you . . . you do not thank them for the reminder of a vital truth, but rather cling to unwise myths of the loving mother earth. Mother earth eats her children, Lesthen. So shall we, should we seek to live on this earth much longer?"

Lesthen said nothing. He was considering. About the *resh'ulan*, many were. Errollyn was surprised. It had been a while since he had stood in a space such as this, and exchanged the *idis'iln*, the force of reason, with his fellow serrin. For so long he had been exasperated by them, by the hypocrisy of a people so proud of their equanimity, yet so lacking in its practice. Had he misjudged his people? Or rather, had he simply grown?

Reynold cleared his throat. "Might I speak my piece?" he suggested. Lesthen ignored him, considering how to respond to Errollyn's *idis'iln*, with one of equal force. Reynold took it for encouragement, and carefully stood. "I have heard often of the justice of the serrin, and I am encouraged, noble serrinim, to see it in practice here today. . . ."

Lesthen made an irritated gesture to another serrin. That man hopped the small moat and struck Reynold to the face. Reynold hit the ground hard, and lay groaning. Not one serrin face, in all those surrounding, displayed any shock nor displeasure.

"Your words are pure poison, Master Reynold," said Lesthen. "You and your kind suffer from the worst disease of humanity, the willingness to subordinate truth, to lock reason in chains and to rape the objective thought, in order to achieve your objective. Never mind if the objective is just, you have forfeited by your methods any right to speak in the *resh'ulan,* for now and ever. Your life belongs to us now."

To the rear of the amphitheatre, some serrin were rising. Errollyn turned, and saw Kessligh walking down the stairs. His eyes were on Reynold, and deadly serious.

"Yuan Kessligh," said Lesthen. "I welcome you. Perhaps you wish to speak?"

Kessligh appeared to be considering it, as he walked to Errollyn's side. Errollyn noted that no one had thought to remove *his* weapons. Kessligh stopped, and looked at Lesthen. Then at Reynold. Everyone waited for him to speak.

Instead, Kessligh stepped across the moat, dropped his staff in favour of his blade, and struck off Reynold's head where he sat. The body fell, fountaining blood. Kessligh examined his blade, critically, as Reynold's head rolled on the stone, then stopped. Finding no blemish, or even a stain of blood, so fast had been the strike, Kessligh resheathed the sword. And turned, to confront the entire *resh'ulan* staring at him, silently.

"What are you doing here?" Kessligh asked, in exasperation. "The purpose of debate is to change opinions. Some humans are not capable of that. In such confrontations, it's them, or it's us. I choose us. Now, Rhodaan is under attack, I submit we all have better ways to spend our time than here."

"The purpose of the debate, Yuan Kessligh," said Lesthen, "is not to convince our enemies. It is to convince ourselves. Serrin are not born wise, we must teach ourselves wisdom every day."

"Wisdom?" Kessligh walked close to Lesthen, and stared at him. "Serrin have had two centuries to prepare for this moment, yet still the main force that defends you is human. Where are Saalshen's heavy forces? Saalshen makes steel unknown to human methods, and breeds fine horses and horsemen, and engineers projectile weapons of terrible force, and flaming oils that can melt steel and crack stone, but still you will not make your own armies save for the *talmaad's* light cavalry! Heavy armies require a change in methods, a change in civilisation, a recruitment of soldiers, a reordering of society. Serrin have refused all this and chosen instead to place their burden upon the shoulders of humans. And why? Because you're too busy fucking debating!"

He glared about at them all, in genuine anger.

"It's wise to learn how to cook," Kessligh fumed, "but a meal prepared over three weeks is inedible! There is wisdom in action! So stop talking, and act!"

He walked up the stairs, between standing serrin who stared at him. Kiel, no habitual friend of Kessligh's, began to applaud. Several of Kiel's *ra'shi* joined him. So did Errollyn, and Aisha. Then some more.

Errollyn followed Kessligh up the stairs, and those applauding followed. It seemed an odd collection of people, Errollyn supposed, within which to finally find consensus with his people. But for now, it was enough.

From upon the crest of a low hill, Sasha sat ahorse and observed the most awesome sight she had ever seen. Across what the locals called Thero Valley assembled the Army of Lenayin. It had been assembling since midmorning, and now the sun drew past midday, and soldiers were still arriving. They filled the valley, a swarm too vast to comprehend. Infantry gathered to the middle, thousands of men from the towns, villages and farms of Lenayin, bristling with swords, with shields to the front. Across the flanks and to the rear clustered cavalry, milling in ragged ranks that had no regard for the thin walls that divided one pasture from another.

A narrow stream twisted across the valley floor, lined with trees. Several small, huddled villages hugged its banks, with little mills and bridges of simple wooden planks. The inhabitants had fled, Sasha heard, upon sighting the first Lenay formations.

The Army of Lenayin's line was directed up the gentle slope of the valley's left flank, on the diagonal. There atop the hill was a castle. Before the castle stretched a thick, silver line of steel, glinting like jewellery in the fall of sunlight through broken cloud. The rest of the Enoran Steel lay out of sight over the ridge, but there was no doubt they were there. The Steel of any Saalshen Bacosh province did not divide its forces, relying on maximum numbers to multiply the fighting power of its formations. And to divide one's forces in the face of any enemy's superior numbers was folly.

Sasha stared now at the slope that the Army of Lenayin must climb to do battle. The diagonal angle was a complication that such a ragged army as the Lenays, unaccustomed to grand formations, did not need. The better news was that the slope was not steep, but for massed armour like the Steel, any high ground was a huge advantage. Koenyg had the option of moving his forces down the valley to the base of the slope directly opposite the Steel lines and the castle, but that could easily have placed him within reach of the Steel's artillery, whose range would be extended by the slope to the tune of a hundred paces at least. Koenyg had chosen well, Sasha thought. But the Enorans had chosen better.

Great Lord Faras of Isfayen came galloping to her side at the head of his entourage. "This shall be a battle unlike any in all the history of Lenayin," he observed. Sasha had expected him to be bursting with excitement, as were all too many of the men she'd observed. Instead, he seemed subdued, as though the scale of what confronted him had reduced him to a state of awe. "Our ancestors shall curse the fates that they lived too soon to see the likes of this. Men shall tell of this for centuries."

"Best that they tell it well," Sasha said grimly. "Should we attack straight up that slope, we're all dead, and our grandchildren will tell only of what fools we were."

"There is no other place," Lord Ranas declared from his friend Faras's side. "North of here is forest, while land to the south is too broken for large formations."

Faras nodded. "The Enorans move faster than we, the Enoran border is all paved roads and bridges. Look how fast they come forward from their border to counter us here. Should we go south, we could manoeuvre for days attempting to find better ground than this, and would be greeted every time by the Enorans atop another fucking hill. I say we go here. The slope is gentle, and we have flanks for our cavalry."

They were still on Larosan land, yet barely so. The Enorans doubtless knew this land nearly as well as their own, having scouted it often. This valley was the obvious approach to the border with a large army, and once their serrin scouts had discerned that the Army of Lenayin was indeed headed this way, it would have been a relatively simple thing for the Enorans to use their paved roads to cut across the Lenays' path, and forward to this point overlooking the valley, thus cutting the route.

"The location is good enough," said Sasha, "but we should not attack here. We should hold, and make them come to us. Our task is merely to prevent them from advancing into Larosa, and attacking the main force engaging the Rhodaanis to the north."

Faras frowned. "This is not a strong defensive position. Should they come, they come down the hill."

"And their artillery comes down the hill with them," Sasha replied. "I learned in Petrodor that artillery does not fire well on a slope. Perhaps they can move it downslope over there," and she pointed to the fork in the valley that turned into Enora, "but that will give us an opening where their main force is undefended by artillery. Either way, it is in our advantage to make them move first."

Sasha was thankful that Koenyg saw matters the same as she. At midafternoon, the army was fully assembled, and growing impatient. A ridge beside a farmhouse had become the royal command post, and Great Lord Faras rode that way to consult, leaving Sasha with the remaining Isfayen nobility. She practised some taka-dans, and wondered just how many serrin *talmaad* were probing their flanks right now, and testing the strengths of Lenay cavalry.

Lord Faras shared those concerns, and with a party of ten nobility they rode back along the gentle valley slope. Across the valley was thick forest, making any leftward flanking move troublesome. It would be crawling with *talmaad*, Sasha was prepared to bet. And now, down the valley, came the Torovans, a great snaking army of metal helms and wooden shields. They rode with a glitter and polish that the Army of Lenayin did not, armour sparkling silver, and great, colourful banners flying. Sasha and the Isfayen galloped close, and were greeted with hearty cheers and waves from the cavalry at the front.

"They look very fine!" an Isfayen nobleman remarked above the thunder of hooves.

"Aye," said Faras, with a twisted smile, "if it made them better warriors, the Isfayen would put feathers in their hats too!"

Upon their return to the main formation, a wild-haired Goeren-yai messenger on a little dussieh came flying to intercept them.

"M'Lady Sashandra," he called, "you are wanted on the field. Negotiators from Enora have requested your presence for parley."

It took a while for Sasha to find the centre of the formation. She galloped along the Lenay lines, jumping pasture walls where they obstructed her, dodging about small camps in fields or milling groups of men who did not seem to know where their place was, or did not seem to care. Banners were difficult to spot amidst the enormous crowds.

Finally, to the front of the formation, she saw a small cluster of men on horses beneath a royal banner. She edged her horse through one of the gaps in the line, and rode to the little group. It was Koenyg, she realised, and Damon, and . . . her father.

The king did not look at her as she approached. Sasha reined up beside Damon, and waited.

"What do they ask?" she asked him in a low voice, above the thunder of hooves, and the roar of many thousands of voices. It would have been too much to expect Lenay warriors to sit quietly and wait. They seethed with anticipation.

"To talk," said Damon with a faint shrug. "It is customary, in the lowlands."

Sasha nodded. In Lenayin, individual warriors might talk before a duel, but rarely entire armies. She did not think that most Lenay warriors would disapprove of the notion, however. To discuss protocols with a man you were about to kill seemed honourable. Oddly, she found herself wondering why Lenays had never adopted the custom for grand battles. Probably, she thought, because there was so little flat ground in Lenayin. Armies did not line up, but struck with the first advantage. An odd case of terrain dictating custom, perhaps.

From the top of the slope near the castle, a small party of men rode forth. Sasha squinted, but could not make out the flags. Sweat prickled on her brow. She thought she knew why she had been asked for. She wanted to say no. To plead off sick, or find some lameness in her horse. But she could not appear weak before the men. And if her horse was lame, they'd find her another.

"It must be them," Koenyg concluded as the party kept coming. The king tapped heels to his horse, and rode with his three children toward the stream and the slope beyond. The stream barely came up to the horses' knees, and soon they were cantering across fields as the ground began to rise. There were three in the oncoming party, two human and one serrin. Sasha nearly turned back.

Koenyg signalled to her and Damon, and Sasha moved up on Koenyg's side, the far left position in their line. Damon took the far right, beside their father. They came to a trot, and then a halt, perhaps ten strides from the opposing line of three.

"I'm General Rochan," said the central man, in Torovan. He wore a helm with a general's crest, and wore chest and shoulder guards over mail. A middle-sized man, with intense, close-set eyes, of perhaps forty summers. "Commander of the Enoran Second Regiment, acting Commander of Armies for this engagement. To my left is my second, Formation Captain Lashel. To my right, Vilan, of the *talmaad*."

Sasha forced herself to look. The serrin had pure white hair like Rhillian's, worn long and untidy. His eyes were nearly gold within a pale face. It gave him the look of an albino, but Sasha doubted that he was. He was simply serrin. Sasha wished he were elsewhere.

"King Torvaal Lenayin," her father replied grimly. "My sons, Koenyg and Damon. My daughter, Sashandra."

General Rochan looked across their line with his sharp eyes. Something about his manner disturbed Sasha further. She had hoped that perhaps some turmoil of Enoran politics would lead the Enorans to place an incapable general in command of this battle. To observe the thoughts racing through Rochan's eyes, she did not think that had happened.

"You come a long way, King of Lenayin," Rochan said finally. He drew himself up, and his gaze held little of respect or fear. "Why are you here? We Enorans have done nothing to you."

"You sin against the Verenthane faith," said Torvaal. "You hold lands that are not yours."

"Truly?" Rochan looked genuinely astonished. "I can trace my ancestry back a dozen generations on this land. How is this land not mine?"

"You sin against the Verenthane faith," Torvaal replied, as though he had not heard the general. "The Archbishop of Torovan has decreed it."

"Ah," said Rochan. "Torovan. And how many have the Torovans sent you? It looks perhaps fifteen thousand from our vantage? Eighteen, at the most? They had promised you thirty, had they not? Why does the Archbishop of Torovan send Lenays to die for his cause?"

"Any Verenthane would serve as well," said Torvaal darkly.

"And barely half of you are Verenthane," said Rochan, giving Sasha a long stare. Sasha looked at the slope behind him, and the castle, large against the sky.

"We have not ridden all this way to debate," Koenyg interrupted. "State your terms, if you have any, or offer your surrender. Should you offer it, you shall be given honourable terms from Lenayin."

Rochan snorted and smiled unpleasantly. "This from a Lenay, who finds nothing honourable in surrender. Have no fear, Prince of Lenayin, we like it as little as you do. Your allies have made it plain for two hundred years that they shall offer no terms. We think it preferable to die on our feet with a sword in our hands than at the end of a Larosan rope, or beneath their torture knives."

Sasha barely repressed a shudder. The serrin Vilan noticed. Again, Sasha looked away, hoping it would all end soon. Battle would be preferable to this. In battle, one did not have to think.

"Do you have terms?" Koenyg repeated.

"Withdraw now," said Rochan, coldly. "Those are my terms. You are foreigners to this kind of warfare. Know that the Enoran Steel has faced armies twice the size of what confronts us here, and left them barely a man alive. I think it an abomination that Lenayin's rulers should lead its sons to die by the thousand upon this foreign field, for this most ignoble cause. You are a curse upon your people, sirs. They will curse you when we are done."

"The wounded and surrendering shall not be harmed," said Torvaal, as though he had not heard. "Whatever your previous opponents may have practised, we Lenays practise honourable warfare. Prisoners shall not be tortured, and shall be returned to their families upon the reaching of terms. Neither do we ransom for gold, nor otherwise partake in hostages, as is the frequent custom here. There is no honour in gold. Submission, by death or surrender, is all that honour requires."

Rochan frowned, and was silent for a moment, considering that. Then he nodded. "I accept these terms," he said, less coldly than before. "We shall reciprocate, when you are defeated."

"I hear you have not in the past," Koenyg accused him.

"No," the general admitted. "Two centuries of dishonourable warfare by our opponents put a stop to it. Ask of your allies of our captured soldiers tortured and disembowelled alive. Ask them what worse things they do to captured serrin. Our captured enemies we attempt to rehabilitate. Some refuse and prefer death. Others are sent to Saalshen. Others still have come to recognise the error of their ways. Formation Captain Lashel here was once a knight of Merraine. Now, he fights for us, by choice."

Koenyg seemed astonished. He stared at the captain, who nodded, and said nothing. Sasha felt that she might be ill.

"Sashandra," said the serrin Vilan. He leaned forward on his saddlehorn, gazing at her with those impossible golden eyes. "You are troubled, Sashandra," he said in Saalsi. His voice was gentle. "You have the look of one lost, and struggling to recognise the path upon which you walk. It seems familiar to you in parts, but then it plunges into foreign mists. You struggle on, more and more certain that you are lost, only to recognise a tree, or a rock, or to think you recognise them. Surely your path is correct. Surely it is true. Is it not?"

Serrin verbs played games through the undergrowth of Saalsi grammar, twisting about to ambush entire sentences unawares. Sasha stared at him, helplessly. She opened her mouth to speak, but nothing came out. Her family all frowned at her, wondering what was said. The Enorans also frowned, but their eyes were comprehending.

"Can you truly fight us, Sashandra?" Vilan asked as though he knew her personally. "Have we caused you such pain in your heart?" A shiver flushed her skin. And she recalled abruptly the battlefield before the walls of Ymoth, and Errollyn talking with her of the Synnich, and of how he, Aisha, Terel and Tassi had known how to come to Lenayin, despite word of the impending battle being a two-month round trip away.

Dear spirits, she realised in horror, she'd never asked him how. And he'd never told her, perhaps sensing that she did not truly wish to know, lest she discover something that would shake her world. Vilan now looked at her as though he knew her, and somehow, she did not doubt that he did. What was the *vel'ennar* truly? And if Errollyn lacked it, being *du'jannah*, how had he known to come to Lenayin when he had? And why had she never asked him how?

"I do not hate you," Sasha replied in Saalsi, her voice straining to make itself heard across the distance. "But my people march to war, and I have seen how the Steel of the Saalshen Bacosh fights. If I do not help them, they may all die."

"And you shall be their saviour?" Vilan asked sadly. "Dear girl, you are but one warrior, and though you have a gift of tactics and command, this army is not yours to lead. Can you save them all?"

"No," said Sasha, more firmly. A tear trickled down her cheek. "I shall die with them."

"And if, by your death, Enora shall fall? And then Rhodaan? And then, left undefended, Saalshen?"

Sasha looked at the ground, and could not speak.

Koenyg broke in, and brought the parley to a conclusion. Riding back to the Lenay lines, he cantered close to her side.

"What did he say?"

"He said we're all going to die," Sasha lied.

"And what did you say?"

"I said that's why I'm here."

The Army of Lenayin did not attack that afternoon. Instead, it retreated up the other side of the valley, and camped across the slope and the hill crest. The men of Lenayin were not happy, and grumbled about glory delayed, but there were enough wise tactical heads among them to keep the discontent at bay.

Andreyis sat by the campfire and gazed across the valley at the fires on the hill beyond. His boots were off, as had become the habit this long march, to allow hardened feet to breathe. Dinner sat ill in his stomach. About him, clustered men caroused, laughed and sang, but Andreyis felt no urge to join in. He never had, particularly. He thought now of Kessligh and Sasha's ranch, and the horses, and how he'd loved to spend time there. Mostly, he'd loved the solitude. And the company of some people he genuinely liked, it was true, particularly as two of them were among the most famous people in Lenayin . . . but solitude, in Andreyis's life, had been a rare and precious thing. Little enough that he'd been getting here.

Valhanan had marched roughly in the middle of the Lenay column, and now occupied the central position in the Lenay front line. It was not such a bad place to be, Teriyan and other, older men had assured him, as in most mass formation warfare, the flanks were harried hardest, not the centre. But the centre, he'd figured, would be the easiest place for the Enoran artillerymen to aim.

Teriyan returned from hearty conversation with others to plonk himself down at Andreyis's side. "Pity the sentries tonight," he said. "They'll have no sleep with these hills crawling with serrin."

"How many serrin, do you think?"

"Oh . . . could be thousands." Teriyan shrugged. "Sasha said just recently, at training . . . she said most serrin don't fight. Don't know how to fight. Amazing, no? All we see are warriors because those are the ones who travel. And svaalverd's only a small part of serrin knowledge. Most serrin know more about crafts, medicine, farming and forestry than about warfare.

"But the *talmaad*'s still big, and there'll be a lot of them coming to help. I'd guess there could be close to ten thousand here."

"That's a lot," said Andreyis. "I spoke with men who'd seen those four serrin fight, the ones who came with us to the north. Errollyn, that was the man's name. And Terel. It was said they fought like demons."

"Aye," said Teriyan. "And here, they'll be fighting for their homes." He took a deep breath. "Sasha says Terel's dead. He died in Petrodor. Errollyn's alive, and the little one, Aisha. Pretty girl she was. Smart as all hells too. Sasha thinks the reason serrin are so smart is their memory. No, she doesn't think, she's certain of it. She says Errollyn and Aisha remember conversations she's had with them word for word, when she can barely recall the topic. That's why your average serrin knows so much, they just learn much faster. That's how little Aisha knows seventeen languages. She learns a word once and doesn't need to repeat it, she just remembers."

"That's amazing." For a while, they both said nothing, but listened to the sound of forty-plus thousand men at camp. Already the air was thick with smoke, from small fires and cooking. "A warrior is not supposed to doubt before a battle," said Andreyis. "But I can't help it."

"Every man feels fear, lad. That's why they drink, sing and laugh, to drown out the fear."

"No, it's not fear. Or at least, it's not *just* fear. It's doubt." He looked at Teriyan, and saw the big man's face troubled. This was one of the only men in all Lenayin he'd have dared express such things to. "We should not be fighting serrin. Nor Enorans. I'm certain of it. And I'll bet Sasha's certain too."

"Aye lad." Teriyan sighed. "She is. But she's Lenay, and she's here because her people need her. If we could turn around and walk out now, all our men would have to fight that much harder to cover our absence."

"I know that," Andreyis retorted crossly. What Teriyan suggested was dishonourable. Like any Lenay, Andreyis was certain he would rather die. "I'm just saying. We fight for honour. But the cause is dishonourable."

"The cause is out of our hands. That's for the king to decide."

"And since when did any Lenay man listen to *him*?"

Teriyan looked at him for a long moment, then shook his head in faint exasperation, but not at Andreyis's question. At the circumstance.

"I wish Sasha had visited," Andreyis said quietly. "I know why she can't, but I wish she had. Tell me some more of her adventures."

"I've already told you all she told me," Teriyan objected.

"Think of something."

Sasha had bad dreams. She dreamed of being dragged from Errollyn's arms, and the bed set on fire, burning sheets scorching her flesh. Of Errollyn screaming, a blade dripping blood, and rattling chains that tore at her wrists. She saw Rhillian, emerald eyes burning with grief and fury, wrestling with a wolf that snarled and snapped at her throat. Kiel fired an arrow, but struck Rhillian instead of the wolf. The wolf retreated to Kiel's side, and licked his hand. Kiel pulled the shaft from Rhillian's side, and blood poured out.

The wolf ran away, and Sasha followed, as it ran down familiar palace halls, and through a wood panelled doorway. Sasha recognised a royal bedroom, with grand furnishings and gilt-edged paintings on the walls. From the huge, four-posted bed came squeals and grunts of sexual pleasure and pain. Sasha walked closer, and found that the wolf had become a man, yet still with a long snout and fangs. Beneath him was Sofy, naked legs about his hairy hide, grunting and crying out as he ravaged her, and his claws reaved her flesh.

Then she was running down a city street, struggling for space in the hot air between oppressive walls. Behind her ran a mob, waving clubs and farm tools, howling like crazed animals. She rounded a corner, and found herself trapped before a formation of Steel, shields interlocked. One lofted a spear, and atop it was impaled Alythia's severed head, eyes wide and mouth gaping. Sasha spun, and the mob behind lofted more spears, each with another head. The one closest was Kessligh's.

She awoke in an eruption of limbs and blanket, kicking the covering away as she surged to her knees. And knelt there gasping, her heart hammering, her old wounds throbbing like fire. She rubbed at the burns on her ribs, and felt no scab, only the smoothness of new skin. It should not hurt like this. But still it burned, like the fire from her dreams.

About, on the hillside, all was black save the occasional glow of a sentry's fire. The moon was new, and Sasha thought of serrin eyesight, and if it might be possible that serrin were creeping through the Lenay camp even now. From nearby came the snoring of Isfayen noblemen. They had camped barely a hundred paces from the farmhouse that was the royal command post, with many other senior nobility. Should an order be given, these men wished to be the first to know. Sasha had been offered a bed in the farmhouse, but had refused, saying she preferred the outdoors. In truth, a bed would have been nice. Yet a bed of broken glass would have been preferable to sharing a roof with her father.

Her heart and breathing recovering, she got up. There were enough fires lit to make for a little light across the long valley slope. Sasha picked her way carefully between sleeping men, and stopped at a small clean patch. She strained her eyes to see across the valley. The lights of the Enoran camp were still there, yet she felt uneasy. She felt like . . . like . . .

She could not find the word to describe it. Yet it was like at Ymoth, during the great charge of horses, when it felt as though there were a formless dark shape moving at the edge of her vision, covering her flank. In fact, she thought she'd seen it, dodging a hidden tree stump, and warning her to do the same. She had seen it, hadn't she? She'd not thought about it in a long time, being busy with other matters, most of them not concerned with old Lenay superstitions. And there'd been a wind, in the second charge of that second fight, when the Hadryn had attempted to regroup. A great gust of wind, that had torn across the flattened fields of crops, and thrown dust and debris into the eyes of the Hadryn soldiers, distracting them from their defence.

It had happened, hadn't it? Or was her memory playing tricks on her, in the aftermath of vivid, horrible dreams from which she had not yet fully woken? A man dreams he is a butterfly, went the serrin tale. When he awakes, he wonders, was I then a man, dreaming I was a butterfly? Or am I now a butterfly, dreaming I am a man?

Sasha squeezed her eyes shut, and put her hands over her face. Her wrists throbbed from recently healed scabs. Memories and pain. She wished that not all memories were painful. She knew she had some pleasant ones tucked away somewhere, but she did not know where to find them now.

She opened her eyes once more, and stared out into the dark. In Petrodor, Rhillian had told her tales of King Leyvaan's army in Saalshen, and how the serrin would stalk them by night, beneath a new moon such as this one, and how no soldier could sleep for the terror of the screams of sentries dying. She heard no screaming now. And she recalled how she'd sat with Rhillian, sipping tea and talking, close as unexpected friends could be, who had known each other only a short time but found some common language of the soul. How had they come to hate each other? Somehow, she found it difficult to recall. Perhaps it was because they were so similar. Like her and Alythia, so similar, so aggressive and self-obsessed, merely the modes of expression differed. She'd hated Alythia, then come to love her. With Rhillian, it was the reverse. Perhaps.

She thought she heard a creaking. A distant squeal, as though of a cart, or some wooden axle. Then nothing. Perhaps something was trying to tell her something. Perhaps through dreams. They called her the Synnich again, in some parts of this army. At Ymoth, she'd felt like this, and seen a dark shadow running through the grain fields. She set off walking toward the farmhouse.

She found Damon sitting on the verandah, and a pair of Royal Guardsmen at watch by the door. Many others stood about, and some slept, watching in shifts. Lanterns were placed further from the farmhouse, not near, as Sasha had instructed—best to make any attacking serrin come out of the light rather than into it, and take away that advantage of a darkened approach. And Errollyn had always said that he found it hard to adjust his eyes from one strength of light to another.

She took a seat at Damon's side, and put her head against his shoulder. Damon said nothing, yet did not seem surprised. He rested his cheek against the top of her head.

"Damon?"

"Hmm?"

"I think they might be moving the artillery."

"What makes you think that?"

"It's a new moon," said Sasha. "They've seen we're too smart to attack immediately. They know they'll have to attack at some point, if they're going to get past us and outflank the Larosans to the north. The longer they wait, the more moon there'll be. Serrin don't see too well in a new moon, but we don't see at all, so it's a much bigger advantage for them than any other kind of moon. Why should they wait, and give us time to scout their forces?"

Damon thought about it. "So you didn't see or hear anything that might suggest they're moving the artillery? Some kind of actual fact?"

"No. It's a stupid hunch."

Damon put his arm around her, and gave her a squeeze. "I'll listen to your stupid hunch. Go on."

"We can't scout the far end of the valley. It's too close to the border, they have artillery covering it, a fast charge down the slope will kill anyone getting too close. The hills aren't that steep either, the Steel ballistas are mounted on oxen carts, those oxen are strong, they could get up or down these hills pretty quickly. Big catapults are oxen pulled too, but those are much heavier and less stable. . . . I'm sure they could do it, though."

"Hard in the dark," suggested Damon.

"Not if each team borrows a few serrin to guide the way. We'd not even see lights moving to know what they were up to."

Damon nodded slowly. "Where do you put the artillery?"

"Along this ridge," said Sasha, pointing along the ridge where the Army of Lenayin was encamped.

"We can outflank them."

"With infantry? We'll have to split our force. . . . I mean, if they send their main force down into the valley, that is."

"Give away the advantage of height? And risk encirclement on their high flanks?" Damon shook his head. "Damn, I'd love it if they did that."

"No, Damon . . ." Sasha sat up and looked him in the eye. "You're discounting the artillery. I've been trying to drum it into your thick heads what it can do, but no one's listening. We won't be able to assemble above the Enoran force in the valley, because the artillery will keep the slopes clear. They'll be guarded, like . . ."

Sasha sprung off the verandah, pulled her knife and began drawing in the dirt. There was just enough light from the nearby lanterns. "You see? The main infantry force in the valley, covered by their artillery on either flank, high on the slopes. Height means extra range, they can fire at us if we go into the valley, or *right* into us if we assemble directly above the Enoran infantry for a charge."

"So all of their cavalry will be defending their artillery," said Damon, kneeling alongside. "What if we concentrate our infantry," and he drew a big cluster on one side of the valley, "and send everyone against one lot of artillery, since they've conveniently divided their force. If we overrun that lot, we not only remove half of their greatest advantage, but we hold the heights above their infantry too."

"They'll move every cavalryman they have to defend that side," Sasha warned. "With all these *talmaad* around, that'll be a lot."

"Yes, but light cavalry," Damon countered. "It's made for attacking, not defending." He considered the squiggles in the dirt. "This would be cunning of them, but it gives us many options. They'd have to be desperate to try it."

"We have them bottled up otherwise," said Sasha. "And if the Larosans are not flanked, Rhodaan may well fall. If Rhodaan falls, Enora loses its defensive line, and will have to fight invasion from Rhodaan, not from Larosa, which is far easier."

"Or from Saalshen," Damon added, "if the Larosans cross the Ipshaal." Sasha nodded, and looked up at footsteps on the verandah.

"What are you two muttering about that's so important you'd wake me up?" Koenyg asked grumpily.

"Sasha has an idea."

"Oh aye," said Koenyg sarcastically, jumping down to look at their scribblings, "this should be good."

He wasn't so sarcastic after she'd explained it, though. He knelt, looking at the squiggles for a long time. And looked up, staring into the dark, as though wishing he had serrin vision with which to probe the night.

"You're probably wrong on the details," he said finally, "but you're right about the intent. If I were them, I'd move soon. Immediately, even. The longer they wait, the worse their overall position."

He got up and strode to a guardsman. The man listened to the instructions, and hurried off. Soon, some cavalry scouts arrived, wild Taneryn men, newly woken. Koenyg instructed more scouting sweeps, in addition to the many he'd already assigned. Those men strode off. More lanterns were lit about the farmhouse, and nearby camps stirred.

The king appeared in the doorway, a black sentinel in a robe. "Trouble?" he asked Koenyg.

"Perhaps. Sasha fears they may be moving. I think she may be right." Torvaal looked at Sasha, long and hard. Sasha ignored him, leaning on a verandah post and waiting.

Yasmyn emerged from the doorway, wrapped in a cloak. Her face, swollen when she had left Sofy's service eight days ago, was now somewhat recovered, though her right eye remained partly closed. Her hair, previously long and loose, had been covered by a red scarf, patterned with ancient black markings. There were new scars on her cheek, that Balthaar's men had not inflicted. It was the *arganyar*, in Isfayen Telochi. In Lenay it translated as "the impatience." The red of the headscarf was for blood. The cuts on Yasmyn's cheeks were for intent. And the two gold rings in her left ear were for two heads, delivered to her father, in apology for the dishonour brought upon the family.

Lord Faras would have preferred an honourable combat, but the daughters of Isfayen were no warriors to deliver such honour. Instead, he spoke of *marysan ne tanar*, in Telochi, "the honour of women," which in Isfayen was a different thing entirely. It was said in Isfayen that by the *marysan ne tanar*, women were far more dangerous to offend than men. A man would at least declare his intention to kill you before he did so, and present you with the opportunity to defend yourself on equal terms. A woman, with honour as pricklish as any man, yet without the option of honourable combat, would achieve her ends however she could. Poison was not unknown, nor seduction followed by a knife in the bed. Yasmyn had been proudly direct, as befitted a daughter of nobility, and ambushed with a blade in the night. It was not by accident that Isfayen women had by tradition the greatest authority of any women in Lenayin. It was a respect built on fear.

Yasmyn came now to Sasha's side. "They move their army by night, yes?"

"Perhaps. We'll see."

"I would ride with you."

"You're not trained," said Sasha. Yasmyn and Sasha had ridden together, these past eight days, at the head of the Isfayen column. Sasha had been impressed with Yasmyn's strength, given her ordeal. Revenge helped, Sasha knew well. It suited Yasmyn's character, and the Isfayen character in particular.

"I am a good rider," Yasmyn said stubbornly. "You have admitted yourself that you are not the equal of most men in cavalry warfare."

"Not an equal in *offence*," Sasha corrected. "But I'm very good at defence. I know how to evade, how to predict, and I know my strengths and limitations. I also have skills of command and tactics, so I have some other uses, even should I not kill many enemies with my sword."

Yasmyn folded her arms, wrapped in her cloak. "I never asked to play lagand," she murmured, gazing into the night. "It is strange. I should have asked, so that I could gain skills like you."

"Why?" Sasha asked. "It does little good for a noble daughter to fight in wars. Her purpose is to produce heirs."

Yasmyn frowned at her. "*You* would say such a thing?"

"That is why I am no longer a noble daughter." Her father stood nearby, doubtless hearing every word. "I have little interest in raising heirs."

"I think a noble daughter of Isfayen should be permitted to fight, should she choose," Yasmyn said stubbornly. "If she has the skills."

"And if all Isfayen noble daughters fight? To be slain before birthing an heir, or depriving her family of the bonds of marriage that bind clans together? If you died on this field, Isfayen could fall apart for the lack of such bonds, and your family ended."

"And also should the men die."

"But you being safe is their guarantee," said Sasha. "You cannot escape it, Yasmyn. I agree that women are capable of more than our tradition allows. But for as long as families rule, and the line of succession is all important, women shall always be shielded from such risk."

Yasmyn thought about it for a moment. More men gathered by the edge of the torchlight, clustered about Koenyg. Damon joined them, but the king remained on the verandah, waiting. Was he truly listening, Sasha wondered? Could he ever admit to listening, and understanding what she was?

"Serrin women fight," Yasmyn said then, thoughtfully.

Sasha nodded. "Succession means nothing to serrin. Family means much to them as individuals, but little as a society. Serrin like to say they are all of one family. It frees women to do as they choose."

"Serrin are not human," Yasmyn objected. "We should not imitate them and expect good results any more than we should live in packs like wolves."

"Aye," Sasha agreed. "Serrin share emotion and thought as humans never shall. It binds them together as humans can never bind. For us to live as serrin do would be to build a great stone house with no mortar, and expect it to stand. But we can think upon our limitations. And we can wonder at what we may learn from their study, not so much of them, but of ourselves."

"I should like to be Nasi-Keth myself," Yasmyn declared. "Perhaps not to fight in wars, though to wield a blade as you do would be glorious. But I would like to think on these things, for the benefit of my people. Perhaps that can be the role of an Isfayen noble daughter. If we cannot fight in wars, then surely we can learn and teach those things that may frighten or offend our lessers."

Sasha gazed at her, in mild surprise. "I think that is a fine idea. Tradition is important, but it is the foundation of the house, not the house itself. For that, we must learn to build, and not be scared of building."

"Would *you* be my uman?" Yasmyn asked.

"I'm still uma myself."

"After," said Yasmyn. "I would be honoured. I have only sixteen summers, I am not too old."

"I'd thought you older. But no age is too old. I'm flattered you'd ask, but it is too early to think on such things. Chances are good I will not live out the day that dawns."

"As I will not likely survive my *arganyar*. Balthaar's cousin Elias still lives, and I cannot kill him yet for the damage it would cause our alliance, and the risk it would cause to Sofy. But eventually, he will die. In the meantime, I shall dream great dreams, and sharpen my darak."

A horse approached, cantering along a line of campfires left clear precisely to guide horses to the farmhouse. The rider dismounted and Sasha recognised Jurellyn, her friend from that first ride to Ymoth, and one of the finest scouts in Lenayin.

"Y'Highness," he announced to Koenyg and Torvaal, "we're fucked." He looked exhausted, and had never been a man for formalities. "I'm pulling our scouts back, I've sent word out for them all to head home to camp."

"You did what?" Koenyg exclaimed.

Sasha saw fear in Jurellyn's eyes, and felt abruptly cold. A man like Jurellyn wasn't scared of much, and certainly not of royalty. "It's the serrin, Y'Highness. They're not attacking the fucking camp like we feared, they're after my poor bloody scouts. I've seen ten dead just this night, they . . . they aren't riding, they're walking and running, all quiet-like, you can't see them coming, they hide in bushes and behind trees and walls, and they shoot for the smallest gaps in a man's armour without a fucking candle's worth of light to see by. . . ."

He took a deep breath, attempting to regain composure. No one interrupted him. "I can't fight that, Y'Highness. No man can. We've safety in numbers, but a man can't fight what he can't see. If I hadn't ordered our scouts back—"

"You did well," Sasha interrupted. "We'll need our scouts later." Most of Lenayin's scouts were Goeren-yai men, foresters with a great respect for the serrin. Serrin, being serrin, would know that. Surely it pained them to do it. But Saalshen was fighting for its right to exist, and serrin for their right to live.

Jurellyn gave Sasha a grateful look. "There's something moving down the valley," he continued. "None of us got close enough to hear. But one of us reckoned he could hear wheels, wooden axles. You could ask him more, but he got an arrow in the neck on the way back."

"How long till dawn?" Koenyg asked no one in particular.

"Soon," said a guardsman, lifting his palm to the horizon of stars. "Another hand."

"Wait until the very first light," said Koenyg. "We'll just make a mess in the dark otherwise. Battle formations, and we'll see what the dawn brings us. Father?"

King Torvaal merely nodded, and folded his arms within the black robe he wore. An assent, that he had faith in his eldest son's command. Koenyg nodded, and strode off to give orders for the nobles to gather. Damon joined him, instructing a guardsman to wake Myklas. Sasha gave her father a final stare, and followed. Torvaal did not seem even to notice. He gazed at the horizon, with all the patience of stone, and awaited the rising sun.

Dawn brought them new silhouettes on the same ridgeline as the command post. The Steel had indeed crossed the valley in the night.

"*All* of them?" Damon wondered aloud, as they stood atop the farmhouse roof, and viewed the enormous mass of glittering steel that now formed a huge line across the rolling fields to this side of the valley.

"Looks like," Koenyg said. "They mean to flank us on our right, and push us back into the valley toward their own border."

"With the forest at our back," added the king, looking at the thick trees that covered the opposing slope. All had been surprised when Torvaal had clambered with his children from a horse's back onto the rooftop. He looked to Sasha more animated than she'd ever seen him. "My son, they will advance on us, and attempt to win around our right flank. We must not let them."

"Aye, Father. But the surest way to defend the right flank is to attack on the left. They have opened up their entire previous position, and we shall divide their attention by taking it."

"Could be a trap," Damon warned, looking out at the formerly surrounded castle.

"If they waste forces setting traps for our cavalry," said Koenyg, "I would not mind a bit." He looked down at the Great Lord Heryd, waiting patiently below in full black cloak and armour. "Lord Heryd! The left flank is yours! Should you win through, recall that the artillery is your primary target!"

"My Prince," Heryd called up, "the north shall bring glory to Lenayin!" He turned and strode to his horses, armoured nobility close behind.

"Is that wise?" Damon asked his brother. "With the primary attack coming on our right flank, we commit our heaviest cavalry to the left." All three northern provinces, refusing to divide their number to fight amongst pagans, had declared that they would form one entire flank together, leaving the remaining eight provinces to form the opposing cavalry flank, and the reserve. The arrangement was not as lopsided as it first sounded, given that the north were almost *entirely* cavalry, and were the heaviest in armour and weight of horse.

"I mean to break through, Brother," Koenyg replied. "We must penetrate their defences and harry their artillery directly. We will achieve it by committing our heavy cavalry to their weakest defence."

"Only look," said Sasha, crouched low on the opposite slope of rooftop, "that weakest defence now means riding uphill from the valley."

"These Enorans improvise well," the king observed. "They appear as tactically astute as in all the tales. Do not underestimate them, my son."

"I shan't, Father. There is no clever move against this foe that could win us a painless victory. We shall fight them, and fight them hard. Damon, our time grows short, I need you on the right."

"Aye," said Damon, with something that sounded more like relief than trepidation. He and Koenyg embraced, and then he embraced their father. "Sasha," he said then, "you're with me."

Koenyg embraced Sasha too. "Good call last night," he told her. "Your details were wrong, but good call anyway."

"I can't be right *all* the time," Sasha said lightly. She paused before her father. Torvaal extended his hand. Sasha took it hesitantly. Her father looked . . . concerned. There was a light in his dark eyes that she could not recall having seen before. It was not a confident light, but a light all the same. Sasha could not say if she found it encouraging or disturbing.

"Daughter," Torvaal said gravely. "Lenayin called, and you came."

That was it, Sasha realised. No mention of fatherly pride, no smile, nothing. Only this, reluctant acknowledgement. She was still the daughter who failed, the one who shamed all Lenay tradition in her choice of life, the one who had abandoned him as Kessligh had abandoned him after Krystoff's death, and had finally led an armed rebellion against his personal authority.

"I've always come," Sasha said coldly, and walked carefully across the roof to the edge, and a short jump to the ground. Damon followed, and she walked with him to their horses. "Why does he always do that?" she asked him plaintively.

"Do what?"

"Make me feel like my entire existence is an affront to him!"

"I heard a compliment," Damon said drily. "That you rejected."

"Where's Myklas?" Sasha asked him, changing the subject.

"He rides with Heryd."

Sasha did not like the thought of Myklas riding with the northern cavalry. But he was too young for a command, he was a good rider, and the northerners should have at least one royal riding with them.

Jaryd was waiting with the horses, and holding a round, wooden shield. He presented it to Sasha.

"What's this?"

"And to think they ever called *me* a dunce," Jaryd remarked.

"I can't ride with this," Sasha snorted. "I'm a girl, it's too heavy for me."

"It's the lightest I could find, and it would barely trouble a fifteen-year-old lad," Jaryd said impatiently, pressing it onto her.

"Take it or I'll have you tied to a tree and left in the rear," Damon told her, mounting quickly.

Sasha scowled, and tried its leather straps. It dragged on her arm, and did horrible things to her balance. She smacked it onto the horse's saddle, and used that weight as a hold to drag herself up. She spurred off after Damon, Jaryd, several Royal Guards and three of Damon's selected nobility. To their left, facing southward, the Army of Lenayin was slowly forming up.

"Sasha, I want you to ride with the Isfayen!" Damon shouted above the noise of their passage. "They have the hottest heads of the bunch, and they're most likely to lose them in a fight! Try to keep them sane!"

"I'll try," said Sasha, "but I can't promise anything!"

Upon the far right flank, the Lenay cavalry were forming. Damon, Jaryd and Sasha rode before the forward line, where vanguards for each Lenay province formed behind long banners that swirled in the gusting wind. A great, stamping, swirling mass of many thousands of horse, stretched across fields, fences and thickets of trees. They formed in provincial groups, nobility and standing company soldiers to the fore. They rode past the Valhanan cavalry, and Sasha glimpsed her old enemy, Great Lord Kumaryn, amidst a crowd of mounted noble riders, armour and leathers polished spotless for the occasion. A little across from the nobility, she spotted the banner of the Valhanan Black Wolves.

Here next were Tyree, behind their green banner. Sasha saw Jaryd give the Great Lord Arastyn and his noble company a burning stare in passing, and saw it returned with equal venom. She'd heard tales of the Tyree nobility's outrage at Damon's selection for promotion to his personal company. A little further, and she saw the banner of the Tyree Falcon Guards. . . . Jaryd pulled his sword to salute them, and a huge cheer rose from the guardsmen. Sasha performed her own salute, and the cheer rose to a roar. This part of Lenayin, at least, was hers and Jaryd's forever.

More cheers greeted them as the line companies, and a few of the nobles, saluted their passing. The line of cavalry seemed to go on forever. Damon and Jaryd rode with her past the royal vanguard, and out along the entire line. And here, squeezed between Lenay horsemen, were the Torovans—rows and rows of tall, muscular horses mounted by warriors in gleaming silver chain and helms. Most of the front row wielded tall steel lances, a forest of spikes against the brightening sky, and they too were arranged behind their provincial flags. Passing the flag of Pazira, Sasha saluted once more, and was received by more cheering. Duke Carlito Renine saluted back.

Riding along the Torovan ranks, Sasha felt her hopes rise. Dear spirits, there were a lot of them. And Carlito was right—while not of Lenay quality on foot, Torovans had long made excellent horsemen. Sasha counted only four Torovan provinces, meaning that Koenyg would be deploying the others on the left flank with the northern cavalry, as the northerners had no complaint riding with foreign Verenthanes, only Lenay pagans. If Lenayin could win this battle, it would be won with cavalry. Gazing out across this great sea of horse-flesh and steel, Sasha thought that surely, now, the advantage was with them.

Upon the farthest reach of the flank, they found the Fyden, Yethulyn, and finally, at the very end, the Isfayen. Sasha peeled off to join Great Lord Faras beneath his waving red, green and blue banners, unable to give Damon and Jaryd any more of a farewell than a wave. They waved back, as the Isfayen cheered, and wheeled about at the formation's far end, to ride back to the royal vanguard. From there, Damon would command the entire right flank cavalry . . . perhaps fourteen thousand horse. The left flank would have about ten thousand—six Lenay and four Torovan, but those six thousand northerners were rightly reckoned to be worth more, man for man. In the middle, fifteen thousand Lenay infantry, with perhaps two thousand Torovan archers and five thousand Torovan infantry for a reserve.

She had ridden to a rebellion in the north of Lenayin, and thought that an impossibly large force. Beside this, it was nothing.

Great Lord Faras did not object to Sasha taking a place at his immediate side, one of his nobles even moving aside to suggest it. He looked magnificent, long black hair immaculately brushed beneath the ferocious, horned helm, mail armour reflecting the sun, his horse's mane and bridle tied with many colourful tuffets.

"Why the far flank, Lord Faras?" Sasha asked, though she already knew the answer.

"In the lowlands, who loses the flank, loses the war," Faras said grimly.

"The Isfayen shall hold this flank." Sasha wondered whose arm he'd twisted for the honour. Or cut off, more likely. "You have a new shield," Faras observed. "It does not like you."

"The feeling's mutual."

"There is no shame for a woman not to ride in war like a man," Faras said confidently. "The glory of the Synnich is on two feet, with no shield. The Isfayen shall protect you."

"Thanks," Sasha muttered. And wondered exactly why Damon had told her to ride here, instead of with him. Clearly they had grown attached to her, and she them. But she suspected something more political afoot.

The Enoran Steel sprawled across a rise of fields, making it difficult to discern their number. A single line gleamed silver in the middle, and darker here on the flanks, where horse dominated. In the distance Sasha could hear horns, high and clear. Communications, she reckoned. Surely more convenient than messengers or flags.

"They're coming," one of the Isfayen nobles remarked. So soon? Sasha frowned, squinting at the line. Surely enough, it seemed to advance. There was no additional flurry of trumpets, no clashing of swords on shields. The Enorans merely came, in perfect formation. This was not an army that relied on threats or bluster to sow fear. This army relied on reputation and capability alone.

Lenay men began noticing, and yells went up, joined by others, until the challenge grew to an ear-splitting roar. Sasha steadied her nervous mare, flexing her left arm against the unaccustomed weight of shield. Great Lord Faras did not yell with his nobles, he merely watched, his narrowed eyes unreadable.

"Confident," he surmised, watching the Steel.

"They've never lost," Sasha reminded him.

"Today that changes."

"They bring their artillery into range. It moves up behind them. We must move now."

Faras smiled. "You worry like a woman. They are not well rested, they spent all night moving." The signalman ahead of them raised his flag. "See, your brother's signal." Faras raised his sword. The flag fell. Faras lowered his sword, and put heels to his horse.

They began at a canter, and already the sound of hooves was deafening. The canter stretched to a slow gallop, as the front rank made to spread the formation for those riding behind. Sasha left her sword in its sheath, trying to figure the best way to steer with this weight on her left arm, concentrating solely on keeping her mare's path straight. If she were jostled in this crush, and fell, the hooves behind would smash her to pulp.

A low wall approached, potential catastrophe if any horse refused the jump and blocked others behind. . . . Sasha's mare cleared it easily, across a dirt road, a farmhouse approaching on the right, and a thin line of trees. . . .

Sasha heard a whistle and looked about, as a horse abruptly vanished from the corner of her vision. She risked a fast look behind, to see a horse rolling, two others falling in collision, others rearing aside in panic . . . what the hells had happened? She saw other riders staring up and ahead, as they approached the foot of the long, gentle incline toward the Steel cavalry. There were dark shapes streaking through the air, fast against the broken cloud. Surely they were not in range already?

She ducked reflexively as a bolt zipped overhead, and risked another look to see a horse fall, and more riders evading desperately behind. How the hells were the furthest flank of cavalry under fire from artillery that should only have been positioned behind protective infantry? And so far out?

Faras waved his sword and with a roar they accelerated up the slight incline, racing at full gallop. Suddenly the air was thick with incoming fire, and Sasha saw at least five coming low as though they might hit her. A noble to her left simply disappeared from his saddle as though he'd ridden into an invisible low branch. Horses were upended, legs folding beneath them, riders catapulted into the turf at breakneck speed. Faster horses were getting ahead of her, and Sasha wove to find a better approach . . . and saw for the first time the Enoran cavalry, a spiked ridge of steel lances, big shields and ridged helms. Dear spirits, there were thousands. The charging Isfayen line was fragmented at the front, where it mattered. The terrible line of lances was lowered, and the Enoran cavalry charged down the incline.

That was it, Sasha realised. The front rank of Isfayen were finished, and she was dead. But she could not stop, for the torrent of riders coming up behind, nor for her honour.

The Enorans were nearly upon them when Sasha realised there were in fact more gaps in their formation than was apparent from a distance. She headed for one, and saw two Enoran lances swinging toward her. She slowed to a fast, high-stepping canter, and her mare, knowing well the lagand field, read her right-feint, then left-dash, as she snapped abruptly across the oncoming Enoran's path. The lance swivelled to track her, but the Enoran rider pulled the reins to miss her, and abruptly he'd passed, and there were horses, riders and lances flashing by to all sides. She nearly died three more times, as fast-adjusting Enorans tried to impale her, but luck and a fast duck saved her. She swung at one man, but struck only shield, and swung about now to find more space than expected, and Isfayen riders fighting clear behind.

The rear Enoran ranks bore swords rather than lances, and laid about them furiously. . . . Sasha threw her shield up to a blow that nearly broke her arm, hauling at the rein and applying heels with wild reflex to lurch past that rider's nose, lengthening his reach, then parrying right as one swung from the other side. Far from annihilated, the Isfayen were everywhere, roaring and swinging with crazed fury, hammering Enoran shields, ramming horses, severing limbs with their huge, curved swords.

Suddenly the Enorans were leaving, a high trumpet sounding, cavalry simply breaking off the fight and sprinting for higher ground. Isfayen flag bearers waved their banners, and nobles stood in their stirrups, calling to regroup. Sasha rode toward one of them, and abruptly there were ballista bolts falling, and that noble's horse took a bolt through the ribs. She saw the bolt simply disappear inside the horse, ripples of impact contorting the huge body like a rock striking the water, and the animal fell as a bag of broken bones. It shocked Sasha as much as anything she'd seen. This was not warfare as she knew it. This was unfair.

She pulled alongside the now dismounted noble, and gave him a hand up to sit behind, searching for a riderless horse . . . but under ballista fire, horses were falling faster than riders. More commotion sounded from the far flank, and Sasha applied heels, the big man behind clutching her with little regard for her modesty. Weaving through the massed, wheeling horses, Sasha found enough vantage to regard the entire far flank of Isfayen riders now racing away from the fight, further to the flanks, in pursuit of light horse. *Talmaad.*

Sasha put her heels in hard, and the mare tore off after them, more Isfayen riders joining her. "Wall!" she yelled for her passenger's benefit, and they cleared the next wall without difficulty. Ahead, she saw serrin riders closing from the left, paralleling Isfayen riders, bows pulled. Arrows fired, and two Isfayen tumbled from their saddles. Another raised his shield high, leaving little exposed flesh to fire at, so the serrin shot his horse instead. It stumbled, reeling, its rider pulling it to a halt.

"Shields up!" Sasha screamed at the riders coming up on her flanks. "Shields up! Archers, archers!"

Those serrin were now falling back, inviting her to chase them. That was death. . . . Sasha waved her sword to the right, where other riders had gone, and wheeled that way. Behind her, perhaps fifty Isfayen had formed, having recognised her. Several ignored her evasion and pursued the serrin.

"Get back here!" Sasha yelled at them, but they either couldn't hear or ignored her. The serrin waited until they were close enough, then accelerated once more to equal their speed. Turning in their saddles, they drew arrows, and fired straight back over their horses' flanks. One Isfayen fell, another clutched his arm, and a third's horse ploughed a nose first furrow in the field.

Sasha skirted a small village, and two serrin barely cantering in the near fields, again inviting pursuit. Sasha waved half of her formation left about the village, herself heading right, and the two serrin took off at fast gallop, realising they were about to be trapped. Others played cat and mouse with Isfayen riders across nearby fields, reluctant to engage directly, seeking only enough running space at close range to fire a lethal arrow at horse or rider.

On the far side of the village, maybe thirty serrin emerged from a line of trees to send long range arrows hurtling toward Sasha's riders. Several clutched at strikes, and the rest charged. The serrin reloaded, cut several more Isfayen off their horses, then split in every direction. Bewildered Isfayen tried to intercept one or another, more arrows coming at odd angles, catching them past their shield alignment. Sasha saw one cut a racing serrin from her horse, only to lose his head to a second with a breathtakingly beautiful overhead. . . . Sasha angled to intercept, but with a passenger she was too heavy, and the serrin darted from range, sheathing sword and recovering his bow. Sasha saw his eyes as he flashed her a stare in passing, green like emerald, hair red like flame.

This, she decided as fast serrin horses scattered away from slower Isfayen riders, was pointless. She reined to a halt, waving her sword for a recall. Eventually the Isfayen came back to her, short another six or seven of their number. Sasha wheeled about and set off back to the Lenay lines.

"We can't fight as light cavalry against *talmaad*!" she yelled at the Isfayen village headman who came up on her right. "They make us look stupid!"

The headman did not disagree, and gave the man riding at Sasha's back a grim look. Only when Sasha returned to the line and dismounted at a small stream by an oak did she see why. Instead of dismounting, her passenger remained astride, clutching the saddle to keep from falling. From his back protruded a serrin arrow. Sasha dumped her shield and with the aid of two men helped him from the horse. They tended to him by the stream, while Sasha watered her horse, and checked her for injuries.

Then she remounted, with still many of her riders surrounding, and galloped off to find Lord Faras. There were a lot of Torovan wheeling about instead, recovering from their first charge, collecting wounded slumped in their saddles and exchanging limping horses. Across the far rise, the battle still raged. Nearer the centre of the fight, smoke streaked the battlefield, and flame flashed at regular intervals. Sasha was very glad she had not been within range of the catapults.

Not seeing anyone she recognised, she instead found the Valhanan Black Wolves, regrouping at the head of a cluster of other Valhanan cavalry. Sasha galloped to their captain, who welcomed her with a wave.

"They've moved their ballistas all the way out to the flanks!" Sasha shouted to him. "We took heavy fire on the approach, it split our front rank so their cavalry could carve us up. With ballistas so far from the central formation, we should be able to pick them off, but I don't know if anyone got through."

"We only had a little ballista fire," replied the captain, sweaty and wild eyed beneath his helm. "I think they may have clustered defensive firing positions on the flanks to break down our cavalry thrusts, they know we have to try to flank them. But we were closer to the centre, we got catapults instead. I lost about twenty men to just one of those fucking things. I think Lord Kumaryn's dead, I saw another hit right in the noble vanguard, lots of burning horses."

"Look," said Sasha, pointing off across the field, "we have to go again, they've nearly halved the distance. They'll be firing into our infantry soon."

More yelling came before the captain could reply. "Serrin in the rear!" came the cry. "Serrin in the rear!"

"Damn my pig-headed brother!" Sasha exclaimed. "I *told* him this would happen if he didn't hold enough cavalry back!"

"What's happened?" asked the captain.

"The *talmaad* have gone way around our flank," Sasha replied in exasperation, pointing well wide of the battlefield. "They were always going to, but it wouldn't have mattered if Koenyg had held a few thousand extra cavalry back. Only I'm betting he hasn't made certain they've stayed put, and some hotheads have decided to charge rather than staying behind. Our infantry will have a few thousand serrin archers feathering their backsides if we don't stop them."

She spun her mare around, waving with her sword to indicate they should all follow. The captain did likewise, and Sasha, perhaps seventy or eighty Isfayen, and several hundred of her native Valhanan's finest, went charging into the rear to cover for her eldest brother's oversight.

Andreyis was frightened. He'd been frightened before, at the Battle of Ymoth. But there, he'd been ahorse, and facing a known enemy. Today, he stood shoulder to shoulder in a mass of Lenay warriors, and heard the sounds of battle draw closer. He could see little above the heads and helms of the ranks before him, but the thunder of cavalry was everywhere. He had no idea how the battle went, save that it drew closer, and louder, by the moment. He'd heard it said often enough that the cavalry would need to win through in the opening phases, and harry or destroy the Enoran artillery, for the Army of Lenayin to have a chance of winning. Yet from ahead, he could smell smoke, and see regular flashes of fire, mostly off to the flanks.

"They've shifted their artillery to the flanks," said Teriyan at his side. "It won't come down so hard on us then."

"Just get ready to run," Byorn said grimly, hefting his shield on one muscular arm. "When they get within artillery range, we're going to need to run like the wind to close on their infantry. The closer we get, the less the artillery can hit us."

They could not go now, Andreyis knew; they had to wait, hoping that the cavalry could turn a flank. About him, men practically bounced on the spot, armour and all, as tense as cats. They were a mixture, these Valhanans— some from Baerlyn, others from surrounding townships, others still from places Andreyis had not heard of. He could only see several other Baerlyners besides Teriyan and Byorn, as all had decided that, in the face of the reputed effects of Enoran artillery, it would not do to have entire villages standing clustered together.

"Ready!" came a yell from the distant front. "Ready!" echoed headmen, and appointed militia officers deeper through the ranks. A war chant started, the location uncertain, but Andreyis had never heard its like before.

"*HEEL*-Chun, *GOER*-Rhun! *HEEL*-Chun, *GOER*-Rhun!" As with most old Lenay war chants, the tongue was forgotten and largely extinct . . . but the words sounded like glory, blood and ancient spirits. Andreyis realised it was a *tsalryn*, a battle cry only to be uttered in war, and unknown by any who had not fought in one. Andreyis's skin flushed hot and cold all over. This was the first time he'd heard a *tsalryn*. Soon they were all yelling, and the noise was like nothing else in the world. It drowned out all the battle, all the world. Warriors beat shields with swords for accompaniment, roaring like men possessed. Andreyis felt his fear fade, swept aside by an intoxication of rage and power.

He did not hear the ballista fire, but he could see it, dark streaks against the clouds. It rained down across the Lenay formation, but none struck near. Men broke off their chants to howl their derision. If that was the famed Enoran artillery, it would have to become a lot worse to frighten the Army of Lenayin. The front ranks began to move, space rippling through the formation until Andreyis himself was moving, no more than a walk. It accelerated to a jog, and then to a run, warriors still chanting, gripping their shields, eyes on the sky for more ballista fire. The force of their momentum seemed unstoppable. Ballista bolts rained about, to little effect. This was the Army of Lenayin, the most formidable warriors in all Rhodia, charging en masse, fearless and devastating. Andreyis felt invincible, and had to fight the urge to sprint madly ahead of his position, so desperately did he lust for an enemy to swing at, to hack, to maim and slaughter.

Something flashed to his left, bright and hot. Another roar from the warrior hoard, and the run increased to a mad sprint. Another flash, then another. . . . Andreyis saw objects soaring across the sky, flames rippling, leaving trails of black smoke like stars falling to earth. One soared straight overhead, and impacted some distance behind him, but close enough that he could feel heat. He ran now in a jostling crush, sword arm held close to his side so that he did not involuntarily cut his neighbours. His shield arm felt heavy, his breath beginning to labour. The artillery range of the Enoran Steel was no inconsiderable distance to run in full armour . . . surely it could not be much further?

Ballista fire increased, like a light rain shower suddenly erupting into a cloudburst of hailstones. Men fell, in front and to the side. . . . Andreyis ducked in sudden fear as one whistled just overhead. The thud of bolts hitting the turf resonated like a drumbeat. Andreyis hurdled a fallen man, his wooden shield pinned to his chest by a bolt that was protruding from his back.

A burning ball streaked to ground not thirty paces to the right, followed by an impossible, eye-burningly bright flash. In that mesmerised moment, time seemed to slow, and Andreyis saw the billowing orange flames actually double, then triple and quadruple their size and intensity, rather than fading. They thrust out greedily, an avalanche of fire, roaring through clustered, running men, engulfing them.

He did not see the next catapult shot coming until the entire world before him transformed to molten fire. He fell, to see the wall of flame coming right at him, blotting out the world. Heat seared his skin, singed his eyebrows, filled his ears with a ghastly sound like a fire demon on eagles' wings. And then it was gone, and the world was full of ash and cinders, black smoke and the screams of men. He stumbled to his feet, and saw men on fire, rolling on the ground, thrashing in agony. A Goeren-yai's long hair and beard had gone up like a torch, a ball of flame now engulfing his head.

A hand grabbed his arm. "Move!" Teriyan bellowed. "If we stay here we're dead!" He hauled Andreyis forward, through the circle of blackened, burning grass and flaming corpses. The smell was appalling, acrid, and burned his lungs. At the circle's far side, men helped survivors to sit, pouring water on wounds . . . one was hit by a ballista bolt through the back, smashed into the turf and pinned like a bug.

Andreyis stumbled on after Teriyan, aware that the charge continued, Lenay men pouring forward like the tide. And now, ahead, there was an advancing, silver line of shields, helms and armour. Spears flew from behind the front line, and more Lenay men fell, or took entangling spikes through their shields. Andreyis ran at them, knowing only that the closer he came to the Steel infantry, the less the chance of being burned alive.

He dodged aside a flying spear, found a gap on the battle line and flung himself onto it, using the weight of his momentum to drive the Enoran soldier back a step. His neighbour pulled his shield aside to stab with the short

Enoran sword, but Andreyis was ready, having drilled many times for precisely that event. He angled his shield sideways, driving down on the thrust, and slashed back for the man's head. The Enoran ducked, and Andreyis's strike smashed off his shield rim. The Enoran Andreyis had run into recovered his place in line, and the shield line attempted to advance. Andreyis backed off enough to gain space, and flashed a low blow to get under the shield. It was blocked, and he reversed immediately to a high overhead. Again the Enoran ducked his head away in time as Andreyis's edge struck the shield's high edge, but this time a space opened between him and his left-hand neighbour. Andreyis thrust his blade through it, catching that man's arm. He faltered with a yell, the shield dropped a fraction, and Andreyis's partner leaped high to drive a blade down over the shield rim, straight through the Enoran's throat.

The next Enoran behind leapt over the fallen man to fill his space, but Andreyis's partner stepped in, using his shield to protect him on one side, hacking at the next man in line to the other. That man went down, and the line faltered. A whistle blew shrilly above the roar and clashing, and the front rank turned abruptly sideways and melted into the gaps between the ranked soldiers behind. Andreyis found himself facing a new, fresh soldier.

"My turn lad!" yelled a warrior behind, pushing past.

"Find the gap!" Andreyis yelled at him as he attacked. "Make the shield move! Find the gap!"

Despite the chaos, a kind of order was developing, Lenay men unable to attack all at once, and awaiting their turn, lunging into space, leaving enough room for their neighbours to swing. This was better, Andreyis thought, fighting to retain his place against the jostle of fellow Lenays behind. The Enoran advantage in artillery was terrifying, but now they were to grips with fifteen thousand Lenay warriors on foot, they'd not find them like any opponent they'd yet encountered. Not merely brave, Lenay warriors studied warfare like scholars studied tongues. They had been puzzling over the Enoran problem for the entire march from Lenayin, and now that they were here, they would put their theories to the test, and force holes in the Enoran line where the Enorans were not accustomed to any holes appearing.

Now if the cavalry could only win out on a flank, and do something about that artillery, the day may yet be won.

Sasha's reward for chasing *talmaad* about the rear of the army's formation was an arrow shaft through her shield. It ended only when reinforcements arrived, whereupon the serrin simply faded back across the fields, their task of forcing the Lenays to divert large forces away from the front largely complete.

Sasha returned to the stream that had become the right-flank cavalry's rallying point, and allowed her mare to drink. Leaving the horse with some Isfayen men, she walked to a paddock wall and climbed up, to gain a slightly better vantage of the fight.

The scale of it defied belief. From horizon to far horizon, formations were engaging. Smoke made a haze about the interlocked lines of infantry, but flashes of flame were relatively few—the Lenay infantry had pressed itself thin against the Enoran lines, making it difficult for the Enoran artillery to shoot without hitting their own men. Even from this limited vantage, Sasha could see the strategic risk—one big push from the Enorans could break a hole through the thin Lenay lines, and split their formation. But for now, the Enorans were struggling, simply unable to inflict the level of casualties upon Lenay infantry that they were accustomed to doing. Tactical ingenuity, Kessligh had told her often, was more truly a matter of knowing your own forces' relative strengths and weaknesses, and deploying them accordingly, than a matter of brilliant commanders winning battles single-handedly with inspired manoeuvres. Lenay infantry simply did not die in face-to-face combat as quickly as the Steel were accustomed. Sasha wondered if the heavily armoured Enorans would tire more quickly, and wished that the cloud would break up further, and the day would warm as the sun rose higher.

She bit from a fruit she'd stowed in her saddlebag. It felt odd to be eating in the middle of a war, but if she didn't keep her strength up, she wouldn't be much use to anyone. Over a vast sweep of rolling green fields to her right, cavalry charged and wheeled like great flocks of starlings above a wheatfield. The *talmaad*, with their swift horses, had succeeded in spreading the massed Lenay and Torovan cavalry far out to the right flank, and far back behind the Lenay lines. She suspected the *talmaad* may have brought fresh horses, and were hiding them somewhere beyond the immediate battlefield, so that they could cover the extra ground without exhausting their mounts.

An Isfayen village headman leaped to the wall beside her in a rattle of mail, and handed her some bread. Sasha gave him her second fruit. She had no idea where anyone she knew was—most of the morning she'd fought by the side of strangers. She thought she liked this better. If she survived, she expected to find many friends dead at the end of the day, and did not know that she could continue fighting if she saw them fall in person.

"We're not breaking through on this side," the Isfayen growled, chewing on the fruit. "I've never seen anyone fight like these serrin. They've got heavy cavalry protecting their damn artillery, and anyone who attacks is immediately outflanked and hit from the side by serrin archers."

Sasha had expected some bitterness, Lenays never having had much admiration for archery, regarding it a coward's art. But the *talmaad*'s horse-back archery was breathtaking, and when one was on its receiving end, terri-fying. Sasha heard nothing but respect in the bloodwarrior's voice.

The fact that much of the right-flank Lenay cavalry were riding smaller dussieh wasn't helping, Sasha reflected. This right flank was superior in num-bers to the Lenay left, but the left was northern, and huge, and somewhat more skilled as cavalry, rider for rider. Against the Enoran cavalry, most Lenay riders were outmatched, and the Torovans, while riding bigger horses and more well armoured, were failing to press home their attacks with the ferocity required. Perhaps the left was where the breakthrough would come.

"Come," said Sasha. "We've had our rest." She jumped from the wall and strode back toward the horses. Riders galloped past, and Sasha spared them a wary look, to be certain they weren't serrin sneaking through the lines once more to cause havoc in the rear. "I think we might be wasting time trying to make a wide flanking move about the far side. I think there might be a way through closer to the middle."

"Against the infantry flank, aye," the Isfayen agreed. "Then there's the artillery."

"We can't become so paralysed with concern for the artillery that we don't dare venture near it. Our infantry are right under it, we have to take some pressure off them."

She didn't dare use the word "fear," or else the Isfayen might have charged straight into the teeth of the worst artillery fire, just to prove they weren't frightened.

On the way in, she found Damon and the royal vanguard, partially hidden behind a cluster of barn and trees. Sasha indicated to her riders, who now numbered perhaps a hundred and fifty, to wait aside while she rode to converse with her brother. Royal Guards pulled aside, and she found Damon and Jaryd pointing at the unfolding confusion ahead of them, seeking an opportunity. Both looked relieved to see her as she halted alongside.

"Hell of a fight, yes?" Jaryd remarked to her. Though it was now midmorn-ing, and they had been fighting since dawn, he seemed yet to overcome his awe.

Damon seemed as grim as ever, yet less anxious than she'd seen him, as though warfare was preferable to waiting. His left shoulder guard was torn, yet from the angle of the cut, it seemed that the mail beneath had deflected it, and his face betrayed no pain.

Sasha explained her trials in the rear with the *talmaad*.

"I'm tempted to try the artillery just to get away from those damn serrin," Damon agreed, eyes searching the way ahead. "I think we erred to suppose that the artillery would be Enora's greatest advantage."

"Sasha, what do you think?" Jaryd pressed. "Perhaps like Ymoth? A two-force feint?"

"Perhaps," said Sasha. "How many are you?"

"Immediately, perhaps two hundred," Damon replied. "If we rally properly, we could collect thousands. . . ."

"But we'll afford the Enorans the same opportunity," Sasha finished for him. "I think that's our next option, if this doesn't look like it's working. We've maybe three hundred and fifty between us, any more may be more hindrance than help. You go first, spring the trap, I'll get in behind and get straight into their infantry. See if we can turn one of their formations, get our infantry an edge."

It worked superbly, but not how she'd thought. Riding out in front, Damon and Jaryd's two hundred cavalry were countered by a similar-sized formation of defensive Enoran heavy cavalry. Thus committed, those cavalry were in no position to stop Sasha's hundred and fifty Isfayen, who tore down on the exposed flank of Enoran infantry. Ballista fire adjusted too late, raining mostly behind the Isfayen charge, and a single catapult shot erupted close enough to singe the leftmost Isfayen rider, but no more.

The redeploying formation of Enoran infantry was caught squarely in the face of the charge, soldiers running madly to lengthen their square into a wide wall as the horses bore down on them. Then, just before impact, the Enorans did the utterly unexpected, and ducked. Soldiers curled up on the ground, shields overhead, and charging Isfayen horses simply jumped, unwilling to risk that metal underfoot. Isfayen riders swung at the Enorans, yet those that could reach hit only steel. Once the charge had passed over and around, the Enorans jumped back to their feet, and completed their previous manoeuvre of widening the flank. Sasha could only be impressed with the discipline.

But now, she could see the Enoran artillery for the first time: rows of wide-armed ballistas on cartback, guarded behind a wall of yet more infantry—the reserve, Sasha realised, doubling as artillery guards in case of a cavalry breakthrough like this one. Men on those ballistas were winding them frantically downward to meet the onrushing threat, and as Sasha looked left and right, she saw no immediate cavalry support rushing to assist. She lowered her sword, and yelled.

The Isfayen roared, and were onto the ballistas before they could winch low enough to fire. Sasha slashed at the Steel defensive wall, again and again, more in hope of a lucky strike than assurance. A few spears soared past, but the Isfayen were too numerous, flanking the defences, spreading them, then driving horses into their midst and hacking about them with huge, curved swords. Steel infantry fell as powerful strokes found gaps in their armour, trying to re-form, clustering back-to-back for protection, shields above their heads to ward the blows that fell on them from all sides.

Other Isfayen jumped from their horses and onto the carts, as mostly unarmoured ballista men abandoned posts to grab defensive weapons, only to be hacked down in fives and tens by furious, howling bloodwarriors. Long-haired warriors then clambered over the ballistas, hacking the taut ropes, stabbing the mechanisms, disabling the weapons, killing the cart oxen along with any remaining men who resisted. No Enorans ran. A group of perhaps twenty Steel, managing to regroup at one side of the carnage, formed a wedge and counterattacked, taking down several unprepared Isfayen in the process. But more surrounded them, attacking from above on horse while those on the ground dropped to a knee to cut under their shields, amputating legs in great scything sweeps. The rest folded quickly, but fought until all were dead.

Sasha did not join in, but circled with the four warriors who had assigned themselves her protectors, watching for a counterattack. Barely two hundred paces to the side, more Steel clustered about the great, swinging arms of the dreaded catapults, oxen teams to the fore, ammunition teams to aft. Not one of those infantry abandoned position to come running to their comrades' assistance. On the forward infantry line, Sasha could see the rear ranks glancing back to monitor the slaughter of the ballista team, but again, none broke their formation. The Enoran cavalry was the artillery's protector in such events, she knew, but the cavalry was vastly stretched, with little or no reserve.

Very concerningly, a pair of catapults were now being turned about to face upon them directly, infantry shifting ahead of the driving oxen teams. Sasha yelled orders to disperse, uncertain if the catapults could in fact fire accurately at such short ranges, but unwilling to find out. Isfayen men finished the last of their carnage, and ran for their horses. For a brief moment, Sasha pondered attacking the catapults too, but she saw horses tearing along the rear of the Enoran line toward them, and figured she'd pushed her luck as far as was sane. Perhaps she and a hundred and fifty Isfayen would be a fair sacrifice for a couple of catapults, but those reinforcements were heavy cavalry against Isfayen dussieh, and besides, she'd glimpsed the Enoran rear, found a tactic that worked, and discovered a key Enoran weakness. She had to get out and tell someone.

Again she rode for the rear of the Enoran infantry line, who were now engaged with Lenay infantry at their front. The rear soldiers turned, and those on the outside made a shield wall, while the ranks behind formed the roof. Isfayen riders crashed their horses into it, making some stumble, and opening holes that others attacked . . . but it was taking too long, and Sasha, again on the fringes, saw that there were indeed hundreds of Enoran heavy horses galloping past the catapults with murder on their minds.

She yelled for a retreat, and enough heard her to follow, which the others copied in turn. They streamed back onto the Lenay side of the lines, Lenay infantry cheering them madly, and pursued in turn by Enoran heavy horse. Ahead, Damon and Jaryd's cavalry were still entangled in a frantic melee with the initial, defensive formation of Enorans. Sasha led her Isfayen squarely into the fight from behind, and for a brief moment, their numbers overwhelmed the Enorans, their cavalry blindsided, cut down unawares by racing Isfayen, or abruptly outnumbered in their various duels. They scattered, wheeling outward, and Sasha was circling while standing in her stirrups, screaming to re-form rather than pursue.

Again, enough heard her to comply, and when the pursuing Enoran cavalry tore into them, they too were quickly outnumbered. This time it was Damon who was yelling at them all to retreat before Sasha did, and they turned and raced from the field as two catapult shots landed in the vacated fields behind them.

The Isfayen had lost men, and others were wounded, but they were whooping and yelling in Telochi as though they'd defeated the Enoran Steel on their own. The village headman who'd stood with Sasha on the wall came alongside, blood flowing down a slashed arm, but grinning toothily.

"You *are* the Synnich," he told her in Lenay, "and I'd follow you to the last hell!"

Sasha felt relief to be alive, but there was no joy. She thought only of the ballista teams as she'd last seen them, crumpled piles of bloodied corpses, killed to the last man in the certain knowledge that defeat was worse than death. Not fanaticism, no. Determination. Selflessness. Pride.

Suddenly she wanted to cry.

Seventeen

THE STEEL LINE WAS ACTUALLY BENDING. Andreyis was so tired he could barely lift his shield arm, but as he took his rest for an uncounted time, he could see beyond the press that this entire portion of the Enoran formation had bent back upon itself. About him, lay Enoran and Lenay bodies in equal numbers, many groaning or struggling to move. He did not know where Teriyan was, and could not see any Baerlyners, yet there were many faces that had become familiar on the march, or in the past morning's fighting. These were his brothers now.

For the third time that morning, the Steel infantry formation began to lose its discipline, as tired Enorans struggled to move into line as the previous line fell back. Andreyis did not see how it happened, perhaps someone tripped, or several in the same place fell to Lenay blades, but suddenly the Valhanans were into their midst with a roar, forcing gaps between the shields, knocking men down with sheer bodily force to cause a cascade that rippled through the entire Enoran rank.

Isolated from their protection, Enorans formed small groups and fought furiously, attempting to fall back. Andreyis's rear formation surged forward, trying to find a way in. . . . He suddenly found a space and darted within, saw an outnumbered Enoran fighting with remarkable skill, felling one Lenay while blocking two more.

Andreyis came at him with an overhead, but the Enoran blocked it, then rammed the shield back into Andreyis, driving him back, then spinning to cut at another on his side. Two Enoran comrades came to help, and pulled him back into the regrouping formation behind. Andreyis tried to cut around their shields, but his aching arm lacked power, and an Enoran shield thrust knocked his own smaller shield aside, with the following short-sword thrust slicing through shoulder leather as he barely ducked away in time.

There were arrows falling now amongst the Enoran rear ranks, Torovan archers braving the artillery zone behind to fire into that armoured mass. It seemed to do little damage, but it kept the rear ranks holding their shields above their heads instead of resting, and the Enorans seemed as exhausted as the Lenays.

"Keep 'em moving back!" men were yelling. "Keep the pressure on, lads! Move 'em, move 'em!" Defeating an Enoran formation by killing a majority of its men hand to hand seemed unlikely, particularly now that exhaustion was setting in. But moving them backwards and out of position would breach the entire Enoran formation, and open spaces for the cavalry. From there, a collapse could occur relatively quickly. Lenay militia knew this for a fact, and motivated themselves and each other without a need for higher command.

Trumpets sounded above the whistles of rank change. Yells from the Enoran officers, unintelligible in that foreign tongue. Suddenly the entire Enoran line was falling back. Lenay men howled in triumph, and surged forward. Too exhausted to join in immediately, Andreyis managed only a walk. As he fell behind the front line, he noticed that the Enoran line to the left was not falling back evenly, but rather pivoting, as though on a hinge. He stared across to the right as Valhanans jostled past around him, and saw that on that side, the formation was doing the same.

"Wait!" he yelled. "Wait, it's a trap!"

Ahead, though he could not see, the renewed sound of battle assured him that the sudden Lenay advance had stopped dead. The Enorans had moved up the reserve, he realised . . . and unlike the Army of Lenayin, with its Torovan reserve, the Enoran reserve would be every bit the quality of its front-line troops, only fresh and itching to fight. The Enoran general had spotted this part of his line about to break, and had shored it up.

And now, the line they had been facing had become the walls of a box, while the new reserve formed the floor. The Valhanans were in the middle, surrounded on three sides.

"Fall back!" Andreyis yelled, pushing forward so that the front ranks might hear. "Fall back, it's a trap!" The roar of fighting resumed to either side, as the walls of the box began pressing in. Other Valhanans took up the cry, and as quickly as they'd advanced, the Lenays were soon fighting a fast retreat as the box's steel walls began closing in around them. Unprepared men who had thought themselves in the rear, suddenly found themselves exposed and fighting on a flank, as the Enorans attacked with renewed vigour. In the confusion, the Lenays lost their spacing, became crushed together, and abruptly the advantage swung back to the Enorans, whose short blades and lightning stabs were far more suited to the cramped quarters. Lenays pressed against that Enoran line fell, unable to defend from two or three possible threats at once, unable to see the blow coming behind its shield, and without the space in which to perform a proper parry in the Lenay style.

Andreyis ran back with the retreat as the Enoran reserve built up momentum, moving at a powerful jog, trampling any who fell underfoot.

The sudden crush of men was alarming, and he held his blade aloft as he ran so as not to accidentally cut anyone.

The Enorans did not stop their advance, as the entire line began to regain the ground it had lost. Andreyis stepped back over the bodies of men left behind, now smothered once more by the shifting tide of battle. Lenays fought furiously to halt the retreat, but footing was hard to attain while moving backwards over bodies.

Above the deafening confusion, Andreyis heard warning yells, and the thunder of approaching cavalry. It was coming from the Lenay right flank, hurtling across the devastated artillery zone. Some galloping horsemen on the far side of the onrushing group were clearly Lenay, and Andreyis felt a huge relief . . . until he realised that they were a minority, and were in fact chasing the others, and trying to cut them from their saddles.

The majority of the oncoming riders, in scattered wheeling groups, were serrin. There had to be at least a thousand of them. And they were firing into the infantry's backs as fast as they could reload.

Lenay men were falling as the racing *talmaad* horsemen drew level. And then, they were coming across behind the retreating Valhanan lines. Andreyis threw up his shield and crouched, trying to hide as much of his body behind it as possible. Arrows hissed and snapped left and right, men to his side took shots through their shields, others less attentive took them through necks, shoulders, chests, legs and faces.

Bodies tumbled, and continued to tumble, as passing serrin riders lifted their aim above those closest them. Andreyis risked a glimpse back toward the Enorans, and saw Lenay men struck squarely between the shoulder blades, one moment yelling in support or preparing to swing a weapon at Enoran infantry, the next clutching the air and falling, pierced through chain mail and leathers by the terrible power of serrin longbows.

The serrin seemed to take forever to pass, those nearest them like Andreyis not daring to lower their shields, while those closer to the Enorans dared not turn their backs on the oncoming Steel. Many Lenays stood to protect the backs of those men with their shields, but Lenay shields were smaller, and many fell with shafts through their legs instead.

Then it seemed the serrin procession was splitting, and Andreyis saw their train mixed with many Lenay and Torovan riders who tried to kill them as the serrin evaded, and continued to find targets. Some horses came racing near, dodging wildly with Lenay riders in pursuit. Andreyis saw serrin tucking their bows into canvas bags behind their leg, drawing swords and charging through the closer Lenay infantry, as much to distract the riders chasing as to cause damage. With shields drawn, and bewildered still from the ferocity of the archery, Lenay men scattered before the onrushing horses.

A man darted from Andreyis's side to swing at a passing serrin, only for the serrin's razored blade to sever his sword arm midlength. Another took an arrow through the middle, and stumbled into the path of galloping horses. Andreyis ran at him, intent on dragging him away from their path, but he'd barely begun to move when a horse changed direction to come straight at him. The last things Andreyis saw were fast, galloping hooves and a swinging silver blade.

Sasha had barely rested from her assault on the Enoran artillery when the serrin began pouring across the fields. Where they'd come from she did not know, nor how so many had managed to slip past as many Lenay and Torovan horsemen as comprised the army's right flank. But come they did, at hurtling speed, a swirling, deadly mass with no respect for formation or self-preservation.

She turned her exhausted horse about and charged at them, her men doing the same, as others tore into the serrin mass's flanks. The serrin kept riding, weaving back and forth, criss-crossing paths with Lenay cavalry to keep them at bay. Sasha held her left-arm shield across her body to guard her right, where most of the serrin were riding. She could see them firing away from her, into the Lenay infantry, and saw men falling by the score. Any of them could have been a friend. All of them were her countrymen. She kicked her horse to greater speed, as several serrin turned and fired her way.

One of them saw her. A man, silver haired and sharp-blue eyed. Their eyes met, and the serrin's fixed, with recognition. He crossed his bow to opposite hands across his saddle horn, nocked and drew with effortless strength and balance. Sasha hauled the mare's reins to the right, but the tired animal was slow to respond. The shield was awkward to use, and left too much exposed. The serrin fired, and as the arrow lunged from the string, Sasha knew that it was her approaching death.

But it was her horse's. The shaft struck somewhere before her hands, and the animal's legs simply folded. Sasha did not even manage a yell as her saddle disappeared from under her, throwing her sword clear and trying to roll . . .

And awoke, hooves still thundering, horses whinnying, warriors yelling, swords clashing on shields and armour, arrows zipping, men shrieking and dying. The music of her life.

She half-rolled and raised her head, and her vision swam. Her left arm hurt, and her shield lay several paces away, its straps broken. She looked about to find her sword, then staggered to her feet, and limped on a wrenched leg to examine her horse. The wretched animal still lived, nostrils wide and frothing, staring at her with the one visible, rolling eye. It kicked and tried to rise, its neck soaked in blood about the serrin's arrow, only the tail of which was visible in its neck.

Sasha whispered a calling to the animal's soul, performed the correct sign to her head and its own, then cut its throat. And turned away so she did not have to watch the blood gushing, and the final, feeble struggles of life.

The last of the serrin incursion was passing now, its final riders weaving in mad evasion of many times their number of pursuing Lenay and Torovan cavalry. Serrin were falling as cavalry blades found them, yet still most paid more attention to targets amidst the infantry than to defending themselves.

Several Isfayen were circling back to pick Sasha up. She extended an arm and one dragged her astride with brute strength, Sasha clutching to his back as they set off in pursuit of the serrin, and possibly a riderless horse.

Peering past the Isfayen's shoulder, Sasha saw the leading serrin riders dividing, then splitting as a wall of charging Lenay cavalry tore into them from the opposing direction. The northerners from the left flank, she guessed. The serrin had charged squarely into the middle of the Lenay formation, and were trapped. Evading riders were decapitated by huge, black-armoured men astride their great horses, who spurred directly into the serrins' midst with little fear of collision. More and more serrin scattered as the northerners worked their way up the line, striking left and right. Others broke off to pursue desperate escapes, serrin cavalry zigzagging madly toward the rear, where five thousand Torovan infantry reserve blocked their way.

"Stop!" Sasha yelled in her rider's ear, as he angled as though to pursue. "Stop here, there's no point."

He stopped, three companions with him, turning his horse sideways so Sasha could see. Many serrin had turned back, and were heading this way, still firing into the Lenay infantry's rear . . . but northern cavalry now overtook them as well, jostling the smaller, sleeker serrin horses, and killing their riders with brutal power. Soon there were but a few visible, each leading perhaps ten Lenay riders in a merry dance around and around, a final defiance of cunning over brawn. Not one attempted to surrender. Several came galloping back past Sasha's position, well wide of her riders, and with many Lenays in pursuit. No Isfayen man bothered to join the chase.

"*Ilayen*," said one of the Isfayen sombrely, and held his sword aloft in salute.

"*Ilayen*," echoed the others.

"That," Sasha's rider said dourly, "is the bravest thing I have ever seen."

The roar from the infantry lines was louder now, and the accent of the voices was not Lenay. Sasha looked, and saw Lenay men being forced back, their already depleted ranks thinned dramatically further by serrin archery. She could see confusion in the rear ranks, men helping wounded friends, others yelling at them to fight instead, wild gesticulations, others gathering support to run quickly to parts of the line that were about to break. All were falling back, an inexorable, gradual shuffle. From the sound of it, the Enorans had their blood up.

"Not only brave," Sasha said tiredly. "It's cost us the battle."

The Isfayen nodded. "A pointless sacrifice is surrender cloaked as bravery. These serrin knew precisely for what cause they sacrificed their lives. Our centre collapses. I salute them."

There were yells now as the Torovan infantry reserve steadied their line and prepared to push forward. The Isfayen turned their horses about and galloped out of the way. Soon another Isfayen rider came galloping, holding the reins of a fair looking, riderless warhorse. Sasha leaped onto its saddle, steadied the nervous animal, and realised from its lovely leather bridlework that it had belonged to a serrin. More of her Isfayen were regrouping amidst the masses of cavalry returning to their respective flanks. Sasha waited until she had as many of them about her as possible, then cast one final glance toward the advancing Torovans.

It was not possible that they could hold back the Steel. They were approaching the artillery zone now, and where Lenay infantry might sacrifice a tight formation for a fast sprint, Torovan infantry relied on that tight formation even more so than the Steel. If they arrived as a breathless rabble, they would need to re-form once in battle . . . nearly impossible against the Steel infantry. Yet if they marched forward in unison, the artillery would cut them to pieces on the way in.

Even as the command to ride came to her lips, she saw something that made her heart stop. Royal flags, galloping to the fore. A cluster of red cloaks ahorse, about a lone man in black astride a brilliant grey horse. And further, to the left, another cluster, red cloaks and noble banners, about another black-clad figure on a horse. King Torvaal Lenayin, and his son Prince Koenyg, riding to battle at the head of Torovan infantry. It raised a cheer from the Torovans, and through the shock Sasha could not help but consider the irony, that it was a king and prince of Lenayin who led them to war, while their own newly crowned king remained safely ensconced in Petrodor.

Sasha's breath caught in her throat to watch them. She had thought the situation desperate, yet if Koenyg was committing himself and their father to the fight to rally the troops, it was surely well beyond that. Her heels urged to kick at her new mount's sides, to race to Koenyg's side and scream that he was being a fool, that even should the Army of Lenayin lose this battle, all was not lost, and they could regroup and live to fight again. The battle, after all, was diversionary, and designed merely to hold the Enoran Steel off the Larosans' far larger, exposed flank. Why did Koenyg risk all in this one battle? Or had it not truly been his choice? Had their father ordered it, overruling his commander of armies on this one, singular point of strategy? Or was it honour?

About her, Isfayen men awaited her next command. She had never truly been her father's daughter. He had certainly never regarded her as such . . . or at least, not since she was a little girl. Why now should she falter? Why should the sight of him at the head of five thousand Torovans fill her with such terror?

"Come now, lass," said a nearby rider, grimly. "There is no greater burden than the honour of a king. A man must bear it alone."

The Torovans let out a roar, and began to run. Ahead of them, the parties about the two Lenay royals accelerated to a canter. From behind the Enoran line, black dots rose into the air like a swarm of bees, and behind them, fiery balls trailing black smoke.

Sasha turned her horse about, and rode with her Isfayen back toward the right flank. If the centre held, only for the flank to fold because she were distracted elsewhere, she would sacrifice everything for which her father risked and fought. She rode on, as fire erupted behind, and did not look back.

Andreyis awoke. He heard cheering, hysterical laughter, the celebrations of victorious warriors. "We've won," he thought dreamily. Then he realised that he could not recognise any words the men spoke.

He lay on his back on the green grass of a Larosan field. His right arm hurt worse than anything he could remember, but at least it was still attached to his body. His head ached and when he put his left hand to his temple, it came away bloody. He recalled the horse bearing down on him, and realised it must have hit him. Better that than the serrin rider's sword.

Thud, came more, nearby sounds. Thuds, and a whistling, fast fading. Another sound, a sharp crack, then a tortured, creaking rush, as a heavy mechanism of ropes and gears unwound. That would be a catapult firing. It sounded close.

He half-rolled, and managed to look up. Sure enough, the Tracatan artillery was near, cart-mounted ballistas drawn by oxen, and a pair of enormous catapults, each behind four pairs of oxen, intricate and frightening to behold at this range. Men swarmed over them, perhaps a dozen to each, carefully lifting ammunition from the trailing cart as others, shirtless and powerful, wound fast at complex gears, creaking the huge throwing arms back into place with remarkable speed. An ammunition shot was loaded into the arm's enormous "palm," a flint struck, and suddenly the shot was aflame . . . yet it was strangely coloured—blue, and barely visible. Then, crack, as the release was pulled, and the arm uncoiled once more, hurling a flaming missile across the cloud-strewn sky.

Still the cheering. Andreyis sat up, his arm cradled as it screamed with pain, yet he did not cry out. He stared instead at the backs of the Enoran infantry, perhaps a hundred paces before their artillery. They were cheering, not fighting, swords waving in the air. Many leaned on their shields, utterly spent. Others dropped back to check on the fallen.

The fallen, Andreyis saw, were everywhere. There were frighteningly more Lenays than Enorans, on his patch of ground. They made a grisly carpet, still writhing and groaning in places, as though the dead themselves protested this fate.

Andreyis struggled to his feet. There was a rise of gentle hillside beyond, and up it, he could see men fleeing. Lenay men. The proudest warriors in all Rhodia, running for their lives as an Army of Lenayin had never run before. Into their midst fell a rain of ballista fire. Nearby, where catapult shots fell, there followed great eruptions of blue-tinged orange flame.

"Stop it!" Andreyis shouted at the nearest ballista crew. "Stop shooting!" Men turned to look at him. "Stop shooting, damn you! You've won! Let them go, have you no honour?"

They ignored him, shirtless, sweaty men winding fast, and placing more forearm length bolts in the empty breaches. More bolts sprang skyward. Andreyis found that he was crying. He looked about for a sword, but before he could bend his injured body to fetch one, hooves thundered close, and an Enoran cavalryman dismounted before him, weapon brandished.

"You, shut it," the Enoran demanded in Torovan.

"Tell them to stop killing a defeated opponent!" Andreyis shouted back. "You have no honour!"

The Enoran advanced, and laid his blade against Andreyis's throat. His eyes were battle-wide and deadly. "You serve evil," he said coldly. "Your masters would kill us all. Enoran mercy was stolen from us long ago."

Andreyis brought his good arm down hard across the Enoran's wrist, kicked at his knee, and twisted expertly. The man fell, and found himself staring up at his own weapon, levelled at his throat. "I am friend to Sashandra Lenayin and Kessligh Cronenverdt," Andreyis hissed, "and I at least have honour! If Enorans do not, I shall teach it to you!"

He turned and ran, as best he could, at the nearest ballista cart. Men saw, and shouted warning, but then another horse blocked his path, and Andreyis found himself staring up at the bright, golden eyes of a serrin. He stopped, trying to imagine a way around this obstacle that might do some good instead of just dying immediately. The serrin shouted something, and waved his sword.

More shouts answered, and artillery fire ceased. A silence hung in the air, as the cheering had faded. It hung like a great emptiness over the fields. The serrin looked down at Andreyis. "You ask much of me," he said grimly. "It has been long since Saalshen or Enora has faced an honourable opponent in battle. And longer still since we have been pressed so hard as this. Many of your countrymen live to attack us once more. I would rather it otherwise."

Andreyis held the sword up before his face in salute. He then laid it on the ground before him. "I am bested," he declared. "My life is yours. I ask only that my honour remain unstained."

The serrin stared at him for a long moment. "Says he's a friend to Sashandra Lenayin and Kessligh Cronenverdt," said the cavalryman, climbing to his feet. "That was a nifty trick. Could be true."

"Are you?" asked the serrin.

To lie was dishonourable. Sometimes, amongst Goeren-yai, that mattered little. But upon a field of battle, surrounded by dead and dying, honour was all. "Yes," said Andreyis.

The serrin nodded. "Take him to custody," he said. "With their king dead, Sashandra Lenayin may figure prominently in the transition of power."

"She may be dead too," the cavalryman cautioned.

"I've a team of artillery on the left flank who might say otherwise, could the dead speak," the serrin replied. "She was alive that late in the fight, we shall assume she lives until we discover otherwise."

Andreyis stared across the masses of fallen Lenay warriors. The king was dead. The Army of Lenayin had broken and fled before their foe. Surely there had never been a blacker day to be a Lenay than today.

A Rathynal circle was already assembling upon the field of battle as Sasha approached. There were too many dead on the field for riders to reach the place where the king had fallen, so Sasha dismounted two hundred paces distant, and walked. The Great Lord Markan of Isfayen walked at her side—a young man, bigger even than his father Faras, with a proud gait and flowing black hair. Faras was dead, struck through the eye by a serrin arrow in the concluding actions of battle, as the cavalry flank had sought to hold back their opposition's thrusts into the retreating Lenay infantry, and prevent the retreat from becoming a total rout.

There had been an Isfayen ceremony for Faras, after the Enorans had granted truce for both sides to collect their dead and wounded. It had been brief, in the way of bloodwarriors at war, yet it had required Sasha's presence, as she was now adopted Isfayen, for the duration of this war. Thankfully the ceremony had required nothing of her save her presence, while a spirit talker had appealed to the spirits to take Faras amongst them, and return him to the earth and the sky, and the world of living creatures between. Sasha wondered where a Lenay spirit would go, so far from home. Would he stay here, to rebirth among foreign plants and animals? Or would he wander the long journey home, in homesick longing for the highland mountains and forests?

The walk to the Rathynal circle was carpeted with dead, men and horses alike. Most were Torovan. Scattered amongst them were Royal Guardsmen. Occasionally, an Enoran, though those were being fast removed from the field. Carts stood near, and Enoran men in light armour, hauling their dead into the tray. Serrin too, with leather bags of medicines, and tourniquets and bandages, searching for wounded who could still be saved. Enoran and Lenay men passed each other in silence—the Enorans wary, as the Lenays were still armed. The serrin, however, seemed less wary. Sasha knew that the Steel rarely granted such truces to Bacosh armies, and would usually hold the field until they had collected all their own dead and wounded, then abandon the defeated foe to their dead, if they dared return. But the Lenay king was dead, and Sasha suspected it was the serrin who had granted this small mercy.

Sasha arrived at the circle as the priest gave incantations. Damon made room for her and Markan. He grasped her hand, and she squeezed back. Before them, Torvaal, the fourth King of Lenayin, lay on his back beneath a black cloak. The blackness of his beard only made his face seem shockingly pale. It did not seem real, that he could be dead. Several men had tears in their eyes. Sasha spied Myklas across from her, at the side of Great Lord Heryd of Hadryn, struggling to hold back sobs. Damon too seemed in difficulty. Sasha wished she could feel something. Anything at all.

It passed in a blur, the recitals, the removal of the Highland Ring from Torvaal's finger and onto the finger of Koenyg. Then, finally, the crown—a thing much unseen in Lenayin, as the first king, Soros, had recognised that such an overt statement of superiority would arouse the displeasure of the proud lords of Lenayin. It was a simple band of metal, made from sword steel. The priest produced it from somewhere, and placed it on Koenyg's head, and all about the circle knelt. Koenyg was grim and bloodspattered. From his posture, Sasha reckoned he bore a wound to his side, however he tried to hide it. It did not seem serious. He made perhaps the perfect image of a new Lenay king, battleworn and unsmiling, civilised yet frightening. The northern lords would be pleased to see Koenyg take full command. Most of the lords would.

Yet nothing could hide the shame of an Army of Lenayin that had lost its king, then run away.

Looking around the circle, Sasha noted who was absent. Kumaryn of Valhanan. Arastyn of Tyree. Her nemesis, and Jaryd's, both dead. She could not feel happy about it. Parabys of Neysh, too. Four of the eleven great lords fallen. Only the Isfayen had been fast enough in handing from father to son to attend these funeral rites. Some of the others, Sasha had heard, had left their sons in Lenayin to tend their estates. Temporary great lords would need to be found, for the purposes of command.

Rites complete, embraces were exchanged with the new king, siblings first. Then all stepped away while Royal Guardsmen came to take the king's body, wrapped in its black cloak, onto a waiting cart. There would be no grieving over the corpse, not for Lenays in war. The great lords assembled behind Koenyg, who walked behind the cart, as it picked its way between the fallen. Sasha walked at Myklas's side. For all his dried sweat and dirt, he seemed to have barely a scratch.

Men talked in low voices of the battle. Sasha risked a look at Great Lord Heryd, walking at Myklas's other side. "I hear tales," she said. "My little brother fought well, it seems."

Heryd's blue eyes were pale, nearly expressionless. "I have rarely seen such skill," he said. "He was the best of us."

Sasha blinked. Hatred between her and Heryd was mutual, yet she knew the Great Lord of Hadryn was no sycophant. Myklas said nothing, with eyes only for his father's body on the tray of the cart ahead.

The cart continued beyond the battlefield, toward where the Army of Lenayin now camped, several hills beyond. The procession did not follow, abandoning that job to a gathering of lesser lords on horseback. Sasha turned back to where Isfayen were following behind with horses, and remounted.

She headed along the great swathe of fallen bodies toward where she figured the centre of the battle had been. Eventually she saw the stag-on-maroon flag of Valhanan, driven into the ground near some parties of men and carts. She left her horse with her two Isfayen guards, and walked to those attending the dead and wounded. Soon enough she found Byorn of the Baerlyn training hall, and embraced him hard. He seemed pale and shocked, his long hair matted with other people's blood. Wordlessly, he escorted her past piled bodies and entangled, bloody limbs, until they reached the body of a large man with thick red hair, a fatal sword wound through his ribs.

Teriyan.

Sasha collapsed in tears, and sobbed onto his shoulder, as Byorn knelt with a hand on her back. This was how she should have grieved for her father, had her father permitted such a thing. But this man had been far more a father to her than her real father had. And he was the true father to one of her best friends.

"How am I going to tell Lynette?" she asked Byorn, helplessly between sobs. "Who's going to tell poor Lynie?" And Byorn, from whom Sasha had never seen emotion in her life, struggled to hold back tears.

"I can't find Andreyis," he said in a low voice. "I'll keep looking, I swear to you. But he's not amongst the living or the dead."

For the rest of the day, Sasha could not speak.

It was without question the strangest day of Sofy's life. She sat at camp and attempted to keep herself occupied with mundane tasks, while beyond the next rise upon the Sonnai Plain, a hundred thousand men and more fought to the death. The wind was from the west, the wrong direction to assist the sound in carrying, yet the din assailed her ears all the same, rising like some unhappy spectre, with wails and cries to chill her bones.

The matrons of the Merciful Sisters insisted on prayer, and so Sofy, her maids, and the other ladies of the camp knelt in the communion tent and recited verse after the men had gone. Then had come needlework, and Sofy attended to some of Balthaar's clothes in the manner of any good wife, gathered with the other ladies in the royal tent. Some had attempted gossip, forced and nervous, against the smothering din of war that lay over the camp. Several of the ladies, Sofy knew, feared for their position in Sherdaine should their husbands fall on the field. Most had returned to family castles, but a few had accompanied their husbands in camp with servants, and now readied to make a fast escape should news from the battle turn bad.

Sofy wondered what the ladies truly feared the most—the defeat of the united Bacosh Army, or the shudder that such a calamity would surely send through their land. Many lords killed, lines of succession called into question, challenges from rivals, siblings, cousins or power-hungry neighbours, and a great rearrangement of feudal boundaries that might last for several years beyond the great defeat. She wondered if such a defeat might teach them, finally, the futility of attacking the Saalshen Bacosh. Such attacks had grown fewer and fewer in recent decades, and consisted mostly of boastful dukes and other, ambitious lordlings hoping to make a name for themselves by demonstrating their courage, and trying to take the Steel unawares. Some had succeeded, in surprise at least, and had penetrated small armies some short distance into Rhodaani or Enoran lands before beating a hasty retreat in the face of advancing Steel forces. Such daring men had gained great reward of prestige for their "successes," thus tempting others to copy their methods. The Steel rarely gathered in full force, as its soldiers rotated back to their families, and others to training, leaving only smaller groups to guard the border. But most often, even such smaller formations had dealt these incursions a crushing blow.

Sofy had now come to suspect that some lords in this great army were happy to see the war not for religious or moral reasons, but simply for the opportunity it presented to grab available lands or claim titles, once so many of those previously in possession had been slain. "The great dice," she'd heard men call it. The great gamble of throwing so many men into battle, and hoping that it was one's rivals who would fall, and not oneself.

Occasionally a messenger would arrive and inform them of the battle's progress. Such messengers never spoke in much detail, and Sofy was uncertain whether that was because they did not expect a group of women to understand, or because they simply didn't know. But she knew the battle was progressing better for the Bacosh because by noon the fighting was still continuing. Both victory and defeat seemed equally precarious outcomes for her personally, and for those she loved. She did not know when the Army of Lenayin would fight its first battle to the south, or how long the word of its outcome would take to reach them. She merely concentrated on her needlework, one stitch at a time, as though by the correct placement of thread and steel, she could stitch all the fates into some more agreeable arrangement.

After noon, the sounds of battle slowly faded until there was only silence. Sofy could stand it no longer and walked out to the camp's edge, accompanied by many guards, wary of marauding serrin behind the lines. Soon, across the fields of eastern Larosa, knights on horseback appeared, their formations ragged. Squires and servants rushed to help their masters from the saddle. Some were wounded and required assistance to walk. Others rode on lame or injured horses.

Then, from amidst the commotion, Balthaar appeared. Servants hurried to him, and assisted his weary, awkward dismount. He looked at Sofy, visor raised, and smiled wanly. Sofy walked to him, her heart pounding. She could not but be pleased that he lived, and was apparently unhurt. Beyond that, she was entirely uncertain of her feelings.

She took his gauntleted hands in hers. Balthaar just looked at her, sweaty and exhausted. His eyes, usually radiating such confidence, were now sunken and dull. Sofy recognised the look. She had seen it in the eyes of Lenay warriors on her march north, following grand scenes of carnage and pain. Balthaar stared at her, as though surprised that his eyes could once again regard something beautiful.

"My father is dead," he murmured. "I am Bacosh Regent now."

Sofy took a deep breath, her heart thudding. She curtseyed. "Yes, Your Highness."

"We suffered grievously," Balthaar continued, as though he hadn't heard her. "Our dead carpet the fields in places so thickly that one could walk across entire paddocks without once touching the ground. I have seen men burned alive by the score, and entire lines of infantry cut down like wheat. The Rakani suffered terribly on the left flank, the serrin devils have taken nearly half their number. I fear many families have ended today, fathers, sons and cousins all slain without any one remaining to continue the line."

"Your Highness," said Sofy, trying to keep her voice from trembling. What did they do now? If they were to run for the safety of ancestral lands, surely they should leave immediately? "We have been defeated, then?"

Balthaar stared. His steel fingers clasped tightly upon her hands, causing Sofy to gasp in pain. "Defeated?" he rasped. "No, M'Lady." He leaned forward, and his dull eyes came suddenly to a blaze, his lips twisting in a smile of vicious, righteous fury. "I bring you *victory*!"

About the Author

JOEL SHEPHERD was born in Adelaide in 1974. His first manuscript was shortlisted for the George Turner Prize in 1998, and his first novel, *Crossover*, was shortlisted in 1999. He wrote two other novels in the Crossover series, *Breakaway* (2003) and *Killswitch* (2004). *Sasha*, the first novel in *A Trial of Blood & Steel*, was published in 2007. *Petrodor*, the second novel in this series, was published in 2008.

Coming soon

Haven

the thrilling conclusion to the

A Trial of Blood & Steel

quartet